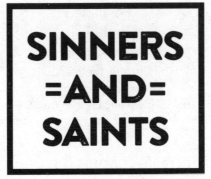

SINNERS
=AND=
SAINTS

BLOOD & BONE: *Book Two*

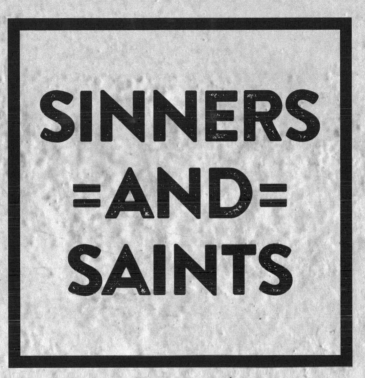

SINNERS =AND= SAINTS

JENNIFER ROBERSON

DAW BOOKS, INC.
DONALD A. WOLLHEIM, FOUNDER
1745 Broadway, New York, NY 10019
ELIZABETH R. WOLLHEIM
SHEILA E. GILBERT
PUBLISHERS
dawbooks.com

This novel is dedicated to

Candy Camin

Brian and Frances Gross

Tom and Linda Watson

for great friendship;

And always to my editor

Betsy Wollheim

PROLOGUE

W ait a minute." I did not want to believe Remi's words. I really, really did not want to believe what he was telling me. "Jack the Ripper? *The* Jack the Ripper?"

Remi, my Texas cowboy semi-brother, or cousin, or beta, or twin-by-heavenly matter—I still wasn't quite sure how the celestial genome expressed itself in human terms—nodded, wholly serious.

I let the letter drop to the table. It landed face-up, showing old-style cursive handwriting, nearly indecipherable. Beside it, placed intentionally face-down, the gruesome photograph that had accompanied it in the manila envelope bearing our names:

Gabriel. Remiel. I was the Gabriel half of the pairing. "Nuh-uh." I shook my head. "No way in hell."

Night, now, and the Zoo was closed, but had livened up considerably, in a sick sort of way, upon delivery of the photograph and duplication of what Remi had explained was Jack the Ripper's infamous *From Hell* letter, and a white styrofoam restaurant box containing not dinner leftovers, but a murdered woman's kidney.

We were upstairs in the wood-walled common room of the Zoo Club. It was an old tin-roofed roadhouse/cowboy dancehall/restaurant/pool parlor/hotbed of annoying country music that had been assigned to Remi and me, strangers but a matter of days before. Our new home was a rustic, utilitarian apartment built over the dance floor, which meant, to my immense dismay, that the thump and twang of live country music wafted its way up the staircase and shook the floors. Modest bedrooms numbered two, plus kitchen, three-quarter bath, and a den doubled as office and dining room containing table, chairs, sofa bed, TV, books, computer.

I switched my attention from my cowboy-hatted "cousin" to Grandaddy, a tall, bearded man with a cascade of springy white hair, standing beside the table. I appealed to him for any kind of sanity that might be found in what was now my new normal. "No way, right?"

Grandaddy's lips in the depths of his pepper-and-salt beard were compressed as he lifted the letter from the table, but he said nothing. Did not so much as acknowledge he'd heard a word. I knew better than to believe he hadn't heard me; when the man held his tongue, the man held his tongue.

Remi's Texas drawl was pronounced as he removed his cream-colored hat and placed it brim-up on the table. "He did go warnin' us, Grandaddy did. Legends come to life, I think you said, wasn't it?" He glanced over, waited for a response from Grandaddy, but none was forthcoming so the attention switched back to me. "Black dogs we've met, and demons. These days, what's to say an infamous human murderer can't climb his way out of hell? I mean, *the Morrigan herself* is living in a motorhome but a half-mile up the road. The freakin' Goddess of Battles."

But. Please, let there be a *but*.

When Grandaddy continued to make no answer, still

examining the letter, I raised my voice. "Look, I get that things are different now, but *the* Jack the Ripper? Seriously?"

Whereupon he shot me an annoyed if distracted glance and walked out of the room, taking the letter with him.

"*That* helps," I muttered.

Remi decided to play pinch hitter in place of our paterfamilias—angelfamilias?—as he finger-combed his short hair compressed by hatband. "I think it's true. That it's the actual Jack the Ripper. Demons gotta come from somewhere, right? Maybe all of 'em are nasty-bad dead humans like Ted Bundy, Jeffrey Dahmer and what-not, now acting as Satan's soldiers. Jack the Ripper would have taken the down elevator to the devil's basement when he died, certain sure. And then those hell vents popped open."

I ran a hand through loose long hair, shook it back. "Well, if it is and we find him, we can ask him who he really is. Was. Solve the whole mystery. 'Hey there, Jack, my man—who the fuck *are* you? People have been guessing for decades!" I yanked out a chair, dropped into it, ignored the queasy roll of revulsion in my gut as I fastidiously pushed the kidney's clamshell as far away as possible. The box squeaked faintly as it slid across the table's polyurethaned wood.

Remi raised one brow. "Well, what do *you* think it is? Some total stranger gaslighting us? Or someone—some *thing*—that knows who, what, and where we are."

The answer was implicit. "Demon." Which still felt a little weird to say so matter-of-factly. "But he doesn't have to be *the* Jack the Ripper. Could be just some surrogate claiming the name and the fame—wait. *Wait.*" But Grandaddy had taken the letter, so I couldn't check. I sat forward, tapped the tabletop with a stiffened finger for emphasis. "It's the same one. The same demon. The woman who tried to strangle me out back the other night. She said I could call her Legion, or even Iñigo Montoya, and that's how the letter was signed. It's got to be her behind this."

He thought about it, then shrugged. "Don't matter. Name's a name. It's the actions that count. Be it him, her, or *it*."

I rubbed at my scarred eyebrow. "Guess that's our new assignment. Find this son of a bitch and exorcise the hell out of it." I preferred to think of it as an *it*. I remembered the woman— the *it*—very clearly, considering we'd damn near become *very* up close and personal in ways generally considered other than evil. "So it's body-hopping. It's not really Jack the Ripper."

Remi was not convinced. "Could be, though. Could just be what's left of a crazy-bad sicko bastard. If souls are real, maybe *that's* what got out. *His* soul, and now he's possessing people."

"And recreating the murders." Deliberately I did not allow myself to look at the styrofoam box containing what we feared was a dead woman's kidney.

For an uncomfortable moment I got stuck on the concept that Jack the Ripper had attempted to kill me. Not because he was a guy and the demon who'd had a hand on my junk was most definitely a female—a body-hopping, gender-swapping demon, apparently—but because the idea of nearly being offed by an infamous murderer *from another century* was hard to swallow.

Remi was aware of my discomfort. "Well then, what else might it be? Grandaddy said demons can make legends real, even actual historical folk. Is the Ripper's soul possessing people, or is it something else playing around with humans? We'd best know, if we hope to kill it. You're the folklorist."

Thus challenged, I ran through possibilities. "Tulpa," I

offered finally. "Could be a thought-form, a figment of imagination."

Remi's tone was dry. "Tulpa . . . not Tulsa?"

"Not in Oklahoma the last I heard, no. It's ancient Tibetan
mysticism, primarily, though there's a small community of
people today convinced they can actually make tulpas real
with enough mental concentration. The belief is that tulpas ar-
en't demonic, and they aren't truly a manifestation of your subconscious. They are *created* but aren't an extension, or subject,
of the devil." I thought more deeply. "Hmmm."

"Hmmm?"

"Well . . . supposedly a tulpa can, at some point, be allowed
to possess its creator's body."

Remi caught my thought. "Sounds like demonic possession
to me."

I chewed absently at my bottom lip. "Supposedly they're
not real, and certainly not considered dangerous. They're *thought*
forms. But . . ."

He nodded, looking pensive. "Things are different, now;
got made abundantly clear when we exploded two black dogs
the other day . . . what did you call them? Barges?"

"No, not barges—they're not boats. Barghests."

"*They* aren't real, are they? Just folklore, right?" Remi indicated the container with its human body part. "Tulpa or no
tulpa, Ripper or no Ripper, might could say that whatever did
this is entirely real and should be considered dangerous."

Yeah, so we might could. And I was done just sitting there.
Done debating, even inside my own head. As I rose, I shoved
away the chair with the backs of my calves, felt the twinges of a
very stiff and sore body—laying a motorcycle down on asphalt
tends to leave reminders—and walked out of the room swiftly

in heavy biker boots, bent on finding Grandaddy, our resident angel, a seraph, an agent of heaven with a direct line to the celestial Penthouse-in-the-Sky and damn well ought to have answers to these kinds of questions.

Such as how to find and destroy Jack the Ripper.

CHAPTER ONE

attempted suicide-by-stairs by heading down them faster than a stiff, bruised body could handle comfortably—I felt eighty-eight, not twenty-eight—played a hasty game of grab-and-snatch with a rough wooden bannister, and finally hit the floor upright on the soles of my boots rather than landing on head or hip. It wasn't a silent descent, but it got me there.

Dim downstairs, and quiet. Dangling string-lights draped at the back windows by the pool tables lent pale illumination. A garland of matching lights stretched along the barback mirror, glinting off glass, copper, and chrome, turned polished wood to liquid. I smelled a melange of alcohol ranging from mellow, tame beer to more robust stout; the thin astringency of wine and the deep, warm odors of Scottish whiskey and American bourbon.

"Grandaddy? You here?"

No answer.

"Grandaddy?" Nothing. I gave the other possibility a try, this time asking for the African god who doubled as a bartender. "Ganji?"

No angelic being. No African Orisha.

The latter, who happened to be Lord of the Volcanoes, was

probably up on the once-burned mountain—part of a dormant volcano cluster—behind the Zoo, soothing her with song, promising life after a long sleep. So long as he *kept* the volcano asleep for a few more centuries, time enough for me to exit the earth in a perfectly normal, boring fashion sans lava or pyroclastic explosions. But I had no idea where Grandaddy might have gone. Or why he walked out in the middle of a conversation while examining the letter purportedly from *the* Jack the Ripper.

I hesitated a moment because, well, while this wasn't exactly a horror movie complete with creepy music, after the discoveries of the last few days of my unexpectedly new life I figured all bets were off. Then I mentally shoved that thought aside and crossed the parquet dance floor to the front door, slid the latch and twisted the deadbolt, pulled it open, and looked beyond the porch and its steps into the darkness of an empty parking lot. Not even the big guitar-shaped neon marquee sign advertising live country music was lighted.

The occasional vehicle hummed its way down Route 66 in the darkness, thumping across cold weather expansion seams in the road, but at this time of the morning, an hour, maybe two, before false dawn, things were quiet. The air was markedly cool, unlike the warmth of the summer day earlier, and made me wish for a little something more than thin black t-shirt. I smelled pine trees, the parking lot's damp dirt, and the heavy moisture of incipient rain.

I reached out. Not physically. But with the—*whatever*—that made me sensitive to places. All I got back was a sense of the color green, flickering at the inner edges of my vision. The Zoo—the *domicile*, in some mongrel hybrid of angelic/demonic-speak—had been cleared of surrogates and no longer could any of them just come waltzing through the door and out onto the dance floor. Whoever had sent the letter and kidney had not set foot in the place.

I did not shout out into the night, after the "vandalism" of a few nights before, when Remi and I had been set upon by a slew of dead animals. As this resulted in us shooting up the place to take out two demons masquerading as ghosts, I figured it was smart not to go calling attention to myself by bellowing into the darkness. Maybe Grandaddy had an understanding with the police, but until I knew that I wanted to play it safe.

Behind me a light flickered. A second pulse caught the corner of my eye. I spun, hand going at once to the butt of the pistol sheathed in the shoulder holster under my left arm, but I lowered my arm when I realized it very well might be Remi, come hunting Grandaddy as well, or our resident African god.

No cowboy, though. Still no Orisha. Beneath more string-lights, crammed back into his corner near the front door the rearing, gape-mouthed grizzly stared blankly out of a broken black-glass eye. I'd shattered it earlier with a hurled cue ball. A trace of a chill touched the back of my neck, slid halfway down my spine. I suppressed a shiver. The grizzly was nothing more than a stuffed animal once again, but still fearsome to look upon. Especially when he—*it*—had done a damn fine imitation of an attack intended to slice-and-dice me.

All of the animals had been returned to their displays throughout the Zoo. Bobcat, mountain lion, even Remi's tusked hava-pig-thing. It was dim enough indoors that I couldn't tell if the bullet holes in their hides had been patched over, but it was downright spooky to see all those glossy fake-ass eyes staring back. Dead, maybe, but they'd been dead *before* and damn near did me in.

As I lingered on the threshold, I reached out again, stretched myself, gathering up the interior stillness necessary to lose myself in parts and pieces, in the architecture of my gift. Grandaddy had guided it, had guided *me*, but for years I hadn't actually intentionally summoned it the way I had upon the mountain at Grandaddy's just the other day. For one thing, I'd been in prison less than two weeks before; I saw so much bad shit on the surface of that place that I didn't care to explore the boiling hostility beneath.

But I was no longer in prison, and now I payed out my senses like kite string. I sensed flickers of green at the edges of my eyes, but also the faintest trace of red. *Off/on, off/on*, as if uncertain. It bled away into nothingness.

I freed the Taurus Judge from its holster, held it down at arm's length against my right thigh. I stood with my back to the front door, then thunked it closed with a behind-the-back push from spread fingers. I felt for the latch, shot it. Took several strides out into the center of the dance floor. String-lights strung throughout the bar flickered. Either trouble with the power, or something far more consequential, maybe.

Consequential it was. As I watched, the illuminated glass globes of the string-lights detached themselves and floated up to perch upon hand-hewn crossbeams like birds upon a wire, ten feet up from the dance floor. Except they weren't string-lights at all.

"Huh," I said, eyebrows rising. "Orbs?" I tipped my head back to follow the dance.

Little by little, more of them detached from walls, from the barback, floated out into the air. Like variegated soap bubbles blown from a wand, some bobbed while others drifted upward in loose ranks toward the roof planks. The glass-like balls sitting on the crossbeams strobed brightly, and I saw some of them were fissured with spider-web cracks.

Yup, orbs. And I knew my orbs. Well, so to speak. As much as you can know when you read up on them in folklore and paranormal texts. Major debates continued, with more scientific types claiming them nothing more than phenomena caused by insects, dust particles, photographic highlights, and so on. But those steeped in the paranormal were convinced orbs were very real, considered them harbingers, spirits, and guides, and certain colors represented specific aspects. I had no opinion other than the ones now gathering in the middle of the Zoo sure as hell looked like more than dust particles or photographic reflections.

And they *winked* at me. I heard the barest suggestion of vibrating chimes, of a subtle singing, like a wet finger rounding the rim of fine crystal.

I gazed up at the rows and clusters, watched the strobe effects go faster, brighter; heard the chimes climbing a nearly silent scale that resonated inside my ears like an annoying case of tinnitus. The orbs quivered and shimmied so markedly that I sensed any second they might spring into the air in joyous abandon like some Disneyfied little creatures.

I pointed a minatory finger at them. "Don't you *dare* start singing 'It's A Small World.'"

A step sounded at the bottom stair, and Remi, still hatless, arrived with his drawl. "Little early for Christmas lights, ain't it?"

"Orbs," I answered, still watching the pulsing lights. "Also rather appropriately known as the Circle of Confusion."

"Well, *I'm* confused." Cowboy boots thumped as he crossed from staircase to parquet. His brows were drawn together as he gazed up at the array of orbs. "Are those suckers *alive?*"

"There is some argument to that effect," I noted, "between those into the whole Orb Zone Theory thing, and those who believe they may well be some form of paranormal life—extensions of energy, that kind of thing. But never the twain shall meet."

Remi stopped next to me, head tipped back. The orbs along the crossbeams quivered. "They seem a mite excitable."

"You seeing the colors?"

"Yup. Green. Peach. Little gold."

"And white."

"I see white," he agreed.

I nodded, mentally counting off the ranks of glass, digging answers from my memory of the texts I had read. "Those are all good colors, they say. And I see colors, *feel* colors, when I reach out." I shrugged; it still sounded weird even to me, trying to explain how and what I felt. "I don't get a sense of sentience, but peach is comfort. White means protection . . . it's holy light, holy power. Gold is . . ." I grinned, holstered the revolver. "Gold is *angelic*. It's unconditional love."

Remi looked perplexed. "So, what—they've come along to hang out with us brand spanking new little half-angels?"

I watched the light display above our heads. "I'm seeing silver, now, too. See? Silver means a messenger."

"Messenger orbs?" He sounded highly skeptical.

"Hey, I didn't write the books. I just read 'em."

We heard a rattle at the front door. I assumed Grandaddy and Ganji had keys, but neither appeared, so this was someone deliberately trying the latch without legal entrance. Possibly even with lockpicks. Rather than bellowing that we were closed, I headed toward the door to throw the deadbolt. And then the latch slid back seemingly on its own, and before I could even reach the door to shove the bolt back into its hasp, the heavy metal-strapped door swung open.

Young, blond, white guy, trim build, maybe late twenties, like Remi and me. He wore pressed dark dress slacks, starched white button-down dress shirt with collar points freed of button containment, top button undone to bare his throat. No tie, sleeves rolled back. Gold Rolex with its characteristic band glinted on his left wrist. He was Hollywood-handsome with clean, striking facial lines, blue eyes, long pale-blond hair pulled up and doubled into a slick-backed high man-bun. And shining white teeth.

"Hi," he said, with a bright go-getter-young-executive kind of smile. "Can a guy get a drink around here?"

"Sorry 'bout that, but we're closed," Remi replied, even as I added it was way beyond last call.

The guy shrugged, hands thrust into his pockets casually. The shoes, I noticed, were black dress and glossy. Probably a thousand dollars' worth of fine leather. "I know it's late, but I'd really like a drink. It's been a hellaciously long trip."

"We're closed," I repeated. "We'll reopen tomorrow at . . ." I had no idea, since I didn't run the place, so I just threw it out there, " . . . eleven."

"Live country music," Remi put in, as if he *were* running the place. "Though the band don't start 'til round about seven."

Our man-bunned visitor showed his handsome teeth in that fine toothpaste commercial dental arcade. "I'd really like to grab a drink before I hit the road."

I wasn't exactly blocking the door, but he did have to step

to the side as if to slide around me. I saw a quick, rippling frown cross Remi's face as he looked at the guy—and the cowboy was the one sensitive to demons—so I reached out, caught the stranger's upper arm.

Fire like an electrical shock kindled into a conflagration, then shunted through my fingers, up my left arm, and set my shoulder socket ablaze.

I fell back a step, clutched my arm against me—the pain and a thumping heart felt like a heart attack—and through gritted teeth called the guy every colorful name I could think of, none of them particularly nice.

"All true," he agreed with unoffended cheerfulness as I ran out of words and massaged my aching arm. Even as Remi took a step, hand going to the Bowie at his belt, the stranger glanced up at the glowing glass bubbles quivering on the crossbeams. He smiled, waited—and every orb in the place strobed yellow, brown, then red, then black. "*There* you go," he said with vast satisfaction. "Better than all those goody two-shoes, pansy-assed pastels." He looked at Remi, at me, and his smile fell away. "I *said* I'd like to have a drink."

CHAPTER TWO

S till clutching my arm, I stared at the man. "You can't—"

"—be in here? Oh, but I can." The stranger looked straight at Remi. Blue eyes sharpened into an almost laser-like directness, pupils shrinking. His body didn't have the obvious posture of a predator, but the impression definitely implied threat. He put up a finger, turned the back of his hand toward Remi, then crooked his finger in a beckoning gesture. "Come over here with that knife and let me slit you open guts to gullet."

Remi appeared in no way intimidated. I guess a guy who rides angry bulls in rodeos—and kills demons—would have more than enough confidence to meet the stranger's eyes straight on. Remi balanced the Bowie lightly in his hand. In the erratic pulsing light emitted from the orbs overhead, the damascened blade pattern was pale, watery ink against the bright steel.

"The fact that you're *warnin'* me says this li'l ol' pigsticker— and what I just might do with it—is somethin' of a concern." Remi flipped it to his left hand, held the blade rather than the handle. A Bowie is in no way made for throwing, but I figured he'd gotten over that handicap years before. Grandaddy would have seen to it.

The stranger was amused. His grin stretched wider, and he slowly licked his lips, left the tip of his tongue showing at one corner. The motion was unsettling, verging on seductive. "You ever been swarmed by lava-hot *sfaira* before?" He lifted his chin, gesturing with it toward the orbs clustered along the beamwork. "Because that's what will happen. Those are mine." He looked at me now, saw how I clenched my fist repeatedly, trying to work away the numbness and dull throb. "Stings, doesn't it? That'll teach you to keep your hands to yourself." He ran tongue across lips again. "Now, hey, how about I get myself that drink I wanted?" He began to turn, slanted a glance over his shoulder at Remi, said something in a language unknown to me, "*Mávro, peiráxtetravíxte ton ánthropo ton vooeidón.*"

"Dammit—!" Remi ducked as one of the strobing orbs high overhead shot off the crossbeam and made a beeline straight at him. It no longer resembled anything so benign as a soap bubble.

My eyebrows shot up. Remi had reacted *before* the orb went after him, which meant he understood what the stranger said.

Still ducking, Remi twisted his torso, tossed the Bowie up-ward. Steel glinted as the big knife performed a heavy looping arc. The orb, strobing through white into muddy brown, then black, with a nuke-bright light in the middle, actually *hesitated*, as if distracted by the Bowie's flash, bull to red cape, and even as the weapon fell, thunked against the parquet floor, Remi came up with one of his tricky little throwing knives and snapped it into the air with a sharp, lateral motion.

Knife and black orb collided in midair. The orb flashed briefly, blinding-bright, then exploded like a dying star gone supernova.

Remi thrust one hand up to ward away sparks and slag, I

backpedaled a step, and then my partner in saving the world straightened and once again met the narrowed glare of the stranger without flinching. "Tease *me*, huh?" Remi offered his own grin. "Hell, son, I got more knives where that one come from."

The stranger flat lost his shit. Lips drawn back, he shouted something that sounded like the language he'd used before, all liquid twists and tangles and atonal emphases.

That it was the same language Remi confirmed by grinning anew, crow's feet deepening. "Nope. My parents were married and my mother was neither a whore nor a bitch, so I can't rightly be the son of one, now, am I right?"

By now I had the Taurus in both hands, left palm cupping the heel of my right. I'd stepped closer, was relaxed but poised, even though my shoulder still felt a little numb. The dull ache went bone-deep. But no more trigger finger along the barrel as a human safety; I rested the finger pad lightly on the cool, curved metal, prepared to squeeze. "Double-tap to the back of the head, execution-style," I suggested. I had no idea if even breath-blessed bullets would work, but you go with what you've got and hope like hell it works. "Your pet orbs aren't faster than a bullet fired into the back of your skull from three inches away."

And then the magic cell phones in our pockets blew up loud with that horrendous ear-piercing flatulent *blaaaat* of an Amber or Weather Alert, and it was enough to startle Remi and me so that we lost focus for just an instant, *just* an instant, but long enough that our visitor spun away from me.

Heat lashed my face, dried my eyes instantly and obscured vision with a wash of flooding tears. Mostly blind, I was aware of movement, of air sucked away, and *heat*, but could not see because my eyes continued to water badly. I heard Remi swearing, wondered if his vision was as poor.

The blast of heat dissipated, but I smelled thick astringent ash and the heavy reek of charred flesh, the metallic tang of hot charcoal. Something whipped across my face, edge on. Mostly air, but I felt a slice in it across the bridge of my nose. In place of the phone alerts, now mercifully stilled, I heard the high, subtle squeaks of cooling charcoal, magnified one hundredfold.

Gun forgotten, I clasped my left hand over my face, swearing into my palm. For an instant the pain in my nose nearly dropped me to my knees, but I did an awkward little hop, skip, and jump to keep my balance and straightened, gun lifted one-handed, trying to find the target through the watery fog in my eyes so I could shoot the asshole.

I still didn't know how in hell a demon could make it through whatever wards existed because we'd managed to clear the domicile—the dancehall—and make it off-limits to demons, but I was taking no more chances in case the rules had changed on us. I was raspy-voiced, but managed a shout. "Remi—exorcism!" And resolved on the spot that I really did need to learn the *Rituale Romanum*. But for now, I just figured Remi would once again jump in to cover our asses.

"Holy shit!" he shouted. "No—no—*it won't work*. He's not a demon!"

I scrubbed the back of my hand across both eyes, blinked hard, trying to clear the remains of tears. And as vision returned, I found our visitor standing *on top of* the bar.

He grinned down at us both with those fine white teeth. "Demon I am not. And I suspect those phone alerts were intended to warn you I was in the area. Bit late, though, wouldn't you say?"

Remi had a narrow slice across one side of his jaw. Blood smeared his cheek. "The son of a bitch is an *angel*."

Atop the bar the stranger laughed. "I might have expected *you* to realize that sooner." Then he spread out both arms in a sinuous motion, made an elaborate, graceful bow as if on a theatrical stage at curtain call, and straightened. Following that, he placed his shod feet in a precise position, something akin to a ballet pose, then bent his back leg and thrust his body upward. He spun into a series of one-footed pirouettes atop the glossy bar in his shiny black dress shoes.

The man-bun came loose and collapsed. Hair whipped around his head and face as he spun, and by the time the revolutions slowed and he stood still before—*above*—us again, thick blond hair fell in tangles and waves around his face. He looked old, he looked young, he looked ageless.

He laughed at us both, clearly delighting in the expressions of shock on our faces. "Baryshnikov—" he began, cheerful again rather than threatening; hell, maybe he was bipolar— "could only manage eleven pirouettes. I just did *twelve*." And then he ran lightly down the bar on the balls of his feet, leaped off into the air, landed beside the jukebox. "Music! *Music*. God, I've missed *actual* music. What's on here?" Dismissing us, he bent over the front panel to browse the listings.

I frowned at Remi as I slid the revolver back into the holster beneath my left arm. Didn't see much use for it now, since I couldn't kill him with so prosaic a weapon. "I thought you could sense angels. *Feel* angels!"

"And I did," Remi shot back. "It just . . . took me a few minutes."

I felt gently at the bridge of my nose. It was sliced and sore. I blotted it gently with fingers, inspected, found no blood. "Well, can you tell if he's the good kind, or the bad kind? I mean, he kind of did a 180 on us." And then the jukebox began to play at exceedingly high volume, and the damn angel was *singing*.

Loudly.

I stared at the angel, then stared at Remi, utterly flabber-gasted, and after a minute or so finally managed a question. "What *is* it with country music and celestial beings?" I tried to make out the lyrics. "And who the hell is Betty Lou Thelma Liz?"

By now Remi was laughing. "He's nuttier than a squirrel turd!" And then he was singing too, also loudly, something about—redneck mothers? And kicking hippies' asses?

He broke it off when he saw the look on my face. "Betty Lou Thelma Liz is his wife. It's 'Up Against the Wall, Redneck Moth-ers,' an old Jerry Jeff Walker song," he explained. "And it is best sung in bars when everyone's half-drunk and *all* rowdy, except the chorus is mostly shouted rather than sung."

And then the music stopped mid-lyric, and the angel once again stood atop the bar. The purity of his features, the planes and contours within the frame of loose blond hair, was strik-ing. He simply was an incredibly beautiful man.

He spun once again into a series of pirouettes. I was tempted to count them to see if he really could out-spin Baryshnikov, but I didn't.

Then he stopped short and stared down upon us. Color come up in his face. He was breathing hard, but with excite-ment, not breathlessness. He wetted lips again. His eyes were *hungry*, and something markedly other than sane.

"Kneel," he said, teeth shining. "What's the *Game of Thrones* phrase—bend the knee? Yes. Do that." He pointed at the floor. "Now. To me."

Remi and I, perhaps five feet away with a checkerboard of

parquet beneath our boots, stared at the angel in blank, open-mouthed amazement.

He didn't say it. He *roared* it: "I am *bene ha'elohi*! I am the *first*, the *first* among them, the *first* among the fallen, the *first* among his servants, the *first* to call him Lord in his Father's place!"

Out of thin air his clothing caught fire. Flames ran up his body and cloth burned right off of him, burned *into* him, left him nude. Now, unshielded, the skin began, too, to burn, to crack open, to melt and char and shrink like blackened parchment curling around his bones. Ropes of burned flesh dripped from his arms, began to peel away and fall. Hair burned off, fat crackled, and the meat on his bones sizzled. The stench of him was thick, and cloying, and foul.

The blue of his eyes was untouched in the travesty of his lipless, toothless face. He flung his arms out sideways and flames played along his bones. He was all black, charred, fissured skin, with faint molten light seeping through the cracks, like magma burning beneath cooling lava. In a shower of ash and soot wings unfurled—*wings*—and snapped aloft. Singed, *burning* wings, dripping gouts of flame like falling feathers.

From out of his melted mouth, the perfect teeth now absent within the bloody arch of his palate, came the shouted command. "*Know* my name . . . *know* it!"

"Holy shit," I murmured.

"*Know* that I am Shemyazaz . . . that I am the *first* among them, the *first* of the *bene ha'elohi* . . ." His expression wasn't angry. It was transcendently ecstatic. "I am *Shemyazaz* . . . and before we fell *we were the Sons of God!*"

CHAPTER THREE

I didn't do as the angel suggested. Rather, as he *commanded*. I did not bend the knee, or, for that matter, bend any part of my body at all. I was too taken aback. I just stood there and stared, like an idiot. The most I could manage was to close my mouth.

Man, the guy in this version of his body was *fugly*.

"Shemyazaz," Remi murmured, as if in shock. As if he knew what that meant.

I darted a quick glance at him before looking back at the burned-black angel atop the bar. In a low voice, I said, "What is it? What is *he*?"

But Remi couldn't offer any answer because the Shemyazaz—whatever, *who*ever that was—began whirling like a Dervish. As he spun, the wreckage of massive wings lofted out sideways, snapped through the air. Ash flew, and soot, and strips of flesh and feathers were shredded from body and wings.

I ducked and dropped, because I was pretty sure that if a wing made contact with any part of me I'd likely be sliced in two. I pressed one hand against the wood floor to keep myself upright despite my squat, but the displacement of the air buffeted me. I rocked forward onto a knee to steady myself.

Next to me, Remi, too, was down, pulling himself up off his ass to crouch there, one hand lifted as if to protect the top of his head. We cast one another abbreviated glances of sheer disbelief and no little apprehension before once more locking our eyes on the still-spinning angel as he shed parts of his skin and wings all over the bar. Gloppy fragments flew out onto the dance floor.

And then he stopped. Just—stopped. With so much skin and muscle missing the bones were clearly visible. And the brilliant blue eyes, even within the wrecked face, remained avidly intense.

Despite the melted rictus, he managed to stretch the remains of his mouth into a wider grin. He gazed down upon us in barely concealed glee. "You *bent the knee!*"

Well. Okay. Yes, I had. Not because he commanded it, but to escape the twin scimitars of his wings. One knee was planted firmly against the dance floor, so yeah. Bent.

Remi didn't stay crouched, and his knees didn't stay bent. He thrust himself back to his feet and faced the angel. "Shemyazaz," he said. "You fell. You *did* fall. And you *were* the first, as you claim; the first among them, the first to call Lucifer your lord, and the first of your people to be flung down into hell for the sin of lying with a human woman. But why are you *here?*"

Warily, I rose from my crouch against the dance floor. I wasn't sure exactly what Remi was intending, but at least he had the ruined angel's attention. Probably safer than the guy spinning again, shedding yet more flesh and feathers. There wasn't a whole lot of him left.

"Morningstar," the angel said.

Remi's eyes were fixed on him. His voice was very quiet. "Why are you here?"

The brilliant eyes blinked. "I came here."

"Why?"

"To destroy the Morningstar."

That caught me off-guard. "You were in hell and all buddy-buddy with Lucifer, but now you're here to kill him?"

Shemyazaz lifted wings and arms, spread his legs. Displaying himself. Displaying the travesty. "Because *this* is what he did to me! I was beautiful, I was *beautiful*, and he grew jealous, just as he did of the Son, and *this is what he did to me!*"

"But—" I shook my head slowly. "You didn't look like this when you came through that door."

He might be an angel, but his voice trembled all the same. I wasn't certain if it were anger, or tears; fury, or abject desolation. Maybe all of them. "That form, that *beautiful boy* I was when I came through that door . . . two hours. That's all I have, to be myself. All the Morningstar left to me. All he left *of* me."

Before I could say anything more he was running the length of the bar again, body shedding gobbets of charred flesh. But he stopped before leaping off this time. Up on his toes he halted, lifted a forefinger in the air, and the jukebox began to play. It was a woman's voice I heard singing, high and sweet on the chorus, but the angel looked down at us both and raised his voice over hers.

"It won't matter," he said in time with the music. "It won't matter anyhow." His arms dropped, and his wings collapsed into folded shreds, like a tattered paper parasol. "The sun's light is dim, and the Morningstar says I've sinned."

I looked at Remi and whispered. "Lyrics, poem, or is he just making shit up?"

"Paraphrased lyrics," he answered. "It's . . ." He paused, looking at the ruined *bene ha'elohi*, the broken Son of God before us, and he swallowed hard. "The song's called 'Angel of the Morning.'"

"Morning*star*," Shemyazaz said.

And then he began to weep.

I've seen many things in my life, including a man bleeding out, dying by my hand, but this . . . this? A burned and broken angel crying? Not even in my wildest dreams.

And then Ganji, the African Orisha, walked out of the dimness from the back of the building. The orbs along the crossbeams, which I'd forgotten in the midst of Shemyazaz's meltdown—*literal* meltdown—strobed bright and white. Their merged illumination gleamed off Ganji's shaven skull. He wore black, as usual, jeans and tight t-shirt, stretched over hard muscle. He paid no attention to Remi or me, just walked onto the dance floor with all of his attention focused on the angel.

Or what was left of him.

"Oh, child," Ganji said, in his resonant, African-accented English. "You are a *malak maksur*. Come with me, come and see Sayida. She will take you to her breast and dry your tears. She will quiet your fires, smooth your skin, put into order your ruined wings. She cannot return all the hours the *Manje* has stolen, but she will ease you. And when you are whole again for those two hours, you may visit among the humans in glory and beauty. *Sawf najid lak alsalam.* We shall find you peace." Ganji stretched out his right arm toward the angel, upturned palm beckoning. Welcoming.

Atop the bar, Shemyazaz stilled his weeping. He seemed irresolute, almost shy, which I found incongruous in a being born of heaven, a full-blown angel. His tone was much diminished. "Can she make me whole?"

Ganji's voice was kind, though his words were not what

Shemyazaz wanted to hear. "Only your God can do that, my *malak maksur*. You are of His making."

The angel said, "I am like Bruno Mars."

For a moment I was certain I'd misheard.

"Locked out of heaven," Shemyazaz added sadly, and I realized he meant the Bruno Mars *song*.

"You are not locked out of Sayida's heaven," Ganji said. "She will share it for a while. Come."

Shemyazaz squatted, slid down from the bar in a shower of soot, placed one charred hand into Ganji's. "Then I will go with you."

I watched them depart the surreal scene in a highly prosaic fashion: they just walked out the back door. The orbs streaked down from the heavy beams and followed god and angel into a quieter darkness.

Remi and I stared after them for a long moment. Then we looked at one another. "But what was that Ganji said to Shemyazaz?" I asked. "That *malak* thing?"

"*Malak maksur*," Remi said.

"And? What does it mean?"

"Got no idea."

"But you knew what the angel said to you when he was talking to the orbs." Talking to the orbs. Yeah, that made me sound sane. So very erudite of a former college professor.

Remi hitched one shoulder in a half-shrug. "Because I know a little Koine Greek. Had to study it for my doctorate, looked a few things up." He grinned. "When he called me *ánthropos ton ageládon*? That was the closest you can come to 'cowboy.' I am '*man of the cows.*'"

"Well, at least that sounds a little more elegant." I stood up. I needed to call Grandaddy, find out what the hell was going on and why he—or whomever—had triggered an alert right when we didn't need one, though I assumed it had to do with Shemyazaz's presence in the neighborhood. I fished in a hip pocket and snagged a phone. Nope, wrong one; I wanted the magic phone that ran on neither iOS or Android systems. Pulled that one, discovered the plain black home screen showed a bright red radioactive symbol.

Frowning, I tapped it. A message appeared on the screen. I promptly looked at Remi. "Check your phone. Hit the red icon, if there is one, and tell me what message you see."

Remi did. His brows shot up and he blinked, then looked at me. "'Danger, Will Robinson?'"

I confirmed mine said the same. "The ring tone is from *Close Encounters of the Third Kind*, and now this?"

Remi shrugged. "Well, one of the explanations for Revelations is that the writers purposely framed everything in imagery specifically designed to grab the audience's attention, to impress upon them the seriousness of the End of Days."

Non sequitur time. I frowned at him. "Yeah. And?"

"Maybe using pop culture references is the kind of language that gets *our* attention, and impresses upon *us* the seriousness of the End of Days."

I stared at him. "That's what you're going with?"

Remi's smile was as slow as his drawl. "Makes sense, don't it? We're fanboys. Unless whoever sent it just happens to be a pop culture fan screwing with us."

For an arrested moment I considered whether celestial beings had personal preferences in music, movies, cars, booze, you name it. I mean, the Bible certainly didn't suggest that as far as I could remember, but you never know.

Then I shrugged it away. "Well, I'll ask Grandaddy about

that, too." I pulled up the only contacts I had: Grandaddy, Remi, Ganji, and Lily—the Irish Goddess of Battles herself— and tapped his name. Waited a while. Whether he wouldn't, or simply couldn't, Grandaddy did not pick up. "Dammit." I stuffed the phone back into my other hip pocket. Carrying two phones was going to get old fast. "I really would like some answers. I mean *some*one sent that Amber/Weather/Burned-Up-Angel Alert. Makes sense it would be Grandaddy."

Remi tilted his head in doubt, lips pursed. "Not so sure about that. He took off with that Ripper letter . . . might could be hip-deep in investigatin' that."

"Then let's go ask the magic computer." I headed for the staircase. "That is, if it chooses to talk to us." The device seemed to be shy, or coy, or downright pissy. And very dictatorial. Possibly, it viewed my questions about this as frivolous, just as it had when we were instructed not to use our magic credit cards for 'frivolous expenditures.'

Like, you know, fighting demons, screwing with the devil, saving the world. No accounting for what might be viewed as *frivolous* in the midst of such minor inconveniences.

Remi followed, but for once he wasn't singing. *I* was the one who had to forcibly stomp on the impulse to surrender to the Bruno Mars *'Locked Out of Heaven'* earworm.

But at least it wasn't country.

CHAPTER FOUR

Upstairs in the common room I plopped myself down in the task chair before the computer. It did not remotely surprise me that I found no indication of the manufacturer on any part of the CPU. Plain old black tower, plain black monitor, plain gray soundbar. Plus a perfectly ordinary power button on the tower, and I depressed it.

I heard Remi's step in the doorway behind me. He'd always been the one on the computer before. I watched it boot up. "Normal browser?"

"Other than when it was showing us unsolicited messages all on its own, yup." He came in all the way, pulled out one of the chairs at the table and abruptly made an inarticulate sound of utter disgust.

I swiveled around to look at him, wondering what triggered the expression. Burned angel glop on a boot? Found him still standing, staring at the styrofoam container resting on the table.

Oh. *Oh.* Blechh.

In the midst of everything to do with a well-cooked angel, we'd forgotten about the ordinary and innocent human who had involuntarily surrendered a kidney. I hoped it had been post mortem. *Ugh.*

Remi just looked disturbed. "What are we supposed to *do* with this thing?"

My stomach gave a little squirm as I grimaced. I was pretty sure I'd never request boxed restaurant leftovers again. "Hell if *I* know." I sucked in a breath, blew it out noisily. "I mean, we don't even know if it's human."

"Pretty sure it is."

"It might be a sheep's kidney, or something."

"This is a *demon* we're dealing with," Remi said. "Why would he—it—send us a sheep's kidney when it can probably drop a shitload of gen-u-wine dismembered bodies on us?"

"Send it to the cops, then."

"That's best," Remi agreed. "But I guess we send it anonymously . . . do you really want to drive over to the closest police station and deliver a human body part?"

I thought of my dad—former Marine, current cop—and how he might react to a couple of strangers walking in with a kidney from a woman whose body had already been found. Or from a body they hadn't *yet* found. "Yeah, that would be a 'no.' Hell, I'll ask the computer about that, too." I swiveled back. "Maybe . . . I don't know, stick it in the freezer for now? I mean, we need to preserve it for DNA. We can get a cooler pack for mailing."

"This in our freezer is downright disgusting," Remi declared, but I heard the squeak of a styrofoam box catching against slick wood as he picked it up and thumped away in his boots. He came back a few minutes later and sat down at the table. "I found some of those kitchen trash bags and wrapped it up in one, stuffed it in the back of the freezer. *Don't* pull it out by mistake. I ain't eating it for dinner."

Oh, God. I *really* didn't want to think about the kidney any more. I wanted to think about why a burned-to-cinders angel had sought us out to do pirouettes on top of a bar, sic orbs on us, and play country music on the jukebox. "Did you do anything special to bring up the magic screen?"

"Nope. Did its own thing. All the other times I went through three different browsers to see if I could get into the deep web—deepest of the deep, I reckon—and I never could."

I stared at the screen, considered things. Finally shrugged. "Ask, and ye shall find." I began checking out browsers just as Remi had.

"Seek."

"Seek what?" Chrome was Chrome, as far as I could tell.

"'Seek, and ye shall find.'"

I was distracted, inputting letters. "Yeah. That."

"The actual verse is Matthew 7:7: *'Ask, and it shall be given you; seek, and ye shall find; knock, and it shall be opened unto you.'* And then 7:8: *'For every one that asketh receiveth; and he that seeketh findeth; and to him that knocketh it shall be opened.'*"

I'd moved on from Chrome to Edge. "Remi?"

"Huh."

"I'm not much interested in Bible verses at the moment."

He was silent as I got nowhere with Edge. But as I moved on to Firefox he found something to say. Or to repeat, at any rate. "You're not much interested in Bible verses?"

"Not really, no. I'm too busy trying to find my way into whatever this iAngel deep/dark web thing is."

"You're not interested in Bible verses even though this

iAngel web thing *is*, I reckon, actually run *by* angels, and coming *from* angels."

I thought that over as I stared at the perfectly ordinary browser screen that offered absolutely no answers, and chewed crookedly at my bottom lip. "Hey, Remi?"

"Huh."

"Go out, close the door, then knock on it."

"Come again?"

I spun my chair to face him. "Go out, close the door. Then knock on it, come back in."

His expression suggested he was weighing my sanity.

"Hey, you were the one who said it: *'Knock, and it shall be opened unto you.'* Maybe we have to do it in physical code, or something."

He seemed no more convinced of my sanity but did as told. Stepped out, shut the door, then knocked, opened the door, and stepped back through. "That float your boat?"

I turned my chair back to the computer. "*'Ask, and it shall be given you; seek and ye shall find,'*" I muttered, and worked my way through every browser window asking what I felt was a perfectly straightforward question.

Remi came up to look over my shoulder. "You're asking who Shemyazaz is?"

"It might be good to know details about who he is."

"*I* know who he is. Shemyazaz, Samyaza, Sahjaza—there's a whole host of versions of his name. He was—or *is*, I reckon, seein' as how he's here among us—a Grigori. The first. *Bene ha'elohi*, the Sons of God, just as he said. He was first among them, and the first to fall, of the Grigori."

"Yeah?"

"*And* the first to share forbidden knowledge when he was

meant only to watch, *and* he had the unmitigated gall to be the first of the Grigori to lie with a human woman."

"The horror," I murmured, trying for Brando's tone. "Any other firsts? Seeking and finding, here."

"He was also the first to sire a child, said child being, therefore, the first Nephilim. *That's* what got a whole passel of Grigori thrown down into the pit with ol' Scratch. And Shemyazaz told us what he's here for."

"To kill the devil?" I shook my head. "He's here like all the demons are: to sow utter chaos, complete with eviscerating humans the way Jack the Ripper did, and prepare the way for Lucifer's return. What Shemyazaz told us is probably what he thought we wanted to hear, for God knows whatever reason. He may be an angel, but he didn't exactly strike me as particularly well-balanced."

Abruptly the browser dimmed, flickered, pixelated briefly, then went out altogether, leaving in its place a black screen with print across the middle.

"Well," Remi said, "there's your answer."

I'd asked, I'd sought, Remi'd knocked, and in bold, gold, bright letters the screen said: *'Unblessed.'*

And below it: *'Anevlógitos.'*

"Is that us?" I asked. "Angelitos?"

"Anevlógitos. Greek for 'unblessed.'"

I contemplated the screen, frowning at it. "Now it wants to teach me ancient Greek?"

"Angelic Rosetta Stone, maybe," Remi offered.

I typed again. *'Why is Shemyazaz here?'*

'Unblessed.'

I typed back: *"But why is he HERE?"*

'Unblessed.'

"I got that part," I muttered, then added a lengthier question with a little bit of melodramatic Bible-speak crossed with Middle Earth mixed in. *"What the hell are we supposed to do about an unblessed fallen Grigori angelito now loosed upon the world?"*

"Might could take out the *'the hell'* part," Remi suggested. "Probably wouldn't go over well with celestial beings."

So I deleted, started again. *'What the fuck are we—'* But that's as far as I got, because the entire screen went black. Possibly I had offended The Man Behind the Curtain. I tapped the escape, enter, and backspace keys, even considered just turning the whole thing off by depressing the power button, then turning it back on. Wondered if we'd have to defrag an angelic device.

"Recalculating," I muttered.

And the screen actually did come back, but no more deep web browser, or whatever the hell it was. Just three minimized browser screens along the bottom.

"Bring one up," Remi said. "Bring one up, type in *Mary Jane Kelly.*"

"Mary Jane Kelly?" I clicked on a browser.

"The Ripper letter," he said. "Those names on the backs of the other photos we received, the names of the Ripper victims. They were prostitutes Jack the Ripper killed. The last Ripper victim, as far as anyone knows, was Mary Jane Kelly. We haven't received a photo of a woman of the same name the way we did with the others. And maybe . . . well, I reckon that kidney might be from the Catherine named on the back of that last photo. Catherine Eddowes was the woman killed before Kelly."

"You know all this how?"

"There're these subversive items called books."

"So, you're a . . . what is it? Some kind of Ripperologist?"

"In my own small way, you could say so. There's no slack in my rope."

It diverted me a moment. "But—never mind." I typed the name into the search field. "And you think maybe we can stop this surrogate masquerading as Jack the Ripper before he kills Mary Jane Kelly—if he hasn't done it already, that is."

Maybe we were spinning our wheels, just like the surrogate wanted, but we couldn't afford to ignore the possibility murder was in the works. "Do you know how many 'Mary Jane Kellys there might be in this country? Or even in this state? This could be a real challenge."

"I do not," Remi said, "but let's start local."

CHAPTER FIVE

I typed, and Wiki came up at the top of the screen along with a string of names tied to Jack the Ripper. Mary Jane Kelly, also known as Marie Jeanette Kelly, Fair Emma, Ginger, Dark Mary, and Black Mary.

"Check the shelves," I said. "See if there's a phone book. Old school, but you never know."

Remi found and pulled out a phone book, flopped it on the table, paged through the thin leaves. It wasn't very thick to start with—Flagstaff, I'd gathered, was not exactly a sprawling metropolis—and contained next to no White Pages. Besides, I wasn't sure it would do any good at all now that almost everyone had given up their landlines. But it was a place to start.

I went back to the browsers, wondering if I could convince the dark web to come up again and say something more than 'Unblessed.' "Try Mary Jeanette Kelly, too." I waited as Remi flipped a page. "Anything?"

He shook his head. "There may still be women who only use initials for their first names so no one knows the listing is for a woman. Means she probably lives alone, right? Doesn't want to advertise that."

I nodded absently, most of my attention on the computer.

"Yeah, my mom said something about that once—that Grandma told her never to list her full name in the phone book. And her mother told *her* no woman needed to be listed at all, if she had a husband. *He'd* be listed, and that's all you needed. Lo, how times have changed."

Remi's tone was thoughtful. "There's a university here. Wonder if they've got their own phone book, or if it's all just virtual these days. It's been years since I was in school, and things are different in England anyhow."

That's right, the Texas cowboy had been a Rhodes Scholar. *Doctor* McCue, Ph.D., graduate of Oxford University. I only had a measly master's. "You think she could be a student?" I stopped noodling on the computer, spun the chair to face him again. "You thinking the victims are age-specific?"

His expression was solemn as he briefly hooked his mouth sideways. "I didn't look that closely at those photos the surrogate slipped us to note what age those women looked like."

"Me, neither." I'd barely looked at the photos at all, in fact, once I'd realized how messily dead the victims were. We'd seen several already, and the gore quotient kept increasing. "But there will be newspaper articles about the murders, and bound to be obits in the paper and online. Ages probably wouldn't be hard to find out." I shook my head. "But we don't know that these victims, outside of the names, are anything like the ones Jack the Ripper killed."

"Prostitutes, maybe," Remi said. "Seems to be a tradition among serial killers. I doubt the Ripper was the first, and we know he's not the last. But obits won't go into that."

"Neither will the reports the police release to the news media," I said. "At least, not at first. So, you're seriously thinking the surrogate is purposely murdering prostitutes with the same names, around the same ages, as the women Jack the Ripper killed? Part of his cover, so to speak? Verisimilitude?"

Remi shrugged. "Possible."

I mulled that over a minute. "I'm not saying you're wrong—how the hell do *I* know?—but you gotta admit it strains the bounds of credulity, that all these victims match up so closely. Besides, Flagstaff's not that big, as far as I could tell on my way in from I-40."

Remi nodded agreement.

"It's . . . wait a minute . . ." I typed, and the computer—a normal browser with normal search engines—gave me the number. "Population around seventy-five thousand," I told him. "Would it even *have* enough prostitutes to match up with the Ripper numbers and names?"

"Nothin' says they all came from here, or that they're prostitutes," Remi pointed out. "We start here, yeah, because we *are* here, but might could be he's killing all over the country and just sending the pix to us. Hell, he could be having other demons do the killings for him, having 'em purposely track down women with the right names, the right ages, regardless of where they're from."

"If that's true, why send the pictures to *us*?" I asked. "We're not the only celestial cannon fodder in the mix. Grandaddy even said so. There're a whole bunch of us little half-angels—or whatever you want to call us; *angelitos*?—running around doing the bidding of the heavenly host."

Remi shrugged. "Maybe *all* of us conscripts across the country are being played this way. Could be one set of photos with copies sent to all of us."

With a twist of my hips I set the office chair in motion, swiveling it back and forth as I thought. "*That* would be one mega mindfuck," I said finally. "All us newbies across the entire country distracted by the murders of women who have the same names as the Ripper victims."

"And all of us tearin' around trying to hunt up info on 'em," Remi agreed. "Mighty big distraction, ain't it?"

"But why would anyone feel we *need* distracting? I mean, how do *we* count for anything?"

Remi nodded. "We are, as my daddy would say, a pair of green pups still wet behind the ears."

"Then why?"

He shrugged. "You're the one who mentioned chaos in relation to demons. It's a state of utter confusion, seemingly random, but maybe highly calculated with surrogates at the wheel. In Biblical terms, *chaos* is also the formless matter that preceded creation."

"Creation . . ." I let it trail off, hooking thoughts together like chain mail. "You know, creation could as easily apply to what Lucifer is after. He wants to create his own particular version of earth, and so the same type of chaos precedes his goal, too. I mean, God succeeded at creating the world in His own image on the heels of that chaos, we know—if one is a believer, that is—so the baddest of His kids might just have decided '*If it works, don't fix it.*' But the concept of chaos as a form of reality, as a true sentient presence on earth, has certainly given birth to all kinds of cultural legends and lore. I mean, with all this ancient Greek language being thrown around . . . according to Greek mythology three specific primordial gods were born of chaos: Gaea, Tartarus, and Eros. Gaea personified the earth, and Eros, love and sex. Tartarus wasn't so benign."

Remi nodded. "A god of the underworld, AKA hell. Or a form of it, anyhow."

"Yup," I confirmed, "and Tartarus is also referred to as a *place*. It ranks below Hades. That's where the monsters and criminals are—Hades is a warehouse for the dead. Well, and also a name for the god himself. Romans called him Pluto, the Egyptians, Osiris. Hell, I don't know—Lucifer's got hundreds of aliases."

"Hades, Pluto, Osiris . . . what's in a name? God knows—" Remi broke it off, smiled crookedly, "*literally*, God knows how many names the devil actually has. Every religion has its Lucifers, Satans. A Tartarus, both location and god. Names are different, maybe, but the end goal is the same."

"Ultimate chaos, ultimate destruction. *If* the stories are true."

Remi ran a thumb across his bottom lip. "But chaos, even if it's the devil's version, doesn't mean there's no truth smack in the middle of it."

I raked a hand through loose hair, let it fall behind my shoulders. "But if this demon's just screwing with us . . ."

Remi turned the photo face up so the image was clear: a woman, limbs asprawl, wearing very little clothing that wasn't torn, that wasn't soaked with blood from the disembowelment. "I think we'd better look for ourselves," he said. "I think we'd best not risk missing a potential victim. I mean, the cops'll be doin' their thing, but they won't be looking at Greek mythology or Lucifer's surrogates."

I spun the chair back to the computer. "I'll start Googling deeper, pull up public records, LinkedIn, social media, try a couple of those pay-for-play search sites—I figure that won't count as 'frivolous expenditures' on the heavenly credit card. Why don't you call Grandaddy, see if he'll answer this time. *Keep* calling him till he does, see if he'll tell us shit and save time. If he doesn't, maybe you could start a search on your phone. If people are dying, we need actual facts. Not alternative ones."

Remi's tone was dry. "Said alpha to the beta?"

That stopped me dead. "What?"

He smiled. "Just joshin' you. I'll step out, call Grandaddy. Check back in a few."

I watched him go, considering what he'd said. Alpha. Beta. It's how Grandaddy had described us when he announced we'd been born, bred, and trained, all unknowing, then conscripted to join the heavenly host as foot soldiers deployed against, well, yeah, melodrama and all: the hordes of hell. I, as firstborn—by split seconds, apparently—was therefore alpha to Remi's beta. Which counted when heavenly matter was coalescing, because it's what fueled the supernatural *primogenitura* Grandaddy'd taught me about. More than just property being passed down, it had ignited in me when I'd nearly gotten my kid brother killed, when I had taken Matty's pain as my own and understood what true stewardship meant. But with Remi, it wasn't brother to brother, older to younger. We *weren't* brothers, not in flesh, not in bone, blood, nor spirit. We were strangers. We just happened to be linked in a bizarre sort of way because we'd both been born in a momentary spasm of heavenly essence.

Or maybe a celestial fart.

A s Remi got on the phone, I stood up and stretched before hitting up the keyboard again. Less than thirty I was—twenty-eight, in fact, only a few days before. But laying down a bike on asphalt at fifty miles-per-hour, leather or no, results in a body feeling more akin to eighty, and a hard-used eighty at that, like Indiana Jones and his quote about mileage over years. I crossed arms, settled palms over the point of each shoulder, twisted side-to-side to gently loosen my spine. Next up was hands hooked behind my neck, elbows stuck out, as I rocked down toward my hips and back up.

"Yowza," I muttered on a restrained groan, teeth gritted, wondering if there were any analgesics stuck away in the modest bathroom. I wasn't going to be walking anywhere quickly for a while.

Of course the bike was worse off than I was. And then that thought, of course, reminded me all over again that my ride was lying half-drowned in the middle of a creek cutting through steep, rocky banks. There was no way of pushing the motorcycle up the sides even with two of us doing the labor; and anyway, there was no path. Both Remi and I, beatin' feet after the legendary La Llorona of Mexican folklore, a mother who drowned her own children, had worked our way down outcroppings of granite and pockets of loose earth, hanging on to grass tufts.

Remi had no more luck reaching Grandaddy than I had, and tucked phone into pocket. "Who was the Irish god of the underworld?"

I rolled sore shoulders. "In Irish mythology? Aodh."

Remi took up his hat from the tabletop, settled it onto his head. "Just who do we know could have some answers about an Irish god who might just slop over into Lucifer's backyard now and then? Maybe pitch a horseshoe or two against one another come the weekend?"

My smile grew into a grin of appreciation. "A certain red-haired, tattooed Goddess of Battles, parked in a motorhome just up the road."

Remi smiled back. "Then let us vamoose ourselves right on up that road."

CHAPTER SIX

Daybreak as we stepped out of the Zoo's interior. Fitful, dour daybreak, and barely registered before heavy skies opened up. Rain blew through the pines and rattled loudly on the roadhouse's tin roof two stories up.

"Ahh, man." I paused before stepping out from under the roof overhang. In the east, the rising sun spawned brief light behind a scalloped scrim of clouds, then dimmed as the clouds closed ranks.

"I thought you were from the Pacific Northwest," Remi said from behind me. "Don't you have to get rained on every day, or shrivel up and die?" He slid by me through the giant split-crotch tree, thumped down four wooden steps into wet dirt and gravel and headed hastily for his silver pickup truck.

I followed, long-striding to catch up and squinting through the rain. The shoulders of Remi's denim western shirt were already soaked dark. I'd left my jacket behind, and within minutes my black t-shirt was going to glue itself to my skin. "Do you even *have* rain in Texas?"

Remi thumbed his remote and popped the locks from distance. "We have no mountains, but rain we do have. Hurricanes, even, in the Gulf. Just be glad you're not aboard your motorbike." He hunched against the weather, then flashed me a quick, sidelong glance as I matched his pace, head ducked. "Guess you'll be wantin' to go haul it up out of the crick soon as you can."

"I was actually thinking we'd do it today." I fumbled the wet door handle, pulled it open on a second try and climbed in out of the rain. "But bike's going to have to wait while we try to deal with what the devil's thrown at us, and to find a Mary Kelly. *The* Mary Kelly."

Remi opened his door, grabbed the wheel and stepped up hastily. His expression was solemn as he buckled up, stuck the key into the ignition.

I settled into the passenger bucket, yanked the door closed to shut away the wet. Rain pounded the truck's roof so hard I had to raise my voice. "Are you thinking Lily might know more than Grandaddy about this demon?"

Remi twisted the key. "I'm bettin' he knows a helluva lot more than most, but since he's not answering his phone we are hitchhiking on the information highway. So maybe Lily can at least get a message to him. I mean, he's got to care about women being murdered."

I stretched the seatbelt across my torso, shoved the tongue home in the latch. "He seemed to be surprised by the picture, like he knew nothing about the murders."

Remi drove out of the parking lot, hooked a left onto Route 66. Still not much traffic, but it was early yet. "Angels aren't omnipotent. He may be high-ranking in the heavenly hierarchy, but none of them is all-knowing or all-powerful, according to the Good Book. So yeah, reading that letter may well have sent him off somewhere to do some checking."

I finger-combed hair back from my face. As hard as the rain was falling, it hadn't taken much for Remi and I to get pretty damn wet just between building and truck. "But he needs us. He's said it. And without the right clues, the right knowledge, we can't be very effective."

Remi's hat dipped with a single nod. "Guess it's up to us to apply some of our ingenuity to finding out what we need to find out. He's never been one for holding our hands, has Grandaddy."

Yeah, ingenuity. We were the two of us highly educated, and we now knew Grandaddy had personally directed that very specific, targeted education right from childhood, starting with *Classics Illustrated*, literature done comic book style, leading into the actual literary texts. After that, for me, came heavy-duty reference books on folklore, mythology, Joseph Campbell, Aleister Crowley, witchcraft, ghosts and goblins, deity pantheons, alchemy, blah blah, woof woof.

"They don't think like us," I muttered.

Remi glanced at me briefly, then switched his attention back to the road as rain pounded down. The wipers could barely keep up. In the distance, lightning stitched light across the sky.

"Demons," I elaborated. "Surrogates. Even if they wear human hosts, rely on human brains—" I shifted in my seat, turning to look at Remi—"if they are agents of chaos, if they are themselves *chaos incarnate*, let's say, there's no such thing as predictability. We'll forever be *re*active rather than proactive. We're going to be running in place a hell of a lot."

"Can't always predict sociopaths or psychopaths, either." Remi hit the turn signal to slot the truck into the left-turn lane leading to the RV park, "but they're not demons."

"How do we know that?" I looked at his profile beneath the hat. "How do we know Bundy, Dahmer, Manson, Jim Jones . . . how do we *know* they weren't demons? Lucifer's advance guard, maybe, scattered hither and yon throughout the world. Doing their bit for the boss."

Remi met my eyes. "Or Jack the Ripper?"

"Or Jack the Ripper."

Lily let us into the belly of her beast, a motorhome echoing an eighteen-wheeler in general silhouette, though smaller, but with several half-rooms that, with a switch depressed, ground outward on a muffled whine of hydraulics, doubling its width. A pregnant house giving birth.

As she opened the door, Lily looked beyond us into the weather, red eyebrows knit. In the storm-grayed light of the day, her choppy Mohawk haircut turned deep auburn until lightning skated across the sky and painted it bright again. Then she stepped aside, made room for us by retreating into the RV.

And it struck me again, as I climbed folding steel steps and ducked inside the narrow door, how incongruous the picture: the Morrigan, right out of Irish mythology—the Goddess of Battles herself—camped out in an RV with an angry-eyed crow and a massive Irish Wolfhound as her road trip companions.

I'd studied Irish mythology on my way to a Master's in folklore. Nothing in the pages of books prepared me for reality. Or, rather, *this* reality.

She stood in the center of the kitchen and looked us up and down. Remi took off his damp hat and hung it on a window valance, eyed the wolfhound lying sprawled across the sofa sleeper.

I settled hipshot against a counter and met Lily's level look. "Grandaddy been by?"

She ignored that. "Coffee? You're lookin' like drowned rabbits."

"Rats," I corrected.

She fixed bright green eyes on me. "Rabbits drown, too."

"Yes, ma'am, coffee'll do us fine" Remi answered on a quick shiver, and when the dog got up and moved over on the sofa to create room, he took it. The wolfhound dropped her head onto one of Remi's thighs with a low-rumbled sigh. A boy and his dog.

Lily's eyes glinted as she looked at me. "Whiskey in yours, then?"

I pulled my wet t-shirt away from my chest, gripped hem and flapped the front in a wholly ineffective attempt at drying the fabric. "It's a little too early even for me."

"The way you're moving, boyo, whiskey may be just what you need. Oil for rusted hinges."

Lily knew exactly why I was moving stiffly; she'd been the one the day before to wash down road rash with rubbing alcohol when I'd have preferred the drinking kind as painkiller.

I refused whiskey, wandered toward the empty recliner, skirted my way around the big wooden perch hosting the bad-tempered crow, and eased my damp, sore self down into leather upholstery. A lap of luxury, Lily's RV. Guess a goddess deserved it. "Grandaddy walked out in the middle of an important conversation and left us hanging. You seen him?"

Lily made coffee, poured mugs full, handed them around. "I have not. But he's a busy man, is Jubal Tanner. You're not his only 'grandkids.'"

"Women are dying," Remi told her flat out. "He took the only real clue we had and walked away with it. Another woman's dead, or at risk to be killed. Supposin' it's the latter, we need to find her first."

The Morrigan was barefoot, wore tight threadbare jeans and a green tank top. Celtic silver coiled around her upper arms above rich, multicolored sleeve tattoos inked into bared fair skin. Lily shrugged, settled herself into a swivel chair, drank coffee, made no further comment as she eyed me over the mug.

I opened my mouth to ask another question, but the rain abruptly ratcheted up into waterfall-level noise. The power of it, the roar of hard-driving water against thin steel overhead, reminded me dramatically that we weren't inside a truly sound structure. I mean, the RV was huge and heavy, but it still stood on wheels, not a cement foundation.

The wolfhound lifted her head sharply. Hackles rose as she emitted a low growl, then she slid off the couch and stood stiff-legged, head slung low as she glared at the door.

The rain stopped abruptly, as if someone turned off the spigot. Lightning lit up the world. A massive crack of thunder sounded directly overhead. Upon the perch next to me, the crow mantled, then about shattered my eardrums with its frantic noise right beside my skull. I shot up from the chair and was in the kitchen before I even realized it.

I felt it come up through the floor of the motorhome, through the thick soles of my bike boots, and recognized the rising power, the promise of violence. I'd felt it before, back home. The RV swayed atop its wheels. Coffee in my mug sloshed. Remi lifted his high in the air as he rose so the contents wouldn't spill into his lap.

Lily frowned briefly, looked fixedly at the dog. Her sister, she'd called her, one of the threefold unity. "Macha?"

The world around us *shuddered*.

"Nemain!" Lily said sharply as the crow shrieked, and the dog curled lips back from her teeth. Everything in the motorhome rattled. Loose items on the countertop slid right off, hit the tile floor.

And then the noise, the shivering of the motorhome, subsided into a suddenly rainless day, into a silence so absolute it felt surreal.

"Earthquake," I said.

Remi, bending to rescue his fallen hat from the floor, stared at me, brows rising. "In Arizona?"

"I don't know if Arizona is subject to earthquakes or not," I placed my half-drunk coffee in the sink, "but I do know that was an earthquake. We've had some in Oregon. Several faults run through the state."

Frowning, Remi yanked his phone from a pocket, probably planning to track down confirmation if any was to be had so soon.

I looked at Lily. "It was earthquakes that started all this, wasn't it? The demon infestation?"

"Hell vents." She stood up, set her mug upon the counter, began to pick up items that had hit the floor. "Or so Jubal told me."

A cold grue ran down my spine. I swore, moved past her at speed and went right out the door. I one-footed it on my way down, then hit the ground with both boots and stopped short.

The old campground wound through big pines, many RVs screened by vegetation. I heard calls and shouts echoing, though none sounded frightened. What I heard was sharp, startled disbelief, and an underlying kid-level excitement.

Remi came down the steps. "I got nothin' so far on any earthquake—"

I was impatient, terse. "It was."

"—but you're hackled up like that wolfhound bitch," Remi said. "What're you sensing?"

I lifted a spread-fingered hand to silence him, and he got the message.

Scent came first. Pines. Vegetation. Wet stone, soaked earth. Damp, dead campfires. No more rain fell, as if driven away by a force more powerful, but the clouds remained, low and malignant. All around me trees and shrubs shed leftover rain into puddles, into rivulets running swift against the ground, drummed uneven percussion on motorhome roofs.

Lightning struck close and low, disappearing behind trees high on the mountain. Thunder followed directly, but the long rumble of it attenuated, died out.

Standing very still, I let the noise of the place, even the shouts and shrieks of overexcited kids, wash away from me.

Lightning flashed, but this time I heard no thunder on its tail. In its place I heard the beat of my heart, heard it slowing, slowing. Heard myself pull in a breath to fill lungs and belly.

Upon the mountain, within regimented parallel lines of young oaks in the midst of towering Ponderosa pines and huge, lichen-sheathed granite boulders, with Grandaddy standing watch and a stranger in a cowboy hat bearing witness, I remembered sensing the deep peace of the San Francisco Peaks. Sacred to the Navajo and Hopi peoples, the former volcano bore only the soothing colors of the earth, the subtle blue-green sheen of abalone in tribute to its Navajo name: Abalone Shell Mountain. Home to Hopi *katsinam*, known more familiarly as kachinas. I'd felt a deep sense of harmony, of unity, that day, upon the mountain. The peace of the earth.

But now? The earth wasn't peaceful. It was *other*.

It needed proper greeting, the other earth, so I might learn its temper. Grandaddy had taught me that. With courtesy and quietude, I reached out to it.

I invited it to come, and come it did.

No grace. No grace in it at all.

"*Koyaanisqatsi,*" I gasped.

And began to cough. To choke.

I wavered on my feet, went down onto one knee even as Remi reached out to grab an arm. I heard him say my name twice, then again even more urgently; felt the firmness of his grip upon my upper arm, fingers and thumb like a vise, and a strong upward pressure as if he would lift me.

But I couldn't rise, even with his hand on my arm urging me to do so. I kept coughing, bent forward now. One knee and the toe of my boot took my weight until I added a hand, a stiffened arm, to prop myself up. I felt wet gravel beneath my palm, and the wicking of dampness up through the fibers of my jeans as I knelt. I thought my lungs might climb my throat and surge out of my mouth like a river in spate.

"*Koyaanisqatsi,*" I repeated, in between painful, involuntary spasms of throat and diaphragm.

Remi was now trying to drag me up. "But what does that *mean?*"

The coughing was abating, thank God, though my chest felt heavy, my throat raw. "Life out of balance," I answered hoarsely. "It's Hopi, it's a Native American concept."

"Well, I think that may well be true," Remi said, "Based on what we've—"

But he broke it off, turned his bare, unhatted head to stare at the mountain, a burn-scarred, stony bulk screened by the pines of the campground.

The hand on my bicep squeezed even harder for just a moment, and then he released the grip on my upper arm altogether, turned away from me to the mountain. He took long strides away from me.

And then he began to run.

CHAPTER SEVEN

What the—?

Startled, still trying to regain my breath and clear my throat, I watched the cowboy unaccountably head off at a run into shadowed, screening trees with no word of warning or intent. I shouted his name hoarsely, thrust myself from knee to feet and absently slapped a wet, sandy hand against my jeans. I took a stride after him as he disappeared into the trees, then swung back hastily toward the motorhome.

We both had knives on us, but I had no gun; it was in my bedroom back at the Zoo, where I'd left it after a quick shower. New heavenly conscript or not, I had never carried a gun but the once, when I killed a man, and now, as a felon, it was illegal to do so. So that was my mindset. Carrying a gun full time wasn't pure reflex yet; it had not occurred to me to slip into the shoulder rig and safe the Taurus home in the holster before heading to Lily's. We were simply to talk.

I was clueless as to whether Remi had his gun in addition to his Bowie and throwing knives. He wore his short-barreled Taurus Judge in a belt holster, less obvious than a shoulder holster setup with multiple straps. I took one step toward the RV,

found Lily was waiting on the top step with an arm outstretched. In her hand was a revolver offered sideways on the
flat, barrel pointed away from us both.

I took it without a word, automatically registered the weight,
the make and model: S&W 686, almost three pounds of steel, a
.357 Magnum with a six-inch barrel. Pretty damn powerful.

Before I could turn back and take off at a run, as I intended,
Lily came swiftly down the remaining two steps, grabbed my
wrist and gripped firmly with both hands. It literally stopped
my breath. In the power of that grip I felt the *other* in her. She
was the Morrigan, green eyes ablaze and fixed on my own.
More goddess than woman in that moment, borrowed body
or no.

"Open the cylinder," Lily said tersely, clamping down on
my wrist harder than ever, "now, or before you shoot. Blow on
those bullets, boyo. If it's a demon he's gone after, the rounds
need to be breath-blessed by a heaven-born soul in order to kill
a surrogate. *Remember* this."

I could move again, and I jerked free of her grip. Something
in me was anxious beyond description, something oddly like
some kind of weird-ass spiritual stress nausea, because it wasn't
physical. My gut was tying itself into knots, but I did not feel
like vomiting.

I left her then, spun away and ran hard. Not just because I
wanted to chase Remi as a natural reaction to a friend poten-
tially running into danger. But because I *had* to.

Because the tsunami of *primogenitura*, the stewardship of
older alpha to younger beta implanted during the spark of my
birth, awakened and confirmed when Remi and I gripped
hands, rings touching, as instructed by Grandaddy but a few
nights before, rose up within me and demanded it.

———

Despite my experience with revolvers, running through the forest and up a mountain, especially at high altitude, while opening a cylinder and blowing on six exposed primers was not recommended in any gun owner's manual, and I was a little concerned not about the possibility of a misfire, but that I might mistakenly depress the cylinder release and dump the bullets altogether. Then I'd have nothing to breathe on, or *bleed* on, and I'd be fucked. Possibly Remi, too. So the bullets stayed put for now.

Blowing on bullets, making holy water out of our spit . . . a summary of my new life as a heaven-sent pest control man. And since what came out of a dead surrogate inhabiting a ghost's body—or whatever that bizarre corporeality of it was— were hell-whelped fugly cockroach-like remains, it was a most appropriate job title.

"Rem*i*!" I shouted, and it echoed back at me amidst dripping pines, oaks, aspens. "Dammit. *Remi!*"

Behind me I heard children shrieking in the RV campground, but recognized the tone as play, not fear or panic. Probably still enthralled with the whole concept of an earthquake on an otherwise wet and boring morning. High-pitched voices faded as I hit the first incline of the mountain's shoulder. I was not yet acclimated to seven-thousand-plus feet of elevation, and I felt the altitude as I clambered up the slope.

Pine needles are slick in any condition. Wet, worse yet. My biker boots had thick grippy waffle soles with decent traction, and I was planting a good 185-190 pounds into the ground through my legs, but slick deadfall offered very little stability. I slipped and slid, swore, kept climbing.

If I *thought* about it, wracked my brain about it, I had no clue where Remi was going. I was totally at sea. But so long as I focused instead on footing and trying to steady my breath, just let myself think about other things, I felt an almost physical certainty where he was, lodestone to North Pole.

Demon. Had to be.

My gift was to sense places, to feel the good as well as the taint of demonic presence. Remi's was to recognize the demon in a *body*, be it human, animal, ghost—hell, whatever. His new-kindled ability was a step slower to come than mine, but was clearly gaining ground. He could also sense the angel in what otherwise seemed human; it was Remi who'd recognized that Shemyazaz was not a demon despite his fearsome appearance, but a fallen Grigori damned by Lucifer himself.

Though it could be Remi was going after Shemyazaz and not a demon at all; maybe he sensed threat in a half-crazed son of heaven. Who knew what Shemyazaz might do? He claimed he'd been inadvertently thrown back into our world when the hell vents opened, and now that he was stuck here, back on an earth he'd walked millennia ago, he was wholly dedicated to killing the devil. But trust the ruined angel?

Grandaddy would say no. Grandaddy *had*.

"Remi . . . come on, man—slow the hell down! We'll take it out together!"

And that was all I had breath for, still climbing, still sliding and slipping, tripping, trying for traction even as wet leaves and needles slid away beneath my boot soles, and trees dumped small burdens of leftover rainwater as I passed beneath. The lower portion of my jeans were wet, growing heavy, and my t-shirt now was completely soaked, slick against my skin. The warmth of a summer day was not in evidence, though I, Oregon-born, would never call this cold, or even chilly. But clammy-cool, yes.

Trees thinned. Conifers now, juniper, and thickets of quaking aspen with lime-green leaves fluttering against white trunks with their black "eyes," striated with dark bars like knife cuts. Still the day was dim behind sullen clouds. I was aware of distant lighting, distant thunder, and prayed it all remained so. Standing high upon a mountain in the midst of an electrical storm was dramatic, maybe, certainly cinematic, but not necessarily compatible with human life.

I slipped to one knee, gasped for air through a throat that still felt raw from coughing and choking. In the midst of that unexpected pause, I depressed the release on the revolver, thumbed the cylinder out into the slightly cupped fingers of my left hand. Smooth, cool, deadly steel. I bent my head, blew. Six bullet casings, six primers, touched now, as Lily directed, by the breath of a heaven-born soul.

Time to go, to still the maddening itch within my body. I rolled the cylinder back into the frame, turned it one chamber to click it into place, then sucked in wind and began climbing hard again through thinning trees.

Two steps more, and I stopped abruptly. Before me, upon the burn-scarred mountain stretched an ancient lava flow from the rounded summit, as if the peak had grown a new and harder skin in centuries past. A younger manmade fire had burned across the flanks, stripping it of splendor and leaving behind the charred remains of skeletal pines.

Like Shemyazaz, the pines had lost their beauty long before, reduced to blackened wreckage. But here had come newer growth in the wake of fire, here was resurrection in the quaking aspen and grass and foliage following close upon the burning.

The mountain was sacred. Gods walked upon it. But there was a taint here, a wash of red in the corners of my eyes. It wasn't yet a domicile and maybe never would be, if the *katsinam* held their ground. But I smelled the odor not of trees, of rain, of stone and earth, or even the sulfur of stories, but the oversweet, cloying, throat-closing fragrance of what Remi had called *kyphi*, an ancient, powerful incense.

Unerring, now, I turned toward the source. Toward Remi and the creature.

Bare-headed, Remi squatted in thin wild grass and deadfall. One knee rested against the ground, a boot heel tucked up under his butt at the foot of three close-clustered aspens. Using merely a thread of voice, he asked, "See it?"

Indeed I did. Neither man nor woman, neither black dog nor ghost. As the gray of the clouds moved apart, permitting a glance of fitful sunlight, the camouflage of tree trunks and foliage withdrew, leaving behind a clear view. Brown, focused, feral eyes; the sleekness of tawny pelt; pointed, triangular ears on alert. Parted mouth displayed an arcade of powerful teeth.

"Not what it looks like," Remi said quietly. "A smidge more than cat."

Cougar, puma, mountain lion, catamount. A plethora of names for a single big cat.

And something more inside. Dangerous on its own. Deadly hosting a demon.

I did not move. Kept my voice barely above a whisper. "We will talk about this, you know."

"I 'spect so."

It was a standoff between cowboy and demon, plain and simple. I had no idea why Remi was squatting with a knee on the ground, as the posture placed him at a disadvantage.

Something nagged. An itch settled between my shoulder blades. "You hurt?"

"Scratch."

"Thought so." *Primogenitura*, again. I knew it better, now. I could lift the wound from Remi, take it into myself, but for now I had another task. I drew back the hammer on the big pistol, felt it click into place. "I'm going to shoot."

"Figured you might. Get to it, then."

"The thing may be quicker than a normal cat."

"It is."

"How fast can you duck?"

"Been duckin' and dodgin' bulls, son. I'll manage this."

Our entire exchange had been quietly conversational. The cat had not even flicked an ear. Not even blinked an eye. Even with me present, its attention was all for Remi.

It's best to shoot from a familiar stance, especially with a big gun, from a comfortable positioning of feet, weight balanced to aid accuracy, hands joined as one cupped the heel of the other on gun butt. But this was neither the time nor place nor situation to depend upon a specific physical posture. We weren't at a range. I needed to shoot the thing dead no matter what it took and as quickly as possible.

One-armed, one-handed, I raised the big revolver, welcomed reflexive instinct. The cat, as expected, leaped.

It came not at Remi, but me.

On a heavy, echoing report and a recoil up the arm that stirred echoes of aches in my shoulder, a single breath-blessed .357 Magnum round entered the cavern of the cougar's open mouth, blew through the back of its throat, exited the skull in gouts of skin and brain and bloodied chunks of bone.

Damn big gun. Damn big round. Damn dead demon.

CHAPTER EIGHT

The cat was dead. No question of that. Not much head left. But I waited anyway, gun at the ready. The *cat* was dead— was its hijacker?

The reek was horrendous. It was the *kyphi*, the ancient, powerful incense smell; the smell of demons. It spread out like a miasmic aerosol, an odor that stung nostrils and eyes. I tasted it in the back of my throat, swallowed convulsively to keep my belly down where it should be.

Rotten eggs, a natural gas leak, the stink of plain sulfur would be easier to deal with. I spat once, twice, then girded my loins, so to speak, and walked closer to the body, prepared to shoot again.

Upon inspection, I lowered the revolver. In the mess of brain, blood, and bone, I saw glittering insectoid carapaces, the sheen of bodies that resembled cockroaches. Feelers, multiple legs, wing-like structures. It was hell's Rorschach test, an amoebic spread of remains.

And then a wave in the midst of the glittering dark sprawl heaved itself upward.

I swore, lifted the revolver, heard Remi say something urgently about *not* shooting, about another way. Then he was beside me. I saw blood on his shirt, saw him yank back a sleeve, ripping it, and press a folded blue-and-white bandana against his forearm. Blood stained the white areas, spread dark across the cloth, and then he dropped it into the midst of demon remains. Remi recited the Latin words of exorcism, the *Rituale Romanum*. The cockroaches—or whatever they were; we really needed a name for them—caught fire.

I'd heard it before, in the Zoo. It was like corn popping, and the splitting open of dark bodies. As one, Remi and I took long steps away, both of us pressing the backs of our hands against noses and mouths. More popping, more stench, and bursts of flame.

I couldn't restrain a hard grimace. "God, this is *foul!*"

Remi nodded, expression disgusted as he stared at the tiny burning corpses. The blood-stained bandana was gone, burned to ash. I saw again the torn sleeve, the stains on his shirt, and before I even thought about it I'd moved, was close to him. I set down the revolver on a stump, reached out for his arm and demanded, with an insistent *gimmegimmegimme* gesture of fingers, to take a look.

Remi refused at first, said he was fine, but I guess something in my tension and urgency got through to him. He lifted his arm, let me take it into one hand while I pulled back the torn sleeve with my other.

It was indeed a real live slice from a mountain lion claw, and it was long, running halfway between wrist and elbow. It didn't go deep enough to separate the multiple layers of muscle, but stitches were needed, I was sure.

"He jumped me," Remi said as I inspected. "I had no clue he was there. I heard him, spun around just as he leaped, and I ducked down—well, most of me ducked."

We had no water to wash out the wound. "Damn lucky."

"Said I was used to ducking bulls, didn't I? You get bucked off of one of those sons of bitches, you'd *better* be ready to dodge. And be damn good at it to boot."

I felt a chill skate down my back. Tried to shake it off. "That's it, though? This wound? No others?"

"That's it."

I tried for levity. "You want me to spit on it?"

He stared at me in consternation. "Why would I want you to *spit* on it?"

"Well, I breathed on a bullet that killed a demon, and we know our spit in water changes it to holy water, so—"

Remi decisively removed his arm from my grip and took a step away, guarding the limb while apparently weighing my sanity.

"—I thought maybe it might act as heavenly antibacterial," I finished. I rolled my shoulders, tried to dissipate tension that was *building*, not fading. "Look, we need to go back to the RV, let Lily clean this up."

Remi didn't dismiss me outright, but he clearly saw no reason for haste. "It'll keep for the time being. I'm wondering if we need to explode this body."

"That's to clear a domicile," I said. "You know, where a demon has set up housekeeping. This is different. These mountains here, these peaks—they can't be a domicile. They're sacred lands to Native American cultures, and have been so for centuries."

"They got here first, huh?"

"Yup. Sanctified it in their ways."

"Then churches? Chapels?"

I knew it, clear to the bone. "Safe."

"Holy ground, huh?" Remi said. "Like TV's *Highlander*? No immortal can challenge another for his head on holy ground?"

"'*There can be only one*,'" I intoned dutifully, then continued, "Remember the Chapel of the Holy Dove?" He nodded. "It had been deconsecrated. Demons could have walked right in, made it a home."

"But we *re*consecrated it." Remi resnapped his shirt cuff, even though a flap of cloth hung down and flesh was bared. Wounded flesh.

My skin, from the nape of my neck all the way down my back, twitched. I felt my hair stand up. A large part of me wanted to shout at him, but I clamped my mouth closed, turned my back, walked away.

"Say it," Remi called out. "I reckon you need to." He paused. "And I reckon I might do the same, wearin' your boots."

I turned back to face him across eight feet of wild grass, weeds, wildflowers. Stuck out my arms from my sides. "What the hell *was* that?" Self-control deserted me as my words began to run together in my haste to get it all said. "What the hell made you take off running like that without knowing where you were going? Neither one of us knows what's out here—" His brows ran up and I saw his point, altered course in mid-rant. "—okay, so we sort of know what's out here, now, but still, what the hell? Remember the whole mutual grip-the-ring-thing the other night, that Grandaddy called 'sealing'? It's two of us, McCue. It's *both* of us. You don't leave me behind, and I don't leave you behind."

I ran out of breath on the last sentence. Damn, I needed to acclimate to altitude in a hurry if I was going to be running up mountains.

But I'd said that before, that last sentence. A couple of years before. To my brother, not a stranger. *'You don't leave me behind, and I don't leave you behind.'*

Remi gazed at me as I sucked in air. "You done?"

The adrenaline surge was dissipating, along with the drive of *primogenitura*. I felt both pouring out of me, and what remained of me was more than a little shaky.

He was safe. He was whole—well, mostly whole. I felt myself settle, like a dog's hackles going down. I closed my eyes, let my breathing level.

Remi said, unevenly, "It was my daughter."

My eyes popped open. "What?"

He looked away from me, staring hard into the trees. "I heard my daughter's voice."

That's right; I'd forgotten he had a kid back home in Texas. I considered saying nothing, then decided to be honest. "You know it wasn't—"

He overrode me. He kept his tone level, but the expression in his eyes was raw. "She called out for her daddy."

That stopped me dead. I forcibly bled every last bit of accusation and tension out of my voice. "It was the demon. You know it was. Had to be."

His eyes were steady. I saw neither anger nor denial. "I know that. Now. But in that instant, in that *moment*, it was all reflex." He shrugged. "You'd do the same."

My head felt heavy on my neck as I nodded, sat myself down on the stump next to the revolver. I watched Remi put his back against an aspen and let it take his weight. Demon-infested or no, he'd been attacked by a wild animal. Probably he was running low on adrenaline and high on the realization of how close he'd come to death.

Butt planted on stump, I spread my legs, leaned my weight

through elbows into my thighs. Damp hair fell forward to hang against my collarbones. "Okay," I said, "now we know they can get inside our heads. We'll have to be ready for that. We'll have to learn how to shut that shit down. Because yeah, I'd have done the same. Exactly the same." And I had, more or less, for my younger brother, when I killed a man to save him. "I have to ask you to do something, then. Okay?"

He was examining his sliced arm again, raised his eyes to meet my own. To wait.

"Trust me, Remi. Just—*trust* me. There's something . . . something that's hard to explain. It's just . . . it's in me."

"What Grandaddy talked about. That you can sense the vibes of places, good and bad."

That's right, he'd been present for the explanation. I grimaced. "Yeah. Look, I'm not planning on being a nursemaid, or a nervous mother—"

He rode right over my words. "But it's all *reflex*."

I knew what he meant. He'd said that about his daughter. Maybe it was all the explanation required. "Yeah."

Remi looked over at the body of the sprawled cat. "You're going to have to ground me, then. If that happens again. We have to figure this out—find the means to deal with this. No one's going to hold our hands. Not Grandaddy. Not anyone. If anything, they'll pat us on the back to wish us well, then shove us out of the airplane without a parachute."

"Which they've already done." I looked up at the roiled sky, the flutter of lime-green leaves against deepening gray, the soft-shouldered highest peak of the lava-crusted mountain not far above us. "Or maybe it's that they give us some ripstop nylon, some paracord—and we have to fashion our own chutes in mid-fall."

Remi nodded. "Kind of a steep learning curve, though."

"Guns," I said. "We've got to keep guns on us. Knives'll do, but we'll need guns, too. Always." His belt was empty of clip-on holster, as my shoulders were empty of straps. I dug at dirt with a boot heel, frowned at the earth I overturned. "All those other things in Lily's RV: stakes, oils, powders, silver, holy wood, water." I tipped my head back, stared directly overhead, wondering what really lay beyond the stars. Form and void? Chaos? A literal Armageddon? "I think, to be honest . . ." I put out my hand, palm-down. It shook a little, until I tucked away the trembles inside a hard fist. "I think I'm scared as hell about all this." I met Remi's steady eyes, saw agreement in them, acknowledgment of the magnitude of what we faced. "I gotta learn me some Latin and Aramaic."

Remi smiled a little. "Just the phrases that count."

I opened my mouth to say something more, only to physically startle when I heard a woman's voice speaking before I had a chance to.

"Who shot that cat?"

Remi straightened up from the tree even as I rose abruptly from my seat upon the stump.

My initial impression was of slenderness, of dark hair in a long braid threaded through the back of a faded blue ball cap, a two-piece rainsuit, pants and jacket, hiking boots.

And in the next moment I registered that although her right arm hung loose at her side, a gun was in that hand.

CHAPTER NINE

chanced a glance at Remi, hoping his sixth sense, or whatever it was, could indicate whether the woman with a gun was a demon, or just a woman with a gun.

Remi darted a glance at me, twice twitched his brows upward just a little, but I wasn't certain if that meant she was a demon, or if he just thought she was attractive and was sharing that opinion the way guys usually do with one another.

But since the revolver was sitting next to me on the stump, and the mountain lion was clearly dead, and the report of a .357 would have been heard quite some distance away, I saw no reason whatsoever to deny shooting the cat. So I copped to it. "Yeah, I shot it."

She nodded, tucked the gun somewhere behind her back as she lifted the hem of the unzipped rain jacket. Beneath it I could see a blue shirt. The jacket hood lay bunched across the back of her neck, hiding most of the single braid. "Okay. Well, it's not illegal in Arizona, but I'd appreciate it if you filed a report."

"Filed a report?" I echoed.

She broke into a blurt of laughter, face reddening. "Sorry, I forgot to say. I'm a Park Ranger." She spread out both arms and made a gesture encompassing the entire area. "*This* is my office." As she let her arms fall she glanced to the cat with its pool of glittering cockroach remains, *cre*mains—hell, maybe even demonic excrement. Her expression was baffled as she stepped to the cat to take a closer look. She picked up a tree branch, began to stir it through the remains. "What *is* this stuff?"

Remi and I looked at one another. I knew he was recalling the same memory: a demon wearing a cop's body in the Zoo's parking lot, telling us he was going to gather up the demon remains inside because, he'd said, 'Everyone comes home.' And once returned to hell, the bits and pieces were somehow reconstituted.

"I've never seen anything like this," she said.

Remi and I exchanged another glance. He shook his head a little, shrugged.

Then she slipped out of her straps, set aside the pack, squatted down to more closely examine the burned bits of demon parts. The unzipped jacket shifted and I saw the SIG Sauer tucked into a slim holster designed for the small of the back, snugged against her spine and held in place by a braided leather belt.

"I need to get samples of this." She stood up, tossed the stick aside, met my eyes. Hers were blue. "Would you mind filling out a report? The ranger station isn't far from here. I mean, it's not illegal to kill a mountain lion in Arizona, so you're not in any trouble, but we do like to keep track of the ones living up here in the Peaks. And, you know—legal matters."

Like lawsuits filed by injured people when wild animals behaved like, shock of shocks, wild animals? I'd bet money on it. "Personally, I believe in live and let live," I said, "and if this is their territory, so be it. But he was looking like he wanted to make dinner out of my friend."

She nodded. "Despite the news reports, mountain lions don't often attack humans. They'll go after dogs who're turned off-lead, but even that doesn't happen much. Usually if the drought's bad enough to drive them down looking for water, but that hasn't been the case lately. Possibly this one was rabid." She turned her head in Remi's direction, frowned a little. "You look familiar. But I don't think we've met . . . have we? I think I'd remember you—wait a minute!" She pointed a forefinger, repeatedly poked the air in his direction. "You were in the Zoo Club the other night, weren't you? And you sang 'Ave, Maria,' which I don't think I've ever actually heard sung in a cowboy bar before." She grinned, and it lit up her face. Pretty girl, if not downright beautiful. "Weird choice, maybe, but a nice job."

Remi dipped his head slightly. "That's kindly of you, miss I do appreciate it."

She smiled briefly at him, then knelt to dig through her daypack and came up with a large resealable plastic bag and a hand-brush. Remi and I watched her kneel again, open the bag's mouth wide, then begin to sweep the burned bits of dead demon into the bag.

Quietly, I reached down and picked up the revolver. Remi and I in unison faded back a few strides, exchanged glances. He tipped his head in a gesture I interpreted as *no certainty but better safe than sorry*,' and I saw the blade of a Hibben throwing knife in his hand even as I lifted the .357 and cradled it in two hands. I didn't point it directly at her, but on an angle toward the ground. It crossed my mind to wonder whether I needed to blow on the bullets again, or if it was one-and-done.

"I didn't realize Park Rangers carried sidearms," I said.

She didn't look back over her shoulder, just kept brushing dead bug-things into her bag. "I'm not actually on duty. I came out because of the earthquake. It's all-hands-on-deck when natural disasters occur. This is a popular area, so best to check for hikers. But some of us carry, yeah." She stopped sweeping, stood up as she squeezed the bag's ribbing closed, ran her fingers along it to snap-seal it. She turned casually to face the two of us. Turned out the braid, as it swung free of the jacket, had a bright blonde streak running through it. "The National Park Service does authorize us to act as law enforcement officers—" And then she stopped talking altogether and stared at us.

Remi and I stood side-by-side but not so close as to encumber one another. We were clearly poised to act, and of course I had a very large gun in my hands. I quoted the demon we'd met in the Zoo's parking lot. "'Everyone comes home?'"

She didn't blink. She didn't speak. She didn't so much as twitch. Just stared at me, sealed plastic bag in one hand. The other hand was empty. Unless she was left-handed or ambidextrous, her gun hand was occupied. Besides, you don't try for a fast draw from behind your back, particularly from under a jacket.

"It's just a 9-mil SIG Sauer," she said with careful clarity, letting no aggression color her tone. "Not enough gun against your cannon. I don't particularly want my head blown off, so I'm not going to try anything. But I would like to ask you what the problem is."

I always got a kind of ironic amusement out of it when people felt their smaller caliber weapon was no match for a larger. A gun was a gun, a bullet a bullet, and you could die from a .22 round to the head as quickly as from a .357. Though certainly less messily.

I said, "Remi."

He took two smooth paces sideways, then began to circle

around behind her. He'd lift that automatic from her and *then* maybe we could have a more casual conversation.

Except before Remi could reach her and slip the gun free, lightning shot low across the sky, lit up the mountain, and a crack of thunder exploded so close overhead that all of us jumped in surprise.

I dove right, ducking behind the stump; Remi dove left behind a broken pine; and she took several long steps backward and dropped down behind another downed tree. The SIG now resided in her hand.

To some extent we all of us had cover, so to speak; that is, we weren't entirely exposed, any of us. But Remi was in no position to dump a knife at her without showing way too much upper body, and while I could poke my head around the edge of the stump just enough to see her tree and the yellow glow of her rain suit amidst the gray of the day, it was easy enough to flush me into the open with a few well-placed bullets shot into my stump. The young woman, on the other hand, couldn't really take a clear shot without exposing *her*self.

And then the blackened skies opened up, sluicing rain upon us, and we all three of us held a standoff while lying on our bellies in dirt and deadfall. Within seconds I was soaked and mud-soggy while lightning strobed directly overhead and thunder deafened us.

In the movies, they don't generally stage gunfights or Mexican standoffs in the pouring rain. I mean, probably it would mess with the actual filming, and possibly even in real life the participants in imminent gun battles would do their best to avoid bad weather if at all possible. And it was completely understandable, because here all three of us hugged the earth in the midst of torrential rain, soaked to the skin with clothing practically glued to us.

And then it began to hail.

"Fuck," I muttered. Then raised my voice. "Remi!"

"What?"

"You can hear me?"

"Since I just answered you, yes, I can hear you!"

Wiseass. I squinted through the hail. "Can't you tell if she is, or isn't a . . . well, you know." I was pretty sure yelling in the middle of a hailstorm about demons and angels would mark me as certifiable, especially if she were just a normal human woman.

"No!" Remi yelled.

Wetter by the moment. "You know, it's not much help, your supposed superpower, if you can't actually *use* it!" Ow. Dammit. *Ow.* The hail was not small. It bounced hard off wet clothing and the skin beneath. I wondered if I'd bruise. "Can you try again?"

"I did! I can't tell if she's either one!" Remi shouted back.

Her turn. "Either one *what?*" she shouted. "Who *are* you?"

I ignored her question and shouted to Remi again. "If she was in the Zoo when you sang the other night, she'd have reacted, right?" I saw the peak of her blue cap show itself above the fallen tree she'd taken shelter behind. "Stay put!" I yelled at her.

She did stay put, but an arm came up and tossed something glinting out in the open. It landed near Remi. "My badge!" she shouted.

Another bolt of lightning cut across the sky very close to us. I hunkered down as low as possible, shoulders hunched up high, placed one spread hand over my left ear. Holy shit, that thunder was loud!

It was Remi's turn. "Why do you want that stuff?" he shouted at her. "Why collect burned bits of—things?"

"To find out what it is!" she yelled back. "I've never seen anything like it, okay? I want to take it to the university, see an entomologist I know!"

It all made perfect sense. Except if a surrogate was riding her, it would know *how* to make perfect sense.

"Gabe?"

"Yeah?"

"Be ready!"

Be ready for—? And then as he raised his voice and began reciting, I knew what to be ready for.

I peered around my stump. We were out of the thick of the trees, on the verge of the lava flow, but there was a fringe of vegetation. I could see no part of the woman, and I would have, had she tried to move away, especially wearing bright yellow.

After another crack of thunder, she raised her voice. It had gone up in pitch. "Why are you shouting the Rite of Exorcism at me?"

Hah, I thought. "So you know what that is!"

"Because I like horror movies, and I heard him singing it just the other night!"

Remi was still reciting, but he eased forward two short steps, bent and picked up the item she claimed was a badge. Then abruptly his recitation stilled. His tone sounded odd. "Your name's MJ Kelly?"

Oh. My. God. I raised my voice over the storm. "*Mary Jane Kelly?*"

She sounded half-baffled, half-annoyed. "Yes!"

I shook my head. "It's too neat!" I shouted at Remi. "Too much of a coincidence!"

Remi shouted back, "I can't get a read on her!"

I felt pummeled beneath the hail. It was known to dent cars. I was flesh, not metal. "Try the rite again!"

"Are you going to shoot me?" she yelled.

Remi was busy calling out the Latin, so I answered. "Are you going to shoot *me*?"

"I don't want to shoot anyone!" she shouted back. "I came out to see if any hikers needed help after the earthquake!" And then she muttered something about the fucking hail, and the ridiculousness of the situation.

Admittedly it *was* pretty ridiculous.

"I got nothing!" Remi shouted. "You see any kind of reaction?"

"Who *are* you?" she shouted.

"Okay, look!" I shouted. "Let's put our guns down, step away from them. I'm miserable, you're miserable, and Remi's miserable, so yeah, let's get under cover and discuss all of this." Discuss a whole helluva lot, in fact, with Ms. Mary Jane Kelly, who appeared to be in possession of both her kidneys. "Look." I stuck my arm out and allowed the revolver to dangle from the trigger guard. "I'll set it down. You do the same with yours, okay?" I placed the .357 on the stump, slowly pushed up to my feet. I was sopping wet, and chilled. Probably if I tried for the gun, wet clothes would bind me. I didn't stand up straight because it's hard not to wince from massive thunderclaps. I just kind of hunched there, hail bouncing off my head. But I had insurance in Remi, which was the reason I was willing to put down my gun. She didn't.

"Step away!" she called.

I took two steps, hands up, fingers spread. I saw a yellow-sleeved arm come over the top of the downed tree, and she placed the SIG in the open. Slowly, carefully she stood up, staring at me. Because she had not had time to zip up her jacket, the shirt beneath it was wet and muddy. Her braid hung nearly to her waist from the opening in the back of the ball cap.

Then her expression changed completely, and she scooped up the gun.

"Oh, *shit*—" I dropped to the ground belly-down as she raised the SIG Sauer.

Guess that answered the question about who—or *what*—she was.

CHAPTER TEN

Remi did not throw his knife. He threw a *rock*.

It smacked into the ranger's hand and ruined her shot. As she cried out in surprise, he made a leap at her and knocked her flat on her rain-suited ass before she could fire the SIG Sauer. He came up with her gun, dumped the clip, tossed them in two different directions while she sat there in the muck, white-faced and staring, holding her hand.

I hitched up on my elbows. "Remi—"

But he began shouting *'No!'* Loudly. Repeatedly. And he was waving both arms around like a crazed man trying frantically to avert a tragedy.

She wasn't looking at me. *He* wasn't looking at me. He wasn't even looking at *her*.

I lunged for and grabbed the .357 off the stump, turned on my knees, saw why Ranger Mary Jane Kelly was so white-faced and speechless, and why Remi was waving arms and shouting.

Well. Yeah. Possibly emptying a clip at—or *into*—an angel is not a wise idea.

Shemyazaz, dripping charred flesh, displaying his lipless

mouth and skeletal rictus, came dancing his way out of the trees. He didn't quite pirouette, as he had atop the bar, but he definitely wasn't walking.

Remi hadn't been yelling to stop her from shooting me, or Shemyazaz. He'd been trying to stop Shemyazaz from harming *her*. Just in case it might occur to the angel to do so, since a woman had been on the verge of shooting bullets at him. *Into* him.

The ruined angel paused at the demarcation between forest and open area. He tipped back his charred head and stared up at the skies above aspens and broken pines. Then he put out a blackened hand, caught a hailstone, brought it to his mouth. Licked it. His tongue was bright red in the burned cavern of his mouth.

His wings lifted away from his body. They were in no better shape than the rest of him, shredded, cracked, weeping bright lava-like streaks and globs. They stretched high, and he shook them, mantling like a bird taking a bath.

His voice cut easily through the noise of the storm, clear and ringing. "I haven't tasted the earth in so long!"

Since Remi had committed to protecting her against a whackjob angel, I figured he had sorted out that the ranger was okay. "She good?"

"She's good," he answered.

I took two steps, bent and caught hold of Mary Jane Kelly's arm, urged her up from the ground. "It's okay," I told her. "It's okay." Of course it wasn't okay, but I didn't know what else to say. I was pretty sure '*Look, he's a fallen Grigori who slept with human women back before Biblical times and made Nephilim, and then he went to hell with Lucifer to pal around with him until the devil got jealous of his beauty and decided to make him ugly'* wouldn't go over well. Instead, I scowled at Remi. "I thought Ganji had him!"

"He did!"

"Well, he doesn't now!"

"It's not *my* job to keep track of either one of them!"

Mary Jane Kelly 's eyes were wide. "What *is* that?"

Well, hell. "He's a fallen Grigori who slept with human women back before Biblical times and made Nephilim, and then he went to hell with Lucifer to pal around until the devil got jealous of his beauty and decided to make him ugly," I said.

The whites of her eyes showed as she stared at me in utter shock. Her face was strained, fair skin snugged tightly over prominent cheekbones.

I met Remi's gaze on the other side of her. Neither of us knew what the hell to do. Grandaddy had explained to *us* what was going on, this whole End of Days/Verge of the Apocalypse thing, but we'd more or less been primed for that realization at some point in our lives from birth. But Mary Jane Kelly?

First she was faced with an actual angel standing right in front of her, who was not currently dressed for dancing; secondly, she had Jack the Ripper—demon, ghost, tulpa, whatever—on her trail. Which obviously meant we had someone else's kidney in our freezer.

"Look," I said, "there's no simple explanation for this. If we give you back your gun so you'll feel safer, are you willing to listen to us? Suspend your disbelief?"

A final gust of hailstones scattered across the mountain's shoulder, then transformed to a lesser rain. She was dry from the waist down because of the rain pants, but her shirt was plastered against her bra. Remi and I were absolutely soaked to the skin. At least rain was less painful than ice.

Just as she opened her mouth to answer, the ruined angel walked out of the trees and paused before her. He shook his wings again, then folded them into something approaching order, if you call a broken umbrella with ripped fabric and spokes sticking out every which way 'order.' Then he spread his arms wide as he looked into her eyes. His voice was a clarion, pure and sweet. "Am I not beautiful?"

She stared back at him. Her face hosted a series of microexpressions running from utter disbelief through incredulity to a flicker of pure repulsion.

Shemyazaz looked into her eyes. His burned brilliant in their sockets. "I am not," he said. "I am *not* beautiful. Because he saw to it I am not!"

A buffet of wind threw rain into my eyes. I reached out, gently grasped her elbow and angled her away from Shemyazaz so all she'd see was me. I could feel her trembling.

I bent, scooped up her SIG Sauer. Remi grabbed the clip he'd tossed, lobbed it to me. I slid the magazine in, clicked it into place and handed the gun to her. I could think of nothing else that might mitigate the shock of Shemyazaz. It allowed her a little control even as I carefully eased her a little farther from the angel.

Lightning lit up the mountainside. Thunder cracked overhead. All of us jumped save for Shemyazaz.

"Will you come with us?" I asked, releasing her arm. "We have a friend in a motorhome not far from here. A woman. We can explain things better if we're out of the storm. Besides, Remi needs to get his arm looked at. The cat caught him a good one."

As I had hoped, invoking Remi's wound diverted her immediate focus from Shemyazaz. She was a Park Ranger, trained to render first aid. As she looked at him, Remi displayed his arm with its torn sleeve. The fabric was so water-soaked that only the faintest trace of pink remained of bloodstains.

She looked at the gun in her hand, then back at the angel. "What is he?" she asked. Then, with a little more determination, she asked Shemyazaz directly. "What *are* you?"

"Fallen," he said, and only that.

"We'll explain," I told her. "I promise. Will you come?"

Her expression was pensive as she nodded, a little unsettled. She wiped the gun as best she could with the stretched-out tail of her t-shirt, snugged it back into its holster at her spine, looked at the ground, found the bag of surrogate remains—we had not after all distracted her from that—and picked it up.

"What about him?" she asked, looking at the angel.

"He's not invited." I had no holster for the revolver, so I just hung onto it. Too much barrel to stuff down my jeans, front or back. I gestured for her to precede us, exchanging glances with Remi every bit as pensive as her own. Well, she'd met an angel. Maybe, eventually, she could handle the truth about demons, too. And she'd better. If she was on Jack the Ripper's list, she needed to know that, too. Because now neither days nor nights were her own.

As we began our slip-and-slide descent of the mud-slick mountain, legs beating back storm-bowed shrubs and flattened wildflowers, I glanced over my shoulder. Paused a moment, struck by the tableau on the slope behind us.

He had called himself a *bene ha'elohi*, the first of the celestial Sons of God. His eyes, as he looked back at me, were no longer brilliant, but dim in the rain beneath lashless lids. He didn't move. Just stood there, alone, in all his ruined flesh.

Yet for some reason I could not explain, it wasn't Shemya-zaz I saw beneath the lowering sky, but *Blade Runner*'s dying replicant:

"All those moments will be lost in time, like tears in the rain."

CHAPTER ELEVEN

I t stopped raining as we reached the halfway point between the high mountain slope and the RV park, but the sun remained no more than a faint watery smear behind still-dark clouds. Trees and vegetation still dropped residual rain. My clothes and Remi's were sopping, though at least my socked feet were dry within my biker boots; Mary Jane Kelly, other than her shirt beneath an unzipped rain jacket, was dry.

At the motorhome we found Lily waiting for us. She had put down a folded rug and sat atop it within the doorway, green shawl wrapped around her shoulders. The woven fabric hid bare arms and all their embellishment of Celtic silver and brilliant inks.

A few children called through the trees, but the excited conversations on the heels of the earthquake had died away. I heard quiet music playing and a recognizable twang in the vocals; did no one in this state listen to anything *other* than country music?

Lily examined us benignly as we approached. First me, quickly dismissed; then Remi, on whom she lingered, looking at the ripped sleeve. And lastly Mary Jane Kelly, who returned the cool gaze with one of her own, weighing Lily as she herself was weighed. Away from Shemyazaz, with a gun on board again, her shock had dissipated, replaced by professionalism.

A brief smile twitched a corner of Lily's mouth and then she rose, resettling the shawl. "Whiskey," she announced, then disappeared into the RV.

Remi stepped aside, made a gentlemanly gesture for the ranger to go up before either of us. He was a rather courtly man when it came to women, I'd discovered. He gave her room to climb the steps, waited for me to go up next. I did, with Remi right behind.

Lily had poured whiskey into short tumblers and handed them out to us. It was a little early to drink—no longer dawn, but neither was it five in the evening. Remi hesitated. Mary Jane Kelly apparently did not wish to be thought rude and accepted the glass, but did not drink. She just held it.

Lily smiled at me, green eyes bright. "Medicinal purposes. Or perhaps you might call it antifreeze, to warm up the bones. You're all of you looking like drowned rabbits. *And* rats."

She waited, one brow lifted. I wasn't entirely certain of ancient Irish customs, but in all the folklore I'd read it was a grave insult to decline food and drink when offered.

Lily's smile broadened. "I'm not Hades, now, am I, tricking you into eating pomegranate seeds and keeping you for four months out of the year?"

"Or the serpent in the Garden of Eden?" Remi put in. "Some believe it wasn't an apple at all, but more likely pomegranate— or even grapes. No one knows for certain. Forbidden fruit regardless."

Mary Jane Kelly was taken aback. "You're saying *that's* what the serpent offered Adam and Eve? Not an apple?"

"He's the right of it, our cowboy," Lily said. "I wasn't there to know for a certainty, but there are differing texts." She raised her own tumbler. "A swallow, no more. Do me honor. *Sláinte.*"

I found it odd, cognitive dissonance in a way, for an ancient pagan Irish goddess to speak of the Christian Garden of Eden. Kelly just seemed perplexed by the entire topic. I drank. Remi also, even as Lily did. The ranger shrugged surrender after a moment, but barely tasted the whiskey.

"There, now. That's something. 'Twill do." Lily set down her tumbler, retrieved Kelly's and placed it into the sink; apparently the one sip was enough for the Morrigan. "Shed your rain suit . . . and that wet shirt. I have dry tops that will fit you."

"Oh, I can go on to the station, change there," Kelly said. "I'm a park ranger—I've got fresh clothes there. But thank you for the offer."

"And in the meantime you are dripping all over my RV," Lily pointed out. "Go on, then. There are clothes in the bedroom. Take what you like. You'll be here a while."

"Actually—"

Lily didn't let her finish. "They've things to tell you, these boyos. And *I'm* telling you to listen."

Kelly stared right back at Lily for a long moment, then looked at Remi, at me. I thought she was on the verge of telling us all off. "And you can explain what that thing was, up there on the mountain?"

"We can," I said.

Remi said, "We will."

"You'll be far more comfortable in dry clothing," Lily said. "I'd offer the boyos clothing as well, but I've none that will fit. They'll have to make do with towels. Go on, then. The bedroom's through there." She gestured to a closed door leading into one of the RV slide-out rooms. "You can return the shirt tomorrow. And when you're dressed, come on through the kitchen to the garage. That's where we'll be. I have a man's arm to see to."

Mary Jane Kelly seemed on the verge of protesting more pointedly, as she evaluated each of us, but instead she disappeared into the bedroom, and Lily gestured for us to follow her into the garage at the back of the RV, then tossed us two thick bath towels each. We rubbed down clothing, scrubbed at hair. Still wet, but damp, now rather than dripping.

Lily stood with hands on hips. "Will you tell her all of it, then?"

"I think we'd better," I replied. "She's in the mix, now."

The Morrigan nodded, then pulled down the wall-mounted bed. She had Remi sit on it, then set up a stainless steel table on casters, rolled it over in front of him. She opened a package of blue towels marked STERILE, spread one on the steel table-top and pointed at it.

Remi took the hint. As Lily poked around in a different cabinet and slapped a notebook and a pen on the countertop, Remi unsnapped his sleeve, rolled it back. The long laceration in his forearm came into view. I couldn't help my grimace and the hiss of indrawn breath, empathizing with the pain.

"Not so deep," Remi remarked. "You should see the puncture scar I have from one of the steers on the ranch, back when I was full of myself and actin' foolish. Right in my butt."

"Pass," I said dryly.

The cowboy flashed the quick grin that set creases into the tanned flesh beside his eyes. "That's what everyone else said, too."

"It's wanting stitches," Lily announced, and began setting out supplies appropriate to the task.

Blood doesn't make me squeamish and neither do stitches—
or, well, such things didn't used to. And I'd had sutures sewn
into an eyebrow not so long before that hadn't bothered me at
all. But I was having a visceral response to Remi's wound, now
that it was bared. Part of me, apparently recalling the whole
alpha thing of birth order, wanted to take the pain for myself.
This *primogenitura* was beginning to annoy the hell out of me. I
hoped it would settle some as Remi and I grew accustomed to
working together.

I turned my back on the first aid procedure and started
hunting through cabinets and drawers, looking not for medical
supplies but for supplies for the task of cleaning a gun. Found
what I needed, pulled over a stool, and onto the spread cham-
ois I unloaded the cylinder, rolled the bullets apart, removed
the grips and went to work with the CLP spray and swabs, soft
cloth.

Into the midst of stitches and gun-cleaning our park ranger
came, wearing her own dry jeans and a dark red borrowed
t-shirt that bore in white, Celtic-style font: *ACTING THE MAG-
GOT.* She'd undone her wet braid and loose hair hung to her
hips, medium brown with that interesting tawny-gold stripe
through the midst of it, starting at the hairline over her right
eyebrow. Maybe dyed; people were doing all sorts of crazy
things with hair dye these days.

Without the rain suit disguising her figure, it was easy to
note she was sturdy through the shoulders and thighs, with
defined muscles in her forearms. Athlete, not model. She carried wet shirt and rain suit folded up, and her daypack was
hooked over one shoulder.

On the threshold she paused, blinked blue eyes slow as her
brows shot up. I guess it's not every day that you walk into what

is a cross between armory and field hospital when the RV park is otherwise full of retirees and a few restless grandkids.

"Chair over there," Lily said absently, mind on suturing.

The ranger glanced around, found the folded camp chair, set aside rain suit and shirt and daypack, sat down expectantly. The huge Irish wolfhound came in as well, collapsed and sprawled with a *whuff* of sound just inside the door between garage and hallway.

"Have you heard of these?" Lily's tone was light. She didn't so much as glance at the ranger. "Black dog. Banshee. Basilisk. Bogle. Cockatrice." Lily raised bright eyes and looked at me. "Your turn, Gabe."

Apparently we were going down the alphabet, though Lily had left some names out. I'd cleaned, reassembled the .357, polished the steel, the rounds, set it aside. I had an idea where we were going with this. "Elf. Gnome. Gorgon. Golem—" I turned my head, gazed at Mary Jane Kelly, "—and no, I don't mean Tolkien's Gollum."

Kelly's expectance had slowly transformed into doubt verging on irritation. She looked from Lily to me, wry hook in the line of her mouth. "Let me guess. I'm a park ranger, so I'm supposed to tell ghost stories around the campfire."

"Reminds me." Remi shot a glance at me across the garage. "La Llorona." He gave it a Spanish accent with the double L pronounced as a Y.

"Hobgoblin," Lily added. "Minotaur. And as I'm Irish, I'll not leave out leprechauns, dullahans, or pookas."

"Ghosts and goblins," I said.

Mary Jane Kelly was clearly torn between utter disbelief, and the memory of what—of *whom*—she'd seen on the mountain.

"Suspend your disbelief." I'd said it once on the mountain. This time I put more emphasis into it. "You saw what you saw, up there. The broken, burned, nightmare of a man. Well—he's not actually a man."

Remi's tone was quiet. "He's an angel, Ms. Kelly."

She drew back in the chair, a visible, visceral denial.

I caught Lily's eye. She was unabashedly amused. Then I looked back at Mary Jane Kelly. "Whiskey?" I asked. "Trust me, it goes down better with alcohol."

CHAPTER TWELVE

K elly didn't want whiskey. She didn't want anything but the truth. And when we gave it to her, she didn't believe any of it.

I couldn't blame her. I couldn't blame her even when I dug into the drawers and cabinets and started pulling items out that a matter of days before I'd believed to be utterly mundane. Guns, knives, bullets, silver shot, powdered iron rounds, stakes, old stained ritual bowls crafted of various woods and metals, sachets of herbs and powders, charms, candles, strung beads, crystals, feathers, small bones, stones, tiny bottles, and an additional infinite array of things I had absolutely no clue how to identify.

Then the sorcerer's wand, sort of: a twisted, carved, polished length of wood as long as my forearm, bisected by silver through the middle with a cross carved into the butt. I picked up and spun it through my fingers as I leaned one hip and shoulder against the cabinetry.

"This?" I said. "This is for vampires."

Mary Jane Kelly, who had moved out of disbelief and denial into annoyance, scowled at me.

"I know," I told her. The stake felt oddly at home in my hand as I flipped it through my fingers. "I do know. A few days ago Remi and I felt as you do: that we were being sold a crock of shit. It's impossible; it's not real; it's all just figments of imagination; it makes no sense; it's just stories, folklore, made up pantheons of differing deities."

Remi's voice was quiet. "All of it's true."

"All of *what* is true?"

"Do you know your Irish mythology?" Lily asked.

To that apparent non sequitur, she said, "Not particularly." Definitely not a happy camper, by tone or expression.

Lily clucked her tongue in mock disappointment. "And you with the surname of Kelly!"

The ranger rolled her eyes. "Listen, my dad hauled us off to Dublin one year for St. Patrick's Day, just so we could stand along a street and watch a parade where the pipe bands were mostly from the *United States*, not Ireland! But what do they say?—everyone's Irish on St. Patrick's Day?" She shrugged. "Kowalski, Kelly—it doesn't matter. So no, I don't really know the ins and outs of Irish mythology."

From more distant parts of the big RV I heard the crow. There was no way of describing the noise it made as anything other than an outraged protest. And the wolfhound rose, took a few steps, sat down immediately in front of the ranger and fixed her with a very hard stare.

"That's Macha," Lily said. "You've insulted her. The racket you're hearing is from Nemain, the crow. But you don't know my sisters, do you? Or who the Morrigan is."

"It took an angel," I said, "to convince *us*." My back-and-forth gesture with the stake encompassed Remi and I. "Hard to deny a pair of wings growing out of a man's back. Plus we took a trip to the aftermath of the battle between Boudicca and the

Romans in . . . AD 60 or 61. *That*, courtesy of the Morrigan herself." I tipped my head toward Lily. "It's real. It *is* real. Ragnarok, Armageddon, End of Days, Judgment Day, Apocalypse. Hell, even R.E.M. nailed it with their song, 'It's the End of the World as We Know It.'"

She shook her head. Shook it harder in abject denial. "I'm not a religious person. What in the world does any of this have to do with me?"

"Murder," Remi said. "That's what it has to do with you. Gabe and I just want to keep you alive, is all."

"*I'm* a target?" Oh, she was frustrated. And angry. And fear was creeping back. "Why the hell would *I* be a target for anything, let alone murder?"

"Because of your name," I told her.

"My *name*?"

Abruptly the wolfhound stood, stared hard at the side of the RV. Even amidst the wiry hair I could see hackles rising. The crow screeched even as the wolfhound growled, and then we heard a knock at the RV's exterior door by the kitchen. Lily got up swiftly, followed the dog out of the garage, back through the kitchen.

Remi and I exchanged a glance. He still sat on the bed Lily had pulled down from the wall, and he leaned back against it, injured arm in its bright blue wrapping cradled in one hand.

"Well?" Kelly said. "What about my name?"

Lily came back and broke up the discussion. "It was but a child," she said, "doing a grownup's bidding." In her hand was a manilla envelope. "Gabriel Jeremiah Harlan and Remiel Isaiah McCue." She flashed the envelope. The writing was in black felt marker.

I dropped the F-bomb even as I tossed the stake onto the counter. Remi thumped his head against the garage sidewall and muttered under his breath.

"Here." Lily held the envelope out to Kelly. "A little proof, perhaps."

"Wait." I moved to reach for the envelope. "I don't think she needs to see that."

Lily's red brows rose. "After all those women with the same names were murdered, and she may well be next? What are you protecting her against?"

Kelly ignored us and tore open the envelope, pulled out a photograph. I screwed up my face, waiting for a reaction to human butchery. Remi didn't look any happier.

She read the writing on the back first, frowned in perplexity, then turned it over. Color ran out of her face, leaving even her lips pale.

I shook my head at Lily, letting my expression tell her I was pissed. The Goddess of Battles was not impressed.

Kelly's hand shook as she held out the photograph to me. I took it, saw not the eviscerated body I'd feared, but the image of Mary Jane Kelly in her Park Service uniform wearing the iconic hat synonymous with Smokey the Bear. She stood laughing amidst a group of kids, expression wide open and thoroughly engaged.

Three words, no more than that, written on the back:

We got next.

CHAPTER THIRTEEN

From Kelly, it was less a voice than a breath. "So, I have a stalker."

I took the few steps necessary to hand Remi the photo. He examined it, then set it on the steel surgical table and looked at Kelly. "'What's in a name?'" he quoted. "And that's it. The name. Nothing more. Mary Ann Nichols. Annie Chapman. Elizabeth Stride. Catherine Eddowes."

Kelly's face was blank. "I don't know those people."

"In the 1880s, in London, there was a series of grisly murders," Remi explained. "Five victims. All women. They think probably there were more than five, but Nichols, Chapman, Stride, and Eddowes are official. The fifth was Mary Jane Kelly."

Her eyes were fixed on something I couldn't see. Then *she* dropped an F-bomb.

I returned to the stool I'd perched myself on while cleaning the gun. I decided to leave out the bit concerning the kidney in our freezer. "Remi and I have been sent photographs of four murdered women with names on the back. All of them match the names of the Ripper's victims. So, we started looking for a Mary Jane Kelly to see if we could get to her before he did."

She nodded. "So some whackjob is a copycat for Jack the Ripper?"

"No," Remi said, blue-bandaged arm resting against his abdomen. "We think it *is* Jack the Ripper."

Kelly now seemed to be a little more angry than she was frightened. I knew many of us find refuge in anger rather than lose ourselves to fear. "So, what—he's been cryogenically frozen for decades, and someone's thawed him out?" She shook her head, dismissing it. "What do the police say?"

Remi and I exchanged a long look. I shrugged. "We haven't contacted the police."

Kelly displayed the photo of herself. "Well, then *I* will."

"We haven't contacted the police," Remi began, "because we don't believe it's a human doing the killing."

She was incredulous. "Not a human?"

With unflagging courtesy, Remi nonetheless was frank. "You came face to face with an angel on the mountain."

Kelly shook her head. "And I still don't believe you."

Remi was unfazed. "Well, this version of the Ripper is likely a demon."

Kelly shot to her feet. "Are you *crazy?* Demons aren't real!" She flung out an arm. "Stories aren't *real,* or the creatures and people in them."

Macha, the wolfhound, had come to sit beside Lily, who stood in the center of the garage with legs spread, inked arms folded across her chest. She was a slight woman physically, but great in presence when she chose to be. She'd said nothing for a while, but now an eerie, unearthly light kindled in her green eyes. "Were I to name myself, were I to *show* myself—would you call me a liar, then?"

I looked at Lily more sharply. The tone in her voice had changed.

"Sit down," Lily commanded Kelly. "Better to see it seated."

Mary Jane Kelly lingered a moment, then slowly sat down in the camp chair. She was completely still, and blatantly unhappy.

Lily's smile was slight. "Nemain!" she called. Then she placed her hand on the top of the wolfhound's skull. "Macha."

It wasn't the crow who entered, called from another room. And it wasn't an Irish wolfhound sitting beside Lily. Women. Two women. Two red-haired women completely nude, garmented only in knee-length hair and a webwork of blue tattoos. Their eyes, as Lily's, were green.

She grinned at me and raised her brows. "No more wondering what's under my clothes, Gabe."

And then she, too, was nude. She, too, had red hair reaching to her knees. But unlike the other women, empty-handed both, she was heavily armed. In her left hand, a spear, and barbed arrows. Hanging behind her back, suspended by a leather loop, was the round Irish shield, the *sciath*, made of brass decorated with concentric circles of Celtic knotwork and animal designs that were echoed in the colored tattoos on Lily's bare arms. In her right hand, a *claideamh*, the ancient Gaelic sword.

"*Ní neart go cur le chéile*," she said. "There is no strength without unity." She indicated the two women. "My sisters. Our tri-part unity. Should you insult one of us, you insult us all." Her tone now was scathing. "Ask the great hero Cuchulainn about the subject."

The story of Cuchulainn, and what became of him, was

probably one of the best known bardic tales in the Ulster Cycle of Irish mythology. But the blank expression on Mary Jane Kelly's face told me she knew nothing of it.

"The Morrigan was Ireland's Goddess of Battles," I told her, feeling back in the classroom again, "and she took a liking to the great warrior known as Cuchulainn, the King's Hound. But he spurned the Morrigan's advances, which pissed her off royally, and so she prophesied his death. Wounded in battle, he tied himself to a standing stone with his own intestines so the enemy would not know he was dying, and thus would not attack."

Kelly made a sound of disgust.

"But the Morrigan took crow-form and perched upon his shoulder, and so his enemies knew he *was* dead, and then, well . . . cut off his head."

"It took him too long to die," Lily said. "But I played no part in the wounding of him. I merely relished the death."

After a long moment, all Kelly could manage was a rather weak, "Oh."

Of no one in particular, I asked, "She's quite the cheery woman, isn't she?"

Lily smiled. "Then if I come to you, Gabe, to take you into my bed, you'll know better than to refuse."

To which all *I* could manage was a rather weak, "Oh."

Mary Jane drew in a very deep breath, then let it out on whooshing breath. "I'll take the whiskey now."

Thanks to Lily's family tableau, Kelly now believed what we'd told her was true, though that belief seemed tentative. We departed the garage and went back through to the RV's living/ dining room, where the Morrigan's sisters once again were crow and wolfhound, and where Lily, once again unweaponed, seemed less intimidating. She handed Kelly the tumbler of whiskey she'd only tasted before, then sat down on the floor where Macha placed a bewhiskered head in her lap. The golden eyes closed as Lily began to stroke an ear, which kind of squicked me out. I mean, she wasn't actually a dog, but a *sister*.

Whiskey wasn't really to Mary Jane Kelly's taste. She managed another sip before making a face and setting it down in the sink. She glanced around for a seat, ended up sliding into the horseshoe dinette across the table from Remi.

"So, up there on the mountain, you thought *I* was a demon?" she asked. "A real live demon?"

"Thought it was possible," he answered.

"And the other night, when you sang the exorcism ritual to the tune of *Ave Maria* . . . that was about a demon?"

"Tryin' to flush one out so we could kill it. Well, that is—if we're actually *killing* them. We're not certain-sure." Remi scratched his head. "What we do know, so far, is that when they *appear* to be dead, when they look like bugs who've been popped in the microwave, other demons try to grab their remains and take 'em home to hell, where they get reconstituted. Or re-something. I reckon otherwise they stay dead."

"Which is why we're trying to make sure the remains aren't collected. But we're still learning," I said. "Remi and I kind of got thrown into the middle of a war we didn't even know existed. We're mostly learning as we go. So when you insisted on scooping up those remains . . ." I shrugged.

"You thought I was a demon."

I nodded. "At *some* point Remi's super powers will wake up all the way and let us know who is, and who isn't, before we have to get that up close and personal, but for now we're just kind of bumbling around trying things. That's why he started reciting the exorcism up on the mountain. You wanted some of the bug-things that came out of the cat's mouth. We didn't know who—or what—you might be."

"I really just wanted to take them to an entomologist I know at Northern Arizona University," Kelly said. "That stuff, the *remains,* came out of the cat? So the *cat* was a demon?"

"Apparently so," Remi said. "Demon snuck into it most likely to go after us."

"Like I said, we're learning as we go," I repeated. "But as it was explained to us, demons can take hosts. So yeah, the cat was basically borrowed. He—*it;* whatever—was going to take out Remi, until I took *it* out with a .357 round." I left out the part about me bathing it in my heavenly breath. One thing at a time.

Kelly nodded absently, thinking things over. "I don't suppose legally changing my name might help?"

I grinned briefly, then looked at Remi. "Do you think he'll still come after her, now that we've found her? I mean, if he was basically gaslighting us—"

"With murdered women."

"Yes, but we've found her. She's protected now. Would he continue?"

Remi was unconvinced. "He had a picture of her delivered *here.* What he wrote on the back can't be anything but a threat."

We got next. Yup. I looked at Lily. "Any advice? You seem to know all the secrets."

A smile lit up her eyes. "I know many things, it's true, but not everything. It's the doing of the angels. I'm just here for the war."

I dug the magic phone out of a pocket, pulled contacts, hit *Grandaddy*. To Remi, I said, "Let's see if he answers this time."

He didn't. Well, he did, but not by live voice. Angels use voicemail, too. I announced that we were to meet him at the Zoo. Then Lily broke in to give him a message, and added that she was bound for New Mexico, that someone in Albuquerque needed help.

"New Mexico?" I asked her blankly as I disconnected.

"I have the entire Southwest Division, so to speak," Lily said, "not just Arizona. I told you that before, that I won't always be here. You'd best load up on ammo before I leave. Heavenly spit on bullets works on demons, but not on werewolves."

Kelly's voice was faint. "Werewolves . . ."

I stood up, Remi slid out of his dinette seat and grabbed his hat from off the valance. We were still damp; back at the Zoo we could shower, change into dry clothes.

Lily tapped the dog to make her move, then rose herself. She smiled at Kelly. "You'll be going with them, for now."

The ranger blinked. "I will?"

"The Zoo Club has been cleared," Lily explained. "No demon can get in there. You'll be safe there. Here as well, but I'm leaving."

Kelly slid out of the dinette and stood. "I have a job. A regular job."

Lily shrugged. "So do they, and it's to keep you alive."

"C'mon," I said. "I'll ask Grandaddy what he thinks we should do." I looked at Lily, could not delete the picture that popped into my head of her nude but cloaked in rivers of hair, weighted by weapons.

Lily's smile was wicked. "Our tryst is merely delayed,

Gabriel. In the meantime, consider poor Cuchulainn's fate. Had he not spurned me, he might not have tied himself to a stone with his own entrails and had me perching on his shoulder as he died."

Remi laughed, the asshole.

Lily quoted William Butler Yeats, Ireland's great poet:

> *Cuchulain stirred,*
> *Stared on the horses of the sea, and heard*
> *The cars of battle and his own name cried;*
> *And fought with the invulnerable tide.*

"He was a fanciful man, was Yeats," she said. "But he did keep his entrails in his body."

I scowled, put a protective hand over my gut, headed back to the garage.

The cowboy was singing, and this time it wasn't country but R.E.M.'s "It's the End of the World." I grabbed Kelly's unfinished whiskey and knocked it back. My head, thanks to Lily, was full of Yeats.

I remembered other words. I'd loved them as a boy.

> *The world is full of magic things,*
> *patiently waiting for our senses to grow sharper.*

But I was *im*patiently waiting, and my senses as yet dulled.

CHAPTER FOURTEEN

A t some point pickup truck manufacturers quit making them with bench seats in the front and switched to bucket seats, AKA captain's chairs. This meant you couldn't squish passengers in between the driver and the person immediately next to the door anymore. But Remi had a dual-cab model and there was plenty of room back there for Mary Jane Kelly, her rain suit, and her daypack.

Also room to set the muzzle of her reloaded 9-mil against the back of my head, or Remi's, were she so minded, but we had established she wasn't a demon. Merely a park ranger, albeit one still mightily confused by matters. We'd made it clear we didn't intend for her to believe this was a kidnapping, that we truly wanted to protect her, but I wasn't sure what was going on in her head.

Grandaddy's white '63 Thunderbird was parked out front of the Zoo Club, so at least we actually were going to have an in-person conversation. I was hoping he had additional information about the demon who was mutilating women and sending us photos of their bodies, and perhaps suggestions how we might keep Kelly safe.

"He's . . . unique," I mentioned as Remi pulled the truck in next to the T-bird; still morning, the Zoo wouldn't open until much later, so we'd have the place to ourselves for quite some time. "But he could be a huge help with this whole mess."

"Who's unique?" Kelly asked.

"We call him 'Grandaddy,'" Remi said, "on account of that's what he told us to call him when we were boys. He's not actually related . . . well, in the normal sort of way."

She blurted a choked-back laugh. "You already introduced me to a blood-thirsty Irish goddess and her shapeshifting sisters. So this guy is, what, King Tut?"

I triggered my door lock. "Maybe we ought to ask him that."

Remi opened the truck's back door before Kelly could, extended a hand to help her out. It crossed my mind to wonder if she'd refuse and climb out on her own—my ex-fiancé had insisted on doing all doors on her own for feminism's sake—but Kelly laid her hand lightly in his, jumped down, thanked him, and let him close the door. Remi did the courtly little you-first gesture again, pointing her toward the front of the building. She thumped up the four wooden steps in her hiking boots and attempted to beat Remi to the big front door. She didn't manage it because his arms were longer. He pulled it open, gestured her in with a warm smile.

"*Such* a gentleman," I said as I hip-checked him out of the way and made him bring up the rear.

In daylight, all the copper, wood, glass, and iron inside blended into rustic simplicity. The ornate barback sparkled and gleamed; the mirror glinted, catching and throwing sunlight across the parquet dance floor. Polished tree trunks and glass stringlights glinted, though the latter reminded me of the orbs Shemyazaz had commanded. I eyeballed the strings wrapped around the trunks holding up the exposed beamwork, but they appeared to be perfectly ordinary light bulbs.

No one was at the bar. Or in the booths. Or at the tables.

And then I heard the crack of a pool table break and looked beyond the dance floor, the dining tables and booths, to the alcoved area by the back door. Ganji was bent over one end of the table, cue stick in hand. Behind the table stood Grandaddy, hands wrapped around a stick with the butt floor-planted.

I shot a side-glance at Kelly. Grandaddy was an imposing man, and looking at him as if I'd never seen him before—as Kelly was—reminded me all over again that he carried an innate power. I didn't know if it was because he was an agent of heaven, or just that kind of guy. And I wondered if his body was borrowed, too. If the body at one time had been an infant on the verge of death, only to have the tiniest spark of "heavenly essence" implanted that grew into Grandaddy. Who were his human parents? And how old was he?

These were things I'd never asked him. He just *was*, like the Rock of Gibraltar. Permanent. Immovable. Could he even die?

Tall, broad, brimming with vitality but also a quietude, rather like power carefully packed away so he could be in polite society without alarming anyone. He wasn't young; silver-white hair flowed nearly to his shoulders, his beard and eyebrows were pepper-and-salt, heavy on the pepper. His face was creased beside the eyes, craggy below. He wore, as always, an old Western-style frock coat, as if he were mimicking Wyatt Earp and his brothers in the middle of a Tombstone street. Blue eyes watched us as we came across the dance floor toward the alcove.

Ganji had broken, and three solids resided in pockets. He

straightened, smiled at Kelly as we reached the alcove. Large, black, shaven-headed, with an affinity for black t-shirts and jeans. His dark eyes had clearly seen the ages pass.

"Was that you?" I asked. "The earthquake? Did you sing the mountain awake?"

"I sang to soothe her," he said, in his African-accented English. "I sang for her to soothe the broken angel."

Kelly looked at him sharply. "He's an African god," I told her helpfully.

She blinked hard, opened her mouth to say something, but Grandaddy's deep tone overrode her.

"The letter is genuine," he said.

Remi was clearly surprised. "It's the *actual* letter? The *From Hell* letter?"

"It is."

"What about it?" I asked.

"The actual letter was lost over a hundred years ago from the police files, along with the kidney," Remi said. "Fortunately they took a photo of it—it's why we know what it said, what the handwriting looked like—but it was never proven to be genuine." He frowned. "Studies suggested if any of all the letters received were the real thing, that one was, but so many letters were hoaxes that it created questions about all of 'em."

Kelly was frowning, clearly on the verge of demanding more answers.

"The letter is genuine," Grandaddy repeated. "Trust us to know better than the police and reporters, particularly of the 1800s when forensics constituted of little more than examining body parts."

Well, yeah, okay. Angels probably had a few more forensic specialists on their side.

"The kidney was legitimately human," Remi agreed.

"What kidney?" Kelly asked.

Remi looked hesitant. Too gentlemanly, I guess, to tell a woman the gory details.

"Jack took a trophy and sent it to the police," I told her.

She was horrified. "A kidney?"

I nodded. "*This* is why we want to keep you close."

"They knew it was a left kidney, which would be obvious," Remi said. "They knew it came from a woman, liver damage proved she was an alcoholic, and it was delivered, preserved in spirits, three weeks after Catherine Eddowes' body was found missing a kidney, so it all fit. And some were certain this letter, from among many, was written by the actual killer. Even modern handwriting analysis backs that up—well, as much as it can, based on a photo."

Mary Jane Kelly crossed her arms and pressed them against her chest.

My turn. "So okay. This guy—this *demon*—masquerading as Jack the Ripper got his hands on the actual letter. How?"

"Many things were lost," Remi explained. "Police files at the time were sketchy, and they were dealing with quite a few hoax letters. It would have been easy for someone knowing what to look for to waltz in there and dig out the actual letter."

"Who would know it was there?" I asked. "Was that letter publicized?"

Remi nodded. "A diary was found purportedly written by one of the Ripper suspects, a James Maybrick, and in it Maybrick refers to the *From Hell* letter and the cannibalism."

Mary Jane Kelly stiffened. "*Cannibalism? Jack the Ripper ate* people?"

Remi nodded. "Seems like. In the letter he says he ate part

of the kidney. And the kidney wasn't intact when it was delivered to the police."

"Oh, this is *disgusting!*" she cried, face screwed up. "Some nutjob masquerading as Jack the Ripper is killing women because their names match those of the original victims, and now a kidney is involved?"

Grandaddy's tone was quiet. "He is not human, this killer. It may be that Jack the Ripper also wasn't human."

Kelly stared at him, then walked away stiffly. She found a chair nearby, dragged it over and sat down heavily. "I can't wrap my head around all of this. I mean, Jack the Ripper is bad enough on his own, but a demon, too?"

"Demons possess hosts," Grandaddy told her, "and pervert them. Whoever he was, the man may have been perfectly ordinary until the demon took him."

"Or he was a perfectly ordinary psychopath," she said. "Men don't have to be demons to do terrible things."

"If it was a demon inhabiting the Ripper," I said, "it means he's been here awhile. He didn't just pop out of hell when the vents opened a couple of months ago."

Remi folded his arms, nodded. "Yup . . . and maybe has been here for decades. Possibly even centuries."

I raised my brows. "And he's running around grabbing innocent hosts for the hell of it, turning them into murderers?"

"Chaos," Remi said. "That was your suggestion: chaos demons."

"What's in a name." Kelly was a combination of concerned and annoyed. "And I'm on his list because he's decided to mimic Jack the Ripper. How cool is that?—*not*."

"Revisiting infamy?" I asked Grandaddy. "His greatest hits, so to speak?"

"Mary Jane Kelly was his last victim, so far as we know," Remi said, "but that doesn't mean she was. Other women were murdered after Kelly."

"Do we know *their* names?" I asked.

"Three of them," Remi said. "One was killed before the five who are Ripper canon, two after. Their names are known. Could be others, though."

I looked at Grandaddy. "The other pictures that came, the ones with the names matching the Ripper's victims written on the back—we don't know that those victims are all local, do we? They could be from anywhere in the state, the country— hell, even the world. I mean, it would make sense if this were happening in London. But why here?"

"Opportunity?" Remi asked.

I looked harder at Grandaddy. "The demon that came onto me that first night, then tried to strangle me . . . we know it's the one sending the photos. Or, at least the notes said so." *Legion*, it had named itself, *for we are many*. "So we're to assume the Big Bad who terrorized London in the late 1800s is here in Flagstaff? Is he assigned to the so-called Southwestern Division, like Lily? Are demons that organized?"

Grandaddy looked down at Kelly. "I'm sorry, but the truth is hard in this matter. The demon's not here because of you, precisely. It's using you, yes, and it will kill you, because that's all part of the game. But the demon is here for Gabriel and Remiel."

She looked at me, at Remi, then met Grandaddy's eyes, blue to blue. "Why is it here for them?"

Grandaddy answered simply. "Because they're not human, either . . . and it has an affinity for them."

CHAPTER FIFTEEN

Kelly stared at Grandaddy for a long moment, then shifted her attention to Remi and me. "Okay. We'll go with that for the moment, just because. So what are they, then? Aliens? Lost mermen of Atlantis?"

"They are between," Grandaddy told her. "Language comes in many forms, including the language of the angels, but it might be easiest to say they are *se metávasi*. Or *ángeloi se metavásai*. Neither is entirely accurate—it's modern, not ancient Greek, but it will do."

She shook her head. "I'll avoid the cheap joke, but I don't speak Greek."

I looked sharply at Remi, because he *did* speak it. "Well? What are we? Because God knows that's more than he's ever told us."

Remi held up a hand. "I know the one word. I was studying religion, not colloquial Greek. Or colloquial Koine Greek, assuming there was vernacular in ancient Greek. *Ángeloi* means angels. I think *se* means 'in.' But I got no clue about *metávasi*."

"You're in transition," Grandaddy said, as if that explained everything.

Kelly's brows shot up again. "Both of you?"

"Not that kind of transitioning," I pointed out, even as Remi's grin stretched wide. "Apparently it's some kind of proto-angel thing. We're apprentices. But Remi and I are pretty much being treated like mushrooms, so who knows? I guess tomorrow we might start sprouting feathers."

Remi was puzzled. "Mushrooms?"

"Kept in the dark," I explained, "with fecal matter for fertilizer. Or maybe *grown* in the dark, since we're but baby 'shrooms." I plucked my tee from my chest, looked between Grandaddy and Ganji. "Look, I'm damp, sore, and tired, and I'd really like to take a shower, change into dry clothes, get something to eat. I'm sure Remi feels the same. So why don't you guys talk all this out, then tell me exactly who—or what—I am when I'm clean and dry."

"Maybe we oughta flip for it," Remi suggested.

"What?"

"Flip for first shower. Only one bathroom upstairs."

I grinned at him. "Alpha trumps beta."

Remi scowled prodigiously, and I headed for the stairs.

Then he called, "I'm going to play country on the jukebox and crank it up high!"

I hit the first two steps. "Fine by me. Shower will cover it!"

And as I went up the stairs, I heard Mary Jane Kelly's raised voice saying, "I need to know more."

The hot shower was damn near orgasmic. The stiffness from the bike accident—coupled with the physical activities on the mountain in the middle of a torrential downpour that became a hailstorm—began to ease. The road rash wasn't too bad, thanks to my leathers, but impact is impact, and I'd hit hard enough to raise some pretty spectacular bruises. Could have been a lot worse, though.

I downed three analgesics, dug through my limited supply of clothing: jeans, heavily-pocketed military BDU pants, couple of t-shirts, long-sleeved Henley shirts. I donned fresh underwear, navy tee, and black BDUs—loose over bruises and road rash; wet jeans had added insult to injury—worked a comb through my towel-damp hair and left it unbound to dry, pulled on boots over socks and headed toward the stairs.

But I stopped when I heard Remi's voice coming from the common room just down the abbreviated hall, speaking on his phone. I paused, poked my head in to let him know the shower was open.

He nodded and gave me thumbs up, thanked someone, disconnected, and stuck the phone into a back pocket. "I thought we could go rescue your bike. I found a Harley shop and arranged to rent a flatbed bike trailer with all the tie-downs, got a bunch of furniture blankets and ratchet strapping, and for forty extra bucks a guy's willing to meet us out there with a winch-truck to give us a hand. Grandaddy's gone again, but Mary Jane is being entertained by Ganji and has no interest in going, which is just as well. She'll be safer here." He headed past me toward his room, then paused. "She's gonna spend the night on the sofabed in the common room. We're trying to sort out what to do going forward about keeping her safe, so if you've got any ideas, throw 'em out."

I was impressed he'd gone to all the trouble, and thanked him. "She's got a job," I said. "Are we supposed to be bodyguards while she does her work?"

"That's what we're trying to figure out."

Remi disappeared, and I headed down the narrow staircase. The jukebox *was* playing country music; I heard the twang, the nasal whine. Something about Ruby being mad at her man and not taking her love to town. I was pretty sure every country song featured cheating in some form, possibly even cheating on someone's pickup truck.

I smelled food as I hit the bottom of the steps, and my stomach sent up its own form of music. Ganji came out of the back bearing a plate featuring a burger and fries, handed it to me along with a beer. We did have a cook for evenings, but Ganji handled food now and then during daylight, tended bar after dark.

Not many people were served alcohol by an African god who sang volcanoes awake. Or to sleep. The sleep part was certainly preferable.

I found Mary Jane Kelly at a table and joined her. Saw ketchup, but no mustard, which reminded me all over again that Remi considered mustard the forgotten condiment.

She'd pushed her plate aside, and now planted elbows on the table to cradle jaw in palms as I sat down and dug in. "So, do you think that mountain lion was meant for me?"

I frowned. "Why?"

"Because if I'm a target, it's predictable that I might rush out to the trail system to check on people and terrain. It's my job."

I thought it over as I chewed, washed burger down with a slug of beer. "Possible," I said. "But I think it was tracking Remi and me. Remi swore he heard his daughter calling for him. It's why he went up the mountain. So more likely you were collateral— except that I took out the demon before you arrived. I'm sure, had it succeeded in killing us, it would have gone for you." I considered that a moment. "Or maybe not—with us dead, what's the point in playing Jack the Ripper with victims bearing the same names? Though . . ." I trailed off, roll-tapped fingertips against the tabletop as I thought further. "I don't believe the demon in the cat is the one who's gaslighting us. There seem to be any number of demon worker-bees. But the other victims I think were the doing of Legion."

"Legion?"

"My name is Legion, for we are many. That's what she/he/it said."

Her face was stark, stretched taut over the bones. "And me?"

I scooped up ketchup with multiple fries. "With us in the mix it's possible it won't go after you anymore."

She brightened. "In which case I'm safe and can go back to my own place, back to my job."

"Give it a couple of days." I used a last fry to draw designs in the remaining ketchup. "We don't know enough yet. Let's not take any chances. As for your job—well, Grandaddy's good at taking care of mundane things like that. Settling troubled waters, so to speak." Such as springing me from prison early, but I didn't mention that to her.

She looked at me thoughtfully. "Remi says neither of you had any idea about what you are."

I shook my head. "Grew up like perfectly normal kids. Well, perfectly normal kids who have a literal guardian angel popping into their lives now and then, though we believed he was just an old family friend."

"I thought you were brothers. You're very similar."

We did indeed resemble one another in hair color, general build, similarities in facial bones. But I opted to forgo explaining the whole two-sparks-born-of-celestial-energy routine and continued. "I don't feel any different. Never did." Except for, well, the *primogenitura*, and sussing out demons and evil in places. I didn't mention *that*, either. "We really are learning as we go."

"Pretty steep learning curve."

I picked up the beer. "Everest. And we're climbing it without bottled oxygen."

Her smile was faint and fleeting. "The descent's the worst part."

From what I knew of Everest, yup. More people died climbing down than on the way to the summit.

And I wondered . . . was Ganji, an Orisha, acquainted with Chomolungma, the Tibetan goddess known as Holy Mother of the Universe whose mountain bridged the border between Nepal and Tibet? Everest wasn't *Everest* to the Tibetans, or to the Nepali, either, who called her Sagarmatha.

Ganji knew Lily, Ireland's Morrigan. Did he know what other gods and goddesses had joined the angels' battle? Did he know which gods and goddesses sided with Lucifer?

The latter information certainly would be handy to have, and I resolved to ask him.

"I'm sorry you got dragged into this," I told Kelly. "I don't know if this surrogate actually *is* Jack the Ripper and has been body-hopping for centuries, or something else riding the coattails of the stories. Borrowed glory, if you will."

Her gaze was serious. "And if you two hadn't found me, I'd be dead?"

I answered her truthfully. "I don't know. Maybe so. Since he's very recently killed women by the names of the original victims, it seems likely."

She nodded, but seemed to have moved on from that answer. She stretched, leaned back in her chair. "So, tell me what you can do. What are *your* super powers, as you called them.

Remi says he can figure out who's a demon, but your ability is something else."

"Remi is *supposed* to be able to figure out who's a demon by sensing them. But so far his ability is intermittent, which is unhelpful. That's why he had to try the exorcism on you."

"And why he changed up the lyrics to *Ave Maria* to the exorcism ritual the other night." Kelly grinned, nodded. "Gotta admit, that was pretty clever. So, *did* you catch yourselves a demon?"

I smiled back. "Nope. Thought so, but it turned out to be an angel. One of three. They dropped by to underscore that we couldn't afford to be stupid about all of this. That we'd better *believe* what we're told."

Though that did remind me of the Grigori, Ambriel, whom I called Greg. She'd dropped by to inform us we shouldn't necessarily trust all angels, which muddied the waters something bad. But she'd also exploded a surrogate's body for us, when Remi and I had no clue how to "clear a domicile." Basically, how to sanitize a formerly infected area.

The next body we'd exploded ourselves, all over the side of a massive volcanic cinder cone.

I wondered, now, if Greg knew Shemyazaz. Both were Grigori, watcher-angels. Though, of course, Shemyazaz had colored outside the lines centuries ago by actually having *sex* with a human woman.

"Do you still have the baggie of demon remains?" I asked.

Kelly nodded. "They're in my pack."

"But you didn't sweep up all of them."

"No. You didn't exactly give me time, remember? But I wound up with a fair amount. Enough for a specialist to examine."

"So the rest is still up on the mountain." I ruminated on

that for a moment. "I wonder if Remi and I should go gather them up. I mean, I don't know if partial remains can be reconstituted into a full-blown demon." Kelly's expression suggested she was utterly grossed out by that picture. "Who knows?" I asked. "Maybe we should gather up the rest that's still on the mountain, add them to your baggie, then drop all of the remains off with that entomologist you know at . . . ?"

"Northern Arizona University. NAU."

" . . . and see what he has to say once he's examined them."

She reached down below the table, lifted her daypack and pulled the baggie from it, placed it on the table. The brown bits glittered through the plastic. "I thought you were going to get your bike out of the crick, as Remi put it." She smiled, dropped her voice deeper and assumed a Southern accent. "I do appreciate a fine Texas drawl."

Okay, then. Like that. And she was spending the night upstairs in our apartment. Hmm. A wingman might be overkill.

And then Remi came down the stairs in a boot-thumping staccato, singing something along with the jukebox about sky-high Colorado and tasting tequila. Which reminded me that while Grandaddy had gifted me with a bottle of fine Talisker single malt, it had been Patron tequila for Remi.

I scootched the chair back and rose, carrying plate and bottle to the bar. "I think we ought to go back up the mountain," I told him. "Take a baggie and scoop up the rest of those demonic bug bodies, add 'em to these, then drop them off with the scientist she knows." I picked up her baggie. "We need to learn more about these remains. I mean, has anyone actually studied them? Then we can go get my bike."

Kelly had pulled her phone from her daypack and was texting. "Remi, I'm sending you the name and directions to Dr.

Hickman's office at NAU. He's got office hours this afternoon. I'll text him, too, so he's expecting you. It'll probably take him a few days, if he doesn't have to send them to Phoenix."

"And there's another reason we ought to gather up those remains," I told him. "The mountain isn't a domicile, and they can't set one up, but they could still go after one of their fallen and reconstitute the bug bits later. Then we can go get my bike."

Remi pursed his lips and nodded. "Okay, I ate and I'm all scrubbed up behind the ears, Mary Jane's safe here with Ganji— let's light a shuck and go."

He'd used that saying before. "What the hell does that *mean*?"

"It means we should put our asses in gear and get the hell gone."

"Okay. That I can do. Just remember that I don't speak Texan."

CHAPTER SIXTEEN

This time we were fully armed: me with my KA-BAR knife and the long-barreled Taurus snugged beneath left arm. Remi had the shorter version in his belt-holster, along with the Bowie and his throwing knives. Both revolvers were loaded with silver buckshot and silver .45 rounds pre-bathed in holy oil and our breath. Before Lily had left, we'd spent time gathering up various items we found prudent, if outlandish.

Under still-cloudy skies upon the mountain, we found the cat but not the demon remains. We got down on our hands and knees to try and find one speck of bug droppings, or whatever the hell the leftovers were, and came up empty, as far as we could tell. We even lifted the dead cat and moved it aside to check underneath.

Nope.

Remi and I stood up, slapped damp knees free of dirt. The mountainside was still wet from the earlier storm. "No one else would have gathered up all that stuff," I said. "Not even kids." Because some kids would have found a tumbled pile of bug remains fascinating.

"And even if it *were* kids, they would not have picked up every last bit."

I swore, looked in all directions in case we were being watched. In a way I kind of hoped we were, because it meant we could do something about it. Saw no one.

Remi leaned down again, seemed to be trying to find tracks leading to or from. But he shook his head.

I wanted to growl. "So we're screwed."

"Looks like."

"Okay. Well, we've got Kelly's baggie—let's take that to the guy. It's something." I looked skyward. "I thought Arizona was a desert. This looks almost like Oregon, with all this rain."

"And earthquakes?"

"Well, yeah. We ought to look into that. It was earthquakes across the world that coughed up a bunch of surrogates and jump-started our new careers."

"You thinkin' the earthquake earlier today was a hell vent?"

I shrugged. "Depends on if anything popped open, I suspect. Some kind of fissure, maybe? We're on top of a volcano, after all. Didn't you say this whole area is volcanic?"

"Over six hundred of the suckers scattered across the plateau. They're just not all as big as these peaks."

I nodded, brushed hands against one another to knock off the last of the dirt. "Then if we're going to campus anyway to see this bug doc, let's check with the geology department."

Northern Arizona University, I discovered, was an attractive, bi-level school built on a broad slope with a slight geologic break between one campus and the other. Plenty of grass and pines, even ivy, but with the patchwork architecture typical of older universities: old buildings mixed with new, and none of the styles similar.

Mary Jane Kelly's bug guy was a Dr. Hal Hickman, and he was indeed holding office hours. His door was one of many along the corridor, but the only one standing open.

On the inside of the door, now bared to the hallway, he'd stuck up a calendar, a small whiteboard, and a quote in bright red calligraphic text on pale paper, treated to make it look aged: *No one thinks of how much blood it will cost.* —Dante Alighieri.

No one thinks the battle between Good and Evil is real, either, nor what blood it might cost. And me smack in the middle of it, to boot. Possibly Dante did, when he wrote the graphic and terrifying *Inferno* portion of the *Divine Comedy*.

Hickman glanced up from his desk as we lingered on the threshold, gestured us in. "You Mary Jane's people?"

"We are her people," Remi confirmed, as I offered the sealed baggie.

Hickman was late-40s by my guess, wavy sandy hair tied back into a frizzy ponytail. Eyelashes framing blue eyes were so pale as to appear nonexistent, and he was heavily freckled. He didn't stand to shake hands, just leaned close to the desk and reached out a long arm to accept the baggie.

Already he was distracted as he unzipped the sealed plastic. "Go ahead and pull those two chairs over—oh, yeah, sorry about that! Just move my leg." He gestured with a thumb at a prosthetic leaning against a chair. "Stick it in this corner by me, if you would."

It's not every day you see a prosthetic leg separated from its owner. Remi treated it carefully, leaned it precisely in the corner within Hickman's reach and made sure it wouldn't fall over.

"I stand on it so much in class I just pop it off in the office." The professor slid out the middle desk drawer, dug up a pair of long tweezers. "I'll get everything under the scope in the lab later." Hickman teased out a fragment of remains. "I just want to get a quick first look."

He placed the bug bit down on the clean blotter, aimed his desk lamp at it, grabbed a handheld magnifier and began an examination. His freckled forehead folded like corrugated cardboard.

Hickman was silent, twisting his mouth this way and that. He used the tweezers to turn the fragment onto different sides and edges. Finally he said, in happy tones, "I am clueless! This is fascinating! I see why Mary Jane said you guys felt it looked insectoid. It may well be part of an exoskeleton. But it has some very odd striations in it. Let me pull out another fragment." He continued the examination, then asked if we'd felt the earthquake that morning. "Doesn't happen often, but now and then, we are visited by the shake, rattle, and roll."

Remi and I both sat up straight. "Any reports of damages?" I asked. "Any new fissures?"

"Matter of fact . . ." He was paying much more attention to the demon remains, and now had a little line of glittering brown bits. "Yeah, they said they've closed a portion of the trail out at Sunset Crater. There's an old ice cave there. An area of it collapsed and the trail went with it. Parts of the lava flow may be unstable, so they're checking it out."

Remi and I looked at one another sharply. Sunset Crater was the massive cinder cone where we had cleared a domicile and exploded a demon in black dog form. Supposedly no more demons could inhabit the place, but did that apply if earthquakes broke open new ground?

I opened my mouth to ask more questions, but was interrupted by a young dark-haired woman in bright red glasses.

She leaned around the doorframe. "Hey, Dr. Hickman—" But she saw me, saw Remi, and stopped dead in the middle of her sentence.

Remi rose abruptly, knocking aside his chair. Her eyes widened and she took off like a shot. He pushed the chair away and went after her.

Hickman and I both stared at the empty doorway, then at one another.

The last thing we needed was a professor sounding the alarm because one of his students, and a young woman at that, was being chased through the halls by a cowboy. I opened my mouth to spin it as best I could, but Hickman beat me to it.

He waved a hand. "Molly does that."

"Molly does that? Runs away in the middle of a question?" Some of my students ditched classes when I taught, but none of them ever *ran away* in the middle of talking to me.

He spread his hands palm up in an *oh well* gesture. "Believe it or not, yes. And it's not really running away so much as it's an avoidance technique employed when she feels cornered by strangers. She's one of those eccentric geniuses—you know, where you give 'em a pass because they're actually much smarter than you are."

Of course that did not explain Remi's leaping to his feet and running after her. So I tried to spin that, too. "Well, he did say his burger tasted a little off. Hope he found the restroom in time." But Hickman was no longer paying me any attention at all, and I wanted to go after Remi because I was pretty damn sure he was chasing a demon. I edged toward the door. "Can we call tomorrow, or stop by?"

"Sure. Or I'll text Mary Jane. I'm going to take these home

tonight, then bring them back in the morning to the big lab. No prob."

Okay, so *Hickman* had no prob. Possibly Remi and I did.

Naturally, just at the moment I hit the corridor, classes let out. I was engulfed by students, most of them grabbing phones out of pockets and purses and paying absolutely no attention to the possibility that a non-student might be trying to find another non-student who was in hot pursuit of someone who *was* a student, even if a demonic student, and therefore knew her way around. I needed Moses to part the Red Sea of social media addicts.

But I had a phone, too, as did Remi, and I checked for voice-mail or text from him as I threaded my way through the masses. Nothing, so I called him, only to reach voicemail.

"Yo." I disconnected, figuring that would be enough. I also sent him a text saying the same thing.

And then I called myself something less complimentary than idiot, or even dipshitiot. Remi and I had not set up GPS apps on our ordinary phone, but I was betting it wasn't neces-sary with the magic phones.

Try Siri? Alexa? Google Assistant?

"Hey iAngel," I said, "where's Remi?"

And to my surprise a nice little nav-map came up on the screen with cool moving wing icons indicating me, and another set of wings that I assumed represented Remi. Mine were red, his blue, and they were pretty far apart. I was supposed to exit the building, according to the screen, so I hit the push-bar on the heavy glass door, shoved my way through.

Around the corner. Along a sidewalk. Crossed a street. Into another building, through another door. I probably looked like I was playing Pokémon GO, though it now was passe.

I chanted swear words beneath my breath. Remi was on the move, which we needed, but I kind of wanted him to pause long enough for me to make up some ground.

"Are you lost?" A woman's voice. "Can I help?" I looked up, prepared to politely decline, and then saw Molly herself in her bright red glasses grinning at me from a distance of ten or so yards. "Boo!" she cried. "Welcome to the war!"

And then she took off.

And I took off.

As I ran I pulled up Remi's contact, hoped he'd answer. Just in case, I yelled to voicemail. "On me!" I shouted. "I'm on her ass—follow my little wings!"

Oh, *that* didn't sound weird or anything. And it was still a man chasing a young woman on a college campus. All she had to do to really screw with us was scream for help.

So I stopped. I just stopped. Molly was familiar with and in control of the battleground, so to speak, and we weren't going to catch her. All we would do was get ourselves arrested. Possibly amusing to Molly, but not so much to us. And I was a felon, so even though Grandaddy would probably come handle the legalities, I'd still have to deal with the red tape in the meantime. Police don't take kindly to ex-cons to start with, particularly murderers, but especially not when caught chasing female college students. *We* might know she was a demon, but they wouldn't. And anyway, trying to explain such a thing to police? Pass. Easier to talk about UFOs.

I watched Remi's little blue wings on the screen get closer

and closer to my red ones, and then they turned purple as his icon and mine met. I turned, and there he was coming up behind me.

"You get her?" he asked, resetting his hat.

I shook my head. "Gave it up for a lost cause. She was just screwing with us."

"Yeah. And even if Hickman has her number or address, he won't give either to us. Student privacy."

"Think she hopped bodies into a real student?"

"Makes sense," he said. "Let's hope it's temporary, and the host is okay."

I nodded, wondering whether a host was aware a demon had highjacked the body, or would have no memory of it after the host was vacated. Providing he or she survived.

"Hickman said he was going home early to look at the remains under his scope, then he'll bring them back tomorrow to the school lab. He'll call Mary Jane if he finds anything of interest." I tucked the phone away. "So, I assume your Spidey-sense started tingling when Molly stuck her head around the door?"

"Like a damn bad weather alert," he said. "One minute I was sittin' there, nice as you please, and then I knew. I just *knew*. I can't even tell you how."

"But you were able to follow her."

"For a bit, but it didn't last. I guess my personal batteries died."

I checked my watch. "Well, we've still got a few hours of daylight. Nothing more we can do until Hickman gets back to us, and even then it may do us no good. Let's call the guy at the Harley shop and see if we can finally go haul my poor bike out of the ravine. I'm just praying it can be salvaged."

CHAPTER SEVENTEEN

R emi drove us out the winding Highway 180 toward the far side of the San Francisco Peaks. At the A-framed Chapel of the Holy Dove, which we had reconsecrated to keep demons from setting up shop, he turned us around. It had been on the way back from the chapel a couple of days before that we engaged with La Llorona, the weeping woman from Mexican folklore. She had been getting her jollies by orchestrating car wrecks triggered by her sudden appearances in the middle of the two-lane road.

I'd been doing 50mph when she popped up immediately in front of me, and I opted to lay down the bike, an action that is beloved of Hollywood and TV because it looks Really Cool, while it is to be desperately avoided in real life. But reflexes are reflexes, and mine went into action when a woman appeared out of nowhere right in front of my bike. I'd dumped it and sent myself tumbling across the highway to the shoulder on the far side. In boots, full leathers, gloves and a helmet, I'd survived without any broken bones and no head injury, but fine I was not. The bike screeched down the asphalt, disappeared on a curve into forest alongside the road, and took a dive off the edge of a steep, rocky ravine, where it landed in the creek.

It hurt just to remember it.

Heading back the way we'd come, I spotted skid marks and shards of shattered glass from the bike's lights littering the asphalt. Remi pulled off to park truck and flatbed trailer on the shoulder. The guy from the Harley shop was supposed to meet us in a half-hour.

I got out, closed the door. "Let's just hope he can get his truck all the way to the edge of the ravine to use the winch. Otherwise we may be shit-out-of-luck."

Remi grabbed a gearbag from the back of the truck and tossed it across the bed to me, then hooked another over his shoulder. "Lead on, Macduff."

"*Lay* on." I slipped an arm through the woven handles, hitched the bag up high. "Everybody gets it wrong, just like the 'Catch me *when* you can' Ripper quote. But that's not what Shakespeare wrote."

"It's '*Lay* on, Macduff?'"

I turned to head out, but threw the reply over my shoulder. "Last words Macbeth says before he and Macduff get into it. He wasn't *following* Macduff into battle, he was telling Macduff to take his best shot."

"Huh." Remi was close behind me as we made our way through trees and vegetation. "I did not know that. So, then, what about 'To thine own self be true.'?"

"The Bible verse? What about it?"

"Which verse is it?"

I laughed. "Don't ask me that! I'm not up on Biblical stuff."

"Shakespeare," Remi said.

"What?"

"It's a quote from Shakespeare, not the Bible."

I marched onward through trees. "Amazing what we go around misquoting."

"Speaking of quotes," Remi began, "I did some reading in the Bible earlier today. It has some things to say about demons."

I grinned. "Well, one would expect that, yeah. Kind of invented the genre, didn't it?"

"You know how our demons say 'Everyone comes home,' and they gather up the remains?"

"Yeah." That had been our first real meeting with a surrogate, when it rode a host body to the Zoo to recover remains.

"It's addressed in Matthew 12: 43 and 44, *'When the unclean spirit has gone out of a person, it passes through waterless places seeking rest, but finds none.'* Then the verse says, *'I will return to my house from which I came.'* There's a little more to it, but that's the salient point. Exorcised demons go home in order to be made whole again. And some bring back seven of its kind worse than it is."

That was a game-changer. "So you're saying this Jack the Ripper demon, this Legion, that if we kill it, the remains are taken back to hell and it will return with *seven* pals worse than it is? Shit. It's like the Magnificent Seven of bad guys."

"More like Seven Deadly Sins."

It was astounding to me. "Can you imagine demonic versions of the Ripper, Bundy, Dahmer, Gacy, Manson, and so on, joining forces in the middle of Armageddon?"

"I reckon that might could be the whole point, and which is why we ought to be concerned about those remains that got scooped up on the mountain today."

Shit. Shitshitshit. "So, from here on out we burn 'em up before we go anywhere else, instead of leaving them lying around."

"Or take them off somewhere ourselves to destroy them later."

"But meanwhile most of those got away from us." I mulled it over as we walked. "Should we have exploded the cat like we did the black dog? Greg said that was enough when she did it for us at the Wupatki ruins."

"Well, that cat jumped me before you got there, and then it went right after you," Remi said, "so I'm figurin' we did the best we could. Besides, it's a public trail system. Shooting a mountain lion is one thing, and Mary Jane said it's not illegal. But chanting a foreign language while sticking our rings together and exploding an animal all over the mountainside might could be a tad much for most folks seein' it up close and personal."

And that took us right to the edge of the ravine. We stood side by side and peered down. It wasn't a sheer cliff, but a cascade of edged rock outcrops and hummocks of soil and grasses, exposed tree roots, divots and pockets in stone. Both of us had managed to climb down to the creekbed without the aid of anything before, though at the time we'd been chasing a deadly figment of folklore and not thinking about ourselves. It's easier climbing down a rocky ravine when lives depend upon it. At this juncture, no lives depended upon it and neither of us was ready to go over the edge without aids.

Which is why Remi dug into his gearbag, took out rope complete with climbing ratchet, fastened it around the trunk of a thick pine and paid out the bulk of it down over the edge. We'd decided against going full climbing harness because the creekbed was not that far down, and the ratchet would be enough for a controlled descent.

I looked around, trying to scope out the best route for a

truck to get in so we could hook up the bike and winch it to the top. But the trees were pretty close-grown, and there were stumps and fallen trees galore as well as plenty of low branches of substantial size. We were going to have to check around, see if we could find easier access for the winch-truck.

Remi went over the edge, gearbag hooked over his shoulder. It didn't take him long to hit bottom. Then I pulled the rope up, repositioned the climbing ratchet, dropped the rope over the edge again and worked my way down.

And discovered that the bike was *not* where it had been. "Ohhh man . . ."

Remi gestured expansively. "I swear it was right here."

"It was!"

"Well, where'd it go?"

I stood creekside, hands on hips. The last time we'd been here we'd killed a woman and her two ghost children. In the midst of that, the fate of my bike was not at the forefront of my mind. But I was certain this spot was where it had ended up.

I watched the noisy creek as it ran over and around stones, splashed against aged boulders. It smelled like home, with trees, moisture, foliage all around. "How many people would go to the trouble to pull a very heavy, possibly very damaged motorcycle out of a creek? I mean besides, you know, the *owner?*"

Remi looked upstream, contemplated something. Then he nodded. "Let's go downstream a ways." When I looked at him, frowning a question, he explained, "We got us a shit-ton of rain this morning, not to mention hail. Got lots of water running right down through here."

"You think it *floated* downstream?"

He started picking his way along the creek. "It doesn't take that much water under a *car* to move it, if the water's running fast enough, and a bike weighs less. You've seen video of vehicles being washed away, haven't you?"

I had. And within a few minutes of gingerly making our way over rocks jutting out of the earth and avoiding loose river stones, we did indeed find my bike maybe twenty yards downstream.

Lying cockeyed on its left side, it had hitched up against some boulders. Most of the gas tank was exposed now, and the front wheel kissed the bank. My right saddlebag stuck up in the air. Because of its position I couldn't tally all the damage, but the lights were broken out, the handlebars were probably out of alignment, and for all I knew the frame was destroyed. I hoped like hell it wasn't totaled.

I could buy a new bike. But you can't buy memories. And this one had a million associated with it.

I blew out a noisy breath. "Okay, let's do what we can to get it up on its wheels, try to roll it out of the water so I can take a closer look, and then we can decide how to do this." I perched my ass on a boulder, removed boots and socks, rolled up my pants. No way of doing this without getting in the water, and Remi did the same. We picked our way out into the creek, risking broken toes and ankles on slick river stones blurred by running water.

Bikes are damn heavy. But we numbered two, and from one side we heaved the bike mostly upright, then hung onto it for all we were worth so it wouldn't unbalance itself and go over on the other side *or* come back down on us. Once we had it upright, I told Remi to be ready and I eased my way around the back end to the handlebars.

Bikes are not difficult to roll when they're upright, not even for one guy, and we had two. But that's on inflated tires with a frame that's nicely aligned and well-balanced.

Well, shit. "Assume it's destroyed," I said. "Assume it will try like hell to fall over. Assume it will take far more effort to move it than rolling it somewhere."

Remi nodded. "Assume it's a bronc bound and determined to pitch me off."

"Whatever floats your boat. Okay, see that white rock over there?" I pointed. "The quartz that's half buried? Aim for that. Once we get there, we'll see if the kickstand will hold it."

"But assume it won't."

"Assume it won't."

Naturally, rolling it out of a stone-choked, hard-running creek with God knows how much damage done to the bike made things much more difficult, even for two men. We wrestled with it, finally got it to the big quartz formation I'd indicated.

The front wheel rim was actually in good shape. The rear was another matter. So the front end rolled while the back end was pretty much dragged. When I went over the bike I found flat tires, a snapped off foot peg, bent rear wheel rim, dents galore, some punctures, all lights shattered, mirrors snapped off, the saddle badly scuffed, ruptured gas tank. But until it was taken apart, I couldn't truly grasp how much damage had been done.

I did grasp that the kickstand was bent and thus the bike wouldn't stand upright without one of us physically holding it in place.

I stared at the side of the ravine. We'd climbed down okay, but from our present location couldn't tell if there was a navigable way up—or down. And no handy ropes.

"Well," Remi said, "I propose that I climb back up, look around for truck access, bring the blankets, and we'll get her wrapped up and ready to go for the shop guy."

"Okay, hang on." I eased a leg over the saddle and straddled the bike as one would normally, hands gripping handlebars, though I had to work a little harder at keeping it upright. "See if you can find a few flat rocks around yay big." I used both hands to approximate what I needed. "Let's stack them under the kickstand, see if we can counterbalance the bike."

Remi nodded, went off to hunt up the appropriate rocks. He came back with four and squatted down to pack the damp sand and soil, carefully stack the stones. It took two tries, but finally I eased the bike leftward a little, rested the kickstand carefully, then rose until I was standing with the bike between my legs. So far, so good. I brought a leg over, stood on the one side, let the bike's weight settle on the propped up kickstand without me making physical contact.

I nodded at him. "Okay."

Remi headed back upstream while I contemplated my poor bike. It was possible the cost of rebuilding would outstrip the cost of a new bike. I had no insurance, since the bike had been sitting at home for eighteen months while I was in prison. So it was all on me.

I squinted across the creek, speaking to the air. "I should ask Grandaddy if this job pays anything. I mean, what does it cost to save the world?" We had credit cards provided by whoever was running things but had been specifically cautioned not to use them on "frivolous expenditures." I wasn't sure if bike repairs entered into that.

Something bounced off the back of my neck. Thinking of insects. I slapped at it. Then again. I turned in irritation, and was astonished to see Molly, she of the bright red glasses and a demon riding her.

"*Boo!*" she shouted. She sat above me at the ravine's edge, skinny jeans-clad legs dangling, and continued to toss pebbles at me. "Dare you!" she called, grinning widely. "*Dare* you to come up here and stop me!"

"Don't have to," I called back, and pulled the Taurus from my holster. "I can shoot just fine from down here."

And I did.

CHAPTER EIGHTEEN

didn't shoot *her*. She was a demon riding a human.

I shot dead center between her swinging legs. Stone chips flew.

"Hey!" She was wide-eyed in shock as she wrenched her legs apart, then grinned broadly. "You shoot the host to get to me, you've got a dead host."

I grinned back at her. "I don't have to shoot to kill. It might not be convenient for the host to be winged, maybe, but it would rid the world of you."

"Nuh-*uhhh*." She sounded just like a young kid. "You can wound the host, sure, but I can heal her. You've got to kill her to get me out."

"The bullets have been washed in holy oil and holy water."

"Oh, ow. I'm all aquiver with terror." She sprang up from the edge of the ravine and brushed off the seat of her pants. As she stared down at me dark hair was loose around her shoulders and the red glasses frames glowed brightly in the sun. She was slim, on the short side, looked about seventeen. And she was apparently whip-smart. Blue-eyed, as I recalled from Dr. Hickman's office. It was an immature girl-next-door look; give her another year or two and she might blossom nicely.

Well, if the demon ever departed.

I raised my voice, let it ring throughout the trees above the sound of running water. *"Exorcisamus te . . . omnis immundus spiritus . . ."* And then I had to stop, because I didn't remember any more of the *Rituale Romanum*. I'd been hoping just the beginning would start the process of expulsion from the host.

Molly laughed very like a hyena, loud and delighted, and it echoed through the trees. "Oh, it's going to be *fun* playing with you noobs!" Then she blew into a flattened palm, closed up thumb and fingers as if to hold the breath, then rolled her hand over and snapped the digits forward sharply.

She pointed at me, and I dropped my gun. Then I fell over. She pointed at my bike, and *it* fell over. By the time I was on my feet again and my Taurus was recovered, she was gone.

Remi, gun in hand, broke out of the trees and foliage and brought himself up short at the edge of the ravine, directly above me. "Gabe—you okay? What was the shooting about?"

I waved him off. "She's gone."

"She who? What happened?"

"The girl we chased on campus. Or, well, the demon we chased on campus. Apparently we have a fan. She dropped by just to give us a hard time. Or, well, me." I motioned. "Can you come back down? The bitch knocked over my bike." And me, but I left that part out.

Remi safed his revolver home in its holster. "I gotta go back and pick everything else up. I dropped it all and ran when I heard the shot." He began to turn, swung back. "Oh, and the guy with the truck can't be here after all. Some family emergency. First thing come morning, he said. But we can at least get the bike all wrapped up so it's ready to go tomorrow. Hang on; I'll be down directly."

While I waited, I examined my gun. Apparently she'd mo-jo'd either it or me, because it just flat fell out of my hand. Which meant one of two things, I decided: One, she really was just screwing with us; or two, bullets washed in holy water and holy oil *could* do a number on the demon inside the host, and she meant only to distract me from that realization.

Nonetheless, I needed to find out how she'd done it so it wouldn't happen again.

Once back in boots, pants unrolled, I recovered my saddlebags—one water-logged, the other mostly okay—and Remi and I heaved up the bike once more, replaced the stacked stones, eased the kickstand down onto them, and refound the balance point. I finally stepped away from the bike, hands set and arms outstretched in case it wobbled, but all looked good.

"You said she knocked it over?" Remi asked. "Did she come down here?"

"No. She was still up top. Did a weird little thing with breath and hand, and it fell over." I kicked a stone aside. "And, well, me, too."

"You too, what?"

"Fell over."

He could make no sense of it. "With her up there?"

I felt warmth in my face. "I would like to remind you that she's a *demon*. Demons can do things."

"But she didn't kill you."

"Apparently not, since here I am in front of you all alive and everything."

He scowled. "It might could be handy to know what she did, and how she did it."

"It might could," I agreed, "but I've got no answer for you. I just—fell over. As if tackled on the football field." I paused. "By an invisible player."

Remi's expression was inscrutable. But finally he mentioned we ought to try and pin Grandaddy down on a few things. "In the meantime," he said, "we'd better . . ."

But he didn't finish. He trailed off, staring over my shoulder, then muttered, "Now this ol' boy has seen a few hard winters, I reckon."

I turned, discovered a man on horseback approaching. Cowboy hat, boots, coiled rope at his saddlehorn, and he wore roughout chaps somewhat similar to biker chaps, but belled out wide at the bottom. He also wore a gunbelt with what I was betting, by its grip and barrel length, was a Colt .45 in the holster. He was mustachioed with a thick brown brush that hid even his bottom lip, and wore a black scarf that hung down in draped folds to mid-chest over a dark bib-fronted shirt. He rode a red horse with three white stockings.

"Howdy!" the cowboy called, still a distance away.

Remi dipped his head. "Come ahead."

"Oh my God," I said, grinning. "Is this a thing? A cowboy to cowboy thing?"

The man came on, actually said "Whoa" when he was about twelve feet away. The horse stopped.

"Oh, it's a thing," I said.

"You got some manners, mind 'em. This man's seen three times the years we have." He nodded at the old cowboy. "Howdy."

"Your pony looks a mite stove up." There was grit in his voice, but he didn't pitch down to actor Sam Elliott's famous rumble.

"She's had a hard couple of days," Remi agreed.

"Burton Mossman," the cowboy said.

"Remi McCue, and this here's Gabe Harlan."

I shot an amused glance at Remi, wondering if he realized his drawl had gotten broader.

"What do you propose to do about it?" Mossman asked.

"We've got to get her up the ravine," Remi told him. "We had a truck and a winch lined up, but he'll be out tomorrow instead of today."

The cowboy checked out the ravine walls. "Can you move her some?"

"Some," Remi answered. "But she's broke down in her rear."

I swear, the two of them spoke like my bike was a *horse*.

Mossman nodded. "How far downstream you been?"

"This far," Remi told him.

The cowboy shifted in his saddle. "Well, if you want her out today, I can get it done for you."

My brows shot up. "You have access to a winch?"

His deep-set brown eyes were rimmed by a network of crows-feet. "I got me a horse and a rope."

"Uhhhh," was all I could manage. Low-voiced, I asked Remi, "What are we doing, now?"

He was grinning. "If we're doing what I think we're doin,' it will make a fine tale."

"But what are we doing?"

The old cowboy took his rope, slung the loop end at Remi. "I reckon you know what to do."

Remi caught it. "Yessir, I do at that." And he proceeded to tell me to make sure the bike didn't fall over, and he ran the loop over the handlebars, did a few things here, a few things there, then nodded up at the cowboy. "I reckon we're ready, sir."

To me, he said, "Hang onto it. Be ready to walk it. He's gonna pull it on out of here."

"He's what?" I looked up at the cowboy. "I'm sorry—what are we doing?"

With that big brush of a mustache, I couldn't tell if he was smiling or not. "Just around that corner back yonder is a path leadin' to the top. You keep her in line, and Jehosaphat and I'll get her up there."

"Jehosaphat's the horse?" I asked Remi.

"I reckon so."

Whole lot of *reckons* being thrown around here. "He's going to *drag* my bike?"

"He's not fixin' to drag your bike, no. That's a cowpony he's riding."

"So?"

"Guess you've never been to a rodeo or ranch, seen stock bein' worked."

"That's a fair observation," I agreed dryly. "Do I look like I have?"

"The cowboy ropes the steer or calf, and the horse holds it in place, keeps slack out of the rope. Horse'll stay put like a four-legged anchor and let that steer or calf tucker itself out and quit, and he'll back up long as it takes while we keep the bike upright."

"If you say so."

Remi rolled his eyes. "Okay, one hand on the handle bar, one hand on the seat. Keep it on its wheels, walk beside it. Let the horse do the work."

I didn't see how this would *not* result in my bike being dragged, but I was willing to try.

Remi's smile was amused. "Cowboy winch."

The old man wrapped rope around the saddle horn a couple of times, lifted long, loose reins, clicked his tongue at the horse. "Go on, then. Get along."

The horse . . . backed up. It took up all the slack in the rope, and stopped. Another couple of words from the cowboy and the horse began backing up again. And pulled the bike.

"Why is he backing up?" I asked.

"If he turned," Remi said, "that rope would cut right across his thigh. Chaps help, but it hurts like a son of a gun."

I began to see what Remi meant. As we steadied the bike and kept it moving straight as we could with a wonky rear wheel, that horse backed us slowly downstream a short distance to where I saw the pathway up the ravine's edge spilling into the creekside. It was well-beaten earth.

"Can he pull us all the way uphill?" I asked. "I mean, it's a *motorcycle*. They're not exactly light."

"How much did you say this one weighs?"

"Seven hundred pounds or so."

"And how much do you figure a steer weighs?"

I stared at him. His expression was smug. I rolled my eyes. "Let me guess—seven hundred pounds or so?"

Remi smiled sweetly.

Mossman moved the horse sideways with the tap of a bootheel. "Go on, then."

And as the old cowboy discussed matters with his horse, from time to time clicking his tongue or tapping with his bootheels and only occasionally moving the reins, that cowpony slowly backed us all the way up to the top.

"Holy shit," I murmured, as Remi and I rolled the bike onto level ground.

Remi slipped the rope, dropped it aside, and the cowboy

began to coil it up. "It was an honor, sir, to see a fine horse at work."

"He's got plenty of arrows in his quiver." Mossman fastened the coiled rope beside the saddle horn once more. "You a Texas boy? You got the sound of it."

"Yessir, I am," Remi confirmed. He poked a thumb in my direction. "He's not. He's one of those Oregon Trail boys."

I thought I saw a faint smile in the mustache. Couldn't be sure, though. "You've done us a favor," I said. "And we appreciate it. But if it's okay, I'd like to ask another."

He resettled himself in the saddle. "Askin' never got nobody killed. Well, most days."

I asked Remi if he could steady the bike, and when he nodded I looked at Mossman. "May I see your gun, sir?" And before Remi could tell me I was a damn fool for asking a man to give up his gun, I lifted mine out from under my arm, popped the cylinder, dumped the rounds into my hand, spun it to show all chambers were empty, clicked it closed and held it with the barrel pointed in a neutral direction. Just as Grandaddy had taught me many years ago. "I would be glad if you took a look at mine."

Burton Mossman considered me a moment, as if weighing my worth. Then the mustache twitched as he worked his mouth, and he unholstered his weapon. He did not unload it, but did offer it butt-first.

We swapped out, while I wondered why he'd left his loaded. It wasn't sound gun handling; the custom was to unload first. And then I forgot all about weapon safety, because I held in my hands a genuine 1873 Colt Single Action Army pistol, the famous SAA Peacemaker. The steel was bright, like new; the walnut grips characteristically dark, but with a little grain showing.

Almost two-and-a-half pounds of steel, and a big seven-and-a-half-inch barrel.

Considering the gun was nearly a hundred-and-fifty years old, it was in outstanding condition. "Damn fine weapon," I murmured, and smiled up at the cowboy. An old man with an old gun. "I've never seen an original model in person, let alone held one."

His eyebrows twitched faintly. "It's what we've got, out here. You a city boy?"

I nodded, reversed the gun and offered it butt-first. He recovered it, handed mine back. "It's a mite puny," he said. "Out here you'd do best with a bigger weapon."

I reloaded, smiling, held up two rounds. "Bullet," I said, "and shotgun cartridge. Two for the price of one."

He considered that a moment, narrowed his eyes at me. "That's just downright foolish. I don't hold with newfangled weapons when all a man needs is a Peacemaker in his hand."

I grinned. "And for a long gun, a Winchester '73. Two excellent guns introduced in the same year." He seemed a little mollified by my tribute. "Thanks again, Mr. Mossman. I appreciate the help."

He bent his head in acknowledgment. "Now, you young men take care. Some of the bad boys from the Hashknife outfit's been rustlin' again, since I turned fifty-four of 'em off the ranch just the other day, sent 'em on their way. It's why I'm up here. You see any loose cattle, I'd be obliged if you sent a telegraph to the Aztec Cattle Company, up Holbrook way north of here. I'm the supervisor there; they'll get word to me."

I got stuck on the concept of *rustling cattle* in this day and age, but what did I know about modern ranching? Meanwhile, something else had Remi's interest. His tone was odd. "Hash-knife outfit?"

Mossman stretched his back in the saddle. "You bein' from Texas, you probably don't know 'em. Some are comin' to no good. But we ain't had a killin' here since last summer. Most of 'em been Hashknife boys or old hands that used to work for the outfit." He nodded at each of us. "I will wish you a good day."

We watched him turn his red horse, head on past us going north. He started singing, something low and sweet. The horse flicked its ears back as if listening. Maybe he was.

Remi frowned after Mossman, took two long steps as if he meant to call him back. But he didn't. He stared after him, then looked at me. He was clearly trying to knit ideas together, and his tone was still odd. "You said the Colt was an original?"

"Yup. The Peacemaker, produced in 1873."

"And in good condition."

"Like new."

Remi nodded after more thinking. "I *have* heard of the Hashknife outfit," he said. "Aztec Cattle Company was founded with cattle and horses from the Continental Cattle Company in Texas. That's how come I'm familiar with the story, and some of what came after. Even as far as knowin' dates."

I took my place at one side of the bike again. We still had to get it out to the trailer. "If you say so."

"Those boys all got fired."

I had no clue where he was going with this. "That's what he said."

"In *1898*."

It took me a moment, and then my head snapped up. "But he said he fired them—" I paused, and together we finished.

"—just the other day."

And he carried an original model of a gun first produced in 1873, twenty-five years before he fired the Hashknife boys. Twenty-five years before his *now*.

Remi cupped his hands around his mouth. "Mr. Mossman! Mr. Mossman, sir!"

The horse and cowboy had not gone far, maybe twenty yards. Mossman reined in, turned his horse in silhouette, looked back at us and lifted his arm in farewell. "I cannot stay," he called. "I have got cattle to find."

And as they stood there, as a long-dead cowboy sang low and sweet, and the big red cowpony bobbed his head, horse and rider turned muddy. The color of them, the color *in* them, bled away, leaving behind a dull afterimage like an old-style sepia photograph; a fading photo of a man and a horse born in and of a time much older than ours.

A man and a horse that now we could literally *see through* . . . see through to the trees behind them, green leaves fluttering, until the photograph faded from sepia to transparency and man and horse were gone.

CHAPTER NINETEEN

For long moments, I just stared at the spot where Mossman and his cowpony had stood but a few minutes before. Then I blinked hard, bent down and scooped up a stone, tossed it into the now-blank space. The stone didn't disappear through a black hole, a wormhole, a mole hole, or any kind of hole at all. It just fell to the earth and lay there being a rock, proving Newton's Theory of Universal Gravitation all over again.

I cleared my throat. "Was that a *ghost cowboy*?"

Remi's tone held an undercurrent of amusement coupled with disbelief. "With his ghost horse."

We stood on either side of my bike, holding it upright. I turned my head and met his eyes. "But he was corporeal. I think. Wasn't he?"

"The rope sure was," Remi said. "And you handled his gun."

Yeah. All two-and-a-half pounds of it. I'd felt the steel, touched the walnut grips. Definitely corporeal.

"I thought demons were taking over all the ghost stories, the tall tales," I said, feeling aggrieved. "They're changing the rules on us. That what isn't real, that what is merely legend, is *made* real only because the surrogates are inhabiting the monsters. I mean, we've been discussing whether Jack the Ripper's soul has been brought back to life by a surrogate inhabiting him, or if he was a demon in the first place when he butchered all those women in 1888 and apparently now is back for seconds." I was struck by something, turned it over in my head. "What if they've been demons all along, all the so-called imaginary monsters like vampires and werewolves, urban folktales? And murderers like the Ripper. What if they've all simply been waiting for Go-Time?"

Remi's brows went up. "You mean—like demonic sleeper agents?"

"Well, yeah. That sums it up. We were told many were cast up from hell just recently, with all the earthquakes and hell vents. But others as sleeper agents, sure. They've been here among us, but dormant."

Remi did not reject the theory. "And now they've been awakened."

Possibly I would not sleep that night. "Okay. So. You said you knew about the Hashknife guys and the cattle company. You ever hear anything about the boss man becoming a ghost after he died?"

"I don't recollect it off the top of my head," Remi replied, "but I can look it up. In the meantime, I'd venture he isn't a demon."

"So he's a *ghost* ghost? A legitimate living ghost—" I waved my hand dismissively before he could give me a hard time, "—or, well, you know, a legitimate dead ghost. Who's going around helping people." I scratched at the back of my head. "'Course there *are* stories of benevolent ghosts, like Martha the Nurse. I just didn't ever expect to meet one in the flesh, so to speak."

"Martha the Nurse?"

"Yeah. Thirty years after her death she was supposedly still working the wards, telling new nurses to check on specific patients who were in trouble. It was always recent nursing graduates, like she wanted to make sure the new kids performed their jobs well."

"So, not a demon, either."

"Apparently not. What time is it?" I checked my watch; the afternoon growing late. "We should get the bike on the trailer, hauled into the Harley shop. And then we can grab dinner at the Zoo. I'm getting peckish." A tactile memory popped up, and I smiled broadly at Remi, wishing he could share the pleasure. But he was a knife man. "That Peacemaker was a thing of beauty. Ghost gun or not, I've now handled an original."

Remi slapped a hand against the bike seat. "Then let's head 'em up and move 'em out, get us some grub."

Sometimes I wondered if what Remi said and how he said it was actual cowboy lingo, or if he was overdoing it for effect. He had mentioned the latter once. And his drawl had definitely deepened when speaking with the Mossman ghost.

Mossman *ghost*.

I shook my head; God, my life had gotten weird.

In sync, we shifted our weight into the handbars and began to push the bike. Or push half the bike. We dragged the back half, since the wheel was all bent.

"I never thought I'd say this," I admitted after a few minutes "but this job would be easier with a good horse."

Remi hooted long and loud. "That is the truth of it. Glad to hear you know it."

We pushed in silence for a bit, and then Remi began to sing, as was his habit. I did not recognize the song. Country, of course. Something about a mighty herd of black, red-eyed cattle, and hooves made of steel, burning brands, and horses snorting fire.

And *yippie yi yays* and *yippie yi oohs*, of course. Remi sang the *yippie yi yays* and *oohs* with particular vigor.

"What is that? That song. What's with the red-eyed cows?"

He broke off the chorus to answer. "'Ghost Riders in the Sky.' Old song. Bunch of dead cowboys chasing the Devil's Herd forever through the ragged, endless skies."

I pursed my lips and nodded. "Huh. Colorful, yet depressing."

But he was singing the swooping, mournful *yippie yi yays* and *yippie yi oohs* again and didn't comment.

When we got the bike unloaded at the Harley shop and went inside to handle paperwork, the guy behind the counter gave me a look, gave Remi and his hat a harder look, then turned his attention back to me. "Twin sons of different mothers, huh?"

Even as Remi sighed, I grinned at him. "You could say that."

He was an older guy, maybe mid-50s. Brown eyes. Carried a pot belly, had old acne scars on his cheeks, wore his gray-brown hair ponytailed and a folded blue bandana tied around his head. Grew scruff in place of a beard. Walked with an odd swinging limp.

He saw me notice it. "New hip," he said. "Helluva way to slow down an old biker." He poked around on a computer with two fingers in a hunt-and-peck style. "I'm sorry Kenny couldn't get out to you boys today to pick up your bike out of that ravine. But you're here, and we'll get her broken down for you, give you a call after we've had a real close look. If you're not up for a full rebuild, we can always buy her off you and part 'er out."

I shook my head. "Whatever it takes, man. She's special."

"Okay, then." He hunted and pecked on the keyboard again. "Well, I've got your information, so I'll be in touch when we know something. Might take a couple of days, though." He scratched thoughtfully at his scruff. "Would you be interested in a loaner? You'd have to pay insurance, sign a waiver, but we won't charge you for it."

I brightened. "Now that is a good man. What model is it?"

His eyes slewed to mine. "VW Beetle. The old orange bug. Last I looked, 45 was her best speed."

I scowled, and he grinned at me. "No, huh? Well, I'm sorry we can't give you a bike, but we'll do our best to get yours back to you soon. Depends on parts."

"I've heard that before." I pulled the spare key off my ring, slid it across the counter. "Anyone ever take you up on your offer of the bug?"

"Hell, no. I haven't met a biker yet who'd hit the road in one of those things. Now, you've got questions, give us a call. Ask for Cisco. That's me."

I nodded, checked him over again. "You ever ride with anyone?"

He knew what I meant. "I was a one-percenter maybe all of a week," he said with a crooked smile. "Turned out I didn't have the stones for it after all."

I answered before he could ask. "Just a H.O.G. with a hog. But I did get the bike off a one-percenter. He taught me everything I know about motorcycles. When cancer got him, he left his ride to me."

Cisco bobbed his head. "We'll take good care of her for you *and* for him, God rest his soul." He glanced at Remi again, then turned back to me. "If you feel like a drink among your kind, so to speak, there's a bar down the road called Hot Tamale, God only knows why. They don't serve 'em. Northeast corner of Route 66 and Steve's Boulevard. You'll see the bikes. Bring your cowboy friend, too."

Remi's tone was smooth as butter. "Thank you kindly, but I'm setting up at the Zoo Club. Protective coloration."

Cisco nodded with a glint in his eye. "You *are* welcome, you know. It's not where the outlaws hang."

Remi nodded his appreciation, but we both knew he wouldn't be going. I thanked Cisco again, and the cowboy half of the partnership walked outside with me.

We were up in his truck and on the way to the Zoo when he asked it. "What's H.O.G. mean? Some kind of biker gang?"

"Harley Owner's Group," I told him. "The 99% that *aren't* outlaw bikers. We're tame, and we have good manners. Mostly. Probably some are RUBs, but most of us just really love bikes. Some are hardcore without quite being outlaws. That whole *Sons of Anarchy* TV schtick."

"RUBs?"

"Rich Urban Bikers."

"Ah! Like 'drugstore cowboys.'" Remi braked, waited for traffic to clear so he could turn into the Zoo's parking lot. It was beginning to fill up. "You have *your* outlaws, and we had ours back in the day. Like the Hashknife boys Mr. Mossman fired. Nowadays, though, you say outlaws to a cowboy and he thinks Willie Nelson, Waylon Jennings, Johnny Cash and Kris Kristofferson. Outlaw country music."

He found us a parking place over by the side of the building. We got out, slammed doors, headed for the entrance. I pulled open the big door for Remi. "We need to ask some questions." I let him go by, fell in behind him. "Such as who actually *runs* this place. Grandaddy? Ganji? Someone else we haven't met? And maybe we need to meet the cooks and the servers."

We skirted the dance floor. Once again, live country music filled the place to the high beamwork and beyond to the pitched tin roof. I smelled whiskey, beef, and beer. "We should introduce ourselves," I continued: "*'Hi there, we're heaven's attack dogs. Don't mind us if we come back bloody.'*"

We made it to the bar. It wasn't the weekend, so not as crowded as it could be. We cut through to the far end, to the station where servers picked up drink orders, and waited until Ganji saw us. He drifted down our way as he wiped his hands on a bar towel.

"Lookin' for Mary Jane," Remi said. "She go upstairs, or hangin' out down here?"

Ganji tipped his shaven head, raised his brows. "That one likes to dance. See?" He gestured with his chin toward the parquet.

I looked. Remi looked.

Mary Jane Kelly was dancing with a well-dressed young man, handsome as a Hollywood star, his features clean and pure, his smile blinding, his blue eyes bright. He spun her one way, spun her back the other. Blond hair, long, loose, and shining, fell around his face.

"Shit," I said.

Remi said worse.

Kelly saw us, and her face lit up. She took hold of her partner's wrist, led him through the crowd to us.

Her eyes were shining. "This is Yaz," she said, "He's a ballet dancer on his way through town. He tells me he can out-pirouette Baryshnikov, but I haven't talked him into showing me yet."

Again with the twelve pirouettes. The guy had a fixation. I went ahead and cut to the chase, looking straight at him. "And how long will you be here *before you have to leave?*"

He knew what I meant, but his eyes were guileless. As old as he was, he'd had plenty of time to perfect his expressions. "Some time yet." He made a sad face. "But always, the time is too short." Then he leaned close to Mary Jane, spoke into her ear, and pulled her back onto the dance floor.

Remi wasn't happy as we made our way to a table, slid into the booth. "Look at it this way," I said, "he can't exactly spend the night. He'll be gone in less than two hours, since the devil allows him only two hours before he turns back into charred pumpkin. At which point a whole lot of people—including his current dance partner—would be utterly grossed out."

Remi didn't respond. Just stared out at the dance floor and chewed the inside of one of his cheeks.

"Tequila time," I said lightly. And that's what I ordered for him when the cocktail server arrived. I made it a bottle.

CHAPTER TWENTY

We took a corner booth in the back of the main area, illuminated by hanging lights and a rusty pierced-tin lantern on the table. Unfortunately the orientation of the table fell in a direct sight line from a stuffed bobcat hunched up on a crossbeam, which reminded me all over again of stuffed animals coming to life to stalk me. I couldn't remember if the bobcat had been one of them, but I nonetheless shifted on the booth seat so I could avoid seeing its glass-eyed glare every time I looked up.

Remi ordered sirloin, I ordered prime rib. He had his tequila, I ordered beer. And Mary Jane Kelly, apparently done dancing with a fallen angel, joined us not long after the server had brought our dinner. Mary Jane asked for a Cobb salad and a beer; whatever was on tap. Then, as our waiter departed, Kelly scooped up her hair in both hands, piled it on top of her head with a haphazard but very long tail tumbling down her back.

"Dancing is hot work," she declared.

"So," I began idly, "what became of the ballet guy?"

Kelly let go of her hair and it fell every which way, thick and dark save for the section of tawny blonde. "Oh, he had to leave. Said he had a few important calls to make and needed to get back to his hotel." She gathered all the hair in a fist, slipped a band around it and tied it back high on her head. "He was fun. A little arrogant—well, a lot arrogant. But fun."

Remi's brows rose just a bit, then settled. His smile was slight, but easy and relaxed. He was definitely sweet on the girl. I wondered if he would inform her that she'd actually already met her recent dance partner up on the mountain, dripping charred skin and showing teeth with no lips. But even if he was that kind of guy—which, on second thought, I doubted—the truth of it was that Shemyazaz had no hope of a relationship with any woman, outside of two hours.

No wonder he hated Lucifer. He was, after all, a fallen angel *because* he'd broken heaven's taboo to sleep with a human woman. And he was still denied because of what the devil had done to him.

Kelly lost her smile a moment, eyes going distant. She looked out at the dance floor, but I didn't think she was looking *for* anything. Just looking. She seemed pensive. Her eyes remained serious when she looked back, caught me watching her.

She shrugged a little, made herself smaller. "Out there on the floor, I could forget. Forget that some psychopathic serial killer with a demon inside wants me dead."

It was indeed a sobering thought. "We'll do everything we can to keep that from happening." Which was the truth. But I didn't tell her the other truth: that we had no plan whatsoever to stop the Ripper.

Kelly looked at Remi as he cut his way into a steak. "Do you dance?"

Gravely, he said, "I have been known to scoot my boots."

She smiled. A big breath lifted her shoulders: relief that she could once again forget for a while. "After we finish eating, we'll have to hit the floor."

Remi smiled back. "Yes, ma'am."

Kelly no longer looked at me. She did not include me in dance plans. I knew very well what that meant, and I was cool with it.

I smiled as I looked down at the remains of a denuded and delightfully pink prime rib. Remi and I had already had our disagreement over doneness quotients. He preferred very well done, while I explained that I wasn't into eating charcoal, thank you very much, but actually like to taste the flavor of *the meat*.

Heresy among afficionados of burned boot leather. He predicted my death from *E. coli* or *Salmonella*—possibly both. I responded that I found it unlikely the offspring of celestial energy might truly be at risk for bacteria.

"But we have human bodies," he'd said. "Flesh and blood and bone, and we both know what it's like to get beat all to hell. You're still movin' like an eighty-year-old man after that spill onto asphalt."

I denied that immediately. "Seventy, maybe. I still have a little spring in my step."

"The point is, you got road rash and bumps and bruises, so of course you can get sick from bacteria. Hell, you were hung over the morning Grandaddy walked us up the mountain."

An uncomfortable memory. I ignored it and returned to the subject at hand. "I've eaten my beef rare all my life, and I'm alive to tell the tale. In fact, I'd just as soon they only just passed it over the flames."

Remi suppressed a shudder and averted his eyes from my plate, taking solace in more tequila.

Kelly's arrival had ended our discussions, and that was okay by me. I listened to her slow conversational campaign to pique Remi's interest, and smiled into my beer as I lifted the mug to my mouth. Remi's interest was already piqued, but maybe she just wanted to put the icing on the cake.

Which 'might could,' as Remi would put it, make things a bit awkward with all three of us upstairs in a modest-sized apartment.

Kelly's salad arrived and she dug into it, drank some beer. I pulled out the magic phone and texted Remi, who sat all of maybe two feet away.

Me: *"You in for the night?"*

Remi frowned, pulled his phone, shot me an odd glance as he read the text. But he answered: *"Yes."*

Me: *"No bike. Mind if I borrow your truck?"*

Remi: *"No, but what for?"*

Me: *"Thought I'd check out that biker bar. Listen to some real music."*

Remi: *"Don't dog my jam."*

Which cracked me up even as he dug keys from his pocket and tossed them lightly to me.

Kelly followed the key-tossing. Her brows rose as she looked at me. "You going somewhere?"

I finished off my beer, set the mug on the table as I scooted out of the booth. "I am going somewhere."

Remi said dryly, "He dislikes country music."

Kelly's mouth rounded. "Oh, don't say that too loudly in a cowboy bar."

"And that's why I'm leaving," I told her, "so I don't have to say it at all. Though Remi and I have had discussions about it."

I looked back at him. "I'm just going to grab my jacket and head out."

He knew exactly why I was going, and it wasn't solely because I wanted to hit up another bar. He smiled crookedly, pointed his fork at the bottle. "Thanks for the tequila."

I echoed Lily's Gaelic toast to health. *"Sláinte."*

CHAPTER TWENTY-ONE

It was, as Cisco had told me, easy to find the Hot Tamale. The bar was perched at the end of a modest strip mall, one side fronting Route 66, and the parking lot immediately in front of the bar was filled with bikes. I pulled in, threading my way, but the truck was Remi's, not mine to risk, and I elected to park a couple of shops over from the bar.

I drove past a small open, tunnel-like breezeway dividing the bar from the rest of the shopping center, and ended up slotting the truck in a space between a beauty salon and a dog grooming shop, which amused me: one-stop shopping for canine *and* human beautification.

The breezeway was narrow and cut through from the front lot to the modest loading dock areas out back, and I had to duck droplets still sluggishly dripping from the overhang despite the storm being well over. I paused briefly to cast an eye across the bikes thronging the small lot in front of the bar, schooling like chromed fish. Harleys outnumbered the others, but I saw Suzukis and Yamahas, Hondas, a BMW, even a Ducati. Nothing chopped; but then, Cisco had said it wasn't that kind of biker bar.

Inside, the Hot Tamale split the difference between dive

and trendy. Just a basic no-frills bar. Dim lighting, tile floor, glossy knotty pine wall cladding, pool tables and pinball machines, darts and foosball, a wall TV showing a soccer game. The odor of French fries, popcorn. I heard clacking balls and the thunks of pinball flapper paddles. A jukebox was playing classic rock, *not* country. I considered the songs oldies, until I looked around and discovered the median age for bar patrons appeared to be forty-five to fifty compared to my twenty-eight, so not oldies to those guys.

A few stools were open at the bar, and that's where I slid my butt onto leather. No Talisker to be had, so I settled for the less-peaty Glenfiddich, a single malt staple of bars. I eyed the soccer game, but wasn't interested; it's just difficult to ignore a TV featuring moving bodies.

"Hey, Harlan! Gabe Harlan!"

The voice came from a table behind me. I turned, surprised, because few people knew me in Flagstaff. Then I recognized Cisco, the Harley shop owner. He waved me over. I collected my drink and change, joined him. As I pulled out the chair, he offered to buy me a bottle of whatever I was drinking.

I thanked him but demurred. "I'm good with a couple," I said. "I borrowed Remi's truck, so best not risk it."

"So, you guys are brothers, right? Twins?"

I'd realized this would likely come up on a regular basis. "Cousins." It was far easier than explaining we were born not of humans at all, but of a brief fart of celestial energy.

"We've started taking your bike apart," he told me, and screwed his mouth sideways in a twist of empathy. "I just don't know . . . more work to do on our end, but not lookin' good. Like I said, parting it out might be best."

"Not if it can be helped." I considered the credit cards Remi and I had been given by the Angel Behind the Curtain. We'd been instructed rather pointedly that they were to be used for expenses encountered in saving the world, in the line of duty such as it was or would be, but my bike was transport. Surely one could consider transport necessary in the fight of good against evil. And one might be correct in assuming the credit line was unlimited. I didn't think angels would be much concerned with credit utilization ratios.

I felt the hollowness again, the pinch in the gut of regret, of grief. "Literally a deathbed gift."

Cisco's mouth opened, then he nodded, poured beer into his mug. I saw empathy in his eyes. "We'll give it our best. I've got a good mechanic working for me—just a kid, but he's talented—and I'm not half bad myself. Just don't want to make promises and have you be disappointed."

I said I understood. "I've worked on some bikes, too . . . I know what you mean. Tommy—the guy who left me the bike—was a genius at rebuilds."

And then, as bike owners do the world over, we launched a long conversation about manufacturers and models, aftermarket parts, technological developments, future versions, you name it. Kept us going for quite a while. I was closing in on finishing my second whiskey when Cisco shifted in the creaking spindle-backed chair and asked me what happened to my friend, if I didn't mind saying.

"You said he'd been a one-percenter," he said.

"He was in Vietnam," I told him. "He came home with a heroin habit and a bad attitude, and joined up with an outlaw club. Did some really stupid things, served time, and while in prison he was diagnosed with cancer, courtesy of Agent Orange. He got clean, got out, stayed straight, and not long after that I met up with him, and we became friends despite being two generations apart. I had an old bike bought with chore money when I was young, and Tommy kept it running when I couldn't. I thought he'd leave his ride to a nephew, but he told me it was mine. He died a couple of hours later."

And six *months* later I'd been sentenced to prison myself. I hated that Tommy was dead, missed him to hell and gone, but very glad he didn't see me go to prison. He'd told me once he expected it of my brother. Instead, Matty walked free while I went behind bars.

Cisco nodded. "Yeah, I served in the Gulf. Didn't come home with a heroin habit, but Gulf War Syndrome, yup. Like I said, I tried an outlaw club . . ." He smiled crookedly, shook his head. "Not for me after all. But I'd saved up a fair bit of Army money, got a loan, bought me the shop. I find peace in working on bikes."

I nodded, too. "My dad was in the service—fought in Iraq—but it was never for me." I remembered our not-so-friendly discussions about it. "He came home and joined the police force, tried to talk me into going military, but I was spending more time with Tommy by then anyway, who had no good opinion of the military, so neither did I. Which really rankled my dad. Said Tommy was a bad influence." I smiled, then drank the last of my whiskey. "Tommy was anything but."

Cisco pushed his chair back slightly, half-rose, signaled the bartender. "Can I get another for my friend, please?" He sat back down, asked me how I'd come to smash up the bike. "Looks like you laid her down."

"Yup. No choice. Someone jumped out into the road. It was go through her, or dump it. But at least I *knew* the wreck was coming. I was able to get loose of the bike, keep my head off the road. It took a little trip through trees, ended up in a ra-vine."

Cisco's eyes went wide. "In a *ravine*? No wonder she's beat all to shit. I take it you didn't go into the ravine with her."

I smiled ruefully. "My trip was across asphalt. Fortunately I was wearing leathers and a helmet."

As I finished, I was peripherally aware of the cocktail wait-ress setting down a fresh glass of Glenfiddich. Cisco pulled a ten-dollar bill from his change for her, and I glanced up to thank the young woman. I broke off abruptly as she sat herself down in the chair between Cisco and me.

"*Boo!*" Molly said, with a broad, delighted grin. "Hey there, Gabe! Thought I'd never find you!"

Three different reactions competed for primacy in my brain. The first: Take Molly firmly by the arm and escort her outside where we might speak in private, except that these days laying hands on a woman could go bad real fast. It was possible Cisco or any of the other guys in the place might decide to intervene, and I could trust Molly to stage noisy accusations of assault. These men would never buy into an explanation that she was a demon inhabiting an innocent host. Hell, *I* wouldn't. If I wasn't me, that is.

The second: Ignore her altogether and every word she spoke, as if she were not present, but she'd already called me by name, and I had no doubt Molly could spin a story that would paint herself a victim and me an asshole.

Third? Play her game, but beat her at it.

Molly's eyes were searching mine avidly, looking for tells, looking for an edge. I had no doubt she might well find one, maybe two, but she knew nothing about my background. She knew nothing of my prison stint, or how a man, if he's lucky, learns to drop casual disinformation, or to present, to inmates and COs alike, a poker face.

I leaned forward toward Cisco, who was clearly startled by a strange woman inviting herself to our table. But a smile was beginning to overtake his mouth and a glint in his eyes kindled. Molly was cute and appealing behind the big red glasses, and could probably charm any man. I used all the excited amusement I could muster.

"This girl is amazing, Cisco! You give her a topic and she can spin a tale like you would not believe. Talented as hell . . . she belongs on *Saturday Night Live*! I'd put her up against any of those comedians, any day or night." I looked at her with a focused, tensile excitement. "Didn't you say you'd been on one of those talent shows? Or you were going to audition?—I don't remember the details. But as I told you before, I *told* you, your improv is unbeatable."

As Molly opened her mouth to interrupt my spate of words, I held Cisco's gaze, assumed a droll smile, and hooked a thumb in her direction.

"She was hitching . . . I offered her a ride in Holbrook after lunch. That's when she entertained me." I sat back, adopted a relaxed posture. "I damn near choked on my coffee when she did a whole routine about Lucifer wanting to get back up top to start Armageddon. I mean, you wouldn't think that's an amusing topic, but she found a way in. Some bit about demons cast adrift, trying to do the devil's bidding when they'd really rather sit in front of the TV and binge-watch *Game of Thrones*."

Molly finally accepted the challenge. She smiled from inside out, reached a hand to shake Cisco's. "I'm not *that* good!"

she said, laughing. "Gabe's just easy to amuse. Infantile sense of humor. The lower you go, the more he likes it. Scraping the bottom of the barrel, most times."

Cisco shook her hand politely, but a flicker in his eyes suggested he wasn't completely buying her insinuations. He and I had spent nearly three hours talking bikes and personal matters, and that's enough to forge a bond predicated on distinct mutual interest. Sure, I *could* be what she described, a not-too-bright enthusiastic fan of low-brow humor, but it didn't jibe with what he'd seen of me so far. Plus, according to my tale, she was a hitchhiker. She couldn't claim an intimate knowledge of my opinions.

I made it obvious that I was checking my watch, my expression reflecting surprise. Then I pushed my chair back and rose. "Hell, later than I thought! I gotta go. Sorry I didn't get to the drink you just bought me, Cisco . . ." I slid the full glass across the table to Molly, who'd served the drink *and* whatever might be in it. "But I think she'll do it justice. She sucked down a couple of beers pretty quickly over a one-hour lunch." I shook Cisco's hand as he rose. "Just give me a call when you've got a good idea about what my bike needs."

Cisco shot a blank glance at Molly, then nodded at me. "Sure thing."

I offered Molly a casual smile, set two fingers against my forehead and snapped them forward in tribute. "Be seeing you." Then I walked myself right out of that bar.

I was still grinning about undermining Molly as I popped the locks on the truck with the remote, and then I heard a noise from the breezeway. Half the exterior lights along the strip mall were out, so I couldn't see anything within the narrow tunnel between buildings. I knew it was possible Molly had slipped out the back door and was coming for me, so I went right to the passenger door, opened it, moved behind a makeshift shield even as I unholstered the Taurus. With my left hand I worked my phone out of a pocket, thumbed the flashlight app, and threw illumination into the breezeway. It wasn't truly powerful light, but even a match in utter blackness can light up a cave.

A person was huddled on the ground, tucked back inside the breezeway about half-way. I saw a tangled spray of blonde hair spilled across the asphalt, darkened by blood, and one spread hand flattened against the masonry wall. A smeared reddish mark on the bricks was either old paint, or fresh blood.

My mind registered female, though I couldn't be sure. Plenty of men, myself included, wore their hair quite long. But the body knotted upon itself with its head down, one hand braced against the wall, was too slight even for a short man.

I shone the cell phone light around the breezeway as best I could, saw that the left hand remained pressed against the wall. The right hand was spread against the asphalt. As my light reached the person, the hand rose, fisted itself into hair.

I heard a low moan. It rose slowly, sustained itself a moment at a higher pitch, then died away. Definitely female. On the heels of the moan came a rising wail. It was a woman's keening, the gut-deep, involuntary sound of an emotional pain so deep it could not be kept in.

The confines of the breezeway lent the tone a hollow, muted echo. I saw movement, saw the hand against the wall tighten, and then fingers scraped themselves along rough brick and left ruddy smears. She attempted to push herself up, to rise. She failed, fell back.

The woman lifted her head. Light bled across her face and showed me one eye puffy and empurpled, a split and bloodied lip. The uninjured eye was wide, fixed on the cell phone's light. Lips parted as she rocked forward, rose to her knees, reached both hands out toward me as far as she could, palms up. Her head was kept low. It was a posture of supplication, of pure vulnerability. She was placing the next moments of her life into my hands. There was no future for her save the one I gave her.

The unbloodied portions of her hair were a true blond, springing from her scalp in long tangled waves. Beneath the hair, as she rose onto her knees, I saw badly torn fabric. One breast was partially exposed within strips of shredded fabric.

With bloodied hands outstretched, she spoke for the first time. Her voice was broken, hoarse. *"Believe."*

Gun in one hand, phone in the other, I approached. All my instincts were shouting to forget self-defense, to think only about an injured woman and not the potential for a surrogate attack. But the first couple of days of denial had been overtaken by a sharp, almost paranoid awareness that this war at the End of Days was legitimate. As Mulder was told repeatedly on *X-Files*: Trust no one. Yet she asked me to believe.

As I came up on her she sat back down, settling on tucked feet. The one eye was so swollen that all I could see were the tips of her lashes. The other eye, a clear, pale blue, was stretched wide as she stared up at me. The pupil shrank down as I played my phone's light across her face. *"Believe."*

My dad, who had worked rape cases with the department, once said that victims of rape or assault usually didn't want to press charges because no one would believe them, particularly if the rapist was well-positioned in society.

This woman's plea for me to believe carried an undertone of despair, not for the act but for the reception she anticipated.

As I hesitated she whispered the word again: *"Believe."*

Okay.

I shoved the revolver back into the holster beneath my left arm and sank down onto one bent knee and boot toe, giving myself over to whatever was meant to happen.

Just as she had.

CHAPTER TWENTY-TWO

kept my voice low. "I'm going to call 911, okay? The paramedics will take care of you. I'll wait right here with you. I'm not leaving." I had the phone in my hand. "It won't be long before they arrive. I'll stay right here with you."

She remained on her knees, but she no longer rocked. No longer positioned herself as a supplicant. She placed trembling hands in her hair, tried to pull it back from her face. It was in complete disarray as she made an attempt to tuck it behind her ears. I saw more clearly the damage done to her features. The right side of her jaw was bruised and swollen.

I wondered if Remi had any kind of first aid kit in his truck that I could use in the meantime. Maybe even a chemical ice pack to place against her jaw, some antiseptic wipes.

"I'm calling now, okay?" I pressed numeral nine, then held off as she spoke again.

"The god must have his way. The god must punish."

My brows shot upward. "A *god*?"

"A god must punish. I angered him."

Well. And just like that, the game changed again. Not a bad-guy surrogate, but an actual deity.

Well, unless she had some kind of mental disorder. But still, these days? I was placing no bets. "A god punished you by assaulting you?"

"He will find me. When he wants me, he will find me."

A week before, I'd have chalked up her words to medication gone wrong, or shock. But an African god tended bar in the Zoo, an Irish goddess lived in a motorhome, a fallen angel danced on top of a bar, and Lucifer's shock troops were on our asses.

I didn't input the last two numerals. This was a woman whom a *god* had assaulted. Where could I take her that was safe? Where could I take her that no gods or demons could track her? A hospital was not the best choice despite her condition, because any of the medical staff could be hosting a demon . . . or, hell, the god could walk right in and drag her out. Same with a police station. There was the Zoo, but it was not quite ten pm, and the place would be in full swing. The back door opened right into the pool table alcove, so even there it would be difficult to take her in discreetly. And shutting the place down, kicking everyone out would take time and cause questions even as it left her vulnerable.

I set down the phone with the flashlight app turned on so it lighted the breezeway in a dim glow. I sat my butt down on the ground and crossed my legs, with mild protest from asphalt-battered muscles. I needed to get her somewhere safe so we could tend her ASAP, but I was concerned that rushing her, touching her with any kind of urgency, might be the worst actions to take.

"He will punish," she said. "The god will punish you."

And now it was me as potential victim. Great. "Because I'm helping you?"

"He came into the temple. He *took me*."

'Took' could mean he took her out of the temple, or raped her there. Possibly 'took' her virginity. It was a turn of speech I hadn't heard for years.

Temple. Temple. Could she mean synagogue? Mormon temple? Hell, *Masonic* temple?

"Believe me," she whispered. And then she looked beyond me, cried out, and ducked close to the ground.

I lunged up from asphalt and spun even as I unholstered the Taurus, aware of twinges in my muscles, a slowed response. I expected to see Molly's host body, or whatever Molly might look like in demon form, but no one was there. No *thing* was there. The truck sat silently with its passenger door open, interior light glowing, just as I had left it. Dim parking lot lighting showed me nothing. No one.

We couldn't remain here. I needed to get her into the truck and moved.

Okay. Zoo it was. I'd call Remi and have him bring out a blanket when I pulled up. We could wrap her in it, hide her against the stares, get her upstairs where we could help her clean up. She might not want two strange men doing anything, but Mary Jane Kelly was there. She understood what demonic threat meant now, knew Ganji was a god and Lily a goddess. Kelly could help her. And as a Park Service employee I was certain she'd had thorough first aid training.

I turned back, lowered the gun. My phone still sat on the asphalt next to her, but was dimming as the battery ran down. "We need to go," I told her. "Will you come with me? Will you let me help you into the truck? I'll have to touch you. I'll have to put my hands on you. But I promise I won't do anything more."

Hell, that promise was all I could think to offer. I could not put myself in a woman's place, particularly one who had been raped. My empathy was intellectual. I couldn't *feel* it.

I holstered my gun, showed her my empty hands. "I won't hurt you. For whatever a stranger's promise is worth, I offer it." I paused, then said the one word that might make a dent. *"Believe."*

She gazed up at me, weighing my words, studying my eyes and expression. Then she looked at her own hands, her bloodied hands, and offered one to me.

I helped her up, steadied her. Bent and scooped up the phone, wincing as I did so. I was going to turn it off, but she seemed to find security in the lighted screen. I gave it to her, began to guide her to the truck. At the open door, as I told her to get in, she climbed up unsteadily, sat stiffly. I debated belting her in . . . for all I knew she'd been bound, tied to a bed or something. A seat belt across her lap, the shoulder strap cutting down through her breasts, might well make her worse. So I resolved to drive very carefully. I raised the window, shut the door, went around to the driver's side, opened the door.

Just as I started to climb up, I saw the envelope on the seat.

Manilla envelope.

My name printed on the outside.

Now I knew that the woman had in all likelihood seen a demon delivering the envelope.

I clamped my left hand around the steering wheel and wanted very badly to rip it out of the truck just to expel some of the rage. But a traumatized victim sat across the console and did not need to see any form of male aggression.

I settled myself behind the wheel. Stared at the envelope in my hands and debated whether I should open it, or perhaps simply dump it out the window and let good ol' Jack the Ripper discover that I wasn't playing *his* game, either. Not anymore.

But it was because of the other envelopes, the other photographs, that we had found Mary Jane Kelly, been able to keep her alive.

I tore it open, slid fingers inside, found the 8x10 photo as expected. As I removed it I took care *not* to view the actual image. It would serve nothing. I'd seen similar. A kidney resided in our freezer. I turned it over, read the writing on the back.

'It didn't end with #5. And any order serves.'

So Kelly continued to be endangered, and others as well. Remi had said it was believed the Ripper killed women other than the five whose names were known. Obviously, this version of him wasn't renouncing his habit and entering rehab.

A woman in comparable danger sat next to me. I had no time to remain here and debate, so I sailed envelope and photo into the back seat with a flip of my hand, thrust the key into the ignition and started the truck. It took all I had to speak calmly to the woman, to keep the anger and frustration at bay.

"I'm taking you somewhere safe," I told her. "It's noisy. Lots of people. But my friend and I will take you upstairs where it's private, and a woman friend of ours can help you clean up. Okay?"

She did not reply. She sat there clutching the phone, staring into its glow.

The Zoo's parking lot was nearly full. I pulled around behind the building where the area was absent of vehicles. I had no clue whether Ganji had a car, or if he even drove. Did a god need to? Or did he just translocate at will?

One yellow buglight outside the back door, one old-fashioned sodium street light hung high on a battered wooden telephone pole, which also bathed the immediate area in pale yellow illumination. While the woman hung onto my dead cell I once again pulled the magic phone from my pocket and hit Remi's contact icon. Hoped I wasn't interrupting anything of an intimate nature between him and Kelly.

He answered right away. "What's up?"

"We're going to have a visitor," I said. "I'll tell you the whole story once we're upstairs, but I'm outside the back door and need you to bring a blanket. I've got a woman with me who's been sexually assaulted and I want to bring her in without exposing her to curious eyes. And tell Kelly, if you would . . . this is going to need a woman's intervention. She's barely speaking. I don't even know her name." I used my lowered tone to underscore the situation. "She did say that a *god* raped her."

He didn't ask any questions and didn't suggest I take her to a hospital. He understood the delicacy of the situation and simply said "Okay" and disconnected.

I looked at her. She sat in the seat with her head tilted downward, staring at the phone.

"You can call someone," I said. "It's still got a little juice."

But she said and did nothing. I couldn't even see her profile because hair obscured it.

"My name is Gabriel," I said. "Gabe Harlan. We're going to go inside, then up some stairs. Remi—my friend Remi McCue, a cowboy—is going to bring a blanket for you, so you can wrap up. And a woman friend, Mary Jane Kelly, will help as well. No one will harm you. I promise that. We'll take you upstairs to our apartment, and Mary Jane will help you clean up. Okay? No one will touch you except Mary Jane, if you want help."

She did not respond.

I unlocked the truck with the remote, stepped out and quickly rounded the front end to the passenger door. I heard the squeak of the screen door hinges and saw Remi and Kelly come out of the building. Mary Jane carried the blanket, which was probably best.

I turned back to the woman. "Remi and Mary Jane are here. Mary Jane has the blanket." I opened the door. "You can come on out. You're safe."

It was Kelly who came up, while Remi hung back. I moved out of the way, let Kelly take point. She stepped closer, nodded at the woman. "You're safe now," she said. "Let us help you. Come on out of the truck and we'll get you wrapped up."

The woman looked beyond Kelly to Remi. With her un-damaged eye, she examined him hatted head to booted toe, but did not seem alarmed or hesitant. She gave Kelly the same once-over. Then she climbed down awkwardly even as I stuck out my hand. She took it, held on a moment, as if she felt better for the contact, then let it go.

She was tall, taller than I expected, and wearing something akin to a long gown, but torn. Yellow light showed a shadowed starkness in her face where illumination didn't reach. Blood, bruises, and swelling altered her face so much that her true features could not be evaluated.

Kelly stepped forward, slowly unfolding the blanket. She shook it out, held it up and made eye contact. "I'm Mary Jane. Will you come with me?"

The woman nodded. Kelly wrapped her up in fabric, then guided her toward the door.

Remi stayed back to ask a couple of questions. "What happened?"

"I found her outside the bar. She's been beaten and raped, is mostly non-verbal. She did specifically say it was a god, but, you know, maybe yes, maybe no, these days." I rubbed at the back of my neck, remembering her words and tone. "She also said he could take her at any time, and that he would punish me as well. Which probably means *us*, since we're working together. But she hasn't ID'd the god, so I have no clue whom it may be." I hit the remote, locked the truck, handed the keys to Remi with thanks. "Oh, and Molly was there. At the bar. She is bound and determined to screw with us, one way or another."

Remi and I walked to the back door. "God Almighty," he said as he opened the screen door, "we have got ourselves in one hell of a mess."

Indoors it was as I had described it to the woman: full of people, full of noise. Jukebox music, clacking pool balls, raised voices, dancers whooping and hooting on the parquet during a very rowdy song. We cut through the pool tables rapidly, went right to the stairs and climbed quickly. Inside the apartment we heard the sound of a shower and occasionally a woman's voice recognizable as Mary Jane Kelly's.

Remi looked startled. "They say don't let a rape victim shower," he said urgently. "Evidence is being washed away."

"I thought about that, but if she reports a *god* as the attacker, they'll probably shackle her to the hospital bed for her own protection, then haul her away to the looney bin." I shrugged. "And, if there *is* one, who is better prepared to deal with a rogue god anyway: us, or police?"

"I'm not so sure *we're* prepared to deal with a rogue god," Remi shot back. "Maybe more'n the police, sure, but I think we're in over our heads if a god is out to get her. Or us."

I pulled the iAngel phone from my pocket, pressed Grandaddy's icon. To my great annoyance, he didn't answer. I left a message:

"We've got a woman here who says she was assaulted by a god. She hasn't said much to us, but maybe she would to an angel. Give me a yell, or just show up. Help would be appreciated."

Remi went poking through kitchen cabinets, pulling things out to look behind them, digging around through drawers. I finally asked him what he was doing.

"I figure there's a first aid kit around here somewhere. Most likely in the bathroom, but I thought I'd check."

I walked down the hall to the bathroom Remi and I shared, tapped quietly on the door with a knuckle. "Do you have a first aid kit in there?"

"I found it," came Kelly's voice. "She's mostly got bruises, some lacerations. Nothing broken. But her clothes are wrecked and she needs something to wear. I haven't been home since you brought me down off the mountain, so I've got nothing other than what I'm wearing. Do you have a washing machine?"

"Uh—I don't know. I can ask Ganji."

"Probably downstairs," Kelly said. "But a t-shirt would be good. She's tall, so with a belt to hold up your jeans she should do okay. Can you find something?"

"Hold on." I went into my bedroom, took a t-shirt and my second pair of jeans from a drawer. I didn't have a spare belt, but rope would do, even a bungee in a pinch. Ganji might know about that, too, whether there was anything downstairs we could cobble together. I tapped the door again. "Here you go."

Kelly opened the door, took the clothes. Her expression was distracted. I asked if the woman would be okay, and Kelly just shrugged. "It's the worst that can be done to a woman," she said, "and everyone reacts differently. She's not saying much. She may never talk about it. We shouldn't push. Maybe get her professional help. But she has no purse, no phone, no ID of any kind."

"Did she at least tell you her name?"

"No. She just says it was a god punishing her, and she keeps asking me to believe her. I tell her repeatedly that I do, but it seems to make no impression. It sounds to me like a regular thing, like maybe her abuser convinced her no one would ever believe her if she reported him." She was silent for a moment. "Do you think it was really a *god*? I mean, we don't know if she's on or off meds, you know?"

Her expression was strained, her eyes asking for a truth different from the one I was coming to understand. I shook my head. "I don't know. But the world we live in now is not what it was . . . I've reached the point where I figure I'd better just accept anything. So yeah, let's say this was a god who assaulted her. We may not have a name yet, but he's obviously working for the bad guys."

"But what can you do?" she asked. "What can you and Remi do against *a god*? I mean—you're just men." And then she realized what she'd said, and to whom she'd said it.

No, we were not "just men." But I didn't know whether what we *were* was enough to fight a god. "Bring her into the common room if you think she'll come. We can try some questions, see if we get any answers. We need to find her people."

"And if you can't?"

"I don't know," I said frankly. "I've got no clue. But we've got to do what we can to keep her safe."

"Like me," she said quietly. "Just like me." She looked at me a long moment, then shut the door with a quiet click.

I lingered, turning ideas over in my head. Then I went into the common room and sat down at the computer. I let it boot, and after a moment I typed in a couple of questions.

What gods are here on earth? How many of them are working for Lucifer?

An answer came in from Wiki by way of Google: *'Lucifer' redirects here, you may be looking for the TV series 'Lucifer.'*

I stared at the screen. It was a perfectly normal page, not black with gold letters and a dictatorial tone. "Not exactly," I muttered at it.

Remi came in with two bottles of beers, handed one to me. I nodded my thanks, gazed at the label absently. Then looked up and met his very serious eyes. "I want a life preserver," I said. "The water's getting choppy and I'm all at sea."

CHAPTER TWENTY-THREE

Cleaned of blood, the young woman's face nonetheless remained bruised and swollen. Kelly had washed her hair. Water-darkened, it lay forward of her shoulders, drying naturally. From scalp to the ends of her hair, even damp, waviness took precedence. As I recalled from the cell phone light in the breezeway, the portions of hair unbloodied were a tawny blonde.

She was seated on the couch, where Kelly had guided her. She'd been given water and a toasted bagel, which wasn't much in the way of food but was fast. She ate it slowly, taking very small bites of torn off pieces, and I realized the possibility was good that a few teeth had been loosened from the blow that damaged the side of her face. My black t-shirt was of course baggy on her, the jean legs were rolled up, and some kind of utility cord doubled as a belt. She was barefoot.

While one side of her jaw was swollen with its complementary puffy eye, from the other side she had an oddly attractive look. Not classically beautiful as far as I could see, but an arresting face with a slightly straight nose bridge. And in the undamaged pale blue eye, I saw a strengthening clarity of purpose.

Her age was indeterminant. Anywhere on the timeline between twenty and thirty, I felt.

Kelly looked at Remi and me, saw the reluctance in our expressions, the helplessness. I had no clue how a man began asking a woman about a rape. Cops were prepared; my dad had received specialized training. Me? I was just *a guy*, and it had certainly never been something I needed to address.

Seated sideways on the couch beside the young woman, Kelly ran a gentle hand across her back, began to rub in careful circles. "Can you tell us?" she asked. "Do you know his name?"

Even if she told us, I wasn't sure the information would help. We'd certainly try to protect her, but despite my familiarity with the pantheons in mythology and Remi's knowledge of specific deities of many cultures, there was a fair chance we wouldn't have the abilities or the means to ward her against a *god*. Or ward ourselves, for that matter.

The stranger shook her head. I didn't know if that meant she couldn't, or wouldn't.

"Can you tell us *your* name?"

The battered woman looked hard at Kelly, re-examined Remi. She was not quite at ease with them, which certainly was understandable. The look in her eye lost its piercing quality when she looked at me, and the set of her mouth softened. I had saved her. I wouldn't say she truly trusted me, but she did acknowledge my help.

Still, she shook her head and did not offer her name. Instead, she repeated an earlier declaration. "I spurned him."

Mary Jane's voice was tight. "You can tell a man 'no,'" she said. "You do not have to consent. He is not allowed to assault you because you rejected him."

"He cursed me."

"Words," Kelly said. "Only words. They don't affect you."

"He said no one will believe me."

"We believe you," Kelly told her. "We believe."

The woman drew herself up. Clean, now, and somewhere she believed was safe, the vulnerability I'd seen in the breezeway was banished. Taut urgency replaced it. "They will come. They will come and destroy. They will breach the gates with artifice. My brother—my *hidden* brother—will bring this upon us. I told him. I told him before he left. But he did not believe me. He did not believe me." The visible eye was angry. "No one believes me. I have told them, I have told them three times. I have *begged* them to believe. Men will die. My brother will die, and in his death he will be ruined. But I am cursed, and they do not believe my words. They say I am a madwoman, that I am god-touched, and do not believe my words."

And abruptly I knew it with certainty, though I couldn't explain why. "She's not from now," I said. "I don't think she's from *now* any more than Lily is, or Ganji." I looked at Remi. "Remember when Lily sent us to the battlefield? The place where the Romans slaughtered Boudicca and the Iceni? She sent us there, brought us back, all to prove a point, to make us believe she was who she said she was. I think this god, whoever he is, has sent this woman here from another time."

Remi was unconvinced. "Why would he do that?"

The woman answered for me. "Punishment. I spurned him, and he cursed me. And no one believes me. No one believes me, and what I see will come to be."

"Is it the demon?" I asked of Remi. "Is it Jack the Ripper? Might he be a god *and* a demon? If so, if he's got the power to send people across time, he may well be the *actual* Jack the Ripper. And we know what happened to him."

Remi frowned. "How do we know that? He was never caught, remember."

"That's it exactly." I stabbed the air with a forefinger. "Never caught, and everyone assumes he died at some point because *everyone* dies. But if he can send himself across time, it would be easy to escape discovery. It would be easy for him to curse her and send her here from a different time. To *displace* her."

Remi frowned. "Because she refused to sleep with him?"

I shrugged. "People *kill* people for no reason at all. In this case, he didn't kill her because leaving her alive was a greater punishment. She *suffers*. That's his curse. To make her suffer."

The woman stood up suddenly, literally surged off the couch. She caught my hand, caught Remi's hand, and pressed them together. Our rings made contact. "Beware the beast." She clung to our hands, pressing them together. "*Believe* and beware."

Abruptly she released us, snatched up the glass of water, spilled it across the table. She dipped a forefinger into it, then drew three shapes:

χἔ͙ς

We could barely see it. In fact, we had to bend down, to catch the glint of light off the wood in order to accurately see the drawn shapes. She was using "invisible ink:" water on wood. And I had no clue what the X and two squiggles meant.

I heard Remi gust a breath of shock. He straightened, looked searchingly at the woman. Slowly he reached out and took both of her hands in his, carefully closed them within his grip. It was gentle, and she did not shy from it.

She stood there looking at him. Waiting.

He said, *"Hexakósioi hexēkonta héx? Sescenti sexaginta se?"*

The woman nodded.

"O arithmós tou thiríou? Numerum bestiae?"

Again, she nodded.

I needed translator microbes, or something, with Remi switching languages at the drop of a hat. And I *really* needed to memorize the rite of exorcism. I resolved to pull it up on my phone later.

"Can you say more?" Remi asked, switching back to English. "Can you say which beast?"

She shook her head, withdrew her hands from his grip, placed them across her mouth.

Speak no evil, I thought. I could translate that just fine.

Remi released a long sigh as he looked at me. "I guess we shouldn't be surprised, considerin' everything that's become of our lives. End of Days, Ragnarok, Armageddon and all."

"Still at sea, here. What about beasts?"

He wetted a forefinger from spilled water, then drew three shapes. Once again I bent down to catch the light so I could see what was written.

I straightened sharply and stared at him. "Six-six-six? Seriously?"

He nodded. "The number of the beast. Or, in Greek: *O arithmós tou thiríou.*"

Mary Jane Kelly, who'd been silent, was clearly at a loss. "What does any of this have to do with Jack the Ripper wanting to murder me?"

Which, of course, reminded me of yet another strand in the sticky new web. I looked at Remi. "Another photo was delivered.

It's in the truck; I forgot to bring it in. I didn't look at the image, just the back, where he'd written a message. He said '*It didn't end with #5*,' and '*Any order serves.*'"

Kelly sounded worried. "What does that mean?"

Remi pressed his lips closely together as he considered what I'd said, then answered her. A tight undertone of anger was present. "There are five women everyone agrees were murdered by Jack the Ripper. Mary Jane Kelly was the last one accepted in canon as a victim. But it's believed he actually killed prior to the canonical five and after. That photo, the message . . . we're being told that he's got more women to kill. And maybe already has." He met my eyes. "We need to look at that image. Everything is important."

Color drained from Kelly's face. "So if *the beast* is really just a metaphor . . ." She swallowed heavily, as if her throat were tight. "Jack the Ripper is what she's warning about? He wears the mark of the beast—or *is* the beast?"

"Or he's a god," I said. "The god who raped her. He just didn't kill her. And of course he could also be a demon appearing as both the god she knows and the murderer we do. He may well become what he feels is best for the particular time period and audience."

"We have to assume he's stealing hosts," Remi continued. "Body-hopping. Well, unless he had the juice to bring the Ripper's *actual* body across time."

"Or the god's, made corporeal." I shrugged. "We don't know. We don't know a damn thing about what he can do." I thought back to the night I'd walked out the Zoo's back door with a woman hot to trot, only to have her nearly kill me as she welcomed me to the war. "That first night," I said sharply, "I broke her arm. *His* arm. Whatever. It means he's physically vulnerable."

Remi's expression was dubious. "The host is vulnerable, yeah. But we don't know that the actual surrogate is. He may just vacate the premises if he's in jeopardy."

"But what if it really was the Ripper? What if he's in his own body?"

Remi's brows ran up. "You mean, preserved it all these years?"

"If he's in his own body, maybe he *is* physically vulnerable."

"Or not."

I sighed. "Yeah."

Kelly's tone was thin. "But what does a woman, one you say may have come from another time, have to do with an English murderer?"

"Maybe nothing," Remi said, then added, "Maybe everything."

That's when our magic phones blew up with an alert, and the computer screen changed to black background with vivid gold letters printed across it.

Chapel of the Holy Dove.

We'd seen that message before. "Why?" I muttered. "Why again, and why this time?"

Remi sat down at the computer and typed in *"Why?"*

Chapel of the Holy Dove.

NOW.

Followed by one last sentence.

Bring her.

"Okay, wait." I stood just off Remi's shoulder, reading from behind him. "That's a little weird, because no one other than

Grandaddy knows she's here. Is this him messaging us? Because I did ask him to come in person."

"Well, he will be in person—just out there instead of here."

That earned him a mild stink-eye. "Why would he? Why not just come here? Then we don't have to haul ass over there in the middle of the night and bring her as well. She needs to rest. And why not just call us?"

Remi turned the swivel chair to face me. "Grandaddy's never been one for answering all our questions, now, has he? Some, sure, but there're plenty he's never answered even when we've asked him directly."

I checked my watch. "It's almost midnight. I think I've had maybe three hours of sleep across the last six days. But since our *angelfamilias* has spoken, I guess we should go."

I looked at the woman. She had not resumed her seat on the couch, merely waited quietly for what came next as she followed every word.

"A man we know wants to meet, and is asking us to bring you, too. We've known him all of our lives. We trust him. You'll be safe." I considered whether we should tell her who—or, rather, what—he was. Or whether she'd even know what an angel was.

Which reminded me.

I turned to Remi. "Hey, what language did you use when you spoke to her? I mean, you wrote the 666, which is Biblical."

"The triple six is not strictly Christian," Remi said. "In the Jewish tradition, the physical world is represented by the number six. The Torah describes a six-part, six-day process that created the universe, and the universe encompasses six distinct directions: *north, south, east, west, up,* and *down.* There are your three sixes: First, the physical world; Second, the six parts of the process; and Third, the actual six-day process."

I huffed a breath. "And now we see exactly why Grandaddy pushed you toward Comparative Religions: for situations just like this. So, were those numerals she wrote on the table Hebrew?"

Remi shook his head. "Greek. But Greek was the prevailing language among many peoples back in the day. Same way English is the official language of the airplane industry throughout the world. Nothing goes out over the radio that isn't in English, regardless of nationality. Centuries ago, scholars, scientists, and royalty, the well-educated upper classes, all spoke multiple languages. I asked her in both Latin and Greek. But I'm not truly fluent in either, outside of the specific words and phrases needed for reading religious writings in the original texts." He shrugged. "I can cobble together some phrases."

I nodded absently, began to wander around the room as I thought, hands on hips. I was still sore, still stiff, and couldn't quite hide a slight limp because my left hip was complaining about how I'd landed when the bike went down.

Kelly noticed. "Are you all right?"

"Yeah . . . I laid the bike down the other day, out on the highway."

She was astonished. "In the middle of traffic?"

"No, no traffic." I patted the air with a hand, tried to calm and dismiss her concern. "I'm fine. Sore, but fine."

"I can get you some ibuprofen. I have some in my pack."

A park ranger would. "I'm good."

After another trip around the common room to think, I paused in front of our visitor, tried to shed the slow-building tension before it could knot up my neck and shoulders. "Would you be willing to come with us?" I felt it was important that she be given the choice, regardless of what Grandaddy had asked over the computer—well, provided that *was* Grandaddy at the origination keyboard. "It's a safe place. Like a—" But I did not, after all, mention the word "temple," since she'd been raped in one. "Remi and I—" But again I stopped short. I didn't consider us holy, but obviously we had some celestial juice in our bodies. I just didn't know how to describe it to her. "The structure has been made safe. No one may harm us there. Remi and I will look after you."

"And me?" Mary Jane asked. She looked to Remi, still seated at the computer. "Do I come with you, too?"

I checked in with him via a questioning glance. I deferred to Remi because he and Kelly seemed to have something going. Or at least something starting.

He considered it a moment, then shook his head. "I think you'd do better to stay here. The Zoo is warded against demons."

Kelly nodded, then said, "But you're taking her."

"She doesn't have a demon after her," I pointed out. "Well, I think."

Her tone was dry. "No, she's got a *god* after her. A little higher on the food chain."

Well, true. "At any rate, we've been formally instructed—"

"By *a machine*," she put in.

"—to go and to take her with us," I emphasized, "—so that's what we'll do. Grandaddy knows what he's doing. He's the man with the plan." I rolled my head, raised shoulders, tried to loosen the rusted parts as I continued. "Ganji's here. He'll keep an eye on you."

She shook her head. "He left a while back. Wanted to go up the mountain, he said, and sing to her. He said the earthquake had disturbed her. The world—life—is out of balance. The Hopi call it—"

"—*koyaanisqatsi*," I finished, nodding. "And I would say that's *exactly* what's happening."

And for some reason that reminded me of Shemyazaz, who was himself markedly out of balance. He'd paid a two-hour visit to the Zoo earlier in the evening, so he couldn't return tonight. At least, not in the guise of a handsome human who liked to spin around on bartops and dance with a pretty girl.

"Well, you've got Remi's number in your phone," I told her, then snapped my fingers. "That reminds me. Did the bug guy call you? The guy at NAU?"

Kelly shook her head. "No, but I'll call him first thing in the morning."

Curiosity made me ask it. "How did he lose his leg?"

She was baffled. "What?"

"His missing leg. How did he lose it?"

Her frown deepened. "Dr. Hickman's not missing a leg. Why would you think he is?"

"Because he wasn't wearing it in the office," I explained. "He said his stump gets sore after standing on it in class, so he removes the prosthesis in the office. We saw it."

Kelly shook her head very slowly. "I've seen him in hiking shorts. He has two perfectly normal legs."

"Then why—ohhh, *shit*!" I turned to Remi. "We left the majority of demon remains behind on the mountain, and they were gone when we went back. But we had Mary Jane's smaller portion. We took that baggie to Hickman, and *he was missing a leg*."

Remi leaned back hard against the task chair, head tipped as he stared roofward and rubbed a hand across his eyes. His tone was resigned. "Molly."

"What?"

"*Molly.* I felt her. I sensed her. With my super power. I didn't sense him because I sensed *her.*"

And there it was, tied up in a bow. Deliberate distraction. I swore. "And she led us a merry chase across campus while the surrogate in Hickman grabbed the missing part of his body and disappeared."

Kelly's mouth was open. "But what happened to Dr. Hickman? The real Dr. Hickman."

Remi and I exchanged a concerned look. "Well, it's possible he only *borrowe*d Hickman's body," I told her, hoping like hell that was the case. We hadn't seen fake Hickman's legs as he sat behind the desk. "He might well wake up with a really bad, really weird hangover, but be fine."

"We don't know," Remi told her. "We don't know much at all."

Her eyes were distant as she sat in silence next to the foreign woman. Finally Kelly rubbed her face, stretched it out of shape as she murmured that she'd call him first thing in the morning, see if he was okay.

For her sake, I hoped he'd answer.

For his sake, I hoped he could.

CHAPTER TWENTY-FOUR

The intended seating arrangement in the truck took an un-expected turn. I'd expected we'd let our visitor ride in the passenger seat while I sat in the back so that she wasn't isolated behind us in the dark. She certainly climbed in will-ingly, but when I stepped up into the back seat she slid out of the passenger seat across the console from Remi, swung the door closed, and grabbed my door hastily to keep me from shutting it.

Um, okay. "No shotgun," I told Remi as he closed his own door.

He turned over the ignition. "Wherever she feels safest."

She climbed up into the back seat, pulled on the door awk-wardly but did manage to close it. She did not sit close to me, but settled right beside the door.

I looked at her. She looked at me. It was odd seeing only one eye open in her face, and made her hard to read. But I saw no fear, no concern. Only purpose, which apparently was to share a seat with me.

As we backed out, I leaned down and rescued the manila envelope and photo from the floorboards. "Do you mind the interior light?" I asked Remi. "I want to take a look at the photo."

"Go ahead. Won't bother me."

I pressed the light panel, and the woman startled in her place on the bench seat. She stared at me a moment, as if waiting for an explanation. When I said nothing, she reached up slowly, placed fingers on the light's surface to explore it.

I raised my voice over engine noise. "Yeah, pretty sure she is not from our time. My phone with the flashlight app turned on seemed to represent something like a talismanic protection, and she's got no clue about the truck's interior lights."

"See if she'll tell you her name now."

I asked her. Once again she refused. So I gave up on that and turned my attention to the photograph but angled it away from her. Seeing the words wouldn't matter—*if* she could read English—but she did not need to see a woman killed very messily.

I read the two sentences on the back again. Before, he had used letters cut out from magazines and newspapers taped to the paper to convey his message, mimicking kidnap notes in movies, but with the *From Hell* letter he started writing longhand.

I raised my voice again. "You know what we need to do? Compare the writing on this photo to the writing in the letter he gave us."

"Probably he can forge anyone's handwriting."

"Maybe so, but we should check it regardless. He's the type to hide Easter eggs in stuff. Could well be a code, for all we know, or might even prove that he *was* Jack the Ripper. I figure we shouldn't dismiss any—oh, holy *fuck*." I'd turned the photo over, viewed the image. My belly rolled. "This is . . . this is worse. Much fucking worse." I swallowed heavily. "He's esca-lating."

Remi was silent a moment. The truck thumped over uneven asphalt. "Have you ever seen the police photo of Mary Jane Kelly's body?"

"Hell no."

"Particularly bad. The worst by far. I'll need to look at this one later on, when we get a chance."

"*Why?* It's horrific. Do you need to know more than that?"

"Because I *have* seen the photo of Mary Jane Kelly—it's on-line; you can just pull it up—and it may be important. He's been either mimicking what the Ripper did, or, if he *was* Jack, recreating what he did in the 1880s. We have our modern-day Mary Jane Kelly in protective custody, so to speak. So did he do to the woman in this current photo as he did to the Ripper's Kelly? Or go another way? If it's the latter, he may be saving that specific method of death for our Mary Jane. Trust me, I'm not interested in seein' it again, but probably I need to. Espe-cially since he personally delivered this to us."

"I didn't see how it was delivered, or by whom, but Molly may have done it. She was here, after all."

"She makes a hornet look cuddly," Remi said in disgust.

When we'd begun searching for Mary Jane Kelly, I knew it was important that we find her, but the photo underscored ex-actly what was at risk. Not just death, but butchery.

I rode in silence for long minutes, trying to sort out my emotions. And couldn't.

The 8x10 was in my hand, image up. The woman reached out, placed a fingertip on the photo.

I hastily pulled the photo out from under her finger, flipped it over and pressed it face-down against my thigh. She didn't need to see that. Not after what she'd been through. Hell, not ever, for any reason.

I looked to her to see her reaction, but there was no horror. No disgust. No shock at all.

"The god," she said quietly.

And I realized that what I read in her face was none of those other emotions because this kind of killing was not new to her. She'd seen this, or something like this, before.

"Hey, Remi?"

"Yeah?"

"Remember Mossman, the cowboy at the ravine? How he was corporeal despite being a ghost?"

"Yeah."

"I think *she's* a ghost. I think she's a ghost and saw Jack the Ripper at his work. I think she may be a ghost *because* she saw the Ripper at his work, and he killed her."

"Sweet Jesus," Remi said blankly.

The woman looked at me out of one clear eye. I pressed the light off and threw the truck cab into darkness, save for the panel on the dashboard.

"Ask her," I suggested. "Ask her if she's a ghost—or, well, a *shade*, since it's Roman and Greek mythology. Do you have the Latin and Greek for that?"

After a moment, Remi cleared his throat. He turned his head just enough so that his words would carry to the back while he kept an eye on the road. *"In umbra es? Eísai skiá?"*

Her single eye glinted with every street light passed. *"Ego mulier tantum. Eímai móno gynaíka."*

"And?" I asked.

"She says she is only a woman."

———

The highway led out of Flagstaff into vast miles of mostly treed but unpopulated high desert, and in the middle of the night was absent of traffic. Pine forest on both sides of the winding road created something akin to a maze. I couldn't see much outside because of the dash illumination, and the brilliance of headlights stretching before us, flashing off asphalt curves, white and yellow lines, and trees.

I told Remi he should turn on the radio, just to break the silence. I also wondered how she would react to music without visible humans playing instruments and singing.

He turned it on, but kept it low. She listened avidly, the one eye wide. I saw her lips soften, part in a very faint smile.

"Oldies station," Remi said. "And yes, it's country. Get over it."

I watched the woman and listened as if I was hearing a radio for the first time, as she was. Then I scowled. "Oh, for God's sake. We're doing the red-eyed cows again? With black and shiny horns?"

"'*Ghost* Riders in the Sky,'" Remi said. "Appropriate, don't you think, in view of the circumstances? And don't you criticize the Man In Black."

"Who?"

"Johnny Cash." And then of course he sang the *yippie yi yays* again.

"I'm not sure she approves of the music," I said. "Or your singing. Or both."

"Why? What's she doing?"

Actually she was smiling. She looked—happy. But I didn't want to encourage him. "Possibly preparing to barf."

Remi ignored that and began to slow the truck. "Well, we're coming up on the chapel anyway. That'll salve your wounded ears."

Tires crunched across cinders and gravel as he eased the pickup to a stop, pulling in front of the small shake-shingled A-frame building. He turned off the radio, let silence settle. As he opened his door the chime went off alerting him to the key in the ignition. He pulled it out, pocketed the remote, and peace reigned again. The woman looked puzzled, which made me contemplate what she was familiar with if not trucks.

"Chariots, maybe," I said. "You think?"

"What?" Remi asked.

"She doesn't know motorized vehicles, and is speaking Latin and ancient Greek. Probably she's familiar with chariots."

"Might could be, I reckon." Remi rounded the truck, opened her door and helped her step out. Even when not jacked up via lift kit, trucks sit high anyway, and if you're not used to a big step down it's easy to misjudge the landing. She clearly had no clue how to navigate lock, door, or step-down, so his help was warranted beyond good manners. Though he had them in abundance.

I slid out the other side, shut the door. The interior light went off as Remi, out of the truck, closed his and hit the remote. I walked a few steps away, looked beyond the modest chapel to the huddled peaks, and let myself go, let myself reach out, to sense what there was to sense.

Beneath the full moon, in the quiet of the night, I felt the colors come. Like a tide across the sand, they washed in, clung briefly, washed out only to be replaced by others. I closed my eyes, tipped my head back, and opened myself to the world.

It began with brown. The richness of the earth, of stability, of home. Comfort was here. Then came green, for nature, for health. Here there was no disruption, no *koyaanisqatsi*—and it wasn't because a reconsecrated chapel stood guardian. The San Francisco Peaks were sacred to Native Americans. Here is where the *ga'an*, the mountain spirits, walked. No solitary religion took precedence here.

Blue seeped in, easing green aside. Sky and water, harmony and unity. Tranquility.

I heard her voice. I heard her ask Remi something. I sensed her coming toward me.

I put up a hand and stopped her. She stood beneath the moon, graced by its light. I sensed purple, rich and royal. A potent amalgam of nobility, mystery, transformation. And lastly of mourning.

I opened my eyes. She waited for me to speak. I couldn't find diplomacy, couldn't call on empathy. My words were weapons, and I could not find the means to turn away the blade. "Someone has died."

Moonlight glinted on the tear welling in one pale eye. "My brother. It was a hard death. No honor in it. Only dishonor. A hero thrown down. I did tell them. I did warn them. *Believe*, I begged. But none of them would. None of them. To die in battle is a great thing. To be dishonored so after death . . ." But she trailed off and did not, or could not, finish.

And was her brother now a shade, too? A *skía*. An *umbra*.

I walked away from her, closer to the chapel. Had to, to collect myself, to think for myself. And then my hip hitched,

I stumbled, but caught myself with a couple of one-legged hops.

"That was graceful," Remi observed.

"Well, keep in mind my specialty was books, not athletics." Actually, I generally moved well, had good flexibility, but not since getting dumped off my bike.

At least it broke the tension. I reached for lightness, for levity, before the colors turned dark and took me down. "I can feel it," I said. "What we did, and where, when we reconsecrated. If I stand here, it's just the mortal world. But two strides *this* way—" I took them, "—and I am elsewhere. We leave behind the mundane world and stand on holy ground."

Remi took three strides, halted, gestured to the ground. "Am I good here? On consecrated ground?"

"You are good."

"I don't feel anything."

"Since *your* super power is sensing demons, and we're on holy ground, that's probably a good thing." I put out a hand toward the woman, gestured. "Come in with us. It's safe. I promise."

The chapel was an A-frame, built narrow and low at the entrance, then broadened and rose skyward on the diagonal similar to a triangle until it ended at tall floor to ceiling windows. The entry door with its small cross-shaped window was not wide enough for us to walk in side-by-side. Remi went first. The woman followed, as I wanted, and I came in behind her, quietly closing the door.

No electricity, thus no artificial lights. We had phones and flashlight apps, but the moon was enough. It lit up the huge windows and flooded the interior.

Before us, the doubled rows of garden bench 'pews' on

either side of the modest aisle ran from door to windows. Hundreds of stapled notes and written prayers from visitors hung like pale butterflies from the roof, covered the wooden walls. And at the broad end of the chapel, above the altar, the hanging cross was black against the glass, save for moonshine and stars.

The draw was obvious. As one, we three walked the aisle and stopped before the altar side-by-side, gazing not at the cross but to the pine-flanked mountains beyond, crowded black against the stars.

Finally I broke the silence, shed the weight of lunar light and looked at Remi on the other side of the woman. "So, we're just supposed to hang out here until Grandaddy decides to show his face?"

But someone other than Remi answered, an unfamiliar female voice. "He wasn't invited."

Remi and I whipped around and by the time we faced her, guns were in our hands.

I couldn't help it. My reflex was to yell at the angel. "Stop *doing* that, Greg! Stop appearing without warning!" I spread my arms wide. "I already shot you once, and that was five shots center mass; want me to do it again?"

Three times. Three times she'd done this, dammit. I shoved the gun back into its holster.

But the young woman between us, whom we'd placed in our care, took a single step back toward the altar. She said one word, barely above a whisper, *"Angeliafóros."*

The new arrival halted just inside the door, let it close behind her. Black hair was cut straight at her chin, an equally sharp line ran across her brow. Black clothing. Black Asian eyes. Wingless at the moment, but that could change.

I glared at her. "*You* brought us here?"

"My name is Ambriel," Greg the Grigori corrected, annoyed. "And yes. I did."

"Why?" Remi asked. "You're an angel, not a demon; you can come inside the Zoo. Why call us all the way out here?"

Her mouth was a grim line. "Because that building reeks of Barachiel. I avoid him. I avoid him at all times, in all ways. I don't trust him. I know him too well. So I summoned you here."

"Who's Barachiel?" I asked.

She flicked a glance at Remi, then back at me. "You behave as children, even as adults, and call him 'Grandaddy.' Barachiel is his true name. He claims himself chief of the guardian angels."

"That's his angelic name?" I asked.

Remi's drawl was quiet, but pronounced. "Ma'am, I believe you may want to modify your words and tone. Because we may be fixin' to have us an argument, you and me, if you continue in this uncivil manner."

Her expression personified utter contempt. "I will say what I will say. I know what he is to you. I know what he's done to you." She fixed me with a penetrating glare. "But recall how I warned you that not all angels want the same thing. Suspect all of them. The war is not what it seems. Good versus Evil is simplistic. Childish. Heaven is not light. Hell is not darkness. They are all the colors of *gray,* and we live in between."

I eased my way one step to the side, putting more space between the battered young woman and me so I'd have room to move. Guns wouldn't work against angels, even with breath-blessed silver bullets or iron powder—Greg was the one who'd told me that, and proved it at Wupatki by surviving my five bullets—but I thought I might possibly need to move even if it wasn't to shoot. Remi did the same on the woman's left. Neither of us had any clue what was coming down, but I remembered very clearly that Grandaddy was no more a fan of this Grigori than she of him.

Now Greg's dark eyes were on the woman between us. I knew what she saw: ill-fitting clothing, bare feet, swollen face, bruises. Ropes of wavy blonde hair verging on ringlets.

Outside the chapel, I heard a sound that literally made the fine hairs on my body rise. It was purely atavistic, a deep, heavy sound rising in pitch until it slid into a shrieking, ear-piercing squeal. The sound repeated, and a second voice joined it. Then a third.

Gun was out again. "What the hell is that?" I spread and braced my legs. "What *is* that, and how many of them are there?"

"I count three," Remi said.

Treble growls, treble squeals. No barking. Just that horrible sound released by a furious dog as he goes feral in an instant, where he growls on the inhale and growls on the exhale, sound and breath sawing in his throat as all teeth are bared, and saliva releases. That savage, primal sound of pure predator.

"He's come for her," Greg said. She strode partway down the aisle, glanced briefly at the cross hanging high over our heads against the window. She walked farther into the moonlight, halted two steps from us, put out her hands to the woman.

In a language I didn't know, the Grigori spoke to her in obvious kindness, in support, in promise. The young woman broke from the physical protection offered by Remi and me by taking those two steps toward the angel.

She knelt. Then prostrated herself and gripped Greg's ankles. *"Angeliafóros."*

The Grigori bent, raised her. Greg put her hands on either side of the woman's face, studied her a long moment as if reading her eyes, then leaned forward, still cradling the weight of her head, and placed a lingering kiss upon her brow. "Be who you are," Ambriel told her, mouth still close to her brow. "Be the daughter of a king, be speaker of the truth."

Ambriel turned the woman to face us. Gone were the bruises, the swelling. The puffy eye was whole. Her jaw was now clean, a pure sweeping line. The straight nose fit the high arch of her cheekbones, the line of brow above two pale blue eyes.

She was not beautiful. The bones were too strong. But it was a face no one could forget.

The beast beyond the door shrieked.

Greg nodded. "He knows who she is, and he's come for her." Her face was grim. "I had not expected this so soon."

Remi: "Who's out there? Demon?"

Me: "Who *is* she? She never told us."

The Grigori answered Remi first. "His name is Cerberus."

I stared at her in shock. "Hades's three-headed hound? Why on earth would he be after *her*? Who is she?"

Ambriel said, "Her name is Cassandra."

"Believe," the woman said. "The city shall fall, and so must the kingdom. Beware! Bring not the horse inside the gates with Greeks in its belly. Give me an axe, and I shall chop it apart. Believe! *I speak true!*"

"Jesus." I could barely speak. "She's talking about the Trojan Horse!"

"And the Fall of Troy." Remi shook his head. "Cassandra did predict it, and no one listened."

"Cursed by Apollo to always speak the truth," Ambriel said, "and never to be believed." She looked at Remi, then again at me. "Hades is here on earth."

Outside the little chapel, his three-headed monster screamed.

CHAPTER TWENTY-FIVE

waited for Greg to say more. She did not. I finally shook my head in annoyance, tucked the gun away, went back to the door and squinted out the cross-shaped window into darkness. Shielded my eyes against the moonlight inside and tried to see Cerberus. Could not. Heard him, though. His voice was harrowing.

"Technically," I turned away from the door, looked at Greg, Remi, and Cassandra standing near the altar, "we can actually go outside and be fine. Within limits."

Remi raised his voice more than a little. "You want to go outside to meet up with a three-headed dog monster?"

"Hey, don't forget the snake for a tail part."

Remi was taken aback. "A literal snake?"

"A literal snake." I wandered my way back up the aisle, fingers of both hands stuffed into tight front pockets. "Cerberus was the offspring of Echidna and Typhon. Echidna was half serpent, and Typhon, depending on which version you subscribe to, had multiple snakes growing out of his body. And also one hundred heads, including a dragon. So yeah, Cerberus comes by the snake tail honestly."

Behind Remi, the bright moon cast enough illumination

through the big windows that I could see his expression as he calculated whether he should believe me or not.

I stuck a forefinger in the air. "But what I meant was, he can't come inside the distance barrier we erected when we re-consecrated the place. Which means we can go outside and ac-tually *shoot* the thing up close and personal without risking ourselves. I like those odds. So, I've got silver and iron in my gun. You?"

"Same, the .45 caliber bullets and .410 cartridges. Will ei-ther kill him?"

"The stories don't say," I admitted, "but the writers knew nothing about gunpowder, bullets, or guns, so it's entirely pos-sible that the rounds alone may do him in. We've got five apiece, so I figure ten should be enough to take him out if we hit the usual places: eyes, brain, heart, maybe go for internal organs as well."

"Did he die in the stories? If so, maybe we ought to use the same tactics."

I grimaced. "Actually, no, he didn't. Or so the writers said; but they're not in agreement." I felt like I was back before my students. "As the last of his Twelve Labors, Hercules went to the underworld to capture Cerberus, and Hades allowed the battle so long as Hercules didn't use any of the weapons he came with. Of course, Hercules was half-god himself and the stron-gest man in the world, so he overcame Cerberus with his bare hands and took him up top to prove his accomplishment. Then Hercules either sent him back to Hades, or else Cerberus es-caped on his own and went back. But I say we rewrite the script and kill the bastard for good. Especially since neither of us is Hercules. Or Kevin Sorbo, for that matter, who played him on TV. Did you watch that series?"

"I did. Though I admit to havin' more of a liking for Xena the Warrior Princess."

"What's not to like?" I looked at Cassandra, who had moved away from us to sit alone on one of the garden bench pews. Then I checked in on Greg, still standing silently before the altar, ignoring Remi and me as she watched Cassandra with an expression of faint regret. I wandered my way closer to her.

"So, what's your suggestion? About the monster, I mean, not canceled TV shows. And just why did you pretend to be Grandaddy and tell us to bring Cassandra out here?"

"I didn't *pretend* to be anyone," she said. "You jumped to conclusions."

"Then let me rephrase: Why did you, as yourself, tell us to bring Cassandra here?"

Greg lifted her head high, which gave her chin a stubborn tilt. "I have a task."

"*What* task?"

"The business of angels," she said, and clearly intended to say no more.

I gave it up and swiped the air with my arm in a broad, dismissive gesture. "Okay, fine; never mind. The bottom line is, you knew Cassandra was with us and manipulated events to make sure we brought her out here. Now I want to know why."

"You can't protect her," the angel said. "Not against a god."

"Why not meet in a church in the city?"

"They are burning. Here it is safe. Here is the power of the white man's belief *and* the Native American."

Beyond the door, in the darkness, Cerberus screamed. The sound ran up the scale into the ear-piercing vicinity. "This doesn't sound safe to me."

"He can't enter. That is safety."

Well, yeah. Sort of. Pretty limited, though.

"Hades wants her," Greg said, "and you two can't protect her."

"Uh, we've kind of already done some of that," I pointed out, thinking of my rescue of her at the strip mall.

"Not adequately," she clarified with precise enunciation. "Not against Hades. He's a god. Your job is to handle demons, and the creatures they animate, or inhabit."

"AHHhhhhh," Remi's inflection rose, then fell in an overdone tone of discovery. "We're sittin' at the kids' table, are we? Allowed to go out after supper and play with the demons, but not the big hat all-grown-up gods?"

I wondered if angels could get constipated, or if Greg had some other reason for always being in a foul mood. "Hades would strip the flesh from your bones," she said, "then crack them open to suck the marrow out. Oh, do be my guest. Follow his pet back to the underworld. While Hades is dining on everything else, Cerberus will eat your livers."

Dramatic and graphic. In response I waved a minatory forefinger in the air. "No liver-eating, no bone-cracking. Our job is to save the world, right? Well, okay, one tiny little portion of it, since we're just-born newbies. To me, that means take out as many enemy combatants as we can. What do you care if we manage it? Wouldn't you thank us? And if we died you probably wouldn't even know it, and you'd miss your chance to gloat."

She pressed her lips together into a straight, flat line of annoyance. "I don't want any of the children to die. Children are meant to grow up apart from violence, to be properly trained before being assigned a mission and a territory."

I snorted to myself. Heaven sounded much like a national conglomeration with a sales force.

Remi nodded. "Children as in heaven's kids? Not humans, right?"

"Humans are not able to fight," she answered. "I've told you before—humans will be collateral damage. It was time to acquaint you with the truth of your births, your gifts, yes. But Barachiel accelerated your deployment for his own goals. It's much too soon, and you're endangered because of it. *This* is why your abilities have not fully manifested, why you cannot rely on them. You are both vulnerable. Fragile, in a way." She stretched out an arm and pointed at the door. "The wards of the rite hold for now, but it's tenuous because the gifts of your essence are weak as yet."

"I thought you said we were safe in here."

"*Inside*, yes. But the buffer outside will fail. Someone higher in the hierarchy, someone stronger, should tend it."

"Then do it," I challenged. "You're an angel. Go out there and strengthen the wards, or whatever, and take out Cerberus for us. Then we can all go home and hit the sack, sleep for a week."

Greg raised her head again. "I will do neither."

"Why?" Remi asked. "You said you don't want us to die, so how 'bout you blow up that three-headed beast the way you blew up the black dog at Wupatki? Then we fragile little flowers won't be dead, and Hades won't kill Cassandra."

"Hades doesn't want to kill Cassandra," Greg said sharply. "He wants to *use* her. And so do Barachiel and others."

I glanced at Cassandra. "Use her how?"

The Grigori shook her head slightly, as if in disbelief that we could be so dense. "She speaks truth to power. Perfect truth to *literal* power."

Finally, I got it. "Cassandra is the scout sent out ahead for recon, to bring back information necessary to formulating or amending a battle plan. Only it isn't a literal scouting job, but visions. Predictions. So Hades, working with Lucifer, wants her, and you say Grandaddy wants her for the same thing, but you don't agree with his goals or his methods. So why are you here? Why do *you* need Cassandra? What's your stake in this?"

"I'm Switzerland," she said.

I blinked at her. "Congratulations. Now tell me—"

"I'm a *watcher*," she snapped, interrupting. "That's what Grigori do: we *watch*. We are neutral." She looked at Cassandra a long moment, modulated her tone to something less assertive, less angry. "I must take her off heaven's chessboard. Enforce neutrality."

Remi shook his head. "The minute you attempt to *enforce* something, you are no longer neutral."

Ambriel lifted her shoulders in a slight shrug. "Call it whatever you like. I'm here to take her with me, to keep her safe. Where neither side can use her." All the annoyance and impatience was gone. What I heard now was empathy. "It *was* a curse, what Apollo did to her, and later Ajax. She is half-mad already. If she is used for the war as they wish to use her, they'll scoop out every last bit of her and leave only a desiccated body behind."

Cerberus cried again, all three heads giving tongue. I felt a much greater urgency now that I knew the warding outside might not hold. I drew my gun, saw Remi do the same. We looked at Greg.

Remi said, "You told us we don't get to play with gods yet. I'd suggest we're not up to playing with their pets yet, either. So how about you call in the guys and gals responsible for animal control."

She shook her head.

My turn. "Taking Cassandra off the board is more than watching, and you're also throwing us—two of heaven's most inexperienced children, according to you—to Lucifer's wolves. Because Cerberus will cross the line when the rite fails, and our livers will be served on the devil's finest china."

Greg looked at both of us for long moments. Then she moved away, put out a hand to Cassandra, and when the woman joined her before the altar in the brightest moonlight, Greg whispered something. Cassandra nodded.

But Cassandra also said something we couldn't hear. She turned from Greg, came to me, gathered one of my hands into hers. She touched the black-and-silver ring, smiled briefly, then met my eyes. "I see no blood," she said, "no broken bones, no crushed skull."

"Well," I said, "that is encouraging news. How long is this happy condition supposed to last?"

Her brows knit as she thought about it. "Time eludes me, though I know what is to come."

"So you can't reliably tell anyone when these things will happen?"

She shook her head. "I saw the city fall. I saw that Paris would bring back the terrible woman from Sparta after stealing her from Menelaus, and I told Paris, but he refused to listen to me. I told him the city would fall, I told him Hector would die if the woman was brought back. But he didn't believe me." Tears welled. She covered them with her hands, hiding her eyes from me. Her voice was uneven, and angry. "I warned Paris. I warned our father. I warned Hector. I told him not to engage with Achilles. I told him."

I knew the story. But I didn't know how much written by others was true.

"I told him," she repeated, "but he fell to Achilles, and Achilles dishonored him. Achilles *destroyed* him."

Destroyed him literally, according to Homer and others; Achilles had dragged Hector's body behind his chariot for nine days. "Have you seen all the days?" I asked. "All the days of the dishonor?"

She lifted her hands from her face. "The days?"

I wondered then if Cassandra could see the future only by waves of visions, or by fragments rather than in sequential scenes. She spoke of dishonor done to Hector, but surely she would know how long Achilles abused the body and would say so.

And yet, all I knew were stories and histories written by chroniclers, and none of them contemporaries. I wondered what they got wrong, and what Cassandra might have forgotten.

"His body was made whole," I told her. "Your father paid the Achaeans for his son's body, and when it came home to Troy the gods saw to it Hector was whole and clean again."

Her eyes were wide, pupils expanded in subdued light. "I have not seen that! How do you know it?"

"I live in a different time," I said. "A later time."

She nodded. "I know this. Your chariots have no horses."

That made me smile a little; engine power was still measured by the number of equines in the equation. "In my time, there are great histories, tales told of your city, of Achilles, Hector, and, well, Helen of Troy."

"She was not of Troy," Cassandra snapped. "The woman was a *Spartan*. She was never of Troy."

I resolved not to inform Cassandra that the story of Paris and Helen was considered one of the greatest romances in history, and the *'of Troy'* was permanently affixed to Helen's name.

But her attention shifted. "My brother's body was clean and whole?"

"It was. He was given funeral rites fit for a great hero, and buried with honor."

She was sad but looked relieved. "Apollo's curse is fitful. It comes upon me, but the loom is crooked-built and all the yarn is tangled."

"Cassandra," Greg said sharply. Then she softened her tone, extended a hand. "We must go before the hound can take you and carry you to Hades."

It was all impulse. I just blurted it out to Cassandra before she could go to Greg. "Stay, if you want. You can stay. You have free choice. Don't let her make you go with her if you don't want to."

"Stay out of this!" Greg cried. "This is too big for you. You lack the capacity to understand any portion of the stakes! You don't matter for anything, the two of you! Don't interfere."

"Your choice," I told Cassandra, ignoring the angry angel.

Cassandra nodded, took my hand again, said something in Greek, then left me and went to stand immediately in front of the Grigori.

Massive black wings burst forth, then swirled down and around, feathers gleaming like oil. First Greg's arms surrounded Cassandra, and then the wings did as well. We saw one more glimpse of Ambriel's furious eyes, and then she bowed her head low. Feathers shifted, wings closed. She was absolutely still a long moment, encased in feathers, and then the wings snapped back.

Cassandra was gone.

A moment later so was Greg.

CHAPTER TWENTY-SIX

Remi and I were left dumbfounded, staring at the space where the two had just stood beneath the moonlight before a cross and altar: Cassandra of Troy—she of the twelfth or eleventh century *Before Christ*—and an ageless angel.

Then Cerberus growled and screamed and shrieked outside, and we forgot about the women and their disappearing act.

"Alrighty, then." I tried to inject lightness into an otherwise dire situation. "I think we can say we've been well and truly 'dissed' by an angel, not kissed. I guess our next step is to try and take out the monster dog before our weak little reconsecration ward fails—we being such useless, helpless, fragile little flowers and all."

"Called cannon fodder," Remi said, in something approaching his own version of a growl, "and I ain't too fond of that title. Time to prove we've got more going on than the Grigori give us credit for."

"I guess then this might be considered *'diss and tell.'*" I pulled the magic phone from my pocket, checked for messages from Grandaddy, found none. So I called him again, got no answer again, left a message again. *"That woman we were looking after because she'd been assaulted? Well, she's Cassandra of Troy—yeah, the psychic who predicted the city's fall—and we got tricked into bringing her out here to the little Holy Dove chapel by that Grigori I told you about—name's Ambriel, remember?—and Ambriel took her off somewhere. She's not a fan of yours, Ambriel isn't. Now we're stuck here at the chapel with three-headed Cerberus outside trying to get in to eat our livers, so we 'might could,' as Remi says, use a little assistance. Sometime this year would be helpful."* I disconnected.

Remi's brows were up. "I'm surprised you got all that on there before it cut off."

"Oh, it cut off about the time I got to *'She's not a fan of yours,'* but I was on a roll and kept going. He knows where we are now and what happened, so maybe he'll come save us from the big bad dog."

"You don't want us to give it a try?"

"Sure I do. But just in case we can't kill it, we ought to have a backup plan." I opened the revolver, rolled the cylinder, judged everything in working condition, gusted my breath over it again, clicked it closed. "How about I concentrate on one of the heads first, and you go for the body. After that it's every man for himself."

Remi grabbed one of the garden benches, dragged it over to the entrance. "We ought to prop open the door, give us a chance to dive back inside if it comes to that."

I look at him askance. "I'm pretty sure that if he comes through the ward, we won't make it back inside. We'll be doggie liver treats."

"The fastest of us will make it inside, 'cuz the dog'll catch the slow one first," Remi pointed out. "And right now you've got a hitch in your git-along, so I'm figurin' it'll be me comin' back through the door."

"Asshole."

"Yessir."

I brought the backlight up on the heavenly phone. I couldn't find a list of apps, just contact icons for a few people, one of whom was here with me. "No flashlight?" I muttered. "You'd think heaven would be all about casting light upon the land."

"Well, unless it's like Ambriel said and there is no light or dark, just grays."

"Bull."

"Well, maybe. But the moon's bright."

"And it casts dark shadows," I said, "heavy enough to provide good hiding places."

Remi turned on his app. On his regular phone, that is; mine was back at the Zoo. I was going to have a talk with Grandaddy about installing proper apps as well as about a rogue Grigori. In the meantime, I opened the door, brought it back as far as it could go, shoved the bench over to prop it open.

We both had our guns in hand. Remi stood beside the door, hugging the wall, and stuck the phone around the jamb on an outstretched arm. I peered around from the other side. The flashlight app really wasn't powerful enough to beat back the deeper shadows. All we saw out front was Remi's pickup.

Which, we discovered, as Cerberus screamed at the heavens, now hosted a Great Dane-sized, three-headed, snake-tailed monster in the bed. He looked for all the world like an ugly-ass ranch dog riding around during chores.

Remi shouted so loudly he damn near took an ear off my head. "You born-sorry no-account looks-like-a-sheep-killer dog! We ain't on borrowin' terms, so you get your ass out of my truck!"

To punctuate that, he walked out of the chapel very close to where I'd indicated the safety zone began, and cut loose with three shots of the .410 powdered iron shells.

Well, okay.

I joined him, giving him room to move as he wanted. But me, I went with the .45-caliber rounds.

I tried eyes. I tried chest. Remi shot into his body. Cerberus just stood there, three sets of crimson eyes glowing and all his prodigious teeth bared while his snake tail writhed. He emitted that horrible growl again, then scaled it up to the screech with all three heads thrown back.

We didn't miss. And the monster didn't die. He didn't go down. He didn't even wobble.

Remi threw every knife he had. I saw them strike point-first, and I saw them fall.

Outrage actually canceled out fear. Well, for a minute. My voice went up an octave. "What, he's wearing body armor?"

And then Cerberus cocked all three heads in unison, as if listening to something. Abruptly he jumped over the far side of the truck bed and took off running. Fortunately it was in the direction going *away* from us. The last we saw of him was the flip of his snake-tail as he ran beneath the moon, and then he was gone.

No predator leaves prey if he is impervious to said prey's defense mechanisms. Predator leaves prey if something even bigger shows up.

And then the ground rippled beneath our feet.

Or an earthquake shows up.

I grabbed the Texas-bred and -born flatlander by one arm and yanked him away from the chapel. He staggered, regained his balance three steps later, jerked his arm out of my hand and scowled at me. "What the hell was that for?"

I pointed at the chapel. "Buildings fall down in earthquakes. Buildings fall down *after* earthquakes, too, if they're
strong enough, or the aftershocks are."

We turned even as the ripple died away and the earth solid-
ified. It really hadn't been much. Just a quiver. But Remi and I
hung around out front for five long minutes just in case—he
inspected his truck and reclaimed his knives, said at least the
dog had not pissed in the bed—but we heard no creaking of
over-stressed wooden structure, no cracking of stone half-walls,
no shattering of big windows in the far end of the chapel.

I declared it safe enough to go back inside, check things
out. I was curious about whether the unique departure of Cassandra and Greg left anything behind that might tell us where
they'd gone, and son of a gun if there wasn't a single black
feather lying in the moonlight.

"Hah," I said. "A calling card."

"Or a warning."

"Warning of what?" I squatted, studied the feather more
closely without touching it. One could not be too careful, especially as Greg had not proven herself particularly pleased with
our behavior. Finally I reached out a hand, poked it with a finger, then actually picked the thing up.

Six inches long, but not, I knew, the longest of flight feathers. To lift a human's mass, even a small woman, the wings
would have to be immense. And while we'd seen only the suggestion and promise of Grandaddy's wings, Greg had unfurled
hers completely at Wupatki, and when she slammed them together it created a humongous thunderclap and a buffet of air
so powerful it had knocked Remi and I on our asses. Here she'd
unfurled them, snapped them open, but then she'd brought

them down into a tight smothering curl around Cassandra's body and her own.

My smile was crooked, but it came. *A feather from an* angel's *wing. Who'd a thunk it?*

And then I managed to give myself a cut from checking out a feather's edge, and I announced to Remi that angels' wings are pretty much razor blades along the edges. Which made sense, because I remember the *zzzip* of Shemyazaz's wing slipping across my nose. Then I put my finger in my mouth.

Remi resettled his hat. "Let's go on back. Nothing for us to do here. I'd say we should *re*-reconsecrate, except the Grigori sure put no stock in our abilities to do much of anything effective. We can let Grandaddy know. Maybe he'll do it or send someone."

"Yeah—if he ever bothers to return my calls." I pushed the garden bench back from the door and returned it to where it belonged. "You know, I was all for sleeping elsewhere if you wanted to entertain Mary Jane, but right about now I just want to go crash face-first into my bed."

Remi sounded surprised. "That's downright generous of you. I wasn't thinkin' tonight, but give or take another day or two and I may take you up on it."

"I know these things." I held up the feather. "I'm your wing-man."

Remi rolled his eyes. "Let's go, son. We got us some sheep to count, even if this is cattle country."

We both climbed back into the truck, thinking various thoughts regarding such things as monstrous dogs, angry angels, and a very *very* old woman from Troy, then pulled our seatbelts across simultaneously and shoved the tongues home in the receivers.

Remi backed us out as I put the feather in the glovebox for safekeeping until we got back to the Zoo. "Big day," I remarked as Remi turned out onto the highway and goosed the accelerator with a heavy foot. "Ghost at the ravine, demon teacher at NAU, Molly the stalker-demon, Jack the Ripper delivering the mail—or one of his hench-demons—and *the* Cassandra of Troy telling me my fortune, plus a pissed off Grigori and Cerberus."

"And an earthquake," Remi added.

"And an earthquake. I think—*oh shit*—" I braced myself. *"Remi—"*

Remi ran into it. He just flat ran into whatever it was because there was absolutely no time to avoid it. I didn't even see it until the split second before the truck made contact. It was a roiling black shape coming out of the night on a very dark highway. The thing flipped toward us over the hood and landed smack up against the windshield.

I'd hit an elk once, back in Oregon. I'd been in a car, not on my bike, thank God, but the big buck had been flipped up onto my hood and smashed into the windshield, making a hole in the glass. The tines of one heavy antler had barely missed me.

Remi stood on the brakes to get the truck stopped as quickly as possible, muttering frantic curses under his breath as tires screeched, and just as he threw it into park we unholstered guns and bailed out our respective doors. The warning chime about the key in the ignition with the doors left open and headlights left on *ding-ding-ding-dinged* repeatedly, but we paid it no attention.

And then the thing sprawled across the hood moved, leaped to its feet, and Shemyazaz, shedding flesh and feathers in the carnage of his hell-burned form, loomed over us from his perch atop the truck. I saw a flock of bright orbs strobing, his glass acolytes, moving in agitation all around his body.

"Where is she?" he shouted. And then he roared it, arms spread. *"Where is she?"*

I was profoundly baffled. "Where is who?"

"Where is the betrayer? I can *smell* her on you. Where is the Grigori?"

Remi sounded downright testy. "Get the hell off my truck. It already had a monster dog in it; we don't need a burned-up angel in it, too. We don't know where she went. She just wrapped herself up in her wings and had Scotty beam her somewhere."

Shemyazaz bared naked teeth in a wide, lipless rictus. "Get her back!"

"We can't get her back," I explained. "We don't know how she got here in the first place. She came, and she went. She's not here."

He spread his legs, lifted his arms, unfurled his ruined wings. The orbs strobed to black, then white. "I *want* her. I want her *here*. Bring her *to me*."

"We can't," I told him sharply, my own anger kindling. "Look, we've got no stake in whatever issue you have with her, but Greg just comes and goes. We can't call her; she's not in our phones. She just—appears."

Of a sudden he dropped into a crouch upon the hood. He leaned outward on two knees and one braced arm, then abruptly wrapped a hand around the back of my neck and yanked me toward him. His thumb sat on my Adam's apple, and I was pretty sure I felt a claw. Our faces were possibly three inches apart. He stared hard into my eyes.

It was the first time I'd smelled sulfur. Always before the

odor had been that sweetish, cloying fug, powerful incense like perfume on steroids. But those had been demons. Shemyazaz was an angel, and I'd never smelled anything of him in his burned form other than a faint charred scent. But this reek was—different.

Remi's tone was exquisitely conversational. "I think we're done here. Let's call it a night. *Gabe* doesn't know where she is, *I* don't know where she is, and *you* don't know where she is. Between the three of us knowin' a whole passel of nothin' much, we're not getting her back here. Gabe and I are, as Ambriel pointed out earlier this evening, pretty much as useful as tits on a boar-hog. So how 'bout you go off and look for her your own self, while we go along home to bed."

Yes, it *was* a claw at the tip of his thumb. I arrived at that conclusion because it pierced my neck. I released a low involuntary blurt of reaction. The charred but living fingers on the back of my neck tightened.

Remi took a step closer. "He doesn't know—"

Shemyazaz thrust his other hand into the air, showing the flat of his hand to Remi. He said nothing, but Remi stopped short. I did not think it was his decision. The orbs flocked around him, as if to keep him in place.

Again the angel stared hard into my eyes. I made certain to meet his and not do so much as move an eyelash. I don't know what Shemyazaz saw in my eyes, or whether Remi's recommendation had an effect, but he let me go. He smiled as he saw the trickle of blood, then shoved me away with a hard thrust of his hand against my chest. After two long steps backward I regained my balance, set a hand to my throat and coughed.

"I want her," the angel declared. "If you see her, take her for me. I will have her." He slid down off the truck, put his hand upon me again and once more shoved me back several steps. "Bring her. Bring her to me."

I stared right back at him. "I'm a fragile little flower, but the merest cannon fodder. How in the hell am I supposed to find a Grigori if the first and the highest of the *bene ha'elohim* can't?"

As Shemyazaz stared at us both, the key-in-the-ignition warning chime dinged over and over again.

"I want her," he repeated.

"We get that," Remi said tightly, "but we *don't know where she is.*"

Shemyazaz, clearly still furious and frustrated, pushed between us, knocked us aside in a petty show of dominance. Remi and I stared at each other briefly, both of us at sea, then turned to watch the broken angel walk out of the reach of headlights. He disappeared into darkness with streaking orbs in his wake.

CHAPTER TWENTY-SEVEN

Remi and I stood in the middle of the two-lane road staring after the now-departed angel. Headlights showed us asphalt, white paint, yellow paint, green pines gone black beneath the moon. Remi muttered something, went to yank the key from the ignition and shut off the unremitting chime, but he left the headlights on as he came back out to stand beside me.

"So," he said.

"So," I agreed.

He turned on his phone's flashlight app. "Let me take a look at your neck—" I lifted my chin. "—yeah, he got you. But not by much. Hurt?"

I held up a finger. "The angelic feather cut hurts worse." I blotted gently at my neck, but found only a smear of blood on my fingers. "So he wants Greg for some reason. Some very important, highly personal reason. And we have now been deputized to find her and bring her to him despite the fact we have no clue where she is or how to do this."

"Sounds 'bout right to me."

"It's the Arizona version of 'Hotel California,'" I said. "The whole checking out but never leaving thing. Because I am fucking confused by everything, and we *are* on a dark desert highway."

Remi scratched at the back of his neck. "Somethin' more to ask Grandaddy, I reckon. Not only about Cassandra and Ambriel, but *Shemyazaz* and Ambriel."

"What did Mary Jane call him—Yaz? Well, why doesn't good ol' Yaz just go look for her himself? I mean, not only is he an angel, while we quite obviously are not, but he's a Grigori! So is she."

"But he's fallen." Remi mulled that over a moment. "He's been in hell. Lucifer's pal, and all. Maybe he really can't find her. Maybe he's banned, in some way."

I snapped my fingers. "Bruno Mars."

"What?"

"Remember? When we first met him? He said that once. The Bruno Mars song. He's locked out of heaven."

Remi looked weary. "Maybe we are, too. Locked out of heaven, I mean. Ambriel has made it pretty damn clear we're good for nothin,' just little baby bugs on the windshield of life."

I shot him a glance. "That's—poetic."

"Let's go." He hooked a thumb toward the truck. "Let's go on, get back to the Zoo. Grandaddy ain't calling us, but that don't mean he won't pay us a visit. And anyway, we both need sleep real bad."

I agreed, turned to head back to the passenger side, stopped because Remi, staring beyond me, put a delaying hand on my arm. "What?" I asked.

"You seein' that?"

I turned, saw, emitted a drawn out *'uhhhh'* of baffled disbelief, then added, "That would be a yes."

Burton Mossman, aboard his red horse, came riding up the shoulder of the road going in the direction we'd just come from. The horse had an easy swing to his walk and a head that bobbed loosely. Mossman came up even with us, reined in.

"Pleasure to see you boys again," he said. "Thought you'd be gone by now."

Neither Remi nor I could say anything immediately, just stared at the ghost cowboy on his ghost horse. Finally I scraped together some form of reply. "There and back again . . . sort of."

Mossman nodded. "You boys seen any loose cattle hereabouts?"

I shook my head. "Only a loose angel."

"And a dog," Remi said, "Mangey ol' critter good for nothin.' You seen it? Screams his *heads* off."

Mossman shifted in his saddle. "More likely coyotes. Well then, if you've not seen any cattle, I will be on my way." He touched his hat briefly, clicked his horse into motion.

Remi and I watched him ride by and head on down the road's shoulder. He'd gone maybe ten yards when he and his horse faded away.

I stuck a finger into the air. "Remember when I counted off everything we'd seen today? The bit about the stalker-demon, Jack the Ripper, Cassandra of Troy, and so on and so forth? Then you added an earthquake?"

"I do remember that."

"We'd better add a burned-up angel and a rerun of the ghost cowboy and his ghost horse." I headed for the truck, climbed up inside. As Remi positioned himself on the other side of the console, I yanked the door closed and fastened the seatbelt. "I gotta say, my life was far less *interesting*, in the

Chinese curse sort of way, when I was in prison. And God knows there were some very, very strange people in prison. But none of them was a ghost."

Remi turned the engine over. "Or an angry angel."

"Or an angry angel."

It was around three a.m. when Remi and I pulled up behind the Zoo. Fortunately Ganji had given us keys, so I didn't have to lockpick my way in. I managed to trip over the threshold and jam my hip, which caused me no little trouble climbing the stairs. I should have let Remi go ahead of me, since I was delaying him up.

At the top landing he asked if I was going to be okay. I told him of course I was going to be okay—and then limped off to the bathroom to dig up some ibuprofen. I swallowed three, did my business, staggered to my bedroom. I dumped boots, got out of my jeans carefully, since it was my hip and the road rash bothering me, but I didn't bother stripping out of boxer briefs or t-shirt.

I'd told Remi I wanted to fall face first into my bed. Well, I was as good as my word. Except I was barely settling in with a long, loud, relieved sigh when my door got tapped by knuckles, pushed open, and my light was flipped on.

I rolled over, scowling. "*What?*"

Remi shrugged. He was still dressed, other than having a hatless head. "Mary Jane's not here."

I stared at him, rubbed my brow. The door to the common room had been closed; I simply assumed she was in there asleep on the sofa. "Well . . ."

"I wanted to see if she was settled in," Remi said—possibly leaving out something of a more intimate nature, but I didn't call him on it—"and she's not there. The sofa bed's pulled out and made up, her daypack's still there, but no Mary Jane."

"Check your phone."

"Did that. Nada."

I sat up, grabbed my phone on the nightstand, now fully charged. "Nope." I frowned at him. "No note, I take it."

"Not in the common room, not in the bathroom, not in the kitchen."

"Did you call Ganji?"

"No answer."

I sat up, hooked my legs over the bedside. "Mary Jane said something earlier about Ganji going up the mountain. Maybe he's still up there. Or maybe he took Mary Jane up there with him, to make sure she was safe." I rose, grabbed jeans, pulled them back on, and boots. "Let's go check his office back by the kitchen, see if there's a note."

We didn't make it as far as the office. Out front we found a couple of tables and a few chairs overturned, and the big door unlocked and standing open by several inches. We hadn't noticed it when turning onto the property because the door was only partially open, and hadn't noticed the overturned furniture because the stairway was back by the pool table alcove and we hadn't gone any farther.

"Oh, *nonono*," I murmured, dread rising. I went out the front door to check the porch and surroundings. Remi righted the tables and chairs, and searched the floor for some kind of note or other sign.

Ganji would have been here when the place closed down. All the tables and chairs would have been put in their places for the next day. This resembled some form of altercation, someone being taken through the chairs and tables against her will.

I hated to think of it, but I went through the bar area and into the back office, afraid of what I might find. But no bodies. After a quick check I wandered back out of the office onto the floor, where Remi was still checking corners. As he looked at me, I shook my head. "No Ganji in any shape or form, no note that I could find."

"Nor Mary Jane." Remi looked at the front door, which I had closed. "You know, it could be either of them."

"Either of who?"

"Jack the Ripper, or Shemyazaz."

"If the Ripper's a demon, he can't come in here. Or any of his little hell minions. But Shemyazaz?"

Remi nodded. "He wants Ambriel."

I realized Remi was hoping that was exactly what had happened, that an angel had taken Kelly rather than a demonic murderer who butchered women.

"Among other problems, there is this," I said. "I'd have no compunction about handing Greg over to Shemyazaz in exchange for Mary Jane, but we don't know where Greg is, how to find her, or how to prevent her from using whatever angelic power she has to stop us. For all I know, she could turn us into a pillar of salt."

"That was God."

"And Shemyazaz doesn't strike me as sane in any sense of the word."

Remi's tone was stark, devoid of emotion because what he felt was *too much* emotion: "If Jack the Ripper found a way to grab her, she's likely dead."

I knew that possibility was likely. "Would she have gone

home for any reason? She said she had no spare clothes. Might she have figured she'd just grab a ride-share home, stuff some clothes in a bag, come right back, only to get snatched?"

"Maybe so. But you don't usually upset tables and chairs and leave a door standing open if that's what you intend to do."

I nodded. "And she knows how dangerous it is. She's not stupid, like in the movies where the female protagonist ignores the hero's warning and walks right into a trap."

Remi was staring at the floor, thinking. "He would have had to send a human."

"Or a god."

Remi lifted his head, frowning. "What?"

"Ganji's here. Lily's been in here. Clearly gods can come and go at will. Now, Ganji and Lily are on our team, yeah, but that doesn't mean other gods aren't on Lucifer's team. In fact, I'm certain of it. Hades is here. Mythologies of multiple cultures are full of gods and goddesses who screw with people, even kill them. Look at what Apollo did to Cassandra just because she wouldn't sleep with him. And Hera was a dyed-in-the-wool royal bitch. In Egyptian mythology, Apep was the ultimate evil."

"How the hell are we supposed to deal with gods?" Remi asked. "Ambriel flat told us we couldn't."

"Ambriel told us we *shouldn't*," I clarified. "Ambriel, I get the impression, probably believes we're incapable of brushing our teeth. But I have an idea. Let's try to hunt down Shemyazaz. Either he's got her, or he doesn't, and if he doesn't he may be willing to help us rescue her from Jack the Ripper, *who*"—I emphasized it loudly to shut down his reply before he could make it—"isn't going to kill her right away."

"Why not?"

"Because my gut tells me he would rather have us living in

fear of what he might do to her, what he *will* do to her, and when he'll do it. We don't know who the woman in the latest picture is. He didn't write her name on the back; she could be anyone. But if he's got our Mary Jane Kelly, then he's got a *real* Mary Jane Kelly, and I think he'll want to keep this ugly, sadistic headgame going awhile." I pulled my phone. "You call Uber, see if they'll say whether they picked her up. I'll call Lyft, ask the same. Then we'll try taxi companies."

Remi shook his head. "They won't tell us anything because of privacy laws."

I smiled broadly at him. "My dad's a cop; I know what to say to sound convincing. You, on the other hand, can probably pull off being a Texas Ranger whose daughter ran away and he's handling this on his own. Be creative. Improvise." I paused a moment. "You learn how to be real good at that in prison."

CHAPTER TWENTY-EIGHT

While we both shied away from discussing whether it was Jack the Ripper who'd abducted Kelly, it was nonetheless a real possibility. So we called hospitals. I nixed calling the cops, though. Too easy to get tripped up. While the police wouldn't take a missing person's report yet, they'd want our contact info. And if we faked that, and if the worst happened and Kelly turned up dead, it would raise red flags about *us*. Anyway, they weren't about to tell us if they'd found a body. And since we still hadn't been able to reach Grandaddy we couldn't count on him to get us out of any official trouble.

Regardless, everything we tried came down to the same answer: No one knew a thing about Mary Jane Kelly. Neither rideshare nor taxi drivers, nor even logged contact. Which left us discussing our next steps.

"We should go up on the mountain," Remi said. "If it's Shemyazaz who has her, I'm betting he'd take her up there."

"Why up the mountain?"

"He's been two places in Flagstaff, that we know of: here at the Zoo, and the mountain. Ganji took him up there that first night—to calm him, he said, remember? And that's also where Yaz met Mary Jane."

"In the rain and hail." I nodded. "Good point. Plus if it's Jack, he'll find *us*, and that will be answer enough." I didn't even want to think about what the Ripper might do to Kelly if he decided to expand his game and keep her alive just to play with. "But we don't know where on the mountain Ganji may have taken Yaz. I think he said there are caves up there, didn't he? That would be ideal for hiding Mary Jane as well as himself."

"Plus we don't know where on the mountain *Ganji* is currently," Remi said. "But we know he walks to the foot of the mountain from here, so that's a starting point. I'll drive us as close as I can, and we'll hoof it from there."

"*Or* we can go back to the trailhead by the RV camp, go up marked trails to make it easier on ourselves, and *then* go off-trail to look for her. We went up that way when we met her."

He considered that and agreed. "I'll check maps online," he said. "It's an organized trail system—there'll be topo maps and others. The caves'll be marked."

I floated the suggestion that we wait until daylight but expected to be voted down. And was. Remi noted that sunrise was maybe three to four hours off, and not only could we get a good start if we left now, but the longer we waited the more danger she would be in. So we went rooting around in the Zoo to dig up whatever might prove helpful on a climb up the mountain at night.

We loaded ourselves with weapons, heavy-duty lanterns, a pair of belt-clip walkie-talkies—overkill, maybe, since we each had two phones, but cell phones have a habit of dropping calls—and grabbed jackets as well, plus found a modest gear bag and tucked into it as many first aid supplies as we could, plus a couple of water bottles and energy bars.

"Man, I wish we knew what could harm an angel." I tucked a couple of extra lantern batteries into my jacket pocket. "Which sounds hella bloodthirsty, but hey. Yaz is not all there, mentally, and he might well harm her without actually meaning to."

"You know—he could even be a relative."

In the midst of jotting down a note for Ganji, I didn't pay Remi much attention. "Who, Shemyazaz?"

"Yes."

"*Our* relative?"

"Have you forgotten the whole bit about us being the off-spring of celestial energy? So is he. Just a hell of a lot older energy."

I scribbled my name at the bottom of the note. "Well. I guess. Which is weird to think about. Are we related to *all* angels? Do they have spawning season? Hibernation? A school prom? Do we all climb out of pods, like Neo in *The Matrix*?"

"No, our little sparks got put into sickly newborns, remember? And I don't reckon our mamas considered themselves pods."

Dying newborns, which still left me feeling a little squicky. Grandaddy had been clear that the human-born infants would not survive, possibly not even last an hour, and that when the parents prayed for divine intercession, as nearly all of them did, those prayers were answered. They raised healthy infants to adulthood, and then we got conscripted into the heavenly host.

I pushed open the screen door. "I guess we're sleeper agents, too."

Remi followed me out. "What?"

"Sleeper agents. You said maybe some demons are here on earth just hanging out, waiting for the signal to go live. Well, you can say the same about us. Because you and I sure didn't know a damn thing about being heaven-born, or that we'd be called to arms, until a few nights ago. And now we're running around exploding black dogs, burning up cockroach-like demon remains with the dreadful power of our spit, and being yelled at by Switzerland."

Remi locked the door. His voice went high. *"Switzerland?"*

"Greg," I said. "Neutral, remember?"

"Oh. Yeah."

"Though the *least* neutral, neutral I've seen, hauling Cassandra off somewhere."

We piled all our extra stuff on the back seat floorboards, settled ourselves in, and Remi started the truck. "What was it she said, back at the chapel?"

"Who, Greg? Nothing particularly kind."

"No, Cassandra. She said something to you, remember? She went over to say goodbye, something about your skull not getting crushed in the near future."

"Oh." I frowned. "I don't know what she said. It was in Greek. I *think* it was Greek. Didn't sound Latin, I don't think." Hell, sometimes we heard Lily and Ganji in English, and other times in their own languages. Now Shemyazaz and Cassandra. Yet *another* question I had for Grandaddy. I think I was at twenty million, now. I tried to recall the syllables. "Something like *theeoy . . . gyno . . . allergies.*" I shook my head. "I got nothin'."

Remi turned onto Route 66. *"Eíhe oi theoí sas dósoun kalí gynaika, pollá paidiá áfthones kalliérgeies, ploúto, timí, sofia, omorfiá, kali ygeía'?"*

I shrugged. "No clue, dude. You lost me around four words in. Sounds a little like it, though."

"'May the gods bestow upon you a good wife, many

children, abundant crops, riches, honor, wisdom, beauty, good health.' It's an old Greek blessing, an *evlogía*. And so you are *makarios*. Blessed."

"Cool beans."

"Of course to be *makarios*, you have to be dead."

I snapped my head around to stare at him. "She wished me *dead?* What happened to no skull crushing?"

Remi waxed eloquent. "I think it's more like a pre-game blessing. You know, just in case something bad happens, like the star quarterback breaking his leg mid-game in the Super Bowl."

"That's a cheerful picture."

He shrugged. "Warriors were expected to die, and if they lived well and died bravely, the gods rewarded them. That's a consistent belief system throughout most cultures worldwide. I mean, Valhalla's a great example. And do you remember the Spartan saying?"

I did. "'Come back with your shield—or on it.'"

"So Cassandra is very aware that we're involved in a battle, on the cusp of something greater than ourselves. You 'did her a solid,' you might say, by finding her, taking her to safety. She's grateful. Gave you a blessing."

I nodded as Remi swung into the left-turn lane. "It's too bad Greg dragged her off so soon. I'd have liked to talk with her about which parts of Greek mythology are just that, myths, and which are partial truths."

I remembered the young woman who had emerged from the bruises, the blood, the swollen jaw. I remembered the pride, the certainty of what she knew, the frustration, even anger, that no one would believe her.

Cassandra could have prevented the Trojan War. Had Paris

believed his sister, had she not been mocked, been dismissed as "god-touched," as she put it, locked away, punished, raped . . . then the Trojan War might have been avoided. Helen would have remained Helen *of Sparta*, wife to the king, Menelaus, and perhaps never known to the modern world. No Agamemnon with his massive navy in the Aegean Sea, no Trojan Horse, no sacking of the city.

Would Heinrich Schliemann have found the ruins of Troy in 1870 without such a tale to drive multiple excavations? Would there have *been* ruins if Cassandra's warnings had been heeded? Certainly Homer's *Iliad* would have been substantially different.

But it was Greek *mythology*. Mythology in and of itself is not a foundation for actual history. Yet because of Schliemann's discovery, some now believed in a historical underpinning to the stories.

Hell, we were dealing with *angels*. Why wouldn't Cassandra tell the truth of Troy? Why wouldn't she be real? Like Robin Hood, like King Arthur . . . fictional tales of composite characters based upon kernels of historical fact. But truth in the tales.

Her icy blue eyes, as she held my hand and gazed at me, had been full of certainty. Of purpose. The woman had been given a gift, just as I had. I knew what I felt when my senses came alive to the world. It filled me up. It wasn't false.

She had given me her blessing. She had given me her trust. Cassandra was a woman who had been mocked, imprisoned. Trust, to the betrayed, is not something they do lightly. If she did it at all.

Remi drew me back to the moment. "If she could tell you— would you want to find out what lies ahead?"

I chewed at a lip as I thought about it. "I'm not sure I'd want to know what lies ahead. First of all, what she sees isn't completely reliable because it's in fragments. But I just think I'd rather take life as it comes."

The entrance to the parking lot was gated. Remi simply pulled up alongside the fence and parked; we could climb through the unbarbed three-wire fence. "But knowing in advance does allow you to put your affairs in order."

I looked at him. "Did you put your affairs in order when Grandaddy told you to come to Flagstaff with no prior warning—and no explanation why? I'm betting not."

Remi pulled the key, stared out the windshield as if lost in thought. Then he looked at me. "If I'd had any idea at all what we were comin' to, the least I'd have done is told my little girl goodbye."

The trail was still muddy in spots, the residue of the morning's hail and thunderstorm. Undergrowth and deadfall had kept the soil damp and, in some places, slick. The lug soles on my boots helped a great deal, but only until the channels got caked with mud. Then I was no better off than Remi in his smooth-soled cowboy boots.

I wasn't certain of the rules about hiking designated trails behind a locked gate, though I imagine if something happened we'd be legally liable.

Because the moon was full, we at first avoided using flashlights and lanterns. But without, it was more difficult to see some of the twists and turns. Once we got up higher, well above the parking lot and road and looking for caves, we'd go with artificial light.

We'd just reached the dual parade of immature oaks lining

the trail when sparks went off in my eyes. Bright flashes of light, and odd pinging pains accompanying each bright pin-prick. Opening my eyes wide or squinting made no difference. Colors were seeping in behind the flashes. Red along the edges, red bleeding in from the shadows. Red in its negative symbology.

I stopped short. In my mind, red was flowing like paint across the floor. Or blood.

I said, "Wait—"

But Remi didn't hear.

The pinpricks of white light strobed crimson, reminding me of the orbs that had accompanied Shemyazaz that night in the Zoo.

"Gabe? You coming?"

I blinked hard twice, then twice more. The red flowed away. No more pinpricks, no more flashes. The night was the night again, darkness mitigated by moonlight, not red paint or blood.

"Yeah." I frowned as I placed my boots more carefully. "Yeah, I'm good. Just—probably the altitude. Still." I was moving again, walking steadily behind Remi. "How long *does* it take to adjust?"

Remi turned his head to speak over his shoulder. "Guess it depends on how high. I know climbers at Everest spend something like thirty to forty days before they try to summit."

"But Everest is over twenty-nine thousand feet! This is, what?—seven thousand? You read up on all this stuff."

"Where we were when we met Mary Jane? About nine thousand. The taller peaks go up to twelve."

"Oh. Well, yeah. Maybe a few more days to adjust." I was out of breath already. "Makes me feel old."

A streak of red suddenly shot across my vision. Inside my

eyeball I felt something like a rubber band pop. It strobed white, then red. Another pop, and something like skin being peeled from the interior of my eyeball.

"Wait," I called. "Hang on a minute." I closed my right eye, stood motionless. With my left eye I watched Remi come back down the trail.

"What's up?"

"Flashes of light." I blinked hard again. I looked at Remi, widened my eyes, let the lids go back to normal. All was well once more. Normal. "Seems okay now. You seeing anything?"

"Nope. But if you need to, you can go back down. It might could be altitude."

"You go up, I go up. I go down, *you* go down. You don't get to do this alone. I know you want to see if Shemyazaz has her, but you're not going alone. We're not doing the movie thing." I put myself back into motion, actually passed him. "C'mon, let's go."

"We're not risking your vision."

I was in front of Remi now, blinking into darkness. "I don't think it's my eyes. I think I'm doing my thing. You know."

"Sensing something?"

"I've got to come up with a cool name for it. Like Spidey sense. Maybe something like angel vision. I could work with th—"

Red. *Red red red*.

I hesitated, blinded by red, nothing, nothing but *red-crimson-scarlet*. My balance was decaying even as I halted and spread my legs to adjust my center of gravity.

To my right were massive granite boulders. I could smell charcoal from old fires, wet mud, aged stone, stone that pressed

down upon me, though when I reached out to touch it nothing
but cool air met my hands.

"You okay?"

"It's like—" I grunted, gritted my teeth. "It's like an
overload—it's too much all at once, too bright, too *much*."

I reached for the turquoise, the yellow, the strength of a sacred mountain.

Red is *violence.*

Red is *war.*

Red is *hatred.*

Red is *suffering.*

I was nearly frantic from it. Never had I sensed this. Never
had the weight of it come down upon me.

"Ambriel." I sucked in a hard breath. "She said our gifts
hadn't manifested fully yet."

"And you think that's what's happening?"

"I don't . . . I don't know."

"Gabe?"

Danger.

Aggression.

Pain.

Murder.

Was Kelly dead? Had our Ripper killed his fifth? Was our
Ripper the original, or a copycat?

"Gabe?" I felt his hand on my upper arm. His fingers pressed
deeply into my flesh. "Gabe!"

"Red," I mumbled. "It's red . . . red . . . rum. Redrum.
Redrum."

Remi's tone was tight. "Is she dead? Is that what you're sensing? Gabe—is she dead?"

"Red room," I said. "Red room, red rum."

And then his voice wasn't tight anymore, but spilling fear and worry. *"Is she dead?"*

I sat down hard, because Remi made me. He just shoved me down and planted my butt on a felled tree. I looked up into his face, then shut my eyes, closed tightly, leaned down, curled my fingers deeply into my hair, elbows on knees.

Everywhere was red.

"Gabe—is she dead?"

"—the rivers . . . the rivers run red with the dead—"

"Gabe, you with me?"

"—blood and fire and billows of smoke—"

"Gabe!"

"'The sun and moon will be darkened, and the stars no longer shine.'"

I felt him then, felt him peeling one of my hands away from my hair. He uncurled rigid fingers, held them open, then filled the palm with something damp, something crumbly. He closed my fingers upon the substance and pressed them closed.

"Green," he said. "Green. All that is good of green, here in your hand. The green of the grass, the green of the trees, the green of new growth, of new beginnings. The green of health and of hope. Be at ease. Be renewed."

I opened my eyes and looked into my hand. Saw soil, and seed, and nothing at all of red.

"I don't know," I said. "I don't know."

"Don't know what?"

I looked into his face, saw a divided concern: for me, for Mary Jane. "I don't know if she's dead. But power is here. Power that doesn't belong. Power that profanes."

CHAPTER TWENTY-NINE

emi made me drink water, eat an energy bar. I told him I
felt fine, which was the truth, but he wanted me to stay put
a little longer. I tried explaining that this was not normal
for me, this was not what I felt when I opened myself to the
deeper workings of the world, but he came back around to
what I had brought up: Greg's statement that our abilities were
not yet fully realized, and thus we were 'weak' in whatever
power mature angels—*real* angels—could tap.

"So it could be two things," Remi declared. "Your super
powers are bleeding out around the edges of whatever blocks
them from full realization. Maybe they need more room.
They're gettin' squoze, so they're knocking at the door."

I couldn't help myself. "You do know 'squoze' is not the
past tense of 'squeeze." I paused. "Even if you are from Texas."

He shrugged. "Kind of like teeth."

I stared at him in astonishment. "*Teeth?* How did we get to
teeth?"

"You know. Baby teeth fallin' out to make room for the
adult teeth."

"Oh." Okay, that made a little more sense. Sort of. "So what
I felt, all the *red*, is an adult tooth coming through?"

Remi looked thoughtful, as if replaying the exchange. "Well, you know. Might could be. All those adult teeth fixin' to settle in and be what you've got the rest of your life, but they gotta make room for themselves."

I squinched one eye closed and stared up at him, expressing profound doubt. "What about you?" I asked. "You've got super powers, too. Are they starting to knock out your baby teeth?"

He considered that. "Well, I did sense Molly at NAU. There was no doubt in me. She poked her head around that door and I just *knew*, with everything in me. But I don't feel reliable yet. So I reckon I've got more baby teeth to get rid of."

"You know this is really stupid, don't you?"

"What is?"

"Using *teeth* as an illustration." I rose, tucked the empty water bottle into the gear bag. "Come on, let's start climbing again."

"I thought you needed to go down."

"No, *you* thought I needed to go down. But I feel fine. Tired?—yes. I haven't had a decent night's sleep for a couple of days and we've been . . . well, 'busy' is an understatement, but it will do. I think the altitude is getting to me. Anyway, let's go." I hooked the gear bag straps over a shoulder and headed out again.

We never made it to the caves. The higher we got, the more I was aware of flashes at the edges of my vision, little explosions of red, now intermixed with black. At first I just tried to blink it away, but a headache set in along with nausea. Apparently I started breathing like a bellows, but I was concentrating so hard on maintaining momentum that I didn't realize it.

Remi caught on and literally stopped me by standing in the middle of the trail, putting up both hands, and letting me walk into them.

I wasn't watching. Suddenly cowboy boots filled my field of vision and I bounced off Remi's hands and stiffened arms, staggered backward. He grabbed a handful of leather jacket and yanked me back before I could fold and do a sprawled, inelegant butt-plant on the ground.

"Whoa," I mumbled.

"Whoa," he agreed, and walked me backward to a pile of granite boulders. "Sit."

I sat, steadied myself with braced arms on either side of me. Under the moon everything was rendered black and white, like an old photograph.

"No red," I said. "No colors. Not like before." I thought about it. "Could throw up, though."

"How 'bout makin' that a 'no.'" Remi had squatted down before me, then thought better of it and scootched over a little. He turned on a lantern, set it on an adjoining boulder. "At least give me a warning before you spew." He peered into my face. "You look like the cheese fell off your cracker. So tell me a story."

"It's different," I said. I rubbed the back of my hand against my brow, felt perspiration. Not being an actual superhero who always hides his true condition, I didn't stint the details when Remi asked. "Headache," I said. "Upset stomach. Little shaky."

"But nothing like before?"

"No. A few flashes of red a bit ago, but that's all gone back to normal. I'm seeing just fine. It's kind of like when you're so hungry you've got a headache *and* upset stomach."

Remi's phone rang, which startled both of us. It was a

regular ringtone, though, unlike the familiar five tones from *Close Encounters* that played when the angel phones rang. His was something country, of course.

He answered, then shot bolt upright to his feet. "Mary Jane?—hang on, I'll put you on speaker." He did so. "You okay?"

"I'm okay. I'm fine." Her voice sounded unsteady, and we could hear noisy breathing. "It was Yaz. He took me to a cave, but Ganji found me and talked Yaz into letting me go. I'm coming down now. He didn't hurt me. Actually, I feel a little sorry for him. Anyway, where are you guys? Can you maybe come pick me up?"

I was puzzled. "She feels sorry for him?"

But Remi was just so relieved he didn't even try to answer. I was less relieved not because I didn't care, but because I was trying to keep my belly in line. "We're halfway up the mountain," he told her via speaker. "We thought—" He broke off, swore, repositioned himself to improve the signal. "We thought of the caves. We're right near a big ol' pile of granite formations, over by the oaks."

Park ranger Mary Jane knew the trails intimately. "Okay, I'm not far." Her tone had a weird echoey sound. She came around a turn in the trail and damn near fell over us. She looked tired, but then she hadn't had much opportunity to sleep, either.

Remi disconnected, too. They stared at each other for a couple of moments, both smiling, but they weren't quite to the point where I'd suggest they get a room. Hell, Remi was so polite he'd probably want to ask her father if he could kiss her on the cheek.

Kelly asked about Cassandra. "What happened with her? Is she okay?"

I thought back over the last few hours. "Long story." But then I frowned, remembering again how Greg had simply assumed Cassandra would go with her. I wish I had asked Cassandra why she was so willing. I'd told her she didn't have to go, that she could choose to stay, but there never had been any indication she truly considered it, that she wasn't willing to go.

Kelly sat down abruptly on the rock next to the lantern. She emitted a whooshing breath, stretched out shorts-bared legs and rolled her ankles in circles. "Tired." Then she rubbed at her temples. "Anyone got any ibuprofen on them?"

"We've got stuff from the bathroom." Remi squatted, unzipped the bag, fished out the bottle, tapped two tablets into his palm, handed them over and followed with the remaining bottle of water.

Kelly swallowed the tablets with a couple of slugs of water, nodded her thanks. "Now, who is this Ambriel person? He went on and on about *wanting* her—and I don't mean in the romantic way. He was angry. Frustrated. Mad about her, not at me. In fact—" she smiled faintly "—he actually apologized. Once his temper cooled, I think he regretted abducting me. Or, as he put it, *borrowing* me. He kept going off on tangents in a foreign language, and he wasn't clear in English, so I have no idea what he was so pissed about. He did say he wanted you to find this Ambriel, and then you'd trade me for her."

"Remi can tell you about Ambriel later." I figured they'd be spending a little more time together, while I crashed. As Remi bent to put down the gear bag, I gestured, caught it when he slung it to me. I dug out the ibuprofen and took a couple. Kelly handed me the water bottle, then winced in apology. Most of the water was gone. I waved the regret away. "'S okay."

"You two ready to go on down?" Remi asked. He studied

me more closely. "You good to go? We can stay put a little longer, if you want."

Kelly looked at me more sharply. "What's wrong? Did something happen?"

"Kinda." I shrugged when she kept staring at me. "We are complicated guys," I said, "with complicated stories and even more complicated explanations. More to come. But right now, yeah, I'd like to motivate out of here and go get up close and personal with my bed."

Remi reached down, pulled me to my feet as we gripped one another's wrists. My sore hip twinged, but I waved that away, too. Before anyone asked further, I said I'd walk it off.

When given the go-ahead to set out at the front of the line, Kelly fell into place, walking easily. As a park ranger she undoubtedly was very well acquainted with the mountains and trails, and certainly accustomed to the altitude. Remi put me in the middle, which I found annoying, but I understood why. Kelly may have been the one kidnapped by an ancient angel, but I was the one moving like I was older than God.

She checked her path, noted footing, then turned around to walk backward briefly. I was concentrating on my own footing, and Remi had the lantern—lighted, now, though I thought we were possibly getting close to false dawn. Down below, across the highway, the big cinder cone was beginning to brighten out of the blackness as faint light seeped over the horizon.

"You know—" Kelly began.

And then something streaked out of the foliage, knocked me hard into Remi so that we both went down, and when we got ourselves untangled enough to sort out what the hell had happened, Mary Jane was gone.

CHAPTER THIRTY

Remi scrambled up from the ground, literally leaped over my legs, and took off after Kelly. I sat up and pulled the phone from my pocket, tried Ganji. Tried him a second time when the call dropped out. Was very grateful when he answered.

"Is Shemyazaz with you? Are you still at the cave? Is *he* still at the cave?"

The light African accent was always pleasant to hear. "The angel is with me, yes. He has told me why he wants the other Grigori. 'Tis a tale."

"Look, something just grabbed Mary Jane." I thought maybe Yaz had changed his mind about using her for an exchange. I reached down, grabbed the gear bag and lantern. "Thanks, man. I have to go. I'll see you whenever." I disconnected, stuffed the phone into my pocket and took off after Remi.

I did not attempt to race down the mountain, which would have ended singularly badly for me, but I did indeed jog as much as possible without tripping over a root or rock and taking a header. The problem was, I didn't think Kelly's abductor had carried her away via the trail. My vague impression, muddled as it was, was that I was slammed into Remi and went down, that something grabbed Kelly and headed over raw terrain, eschewing the trail. Remi may have done the same, hoping to catch up. I cut corners where I could, but I was in no in shape to handle cross-country.

Had to be Jack the Ripper. Yaz was out of the picture. I seriously doubted other demons would be going after Kelly. She didn't mean anything to them. She had value for the Ripper.

Lantern light bobbed and swung as I made my way down, sliding now and then with so little grip left in my bootsoles. Remi in his slick-soled cowboy boots was likely having a much harder time. I was huffing hard, trying to catch my breath and very aware of an unhappy belly. And every time I jammed boots against the ground it reinforced the headache.

Then my phone rang, and I stopped, dumped the bag so I could pull the cell from my pocket. The screen flashed Remi's name. "You got her?" I asked urgently.

He was breathing hard. "She's gone. She's *gone*, Gabe! Tell me it's Yaz, okay? Let it be that son of a bitch burned-ass angel."

"It's not," I told him soberly. "I called Ganji. Yaz is at the cave. Has been."

"Oh, damn. Oh, dammit. It's got to be the Ripper. God *dammit!*"

"I'm coming down," I told him.

"I'm near the parking lot. That trail will feed right into it. Look for my phone's flashlight."

And then he was swearing again, and I didn't blame him. We had a human kidney in the freezer, and Remi had said the original Mary Jane Kelly in London was cut up worse than any of the preceding victims. I just hoped like hell Jack wanted to keep our Kelly whole for a while.

That set my belly to rolling again. I tucked the phone back into my pocket, grabbed up the gear bag, hit a jog once more. At the steeper sections I had to slow and lean back so gravity didn't tip me into a face-plant.

By the time I saw Remi's flashlight I had little left in the tank. Loose hair slapped against leather jacket, my uneven breathing was noisy even to myself, and my throat kept sticking to itself because I was sucking in air, swallowing, and shoving it right back out again.

As I arrived, Remi took one look and grabbed the gear bag. "Can you make it to the truck?"

I was hoarse, but got it said. "Just go!"

He went, and I went.

In the truck, as he threw it in gear and swung the big vehicle into a hard U-turn, he told me we were going straight back to the Zoo, and he was getting on the computer to see if he could get through to whomever in heaven sent us messages. Before he could suggest it, I was already on the phone to Grandaddy.

The message I left was not polite.

Remi did immediately head for the common room and the computer. I went in with him to drop off the bag, the lanterns. Both of us had mud smears on clothing and skin from being knocked to the ground by the demon. In the kitchen I grabbed bottles of water, took one in to Remi while I sucked down the other.

The sofa bed remained extended, made up for Mary Jane. Her daypack was on the floor by the side table. It just served to underscore how worrisome was the situation.

I left Remi to the computer, hit the bathroom and my bedroom to clean up, change clothes. I had little left; Cassandra
had disappeared wearing tee and jeans borrowed from me, and
I wore my other tee and jeans. This left me with a couple of
long-sleeved Henley pullovers and the many-pocketed black
BDU pants popularized through use by tactical units, or my
road leathers. I went with the BDUs, ponytailed my hair, went
back in to see if Remi had any news.

He heard me come in. His attention remained on the computer, but he brought me up to speed. "I can't get into the deep
web, the dark web, or whatever web it is heaven uses to contact
us. All the browsers just bring up the usual home tab screens.
But there's bad news on all of them." He swiveled the chair to
look at me. "Someone is burning places of worship again. And
it crosses denominations, as happened the other day: church,
synagogue, Mormon temple, a mosque, even a Quaker meeting house."

"Demons," I said. "Equal opportunity arsonists. And I'm
betting we know why: they're taking holy ground out of play.
No safehouses for us."

Remi nodded. "They can't enter; we know that. But investi-
gators are finding bits of highly incendiary Molotov cocktails
among the remains. Plus what's to stop surrogates from finding
actual human pyromaniacs? They'll do it for kicks, and they
can go two-steppin' right on up the aisles to set their fires."

I pulled one of the dining table chairs over closer, sat my
ass in it and sprawled. I was beat, and the headache remained
nagging background music. "It will take time to rebuild all
those structures, and they won't be consecrated—or whatever
is done with the various faiths—until they're whole and ready
for worship."

Remi looked thoughtful. "I wonder . . . any way to suggest to the preachers and priests, imams, rabbis, etc., to do whatever they do early?"

"Coming from us?—probably not. I mean, we could write letters, e-mail them, call them, but I'm betting that's the kind of thing that should be handled by those higher up the angelic food chain. Would you listen to a cowboy and a biker telling you to hold whatever rites and ceremonies are usually done? And, you know, claim to be kid angels with training wheels?"

Remi nodded. "And that may well be what's got Grandaddy so tied up. He's said we're not his only 'grandkids,' so to speak. Might could be he's travelin' hither and yon trying to sort things out."

"He took the Ripper's handwritten letter with him, so we can't even have it looked at by an expert. We can with the last photo he sent, though, because Jack wrote on the back of it." Then I winced, because the most recent photo was of Mary Jane Kelly. And that reminded me. "Picture's still in the truck." I pushed myself out of the chair. "Toss me your keys; I'll go down and get it."

Couple of minutes later I was tromping down wooden stairs, hanging on to the bannister. I exited under the back door bug light into the darkness, popped the truck locks, leaned into the back to find the photo and envelope. It was as I was doing that, with my ass hanging out in plain sight, that I heard the growling. Deep and low and threatening.

Oh, shit.

Frozen in place, I reminded myself that everyday ordinary dogs growled, not just Cerberus. Everyday ordinary dogs sometimes wandered randomly and might even show up behind a cowboy dancehall. Everyday ordinary dogs might be scavenging around the dumpster for scraps. And they might even feel they had a right to guard those scraps. Maybe even claim the dumpster itself as territory.

I made a giant leap for Gabekind up into the back seat and slammed the door behind me. Which naturally trapped me inside the truck, but I wasn't too proud to admit that I was not prepared to brave the dog-populated outdoors quite yet. Not until I at least put an eye on whatever beastie was nearby.

I called Remi and got voicemail, so I left a very brief message as I unholstered my revolver: *"Cerberus is out back. I'm in the truck. I'm not sure tempered glass is good enough against Hades's pet monster."*

As I disconnected, I reflected that I'd better do some research on gun suppressors, since I was pretty sure the local constabulary would not be thrilled to know there was gunfire at the Zoo *again*.

In general, except for some specialized models, silencers—suppressors—aren't effective on revolvers because of the gap between cylinder and barrel. Gap equals noise. And while I was somewhat of a gun specialist thanks to Grandaddy, I'd been in prison for eighteen months and had no clue what the manufacturers were up to. The Russian Nagant was out there, but I didn't know if anything had been done with the Taurus line.

Of course, last time I shot Cerberus it hadn't fazed him.

Well, hell. How do you get rid of a mythological but apparently *real* three-headed monster dog who couldn't be killed by bullet or knife blade, even specially treated? I was pretty sure the earthquake had sent him heading for the hills last time. But I was also pretty sure my angelic spit would not summon a quake.

My phone rang. Remi wanted to know if Cerberus was still there. Because, he said, he'd actually grabbed a machete from Lily's armory and wiped it down with holy oil.

Huh. Decapitation might work. But. "Are you good enough to lop off *three* heads at the same time?"

"I don't know if I'm good enough to lop off *one* head," he answered, "but it might could be a tad more effective than bullets and knives that do no damn good against him. Anyway, I'm headin' for the door. I have an idea, but you won't like it."

"Let me guess—you need me to play bait."

"Well, I can't really get at him if he's tryin' to dance with me."

I dropped an expletive. Remi said he understood my feeling that way.

So I stuck the key in the ignition and turned it over far enough to work my window. I lowered it a third of the way down and placed my right leg on the seat with my knee bent under me, and my left leg braced against the floorboards, gun at the ready.

I saw the porch light blink off and on to let me know Remi was heading out the door. I released a noisy breath, muttered, "Praise the Lord and pass the mashed potatoes," then banged around inside the truck in hopes of attracting a monster.

The dog shot out from behind the dumpster, jumped up against the truck door, bounced on his heavily muscled hind legs, and licked the truck window with a giant tongue.

One, and only one, big tongue.

"Well, *you're* not Cerberus," I said from behind the window.

The dog continued bouncing and licking glass, anointing it with substantial swipes of saliva. He was a big, muscled, steel-gray male, crop-eared and huge-headed, with a long, whippy, madly waving tail and large die-for-you brown eyes.

I stuck the gun back in my holster. The dog whined at me through glass as his tail beat the air. I opened the door slightly, intending to work my way out with heavy boots first. The dog stuffed his big nose into the crack, followed up with his massive head, and shoved the door completely open.

Then he politely sat down in the dirt and stared up at me, waiting for God knows what.

I heard the screen door and saw Remi come out with the machete. The dog twisted his head on a thick neck to give the interloper a quick examination at distance, then turned back to stare at me. Again with the eager waiting.

"I am fresh out of dog cookies," I told him. He continued waiting anyway.

Remi ambled up, machete dangling. "Looks like you caught yourself a big bad pit bull."

The big bad pit bull just grinned at me and raised a duststorm out of dirt with the power of his tail.

Remi smiled slow. "Or maybe he caught you."

CHAPTER THIRTY-ONE

said, "He looks too nice to be a stray."

Remi just looked at me, expression utterly bland, brows raised slightly.

I felt wholly justified in my defensiveness. "Well, he does."

Remi still just looked at me, expression neutral and brows raised a little bit higher.

I, on the other hand, scowled. I recognized the expression, the classic *I know what's coming.* "Look," I said. "I'm not leaving him out here to maybe get hit by a car on Route 66. Tomorrow morning I'll find the animal shelter, take him in to see if he's microchipped."

Remi lifted one empty hand and the machete, body language all hands-off, no argument. "Fine."

I scowled a little harder. "Why are you acting like a parent?"

"I'm not acting like a parent. I'm acting like a guy who's got no dog in this hunt—" And of course he smiled broadly, the asshole, "—and has no comments on the matter." And then the smile fell away as he saw the envelope in my hand. "You found it."

I hesitated until he extended an open hand, then gave it to

him. His expression was no longer neutral. Probably mine wasn't either.

Remi headed back to the door. I looked down at the pittie and found bright canine welcome in his expression. I told him he could come along but just for the night.

He laughed at me. He did it silently, but he laughed at me. I could see it in his wide, upturned mouth and bright eyes.

Someone was missing him. I knew it.

Inside, I went through to the restaurant kitchen to find a metal bowl, filled it with water. I had no proper dog kibble, but did carve him off some cooked chicken breast I found in the big industrial fridge, cut it up into smaller chunks. He might have found plenty of scraps around the dumpster, but I wasn't taking any chances.

I turned to find a good spot in the kitchen to set out food and water and found the pit sitting politely. He had a big white splotch from belly to chest, tan points on his cheeks and legs, and the rest of him was a blued-steel color. The brow wrinkles twitched as he looked from the bowls to my face, and back again. He was fit and sleek. He did not have the heft and height of a mastiff breed, but I was betting eighty pounds of solid dog.

"Someone," I said, "has trained you very well, and I'll bet they are missing you something fierce right now."

I stuck both bowls down on the kitchen floor for him. He waited. I told him he could eat, and he dove in with tail waving. I made myself a chicken and mayo sandwich, then wandered back into the bar to grab a beer and headed to a booth. I half collapsed into it, took stock of my condition. Headache, check. Belly ache, check. Aching joints, check. Road rash and bruises, hell yes.

The beer tasted bad. The sandwich tasted bad. I pushed

both aside, stared blankly at the table a moment and realized in my head I heard my own voice saying, "*—red rum red rum—*"

It was considerably easier to just slide down sideways and end up flat on my back in the booth, legs hanging out and feet on the floor. Which is where I stayed until the dog came out, sat down close and rested his massive head on my knee.

I pulled myself upright. "Okay. Yeah, you probably need to go out. C'mon."

As I crossed the floor to the back, I realized the mud dried into the channels of my lug soles was falling off in little clumps. Well, I'd poke around looking for a broom once the dog's business was finished.

I opened the back door, the screen door, stepped out as the dog pushed by me into the watery yellow light. But I stopped short, because lying on the abbreviated back porch was yet another manilla envelope.

I made several pungent, vulgar comments about Jack the Ripper, bent and picked up the envelope. Much as I wanted to, I couldn't ignore it. I also couldn't just hand it to Remi without viewing it myself.

I planted my butt on the edge of the porch, legs propped against dirt. I used the KA-BAR to slit open the envelope, then dipped inside to grasp and pull the photo free. Purposely I looked at the back first, to read the message and put off a little longer looking at the image.

Jack's message was written in long-hand. He'd given up on letters clipped from newspapers and magazines.

'Anyone. Anytime. Anywhere.'

My stomach did a slow roll. I remembered too well the image of the woman he'd killed in Mary Jane's place. He had said the order didn't matter.

The dog came back from his outing, pleased to find me down on his level. He snuffled at me, pushed a nose into my free hand, snuffled more. I ran a hand over his big head. "Okay, guess I'd better take a look."

I turned it over. Mary Jane Kelly. Our Mary Jane.

She was seated in a plain wooden chair facing the camera. She was clothed, thank God, but buckled into some kind of harness on her upper body. Her arms were crossed, wrists fastened to the harness up high by her shoulders. Ankles were in leather cuffs and buckled to the chair legs. She was gagged. Her eyes, as she stared out of the photo, were absent the bright sparkle I'd grown used to. They were dark. Lost. The visible portion of her face was drawn. She did not appear to be drugged, but terror lay in every line of her body, in the stark contours of her face.

She was whole. She was unbloodied. She was alive.

Behind her stood a man dressed in black, in a coat I recognized from readings as a Victorian-era greatcoat, a long wool garment with a short cape and heavy cuffs, buttoned from throat to knees. These days it was considered steampunk style. He wore a black top hat. One gloved hand he rested on Kelly's shoulder; in the other was a short-handled, narrow, long-bladed knife, one edge held against Kelly's throat.

In place of his face was a mask. The white Guy Fawkes mask with thin upward-curved black moustache, trimmed goatee; eerie, compressed cat-got-the-canary smile; slits for eyes, and arched black brows. I'd seen it featured in the movie *V for Vendetta*. I'd always thought the mask downright creepy.

The dog sat, placed his head on my knee. I stroked his head, then leaned down, rested my forehead against his broad skull. I wasn't one for talking to God—I'd been an agnostic throughout my adult life, though those foundations were now eroding—so I talked to the dog.

The screen door creaked open behind me. Remi said, "Another one."

"Yup." I sat up, handed him envelope and photo over my shoulder. "She's alive and appears unharmed. The message does not threaten her, does not make promises about what he might do to her. It's a warning about *other* potential victims."

Remi's posture was rigid as he viewed the photo.

I tried to offer some form of reassurance. "Demented as this sounds, I actually count it a good sign for Mary Jane. He has her, he's made his point. We saw the photo of what he did to that other woman in Kelly's place, but he *hasn't* done it to Mary Jane. The impact was made with that other photo. There is no need for him to kill her, now." At least, not in the same graphic manner, but I didn't say that.

Remi disagreed vehemently. "Sure there is. Just to *do* it. You said these are chaos demons. They just do whatever they can to mess with us. Don't matter what."

"Yes, but this guy—*this* demon—doesn't strike me as being like the others. The Molly-demon's just teasing us. It's annoying, but not dangerous. Not physically harmful."

"So far."

"So far. Now, we're to assume Jack is also Legion, the demon in a woman's form who damn near got into my pants our first night here. But she, he—whatever—didn't try to hurt me."

"She tried to stab you, then *strangle* you."

True enough. "Well, there is something we need to do. We need to somehow make a buffer around this place, like we did with the Holy Dove chapel."

"You want to consecrate a *dancehall*? Make it the High Holy

Temple of Taxidermists, or some such fool thing? Besides, demons can't come in."

Patiently, I said, "I would just like to be able to *enter or exit this place* without worrying if demons are lying in wait right outside the door. They don't have to be *inside* to attack us. But every time we walk out to your truck or my bike, we're vulnerable. I mean, yeah, they can go at us elsewhere. But knowing we have one spot in the world where we can rest our heads without fear of attack would ease the mental load, you know?"

After a minute, he said he reckoned that was so. Then, "You look pitiful as a three-legged dog."

I squinted up at him.

He translated. "You look like shit."

"Truth in advertising." I pushed myself to my feet, grabbed a post to keep myself there. "I think I am pretty much done for the day, and the day isn't even started."

Remi opened the screen door. As I stumped in past him, he invited the dog as well. "Come on, son. We've got to get you sorted out."

By way of the bannister I practically hauled my body up the stairs, made it as far as the common room. Remi had folded the mattress frame back into the sofa bed. I took that as permission to collapse on it and put my head back to stare at the wood-beamed ceiling. The pittie got up beside me and dropped like a boat anchor onto the cushions.

I patted him. "Either you're allowed up on the furniture at home, or you're writing your own rules here hoping we won't catch on."

Remi returned to the computer, sat down with the photo. "Dog hair never hurt anyone."

"Unless you're allergic."

"Are you?"

"Does it look like it?"

"You're not. I'm not. 'Nuff said about that. Besides—" I was learning his pauses, so I waited for it, "—dog hair is a condiment."

I grinned, stroked the pittie's big head. He lifted that head, stared hard at me, and whined. Then he stood up, leaned close to sniff my ears and eyes, and whined. His brown eyes were telling me something, but I couldn't translate.

He whined again, waited for something, then jumped down from the couch and went to Remi sitting in the task chair. Remi was busy on the computer and just patted the dog absently a couple of times, went back to the keyboard.

The pittie emitted a huge, deep bark, shoved hard at Remi, then came back to the couch. There he barked right into my face and damn near shattered my eardrums.

Remi rotated the chair toward me and frowned. "You gotta slow your roll, dog."

I smiled, then stopped. My heart thumped hard. Oh *shit*. "Something's wrong . . . Remi, something's—"

And I was gone. Lost in a wash of red, rising like a tsunami.

"Gabe?"

Something's wrong.

CHAPTER THIRTY-TWO

—drowning—
  —drowning—
  Down.
  Down.
  Down.
  And everywhere was red.

I take anyone. Any time. Anywhere.
    I was aware of sound, but it was muffled, distorted. Pressure in my ears, in and out like someone breathing inside my skull. Breathing inside my *brain.*
    Too much color. Too much sound. The hairs stood up on my arms. My skin ached. Muscles twisted on my bones.
    I tried to speak, tried to make words. All were absent.
    Every one. Every time. Every where.
    My mouth moved, but no words, no words.
    I opened my eyes, saw the rush of everything surging toward me. Upside down. Rightside up. Sideways and inside out. Taking me down, down. Down.
    Every thing. Every one. Every where.

Shivering.

I smelled pine, I smelled food, I smelled aftershave, dog, mud, leather, alcohol. I smelled myself. Every *molecule* of myself.

Too much. Too much everything.

Voices.

The first voice, to another: Sharp and deeply concerned, underscored with a note of rising anger: "Is this what it is, his so-called gift? Gonna be like this for the rest of his life? Because Grandaddy never said anything about this. Not like *this*. Ambriel warned us. *She* did, not Grandaddy."

Hands were on me, bending me down, bending me over.

The second voice, to me: Deep tones, slow and soothing, unperturbed, an African accent. "Let it go. Let it go. Rid yourself of it." Large hand on my forehead, another on the back of my head, holding me in place, holding me up. I was bent over the broad hand on my chest. "I have you. You are in the hands of a god. Let it go."

Involuntary tears ran from my eyes, dripped off my face. My belly heaved and heaved.

"Is that *blood*?" the other person asked.

"Purge it," said the deep voice. A hand smoothed my hair. "This Orisha tends you."

"Do I need to call 911?"

"This is not enough blood for hospitals. From the throat; the small vessels have broken."

Little by slowly, the heaving of my belly settled. Residual quivers startled a blurt from me, but it seemed the worst was over. The palm of a very large hand smoothed hair over the crown of my head.

Of the other person, he asked for a damp towel and an ice-pack.

Ganji. That's who it was. And Remi.

"Anything for him to drink?"

"Bring water, yes. We'll see if he's ready."

I realized then that I had *let it go* all over the floor. The taste in my mouth was vile. I spat, spat again. Felt the tremor in my muscles. I reached up and tapped a hand. Tapped it a little harder when he didn't let me sit up at once. Then he placed a big hand across my chest, lifted me upright. I fell back against the couch.

The interior of my head was banging like a bell clapper. My belly seized, and I thought I was on the verge of vomiting again. Happily, it was a non-starter.

Remi came in with water bottle, washcloth, something wrapped in a hand towel. Ganji limited me to two sips to swallow after spitting again. I managed to wipe my mouth and face with the damp washcloth, then was urged to put my legs up regardless of boots, stretch out with my head on the couch arm. Ganji arranged the wrapped icepack on my forehead. I closed my eyes, held the icepack in place with one hand. The other I let fall across my chest.

"You are well," Ganji told me. If anything, it sounded more like a command than an observation. "You are clean of it."

I remembered him speaking so soothingly to Shemyazaz as the broken angel stood atop the bar weeping for his lost beauty.

I was cold, I was hot, I was utterly enervated. "What—?" I took a breath and tried again. "What was that? What the hell?"

Remi squatted as he dropped a big towel over the splashes of vomit, cleaned it up. "I got no idea," he said, "but you were spoutin' off about red again, and *red rum, red death.* I don't know what the hell it means, but you clearly have a fixation with the color."

I had to start twice to get my voice working. "It's what I'm seeing. Usually it's more colors . . . not just one." I hitched myself up on one elbow, asked for more water. This time Ganji let me have *three* slugs of it. So generous. I lay down again. "Color symbology is complicated." I barely recognized my voice. It was hoarse and cracking, and my throat felt bruised. "In folklore, in various cultures, every color represents multiple aspects."

"That is so," Ganji agreed. "I have my colors, special to me, and patterns. Nine beads in two of brown, one of red, one of yellow, one of blue, one again of yellow, one again of red, and two again of brown, you see."

I swallowed painfully. "In the white man's culture, red can be hearts on Valentine's Day. Or anger. Rage. Negativity. To me, in my head, the colors are actually tangible. Remember you grabbing up soil and grass and pressing it into my hand? Telling me it was green and therefore good?"

Remi nodded. "I wasn't sure you heard me."

"I did. And it was the right thing to do. But remember—Lucifer is often depicted as a red creature." I cleared my throat, winced. "And red is also blood. We say 'bad blood' about a feud, people disliking one another. 'Seeing red' is anger. But blood saves lives. Red is Christmas. Red is Santa." I smiled. "Red is sexy lipstick."

"And the red death?"

"Sure." I waved a hand, dropped it back. Closed my eyes. "Edgar Allen Poe's story, 'The Masque of the Red Death.' The Red Death was plague. It walked through rooms killing people with a touch."

"Red rum?"

I cracked an eye. "You ever see *The Shining*, with Nicholson?"

"Sure—oh! *REDRUM*. Murder spelled backward. The kid writes it on the door."

I took the ice pack off my forehead, tucked it beneath my neck. "Obviously my associations are with the bad aspects right now. And for some bizarre reason, movies and literature."

"So, you think this is tied in with your abilities getting stronger?"

I looked at Ganji to see if he had any ideas.

He shrugged. "It is not my world." He tapped his chest. "Not my heart, but yours."

I sighed and scratched an eyebrow. "If it *is* my abilities getting stronger, I wish my subconscious would pick a neutral color. A *happy* color. Like yellow!" I eased my way into a sitting position, nodded my thanks at Ganji. He smiled back, said he would return with a special thing for me, something that pleased him as a god and would set me to rights. Perhaps the beads, in his specific pattern.

Remi stepped out with the soiled towel, then returned. I rubbed my forehead. Sweat was drying. I actually felt semi-human again. "Thanks for that." Still croaky. I looked around. "What happened to the dog?"

"He's locked in the bathroom."

"Why is the dog locked in the bathroom?"

"Apparently he felt that dog slobber would fix you right up. He wanted to lick you in the midst of—everything. He kept interrupting and getting in the way."

Ah. Good decision. "Well, I sure hope he hasn't eaten the toilet."

"I checked on him. He was lying in the bathtub."

"He's *in* the bathtub?" I waved a limp, dismissive hand. "Never mind. He's going to have to vacate, though, because I want a shower. When I can maybe walk again. Holy crap. That was something I don't ever want to experience again." I drew in a deep breath, blew it out on a gust, which I regretted because my throat was really sore. "Add this to the list of topics we gotta bring up with Grandaddy. Because we need to know what *you'll* be going through."

Remi looked taken aback. "Here's hoping it's not like this!"

Ganji came back in. He handed me a bottle of beer. "Drink up!"

I gazed at the bottle a moment, blinking, then assumed a neutral expression as I looked at him. "This is the 'special thing'?"

"Beer and beef!" he said. "Vastly satisfying. Superb offerings for a god. I will cook you steak tomorrow, prepared my way." He patted me firmly on the shoulder. "Have the beer. Always do the drinking of the beer." And then he departed the room.

Remi and I exchanged blank looks. Abruptly, he went to the computer and sat down, typing. After a moment I heard a blurt of surprise. He swung around, grinning widely. "Aganju the Orisha is said to prefer beer and beef . . . and often he eats the bottle afterward."

"He eats the *glass bottle*?"

"That's what it says."

I examined the beer. "The eating of the glass bottle is not going to happen. But I will do the drinking of the beer."

I showered. Hung on to the curtain rod the whole time, too. No way it would hold me if my balance decamped, but the psychology of *knowing* it was right there, that I could *touch* it—well, just no accounting for the brain. The dog, whom I'd allowed in because he scratched at the door incessantly, kept pushing his head into the shower curtain trying to move it out of the way. I would squirt water at him, yank the curtain closed, and then we did it all over again.

Went to bed. Was too tired to insist the dog stay on the floor, so he grabbed half the bed. I woke up a few times, registered that it was daytime, which confused me. My brain was convinced it was the middle of the night. I was cold, I was hot. I shivered, I sweated. The dog licked my face intermittently, stuffed his blunt muzzle into my armpit, or nibbled on my chin.

Then someone tapped on my door. Remi opened it, put his head in.

One look at his face, and I knew the news was bad. "Picture?"

He nodded. The color was out of his face.

I had to ask it. "Is she dead?"

For a wonder, he shook his head. As I shifted into a sitting position with my back against the headboard, one hand blocking the dog, Remi stepped in and handed me the photo. "Leastaways, she was alive when he took the photo. Can't swear to it now."

The photo was of her head only. Her hair had been hacked off, presumably with that nasty knife in the prior photo. It was all tufts and streamers. Deep circles underlay her eyes. She was conscious, but clearly in shock.

Remi's phone rang. He frowned at the screen, stepped away from me as he answered. He listened, said 'Yes' a couple of times in a puzzled tone of voice, followed by astonishment. He swung around sharply and looked at me, even though his mind was clearly still on the telephone conversation.

When he disconnected, he said, "She's at the hospital! My name and number's in her phone. They couldn't reach anyone else. Said I could see her."

"Okay." I peeled bedclothes back, swung my legs over.

Remi was startled. "You don't have to come."

"Yeah I do." I pushed myself up, suppressed the winces and grunts I wished to make. Flapped hands to urge him out of the room so I could get dressed. "What's to say he won't try for you next?"

"All his victims have been female."

"That could change," I pointed out.

Remi scowled at me. "And you'll do what, exactly, if he does come after you? Throw up on him?"

Had to admit, the image was—colorful. She was alive, she was safe, and on the crest of extreme relief there was room now for irony. "Heavenly spit works, and heavenly breath. Maybe heavenly barf will eat up all the roach bits so he can't reconstitute."

CHAPTER THIRTY-THREE

Clean clothes, huzzah and hallelujah. Shoulder holster, KA-BAR knife, Bowie, extra warded rounds tucked into a pocket; revolvers don't have clips, so it's loose ammo unless you go with a speed strip or loader. Possibly a good idea when wearing a jacket, but bulkier than semi-auto magazines if you want to stuff them in jeans pockets. I threw on my jacket because of the holster harness.

The dog followed me out of the room. The dog followed me everywhere. I met up with Remi in the common room where he was once again on the computer.

It was 8:30 p.m. My brain swore it was 8:30 in the morning. I wasn't sure I'd ever get the space/time continuum straightened out again. I felt like I'd been shot through a wormhole.

"Anything new?" I asked.

Remi gusted a laugh. "*Oh* yeah. There's a rodeo in town, and one of the bulls staged an escape. Guess they are chasin' him all to hell and gone out in the sticks. But he's a smart old boy, and he's using the terrain to his advantage."

"Can't be *that* hard to catch a bull. I mean, they're cows."

Remi's drawl was pronounced. "Uhhh-huh. Your vast knowledge of All Things Rodeo teach you that?"

"Seriously! I've seen cows at the state fair."

"Seriously. Some are mean suckers, and particularly good at figurin' ways to get around humans." He rose, bent over to finish the shutdown sequence on the computer. "At any rate, no angel stuff. But I did read up on the arson fires. No leads yet beyond knowing the accelerants. No claims of responsibility. But this is the second batch of places of worship burned down, and we have to assume this will continue. Because it *is* all about the surrogates getting rid of holy ground." He straightened as the computer shut off, popped me on the shoulder as he walked past me. "Let's hope Mary Jane can give us some insight into this asshole, whether he's playing at being Jack the Ripper, or he *is* Jack the Ripper."

I followed. "Isn't it past visiting hours?"

"They said we could see her. And anyway, we need to ask her some questions." Remi put his hat on. "She may not be up to it quite yet, but doesn't have to be tonight. Just sooner, I hope, than later. Let's vamoose."

The stairs were wooden and a little slippery and dogs can't generally reach bannisters, so Remi and I nearly got bowled over when the pittie came scramble-sliding down the stairs behind us. He splatted on the floor as we watched and winced, but bounced right back up again, grinning and wagging as he accompanied us to the back door.

"Uhh," I said. "I think *he* thinks he's coming."

Remi considered. "We leave him here, he might eat the tables. We take him with, he might eat my truck."

"He didn't eat the toilet last night. Or my bed. When he applied teeth to anything, he just nibbled on my chin."

"I thought you were going to take him into a shelter to get him scanned for a chip."

"Hello? I was in the throes of the red death and red rum and red everything last night, remember? I'll get it done tomorrow morning."

Remi opened the door. "Uh-huh ."

"I will. He's too nice a dog to be a stray. Someone's missing him."

The dog was allowed all of the back seat, and not once during the entirety of the drive to the hospital did he attempt to eat Remi's truck. He just stood with his front legs braced on the console between the front seats, panted a lot, and dripped saliva everywhere. Including down our arms.

"Sliming is not eating," I pointed out, wiping at my jacket sleeve.

Remi shot me side-eye. "And dog smears on windows is nose art."

"Yes."

Remi was required to show ID at the nurse's station in order to get clearance to see Mary Jane. He did inquire as to whether she had family already there or coming, and was told family lived across the country and it would be another day before their arrival. Boss and co-workers planned to come the next day, but until then, he and I were it.

The nurse would not address Kelly's injuries with us, which made sense; that was a family matter. Stable condition, lightly sedated, monitored. Sleeping, mostly. That was all the intel we were allowed.

So as we walked into the two-patient room, we found the first bed empty and Kelly in the other, next to a large window. The view of the Peaks at night was mostly black silhouettes against stars, but I knew the daytime panorama of brilliant blue skies, bright sun, rich green-and-gold slopes. Unfortunately what I mostly associated with the mountains was a demon-possessed mountain lion, a broken Grigori angel, African volcano god, park ranger, two guys still fumbling their way around the End of Days. And Jack the Ripper.

Typical hospital room: bedside hosted a couple of rolling machines featuring blinking, bouncing lights, with leads running to Kelly under the top sheet; orders written on a whiteboard; IV cath and tubing. Her head was bandaged, all wrapped up in white gauze. She slept. Dark patches discolored the fragile flesh below her eyelids and lashes, and her bottom lip was swollen. But otherwise her face, though pale and hollowed with fine bones more in evidence, showed no injury. She did have bruises on her wrists and forearms from being harnessed. But if the Ripper had used his knife anywhere besides shearing her hair away, the sheet and thin blanket hid the results.

Having seen the photo of what Jack had done to the prior victim, I counted this a win. Kelly was damn lucky.

Remi moved close to her bedside. He removed his hat, held the brim in both hands at belt-level. "Hey," he said quietly.

I let Remi take precedence and stayed back from the bed. I couldn't help but think that Mary Jane Kelly might actually blame us for allowing her to be abducted. Supposedly she was in our care, but first Shemyazaz dragged her out of the Zoo to a mountain cave, and then Jack grabbed her on the way down while she was in our company.

I found I much preferred it when the only ones at risk, the only true targets, were Remi and me.

"Hey," he repeated.

She moved her head slightly, made a small sound. After a

moment her eyes blinked open, slowly focused. She swallowed, licked her lips, swallowed again.

In that moment, seeing a woman I actually knew on the receiving end of a demon's demented appetites, in the battered flesh and not in imagination, I realized the enormity of the burden laid upon us. Not to resent it, to deny the concept, but to *understand* it, to grasp the deeper implications. Remi and I running from demons, ghosts, and beasts? Not what we ever imagined, certainly not what we wanted to do, but according to Grandaddy we were literally *made* to do this. Spark, glob, fart, a celestial Petri dish of heavenly cells, whatever. We were bred for it, born for it, raised for it, trained for it. But Mary Jane Kelly wasn't. And she and all the other ordinary humans were exactly what Ambriel warned they would be: collateral damage.

We were not ordinary humans. We were of the heavenly host, and expected to do our duty, whether we liked it or not.

Lucifer wanted the planet for himself. The angels wanted the planet for humans. The devil didn't care who or how many he killed. The angels did—but people would die anyway.

Whether Jack the Ripper from the 1880s was a sleeper demon in human drag, or a human born an ordinary but evil man, he'd carved up people then, and he carved up people now.

'*Call me Legion,*' he'd told me that first night outside the Zoo while wearing a woman's form, '*for we are many.*'

'*Call me Iñigo Montoya.*'

Maybe Ambriel was right. Maybe Remi and I really *weren't* ready. Maybe Grandaddy should have waited to deploy us, should have trained us longer. Made us *better*.

But the world had cracked open and hell belched demons. You field whatever army you can in such circumstances. Maybe all of the newbies like Remi and me were, in military parlance, the 'forlorn hope,' the band of soldiers undertaking a suicide mission for the good of the army. But someone had to be. And sometimes that forlorn hope made the battle winnable against seemingly insurmountable odds.

Kelly's eyes were clearing. She saw me, but vaguely, I thought; true focus came when she looked at Remi.

She swallowed heavily. Her lips parted. Her voice was weak, but the words were decipherable. "He wants you," she said, "and he's going to have you."

I moved close to the bed. "Why us? Why us specifically?"

"He said . . ." She was clearly fading, blinking long and slow. "He said he picked you in the fantasy draft."

Remi and I were quiet on the drive back to the Zoo. The dog, who had not eaten any part of the truck but *had* created much imaginative nose art on the insides of all the glass, took advantage of the half-lowered window behind me to catch scent upon the breeze as we drove. Eyes slitted, tongue hanging, the loose skin of his mouth and cheeks flapped. He looked ridiculous—and ridiculously happy.

It was about 10:00 p.m. when we rolled in. The parking lot was emptying, as the kitchen closed at 9 p.m. Ganji had promised to cook me a steak, but I wasn't really in the mood for a big slab of meat. Remi took the truck around back, pulled it close to the sodium light hanging on the old telephone pole, shut off the engine.

The dog went berserk. The dog went absolutely batshit crazy with growling, snarling, and frantic, eardrum-imploding barking. Since he did this from directly behind us, Remi and I both about went through the roof.

I twisted in my seat. "Hey! *Whoa whoa whoa!* Easy! Knock it off! You just took ten years off my life!"

The dog did none of those things. The dog was an explosion of bone, muscle, skin, and teeth, scratching and digging at the window. The noise he made was horrendous.

And then Cerberus paced out of the shadows into yellow light.

This time the snake tail was obvious as it writhed and coiled, mouth opening to display fangs and forked tongue. The three canine heads worked independently of one another, but in this case all were lowered. He was shoulder-heavy, bulked up like a body-builder because the three heads tied into his body there. Massive muscle across the withers was defined as hackles rose. Hair stood up in a stiff line along the spine from neck to tail root. Pointed ears were pinned to his heads. Three sets of lips drew back from three monstrous dental arcades. The canines were massive fangs. Cerberus licked his lips repeatedly, muzzles accordioned into folds from noses to lower eyelids. The eyes themselves were bright red against black, mottled hair. Overall his body mass, not including the heads, was the size of a Great Dane on steroids.

One head went up to make the horrific screeching noise, but we couldn't hear it. We could see the other heads rise, tip back, see the monster assume a splay-legged, balanced posture and we knew all three throats were screaming, but the pittie was so loud in the seat immediately behind us that we couldn't hear anything else.

"Got the machete?" I shouted over the frantic dog.

Remi shook his head. That left us with guns and knives, which had already proven useless despite being blessed by holy oil and our breath.

We were not getting past Cerberus to reach the building.

Remi looked over his shoulder beyond the furious pittie. His gunrack carried a Winchester '73 rifle, a shotgun, and a coiled rope similar to the one ghost cowboy Burton Mossman had used to haul my bike out of the ravine. I'd learned, thanks to Remi's instruction, that these were not soft ropes, not flexible ropes, but somewhat stiff and rough, intentionally shaped into loops at their manufacture. If you dropped one of these, the coils would loosen, enlarge, but the general shape remained, so that it was easy for a cowboy to coil his rope back into something akin to a wreath to tie onto his saddle.

I was astonished. "You want to lasso it?"

"No. I want to *rope* it." He was deadly serious. "If I could get a big enough loop around two of those heads, or even all three, we'd have him. Or I can heel him like a calf, stretch him. Try, leastaways. Tie 'im off while you grab me the machete and then I'll have at those heads one by one."

I gave it another go. "You want to *rope* a three-headed, snake-tailed, hell-born monster dog?"

"Not sayin' it would be easy. But—"

He never got to finish. The frantic pit bull in the seat behind us finally broke out the half-dropped window and piled himself like a guided missile right into Cerberus.

CHAPTER THIRTY-FOUR

Remi and I had the F-bombs drop right out of our mouths at the same time, and then we dropped out of the truck. I had my gun in hand, Remi had his in hand, and I suspect he knew as well as I that we could do nothing. It was now between the pittie and the monster, no humans wanted. Primal instinct, predator and prey, two male dogs hopped up on testosterone blind to anything but the desire to kill one another.

We kept shifting position, trying for a new angle *just in case* the dogs tied themselves up so tightly that, like Greco-Roman wrestlers, no one could move, and we'd have clear shots. But there also existed the possibility that Remi and I might shoot one another.

It was horrific. That we didn't have onlookers piling out from the Zoo was due to the hour, the noise level inside of jukebox, pool balls clacking, people talking loudly. And because now that the dogs had fully engaged, their mouths were full of hair, skin, and muscle. They growled. They did not bark.

Tommy, my mentor in bike rebuilding and, basically, life in general, had owned a pit bull. Peter was a good old dog, broad as a barn, massive of head, giant of heart. He loved greatly. And he was literally a weapon.

Hell, even a Chihuahua can be a weapon. Anything alive with teeth, courage, and dedication can be a weapon. A full grown pit bull, one of the strongest breeds in the world, brought to battle a mix of mass, muscle, and momentum, and sheer determination to dominate its rival.

But a pit bull does not have a snake for a tail nor three heads.

And then I realized the dog—*our* dog—was drawing away. And I realized also, to my shock, that he had selected not Cerberus's throat, of which there were three, along with three sets of teeth, but the single abdominal cavity.

I knew Cerberus was dead, with his belly torn apart. Also, the pittie would not have walked away otherwise.

So much for heaven-born men with guns and knives. Just leave it to the dog.

He was done in, poor guy. Bleeding, limping, head hanging, licking repeatedly at his lips. But he was on his feet. He wobbled his way to us, then sat down. And waited.

But only for a moment. As Remi and I both surged toward him, his front legs slid apart and he went down.

"Truck box!" Remi said urgently. He tossed the key-fob to me. "I need the tarp, the incontinence pads, and there's a green toolbox, big. Bring it all."

Incontinence pads? But I clambered up into the truck bed, unlocked the hinged metal box that ran from one side of the truck to the other just behind the cab, started pulling out what Remi had directed me to bring. I scrambled back down, took four long strides to the dog. Knelt down.

"Alive?" I asked.

Remi's hands were moving over the dog swiftly and with competence. "So far."

"What else do you need?"

"I need you to spread the tarp. Then, get into that tool box and you'll see a spray bottle marked ALCOHOL. Spray down the tarp. Put the incontinence pads down; they'll keep the field sterile, more or less. We're going to lay him on 'em, doctor the one side, then do the other. I don't see any gaping wounds, but we gotta get everything flushed, cleaned out, treated with anti-biotic ointment. Dirt's bad enough, but we don't know what kind of saliva Cerberus had."

I did as instructed with the tarp, sprayed it with alcohol, then spread the plastic-backed incontinence pads and told Remi all was ready. He picked up the dog just enough to get him off the ground, shifted him to the makeshift 'exam room.'

"What next?"

"There're a couple of bottles of saline eyewash in there, like for contact lenses. Also large syringes, no needles. Pull those out, start filling them with the saline wash. He's mostly lacera-tions and punctures. We are going to start flushing everything, try to lift out the dirt and debris. This side, other side, butt, legs, and chest."

The two of us spent some time doing the flushing routine carefully on the one side. The dog whined, scrabbled at the tarp in an effort to rise, and I pressed him back, stroked him, talked to him. Soothed as best I could.

"Okay," Remi said. "Look for boxes of Triple Antibiotic Ointment. We're going to pack each laceration with the oint-ment, but the punctures need to stay open for now. Then I need you to get on your phone and see if there's an emergency vet in town. If not, what regular vet opens earliest in the morning?"

We tended the dog with the antibiotic ointment. Then we lifted him as best we could, turned him, lay him down again.

As Remi began the flushing and packing routine all over again, I got on my phone and checked Google.

I shook my head. "No emergency clinic. Got a vet opening at 6 a.m."

"Okay. I need you to go get me a t-shirt. Otherwise he'll goober up whatever he sleeps on tonight."

I started to say I had no t-shirts left, but did not. I just went inside and right to Ganji, asked for one of his. He had an extra in the office and gave it willingly, came outside with me.

Remi saw him. "Ganji—can you go cut up a chunk of cheese, bring it back out?" To me, he said, "There's a box of Benadryl in there. I need you to get me . . . oh, say, three of the 25 mg tabs. This bad boy's probably 70-80 pounds, I'm guessin'."

When Ganji returned, Remi tucked all three tabs inside the cheese, then let the pittie sit up. He fed him the cheese and tablets, scritched him around the ears, spoke to him calmly in a low voice.

"What now?" I asked.

"Now we put the t-shirt on him, take him up to your room. Benadryl's used for anxiety as well as allergies and insect stings. He'll sleep. Vet first thing tomorrow morning. You go on with him; I'll clean up here." He cast a glance at the body of Cerberus, a misshapen heap beneath the sodium light. "I'll wrap that up in the tarp, drop you off at the vet's tomorrow, then take it out and bury it. We don't need anyone coming across a three-headed, snake-tailed corpse."

I leaned down, told the pittie he got to sleep on my bed again. Watching him walking slowly in a human t-shirt was mildly amusing. He did need help getting up the stairs, but amazingly had enough oomph left to get himself up on my bed, the malingerer. This time he curled himself up right in the center. I resolved that I could bend my limbs around him one way or another.

I t was a fitful night, to say the least, and by the time dawn arrived I'd given up on restful sleep. At six a.m. I called the vet's office and explained what had happened, what we'd done for the dog's comfort. They said they'd see him at six-thirty.

Remi was up, too, and fixing coffee in the modest kitchen. Bagels were in the toaster, and he'd pulled out a tub of flavored spread. "There's a lead rope hanging from the back door handle downstairs. Figure you can use that as a leash to get him into the vet."

I shook my head. "What else do you have packed away in that truck box? Reminds me of Dr. Who's TARDIS—larger on the inside than the outside!"

He shrugged. "Just basic stuff anyone working around animals needs. On the ranch I'm dealing with cattle and horses, mostly, a dog now and then and maybe a barn cat fracas. You live far enough away from a town and a vet, you gotta know how to tend injuries till you can get the vet out to see the animal."

"Comes in handy with humans, too, I imagine."

Remi smiled crookedly. "I have been known to slap livestock liniment on me now and then."

"Okay, I'll take him down to do his business, then put him in the truck. Appointment's in twenty minutes."

Remi nodded. "I'll drop you, get Cerberus buried, then head on over to the hospital to see Mary Jane. I figure you can catch a ride-share." I nodded. His eyes were troubled. "Sure hate that she got dragged into all of this."

"Hazards of the wrong name." I swallowed a couple of slugs of coffee, stuck a bagel between my teeth, rounded up the dog and began the laborious descent of steep, narrow stairs carrying a canine who apparently managed to gain two hundred pounds overnight.

W ith the nav app providing directions in a sexy Scandinavian voice—Remi said her name was Helga—we got to the vet in no time. Once the dog and I were on our way inside, I waved Remi off to visit Mary Jane. I matched my pace to the dog's, who watered a plant along the drive, then allowed me to lead him inside.

And as we entered, I saw the receptionist look at us with a professional smile, then stand up quickly. "I think that's—just hang on a sec." And she was out from behind the counter and gone.

After a moment she was back with a guy wearing a lab coat and a hopeful expression on his face. I couldn't read the entire name embroidered on his pocket, but the DR. and DVM were obvious.

"Yep," he said, relief softening his face. "Let's scan to be sure, but it's him." He knelt, put gentle hands on the dog, looked up at me. "What's the story?"

"Found him out back scavenging near the dumpster," I explained, then decided to excise pretty much the rest of the story other than the dog fight. "My friend's a working cowboy so he knew what to do before we could bring him in."

"Okay." After scanning and checking the chip's data, the vet told the receptionist to give someone named Mac a call. "Tell him we've got Bosco, and he'll be fine." He rose, gestured at me. "Come on and bring him back. I have three clients who will be *very* glad to get the news that their dog is okay. They were in a car accident, lost Bosco in all the excitement. Thank you for bringing him in."

I wanted to say it was better to thank the dog for saving our lives, but that was another tale.

We got Bosco settled on the floor in the exam room for a preliminary exam. He was quiet and receptive as the vet went over him, blinking slit-eyed at me as I stroked and spoke to him. In the midst of that, a man with a young daughter—aged six? seven?—was escorted into the room. Tall red-headed guy, maybe thirty, and the girl had the same blazing hair. Her left arm was in a cast. She saw the dog and promptly burst into tears, dropping to the ground.

The dog had been lying still. Now he sat up, thumped the ground with his tail, tried to rest his big head on a much smaller shoulder. The girl threw her arms around his neck and hugged him, still crying. The hug didn't last long because he decided to clean the tears with a few swipes of his big tongue.

I cleared my throat, gave the father a weak smile. Tears stood in his eyes.

"Thank God," he said, "thank God. And thank *you*! My wife's in the hospital—she'll be okay—and Mercy has been crying nonstop because Bosco was lost. He's *her* dog, you see. Or maybe it's that she's his kid."

Bosco gazed up at me with those expressive brown eyes. I knew it was time to go. I had no place here. He was home.

I asked for a pen and paper, wrote down my name, number,

and e-mail address. I squatted and gave the slip of paper to the little girl. "Would you let me know how he's doing? He's a really good dog. Would you, please?"

She took the paper, nodded, gave me a watery look out of big blue eyes and went right back to hugging on the pittie. In this moment, only the dog mattered.

I smiled at him, scratched him under his jaw. I bent down close so what I said was private between the two of us. "Good boy," I said, "and thank you. *You* know why."

The pittie grinned and thumped his tail, then snuffled the little girl's ear.

I shook the father's hand, wished his wife a fast recovery, and left the room. As I slid the door closed, I heard the little girl asking if Bosco needed a cast, too.

Yeah, a happy ending. And I was glad, relieved, happy especially for the little girl—and more than a little wistful. I didn't realize I'd kind of been hoping no owner was found. There were such things as motorcycle sidecars, and dog harnesses, dog seatbelts, dog goggles . . . but clearly he was where he needed to be.

I was about to call a ride-share when my phone rang. Not Remi; I didn't recognize the number.

The voice on the other end, when I answered, told me my bike was ready.

CHAPTER THIRTY-FIVE

The kid from the Harley shop rode my bike over to the vet's office to deliver it personally. I would have preferred to come in and pick it up, discuss with Cisco what had been done, but the kid said his boss was out of town. Plus, I remembered that Cisco himself had said the kid was a real good mechanic. Kenny! That was it.

Kenny was skinny and sandy-haired, around eighteen, I judged. He had a lazy eye and stuttered. Certain tics suggested possible developmental or emotional challenges, and I remembered Cisco saying something about the boy being 'a little special,' and excellent with his hands. It was entirely likely Kenny preferred *not* to talk to clients and was highly uncomfortable right now, speaking with me.

Then I asked him something technical, and he was off and running. Bikes were his love, obviously, and the physical and vocal tics mostly disappeared as he talked shop. The upshot was that he had done most of the work on my bike—he hastened to say it was under Cisco's supervision, and Cisco always checked his work. He was able to spell out in detail how he had handled the repairs. Definitely knew his stuff, and we "talked bikes" for around twenty minutes out in the vet clinic's parking lot.

Kenny handed over the invoice and receipt, and when I offered to give him a ride back to the shop he said his mother was coming to pick him up.

And then he surprised me when he volunteered he had a doctor's appointment with a neurologist. "Bunged up head," was all he offered. No additional details.

"Bike?" I asked, and he nodded. "Yeah," I said, commiserating. "I laid this one down—that's how she got wrecked—and I'm a little bunged up, too." I tucked the paperwork into a pocket, thanked him again—offered a $20 tip he refused—swung a leg over the saddle and felt vast contentment settling into body and spirit as I let my weight down.

God, it felt good! Freedom from prison. Freedom of the road.

Hell, just freedom.

I turned over the key, nodded to Kenny as the engine caught and settled into a smooth rumble, took my sweet ride out onto the street.

As I pulled the bike around back to park at the Zoo, I was, of course, reminded of the battle the night before between Cerberus and the pittie. It did make me smile—which was a luxury in view of what could have happened.

Bosco the Pit Bull, *One*. Cerberus, the God of the Underworld's Pet, *Zero*.

I wished Tommy was alive so I could tell him his bike was back together again, and a pittie who barely knew me had saved my life and Remi's the night before. He'd have been proud of both.

Parked, I headed in the back door. I still wasn't entirely

comfortable under the glass eyeballs of the animals on display throughout the Zoo, especially not after my dance with their *live* versions. But at least they were inanimate again.

I called out to see if Ganji were present. No answer was an answer. As I made my way slowly into the dancehall proper, I found a text from Remi saying he was on the way. I went ahead and texted back to let him know the dog was with his humans, the bike was with *her* human, and I was back home. How was Kelly doing? Any insight into Jack the Ripper?

An answer came, but terse: *'Almost home. Talk then.'*

Home. Huh. Guess that's what the Zoo *had* become.

As I hit the power button I glanced up just in time to register that a man stood right in front of me, and that his fist was on its way to my face.

I went down. Hard. The phone whacked the parquet floor and slid some distance away, and even as I tried to reassemble splayed limbs so I could get to my feet, grab for my gun, the guy bent down, locked a hand into my jacket, and dragged me up from the floor.

Oh. Shemyazaz, in his human form. No wonder my jaw hurt so badly. No wonder he was so strong. No wonder he could snatch the gun out of my hand and hurl it across the room, rip the knives off me as well. They, too, were tossed away to clatter against the floor.

"Ambriel!" he cried. "*Ambriel!* I gave you your human back. I gave you the woman. I want Ambriel!"

Even in his normal human-looking edition, the angel was formidable. It had nothing to do with height, nor weight—we were probably close in that—nor his overall fitness. It was something incandescent that had come to life in him. He was set apart from mankind. He was *more* than mankind. He filled the room just standing there. And he was pissed as hell.

I noticed the orbs perched along beamwork as the angel curled his hands into the unzipped flaps of my jacket and *shook* me. My arms actually flopped until I stiffened them, and my head snapped once before I recovered control of my body. He still held me in place with his grip upon my jacket, but at least I wasn't ragdolling anymore.

I set my hands upon his wrists, hung on hard as I tried to loosen his grip. When he finally paused and I refound my voice, I didn't hold back the anger. "I don't know *what* the fuck you want with Ambriel, and I don't know *where* the fuck she is! She left! We were in that chapel, she closed up her wings, and she *left*. Got that? You could try Spock's mindmeld on me and you'd get nothing more than that, because it's the *truth*, you angelic asshole! I *get* that Lucifer beat you with the Ugly Stick and you're pissed about it; and I *get* that you're pissed about the girl who got away; and I *get* that you feel some kind of competition with Mikhail Baryshnikov over the number of pirouettes you can do—he's retired, by the way—but *I can't tell you what you want to hear*."

He let go of me fast and hard. I staggered a moment, caught my balance, shrugged my jacket into its proper fit. Then we just stared at one another for several very long seconds. It reminded me a little bit of Bosco and Cerberus, except I knew that if Yaz got really worked up *I'd* be the one missing my guts and wrapped up in a tarp for burial.

Yaz really was a beautiful man, and I could definitely see why he'd be pissed to lose the looks for any reason, let alone so disastrously to Lucifer's fit of jealousy. I assumed he was in pain when his body burned and melted twenty-two hours out of every day, and that coupled with the psychological pain of knowing what he had been and now what he was . . . yeah. Enough to knock a guy's mental train off the tracks.

His eyes blazed. "You are *no help at all!*"

Wings, and his were pure and white not Ambriel's black, shot free of his back—or shoulders, or spine, or whatever portion of his anatomy held them, or maybe like the swords on *Highlander* they lived in a pocket universe and appeared only when needed—stretched endlessly across the dance floor.

Then he wrapped himself up in them and he, with the orbs, disappeared.

I put a hand to my jaw. "Shit, that hurt."

"Gabriel," she said from behind.

Swearing, I spun. It was Greg. "Oh, *now* you show up! Great. It would simplify my life considerably if you and Shemyazaz got your damn timing straightened out!"

Greg's face was stricken. "Shemyazaz was here?"

"Like, *just* here. What, you angels can't feel one another? Maybe ping your sonar?"

But she ignored me, was looking around frantically as if she'd lost something. "Did he drop a feather?"

"A feather? How the hell do I know? I don't see one; do you see one? So no." I realized I was in a really foul mood. "And what is it *you* want?"

"I need a feather," she said blankly. "If I have one, I can hide myself from him."

"I don't know if he dropped a feather," I said. "I don't see a feather. Is that what you came for? A damn feather?" I paused, remembering. "I have one of yours, though."

Her head snapped around. "You have one of my feathers?"

"Yes. You dropped it at the chapel. Or shed it. Whatever it is you guys do."

"Where is it?"

For a moment I drew a blank. "Oh. It's in Remi's truck. Glove box."

Ambriel, a Grigori like Shemyazaz and possibly related, put her hands on my jacket. "Let no one have it. Do not give it to Shemyazaz. Do not give it to Barachiel. Give it to no one."

"Barach—?" Ah. Grandaddy. "Why?"

"I have to go," she said. "I mustn't stay. Barachiel is chasing me, and Shemyazaz will kill me. Keep the feather safe, and keep *this* safe."

"Keep what—?" I frowned at the object she pressed into my right hand.

"It will be of use. Use it. Let it tell you the truth of things when others don't. You are its protector now. The *prostátis*. Do your job." She grabbed my jacket again. "Barachiel mustn't have it."

"This?" I displayed a flash drive, of all things, on the vertical between thumb and forefinger. The stub of a USB connector was tucked away inside the small silver case, like the folded blade of a Swiss Army Knife. "You do understand the man practically raised me, in his own way. Or at least mentored me. Do you expect me to just assume everything he says is a lie? I won't. I won't do it."

For a moment, all the urgency and tension dissipated. She released my jacket. "No. No, I shouldn't expect that. He was kind to you; of course you trust him. He will have to prove to you what he is before you learn not to trust. But believe me in this: You hold my feather—I won't lie to you. Keep it safe. Keep both safe. Let no one have them." And then her eyes were frantic again. "He's coming."

I opened my mouth to ask her another question, but she stepped away from me, sheathed herself in wings, and disappeared.

No feathers left behind. Black or white.

"Jesus Christ," I muttered. I looked at the drive, moved a couple of slider buttons on the small case, discovered it was a dual USB with retractable A and C connectors, one at each end. I stuffed it into a pocket, made a perimeter search of the dance floor to collect my gun and safe it back in the holster. I needed to take it apart, check it for damage since Yaz had actually thrown it, then gathered up my phone and two knives.

As I sheathed the bladed weapons the front door was thrown open and Grandaddy stalked in. "Where is she?" he asked. "Where is Ambriel?"

I lowered the gun I'd snatched from the holster. "What is this, Grand Angel Station? How many more of you are arriving today? Should I set an extra twenty places at the table?"

In his Western-style frock coat and boots, the sun behind him lighting up his long white hair, he appeared part avenging angel, part movie hero arriving just in time to deliver us from evil bad guys. Except that no one was wearing black hats, so I wasn't sure who to root against.

Grandaddy was not a demonstrative man. He laughed, he got annoyed, could be impatient, yet never to excess. But he was pissed as hell.

Maybe I should have kept my mouth shut. But I didn't. I was pissed, too. "She's not here," I told him. "She's gone. I don't know where she is. Seriously. So you and Yaz can go off to a bar together—some *other* bar, please—and commiserate."

He stepped closer. The avenging angel version had taken precedence. "Do you think this is funny?"

"No." I dropped the wiseguy act. "No, Grandaddy, I don't find it funny. I find it deadly serious. I find it *deadly*. I'm at risk, Remi's at risk, and we lack a whole lot of information that would be helpful to have. You threw a lot at us that one night, the night you had us so dramatically shake hands and clasp rings together, but we don't actually *know* anything. Basically it was *'Go thou and battle demons.'* Seriously? Did you ever think that maybe Remi and I aren't ready? That maybe we needed more time to assimilate, more time to truly understand the yellow brick road that lies before us, *before* you deployed us?"

His expression was grim. "She told you that. Ambriel. She told you that you're not ready."

"Yes. She did."

"Are you alive?"

I blinked at him. "So far."

"Then you're ready."

"Grandaddy—"

"What she told you is a *labrys*, a two-sided axe. It can build you up, or tear you down. Some are told they're not ready, and they fail. Others are told they're not ready and they *work harder*. So which are you, Gabriel? Which is Remiel? Children destined for failure because you believe a Grigori who refuses choices and perches on a fence? Or men who take on the burden, who prosper under that burden, and literally help save the world?"

I shrugged. "She said she is neutral, like Switzerland. That Grigori *are* simply watchers. They are not to act."

"In World Wars that are not truly wars of the *world*, in our terms, Switzerland and other countries may remain neutral. But this battle, Gabriel . . ." He shook his head. "This battle is for humanity and the hereafter."

I squinted at him. "Don't you have to be dead for the hereafter? Can we avoid the dead part?"

"'Hereafter' means *after here*. Later. In the future. At a time that is not now."

"You mean the battle is about what happens later."

"The battle, if won, means we will *have* a 'later.' We will have an after that is here."

And thus here I was, approaching the End of Days and discussing semantics with a seraph. "Okay. No neutrality when the world may end. Or at least our version of it. So, what, you figure you can talk Greg into surrendering her neutrality because you need every single angel on the payroll? Is it Greg specifically, or all the Grigori? If it's the latter, what happens to Shemyazaz? He's a Grigori."

Grandaddy's tone was dismissive. "Shemyazaz is fallen. Shemyazaz is Lucifer's."

"He says he's here to *kill* Lucifer."

"Shemyazaz isn't capable of killing Lucifer. He is a *fallen* angel, Gabriel. He gave over his soul to Satan. He is the devil's *pet*. And Ambriel, by interfering as she is—which I must remind you is *not* being neutral—is getting in the way."

The grays. The grays, she'd said, not the blacks, or the whites. "Angels live among the grays."

"Not anymore," Grandaddy said.

I stuffed my hands in my jacket and felt the flash drive. It would be so easy just to hand it over, to surrender complexities and simply stick with *'Go thou and battle demons.'* And not get

involved in internecine warfare among the angels. Easier just
to trust the man who'd meant so much to me.

In my pocket, I turned the flash drive in my fingers. Part of
me wanted to approach the subject, part of me wanted to forget
it altogether. "Well, what about Cassandra, then? Why do you
want her?"

That changed the look in his eye. "She told you about Cassandra?"

"I rescued Cassandra, Grandaddy. I picked her up from the
ground after an assault. I have a little something invested in
her. So, why do you want her?"

Grandaddy's eyes flickered a little. "Cassandra is mad."

"So what does a seraph want with a madwoman?"

He maintained a fairly even tone in his voice, but now his
eyes were angry. "In dreadful times, people may believe the
wrong things. The wrong people. *Drákon*: The dragon. *Thirío*:
The beast. And *pséftikos profitis*: The false prophet. All mislead."

Dragon, beast, false prophet. Triple-six, written in water on
wood. "And you believe Cassandra is the false prophet?"

He said it with infinite simplicity. No thundering from the
mount. No roar of rage. Just a quiet, "We take no chances."

"So you're not certain of it."

"We take no chances."

"Ambriel may be right, then, and Cassandra plays no part
in this. She's just a collateral nutcase."

Grandaddy said nothing.

I nodded. "You take no chances."

"Can it be afforded, at the End of Days?"

I fingered the flash drive that Greg had begged me not to
give to him, to the man I had always trusted more than my
own father.

Sleeper agents. Assets in abeyance. That could apply to so many, in all the shades of gray. Apply to Remi. To me. And I had a flash drive and a feather that apparently meant a great deal to Greg.

Grandaddy said, "I trust you to do the right thing, Gabriel. I made you for it."

And so he had, mentoring me, grooming me for battle. I searched his eyes for the truth. I *knew* this man. I barely knew Greg at all.

He stood tall and formidable, as he had that day on the mountain when he allowed us to see the suggestion of massive wings. Greg had called him chief of the guardian angels.

I didn't have to give him the flash drive now. I could view it for myself, decide then who should have it.

"Yessir," I said. "I will do the right thing."

He didn't fly away. He left no feathers. He simply turned away from me and walked back out the open door.

I stood on the dance floor for long minutes, trying to figure out what I was. Then I removed the flash drive from my pocket. Possibly *it* could tell me what I was and what I was to do. But first?

First, close the door. Pour whiskey. Swallow ibuprofen.

A nap would be good, too, but I was pretty sure that wasn't going to happen.

CHAPTER THIRTY-SIX

I patted myself down: revolver, both knives, phones. The only thing left lying on the floor was my pride, but that I could deal with. Well, at some point; right now it was a little tender.

If the flash drive was so important and now entrusted to my keeping as its *pros*-something—protector; English was easier—it was about damn time I stuck it into a computer and viewed the data. I mean, it could be a list of all the sleeper agents—angelic or demonic—in the country, or the world itself; and photos, and dossiers, and possibly blueprints of a dam we were supposed to blow up, or maybe of the Japanese-owned highrise in L.A. that would be compromised come Christmas, saved only by the skin of Bruce Willis's feet; or, for all I knew, the video of the original ending of *Thelma and Louise*, where they *didn't* drive off the rim of the Grand Canyon.

I jogged up the stairs, pulled out my phone to text Remi again and fill him in—and discovered the screen had more cracks than my vertebrae on a bad day. Also, the phone part of it was just flat broken.

Okay, I still had the iAngel phone. I called him, but received no answer. I did skip the whiskey, but in the bathroom I swallowed two ibu tablets and stared at my face in the mirror a moment.

I affected a drawl to mimic Remi, "'Son, you look like you were rode hard and put away wet.'"

Back in the common room I sat down, booted up the computer. A physical examination of the small flash drive in its closed silver metallic case offered no answers as to why Greg felt it was so vital—it certainly lacked the charisma of WWII's Enigma encryption machine—or why I wasn't supposed to show it to anyone, least of all Grandaddy.

Just as I was about to slide one of the buttons to release the connector and insert the drive, I hesitated. This computer was perfectly ordinary, capable of presenting information as prosaic as ads for various items made in China under the guise of an English-sounding company name. And at times this computer presented us with an angel-operated dark web, providing vital information via photos and text, not to mention missions, and answering limited questions with obfuscation.

Greg planted doubts about Grandaddy. He planted doubts about her. If she were *not* on the fence but was playing a long game, the drive she'd given me could very well fry a network vital to the war. I was no computer nerd or geek. I didn't know various ways of doing assorted bad things on the internet, other than knowing it could be done. As an eight-year-old I'd heard all about Y2K and the potential for world domination when the clock ticked over for the new millennium—except it turned out to be a total bust.

Then again, the drive contained a microUSB connector in addition to the 3.0. I could insert it into my phone—except, yeah, my phone was broken. Which left the angel phone, also plugged into whatever celestial network the computer used.

Well, they *were* angels. Probably they had a heavenly Geek Squad on call for repairs. I plugged the drive into the desktop's port.

Zero. Zip. Nada.

And then her photo came up on the screen: long, wavy blond hair, ice-blue eyes, strong features and a straight nose.

No, not a photo. "Cassandra?"

She looked stricken. She spread a hand on the screen. The monitor was so clear I could see the pads of her fingers. Pads of fingers that lacked the whorls of fingerprints. "Gabe!"

"Where are you? Where'd Greg stash you?"

"I am here. I am *here*."

"Where is here? Some kind of safehouse?"

"Here! I am *here!*"

I shook my head. "Cassandra—listen, I think we've got a language issue. Greg—Ambriel—has taken you somewhere safe. I'm apparently your angel-appointed protector. You can tell me."

Now she spread both hands across the monitor. One she smacked on her webcam over and over again. "I am *here*! Inside! I am in the labyrinth!"

"What labyrinth?"

"All the lines. All the colored lines." She smacked the webcam again. "The labyrinth! The way to talk to you. The way to provide . . . *data*? To tell you what I see! I will . . . overwrite? Yes, *overwrite*—the bad prophecies. To provide correct data."

I stood up so fast the task chair rolled hard into the table and fell over. "You're *inside the internet?*"

"I am here," she said, and took her hands away.

It wasn't a webcam. It wasn't the ordinary internet, or even iAngel.

I was absolutely horrified. *"Cassandra . . ."*

"Protect me," she said. "Be my *prostátis*."

I couldn't move. I could summon no other word. I could only stare at the woman on the screen. The woman *in* the screen.

The woman reduced to data stored in a modest little flash drive with two USB connectors.

I finally rediscovered language skills. "Cassandra—do you know if you can be moved? If you—the you that's in the thing I plugged into the computer—can you be transferred into additional devices?" I knew I wasn't getting through to her. "Are you stuck in the drive, or can you put yourself into *different* computers and phones?"

"I am in the—thing. The thing."

"The drive."

"The data thing. Only there."

"We can contact you if we insert the USB drive into any device?" I tried again. "If we insert *'the thing'* into any device, we can reach you?"

"I am wherever the thing goes."

I nodded. I felt sick to my stomach. "Can you contact us? If you need us?"

She shook her head wildly. It wasn't a *'no'*; it was an *'I don't understand what you're saying.'*

An odd bit of memory floated into my brain, a disembodied voice asking the first of many questions in times of computer confusion; the question that frustrated so many: *'Is the computer plugged in?'*

"Okay," I said. "Listen, you must get a message to Greg—to Ambriel. Can you do that?"

She stared at me like a deer caught in the headlights. Except she wasn't seeing me, I didn't think. Well, maybe she was. I didn't know what kind of tech existed among the angels. But I would certainly ask Greg the first chance I got.

I tried another way. "Can you give Ambriel my data? If I type or text—scratch that." I thought a little further. "If I give you words, can you remember them? Can you tell them to Ambriel?"

"Yes."

"Okay." A little relief came with that. "Tell Ambriel to call me. She knows what that means. Tell her I have many questions."

She nodded jerkily, clearly not quite certain what I meant.

And then I cast aside compunction. I had to make sure Greg understood how serious I was. So I used what I had. I used what she feared could harm her in the wrong hands to force a response. "Tell her this exactly—*exactly*, Cassandra. Say: '*I have your feather.*'"

This time her nod was of comprehension.

"Tell her that my data is: '*I have your feather,*' and '*call me.*'"

She began to speak again, then a wave of pain passed across her face. She set both hands to her head and squeezed her eyes closed. I wanted to yell questions for Greg, things like: "*Do you know if this is safe? Do you know if this will harm her? Don't tell me to protect her if this is going to harm her!*"

A safehouse. I'd thought perhaps Greg would stash her in a safehouse, not in a flash drive!

A prophecy was of no use if it couldn't be passed along *in advance* of the events. We needed tech that would allow Cassandra to initiate texts on her own.

"Cassandra—if you're in pain, you need to shut down." I rephrased. "You need to rest."

She lifted her head and looked at me in shock. "I can't see all—can't see all." She sucked in a breath. *"Remi!"*

The only phone I had was iAngel, beside the computer. I grabbed it, pulled up the screen, hit Remi's icon.

Zero. Zip. Nada. Not even a voicemail greeting.

I turned away and took one long step, then swung back. I initiated Eject Media, plucked the drive out of the USB port, stuck it into an interior jacket pocket and zipped that closed.

Hospital. Last place he'd been. And I had wheels.

In my room I swapped out BDUs for leather bike pants, grabbed gloves and helmet, thundered down the stairs and snatched the back door open, took the two steps, another two strides—and found a manilla envelope taped to the bike saddle.

Ohnonononono.

Remi had been with Kelly at the hospital.

Mary Jane Kelly, Jack the Ripper's number five.

I ripped open the envelope, found the message on the back of the photo.

'My name is Iñigo Montoya. You keel my puppy. Prepare to die.'

"No-no-*no*," I said blankly.

I knew what the Ripper had done to the Mary Jane Kelly of 1888. I'd seen the photo of a woman he very recently had carved up. And now he had *our* Mary Jane.

I took a breath, held it, turned over the photo.

Not Mary Jane.

Remi.

Alive in the photo, but written in red were the words: *'Come and take out the trash.'*

After a moment of paralysis I yanked the angel phone from my pocket, fished out the flash drive—and just barely stopped myself from inserting the microconnector. Plugged in,

Cassandra would be using the OS of the magic phone and thus extending herself into the angel network. Cassandra was data, not a microprocessor. If she accessed the angel phone OS, Grandaddy could track her.

Damn Ambriel for making me question his motives!

I crammed phone and drive back into a pocket, fired up the bike and took off like a bat out of hell.

Burner phone. Burner phone. *Any* phone—so long as it could take the Cassandra drive right now as it was and didn't need an external On-The-Go adapter. That could come later.

I prevented myself from speeding by the application of sheer willpower because being pulled over would delay me even more. But it was minutes only before I pulled in to the Harley shop, and then I was off the bike before it settled firmly on the repaired kickstand.

The kid was in the shop wearing stained overalls, working on something with a sound system blaring. I went in underneath the rolling door, walked right up to him, scared the daylights out of him as I clamped a hand on a shoulder.

"Gotta use your cell!" I shouted, miming fingers to ear. "Emergency!—sorry, please—"

Kenny was wide-eyed, mouth working, but he nodded jerkily, slapped a pocket, showed me a greasy hand and a panicked expression. I shoved my hand down into the overall pocket and pulled the phone out, took the flash drive from my jacket, prayed it wouldn't fry the phone. I could buy him another cell—what I *didn't* want is for any part of Cassandra to be damaged *or* to get into the telephone provider's network. I hoped, too, it had an internal OTG, or I'd have to go buy an adapter and I *didn't have the time.*

I walked away from the kid hastily, pressed the power

button, waited for the home screen. When it came up I inserted the C-type microconnector.

Cassandra was now a heaven-built device with her own autorun.exe program. But I didn't know if she realized that. I doubted it. "C'mon, c'mon, c'mon."

The screen flashed blinding-bright, went to black.

"Nononono."

It came back up, and I saw one ice-blue eye filling the screen, staring at me.

"Cassandra. Cassandra, please—can you tell me anything about Remi? Where he is? Anything at all?"

The eye withdrew. I saw both eyes now, pupils spreading to fill the iris. Black black eyes.

"Cassandra—"

"Sun goes down," she said. "Sun goes down—sun goes down—*sun goes down*—"

The screen flashed again, went black.

I set the phone's edge against my brow, feeling empty and scared and helpless, and on the verge of sudden tears. "I don't need to know when. I need to know *where!*"

Kenny had come up. He hung back a little, but was on the edge of my space. He rocked a little from foot to foot, staring at the phone I had pressed against my head.

He'd said, *"Head bunged up."*

Phone bunged up, I thought. I pulled the drive, slid the connector inside the little case and handed him the cell. Thanked him, made to pull out my wallet but he shook his head hard and took a big step back. I put out my hand to shake his, but he wouldn't do that, either. His was too greasy. I smiled at him, and for the hell of it said, "By any chance, do you know what *'Sun goes down'* might mean? Besides the sun setting, I mean."

The kid with the bunged up head stared at me like I was an imbecile. "Sunset Crater."

I felt a chill sweep over me. I *was* an imbecile.

Remi was maybe twenty minutes away.

CHAPTER THIRTY-SEVEN

As I drove out Highway 89, I wanted badly to shout that it wasn't fair, it wasn't right, it just shouldn't be happening because Remi and I had been to Sunset Crater before and had cleared the domicile. No more demons allowed; in a way it was a secular version of holy ground. I had sensed something there as I drove by that night after we'd cleared the Native American ruins at Wupatki, and we had discovered a black dog as we climbed the side of the ruddy-hued cinder cone.

We'd killed that black dog, we'd exploded it. We'd done the rite as Greg, of all people, of all angels, had shown us at Wupatki, when she'd blown up the body of a black dog who'd been murdering humans. Remi had killed it with blessed rifle bullets, but we hadn't known what to do with the body. Within thirty minutes we'd killed a second black dog at Sunset Crater and made the cone all nice and shiny and safe again. No demons could return to it. So how was the Ripper demon holding Remi at Sunset Crater?

In the photo, Remi didn't appear to have been seriously harmed. Maybe the Ripper had taken his knife to another portion of Remi's body, maybe fingers, as he'd shorn Mary Jane Kelly's hair, but Remi's face and hair were intact, and his expression—eyes open and lucid—had been stoic, not like he was hiding pain.

He'd said rodeo cowboys were tough, and in general tended their own injuries without much said about them, often avoiding professional medical care altogether. So possibly he *was* hurt. But my *primogenitura* hadn't twitched. My link to Remi had not indicated injury, and it had before.

Then I muttered between my teeth, "Don't do that. Don't *do* that."

I shut down my brain the next few miles, until the big cinder cone rose high and close on my right: black and bloody-red, lower slopes studded with dusty green vegetation. The cone edges up top broke inward into a true crater hollowed down toward the original volcanic vent. Officials had stopped allowing visitors to climb the cone because of erosion.

Before, Remi and I had stopped along the highway, then hiked in to the cone along the lava flow. This time I took the normal turnoff to the loop road into the monument. I rolled up to the gate, discovered a sign explaining Sunset Crater was closed due to earthquake activity.

Huh. Yeah. I remembered the demon possessing the entomologist professor had said something about one of the trails being damaged by the first morning quake, that it had collapsed into a cave. And there had been another quake since then. Remi and I had been at the chapel with Cassandra and Greg clear on the far side of the Peaks for the second one, and I hadn't thought to look up information on secondary earthquake damage at the crater. No reason to.

Well, till now.

Sitting on my bike, engine idling, my entrance blocked by steel, I pulled up the iAngel phone and Googled for news. What

I found was pretty much what the sign said: The monument was temporarily closed to visitors until all damage could be further investigated. Details were sparse, probably because they didn't want lookie-loos sneaking in. Naturally such declarations meant nothing to demons.

However, I had an angel phone, and Remi had an angel phone, and probably we had angelic GPS. I smiled, then arrived at the obvious conclusion and the expression dropped away.

Probably the demon had taken Remi's magic phone, may even have texted me on it *as* Remi, and very likely would use the GPS feature to track mine, so he'd have us both.

I drove off the main visitor road, rolled slowly down the fenceline until I found vegetation that would shield the bike against a casual look-see. I climbed off, checked all my pockets for additional breath-blessed bullets and shells, checked the KA-BAR, the Bowie, checked the Taurus Judge in the holster beneath my left arm.

I had nothing else. I couldn't *smite* anyone, demon, angel, or human. I had weapons that could be taken away from me. The only thing I held in reserve was something kindled in me years ago as a kid, the day I had taken my brother's pain for my own. Grandaddy had called it the stewardship of the younger. My brother Matty had stood proxy for Remi that day, until the night at the Zoo when Remi and I had clasped hands, touched rings, and sealed ourselves to the battle by blood and bone, life and limb.

Primogenitura.

I left the bike, worked my way through the 3-strand fence—I didn't have Remi's nippers to cut the wire, or I'd have taken the bike in farther—and began walking the road's shoulder. It ended in a parking lot, and the trailhead was clearly marked.

I turned off the Location setting on the phone, pulled the SD and SIM cards, tucked them away in a hidden pocket but kept the phone in an obvious place on my person.

So, okay. If I was found, they'd take a non-working phone from me. I'd still have the guts and a way to contact Grandaddy if he deigned to answer—or even Greg if I inserted the Cassandra drive—using someone else's phone, if I could get my hands on one.

I traded asphalt for soil and cinders, started hiking in.

The cinder-heavy soil was broken by ancient lava, hardened into blackened and shirred folds, squared blocks, and jagged protrusions. The trail in places led over strands of lava, or ran beside it like a cartpath on a golf course. Tumbled piles reached knee level, or higher. There was no kindness about it, no rain-and-sun-softened stone. Here lay the bones of the earth, built of petrified lava. But here, too, were trees, copses of piñon and ponderosa pines, quaking aspen, where cinders and ash freshened the earth to grow again. At one stand of aspen I stepped off the trail, closed my eyes and let myself go. Let myself reach out:

I want Remiel. I need Remiel. Beta to my alpha. The man, the soldier, to whom I was sealed for the brotherhood of battle. I can lift the pain from him, renew his body, renew his soul.

It was a stewardship, not a selfish rite of passage that gave all to the older and left out the younger. Not in the ways of heaven.

Remi sensed demons in human hosts. He was likely imprisoned by demons now, at the very least by *one* demon more powerful than others. Among them, or kept in the company of

Jack the Ripper, Iñigo Montoya, Legion—whatever it wished to call itself—he might be able to sense one strand of what is clean about the world, the purity of the earth and all its many parts. He might be able to find the *me* in the strand and follow it until he was close enough to tell me where he was and how I could find him.

In the midst of quaking trees and green-coin leaves, in the shadow of a volcano, I extended my senses again, reached again, requested willing guidance.

I extended, I reached, I requested . . . and felt needle-like pain enter my right eye. When in the interior of my skull it exited the eye, it entered the brain proper as an Improvised Explosive Device.

I'd experienced migraine headaches maybe six times in my entire life. Enough times to know just how bad they can be, but so far apart that it was easy not only to forget just how excruciating they are but also to forget to stock up on any kind of migraine-specific medications to keep around. Aspirin, ibuprofen, NSAIDs were all I'd ever taken, and I had none on me. I'd swallowed two ibu tablets not long before I left, but there was not enough oomph in them to counteract this degree of head pain.

Flashing lights, a watery aura, nausea. Involuntary tears poured from that eye. I found myself kneeling on the ground trying to keep down the last meal I'd eaten, right hand clamped over eye, cheek, and brow while the braced left hand and arm kept me from doing a face-plant.

Migraine pain can reduce an adult to infancy, begging internally for someone, *any*one, to bring relief. Even for a parent when you're two years short of thirty. I didn't beg for that, but if the pain continued, I might.

I breathed hard and hoarsely until I feared it might worsen matters. Then I breathed very, very quietly. I wanted badly to fool the world into believing I wasn't present, so that the pain couldn't find me.

Of course it already had. But the goal was to find time to control the current discomfort before the world added more.

Finally I gave up and just lay face down in the grass, dirt, and cinder ash, folding arms over the back of my head to block out sunlight. Little by slowly, I felt the pain begin to recede. Seconds feel like hours when pain is involved.

I bent an arm and slipped it between my chin and the ground, so I wasn't puffing dirt with my breaths and sucking in ash. "Okay, could have done without this experience." I lifted my head, felt the pupil in my right eye contract sharply. Grass rustled at eye level.

I pushed myself up into a sitting position, thought over what had happened. The trigger, I was certain, was when I reached out for Remi, or for something that could indicate Remi's location. Which meant possibly it wasn't happenstance, but an actual intentional block.

"Okay, then." I got up unsteadily, brushed off my leathers, closed my right eye as I peered across the vista. The relief from migraine pain left me repeatedly thanking whatever power was responsible.

So. Maybe the trick was not to engage my sensitivity until I really had no other choice. I was counting on the organic GPS of *primogenitura*. It hadn't entered my mind that instead of giving me an edge, it would be an impediment.

I felt a little fragile as I got back on the trail. Migraine pain took the legs out from under a person, and while everyone could empathize with a broken limb, even if only in the imagination, a headache surely was not so debilitating as to interfere with actual activities.

Sunglasses. I should have brought sunglasses. Because my right eye was squinting against daylight. Hat with a bill on the front. Maybe even a cowboy hat.

Well, no. People would expect me to like country music if I wore a cowboy hat.

I toiled along the trail, keeping my head bent as much as I could without cutting off the view of where my feet needed to go, blocking the glare with a raised hand. And then, after a tight turn down into a narrow portion of the trail, wending its way through clusters and bends of lava, I came up to an area marked by yellow caution tape and highway construction barricades.

Yup, the trail stopped abruptly, tipped down into a giant hole. Looked like a massive animal had bitten out mouthfuls of the earth. Perhaps twenty yards on the trail picked up again. But in the meantime, as I made my careful way around the perimeter of the tape, I saw the chasm in the earth. Felt an actual chill. The earth was breathing here, but in the midst of hardened lava, the dragon in the earth's core, the breath was markedly cool.

Beyond the tape and barricades, about twenty-five yards along, I saw a metal post. At its top was fastened a metal plate, tilted. A trail marker of some kind, or a sign providing tourist information. I skirted the tape, climbed up on piled lava to avoid the collapsed trail, made my way around to the post and plate.

My eyebrows rose. Seemed an odd cognitive dissonance: a massive lava flow, and in the midst was a large lava tube now tagged an ice cave because the interior was cold enough to maintain some winter ice through summer.

The sign also announced that while visitors were once allowed inside the cave, it had been closed for years, sealed by iron grillwork.

Not anymore. The grill was a twisted remnant, more crude sculpture than serviceable barrier broken out from cement and stonework. The cave now gaped open, hemmed in by freshly broken rock and static stone formations, but open to the sky.

I made a visual examination of the immediate area of the ruined grill, because a fair number of rocks were loose. The corrosion of the earth, broken up by two earthquakes, funneled the remains down from the higher point of the trail. The earth and stone forming a roof over the cave entrance had not been broken apart, but held up part of the lava flow as well as other boulders. No sign remained to provide information on how large the cave was when it had been closed, or where the lava tube collapsed under the earth's surface to form a finite cavern rather than continuing tunnel-like access deeper into the ground.

Maybe I had pulled the SD card a little too quickly. It would have been helpful to Google the monument and pull up photos of the original entrance and cave, see what it looked like before being blocked by the iron grill. But I wasn't going to slip the card back into the phone now, not here.

Because, face it, an old cave with a formerly blocked entrance in the midst of an ancient lava flow from a 900-year-old volcano made a really effective lair.

Maybe even a prison for one Remi McCue.

CHAPTER THIRTY-EIGHT

I made a rather clumsy trip down from the blocked off trail to the cave entrance, trying to avoid loose rocks. The cave wasn't a vertical hole, so if I lost my balance I'd merely fall down flat, not disappear into the depths of the earth. But if I was a fantasy hero setting off to rescue my battle buddy bestie—provided I wasn't the kind of Hollywood hero who was forced to lose his battle buddy bestie to death for emotional motivation—it would be helpful were I to arrive whole.

At the cave opening, beside the twisted grill, I unholstered my revolver, closed the grips into the palms, examined the sight atop the barrel. Shemyazaz had tossed the gun hard away from me and it had struck a parquet floor. Revolvers were difficult to seriously damage—you could chip the hammer, a grip, maybe—and unlike some semi-autos they did not discharge on impact. But the sight could be damaged, which would affect one's aim.

I couldn't be sure. A migraine can affect visual acuity for a while, and it was possible the gun sight could be slightly off. Short of shooting it now, I couldn't know, and that was not going to happen. In the midst of conflict one shot would provide the information I needed, and I'd have four loaded chambers left to get my business done. But five would be better.

The entrance was low and I ducked my way in, but once past it the cave expanded. Not much room, and a lot of tumbled stone. But if the lava tube beyond the entrance chamber had once been blocked, occasioning closure, it wasn't impassible any longer.

Sunlight still reached the cave proper. Once I ducked down and climbed over rubble into the actual lava tube, sunlight would at some point cut off, unless there were cracks in the ceiling. Which I'd rather there were not.

I lacked my regular phone with its flashlight app, and the angel phone didn't have that app, but without cards in it for now it didn't matter.

But who needs flashlight *apps* when he has an actual flashlight? "Not such a dummy," I muttered, pulling the mini Maglite from a pocket. "At least, not always."

About ten yards beyond the remains of the blockade, still gathering some sunlight from the cave entrance, the tube expanded into a cavernous avenue. Astonished, I stood inside a natural volcanic structure that resembled a huge manmade tunnel. You could drive an eighteen-wheeler through the middle of the thing and still not risk rubbing sidewalls or ceiling.

Lair, indeed.

Alas, the tube did not maintain that initial size and shape as I hiked. At points the ceiling lowered—or perhaps the ground rose—the sides closed in, and rubble choked certain areas, though it remained passable. Sunlight was long gone, but in the absence of all light, in the pressure of utter blackness, the Maglite, though small, was highly effective.

The tube went on and on, driving through the earth. I could see it doubling as a highway for the great sandworms of Frank Herbert's *Dune*, burrowing beneath seas of sand.

When I reached the first tube split, I stopped. The eternal debate, at a fork in the road, in a maze, concerning which way to turn. Left, right, up, down. Flip a coin. Draw straws. Rely on instinct.

I drew in a long breath, sat down on stone and ash, crossed my legs with bent knees extended, bootsoles facing sideways. The split was precise, like a Y. I placed myself at the head of the stem, facing both offshoot tubes. The flashlight lit up the Y—and told me nothing.

I set the Maglite in my lap, scraped up pebbles and ash in both hands, closed my fingers. It was cool, verging on cold, in the tube. I was thankful for my leathers.

I took another breath, closed my eyes. I couldn't be tentative. I had to let myself go, to risk it. Let my senses drive through the tubes as lava once had.

Black/black/black.

Bright red/dark red/brown red.

Orange so brilliant it blinded.

Brown/tan/silver, pink, and olivine.

Ash over it all, and the sheen of metal in edges, the clean steel of knife or sword, the blued metal of gun or damascened whorls.

'*We live between the grays,*' Greg had said. '*We live between the black and the white.*'

It came in on a rush and knocked me flat, a torrent of *here/here/here.*

And also, '*Hic sunt dracones.*'

It made me smile. No question that it was Remi.

I rose.

I threw down the ash and stone.

I took the right-hand tube, thinking, *'Here be dragons.'*

Pain came, of course. It pierced, then dove into the eye, thrust through, exploded inside my skull. It knocked me down, it knocked me flat, it knocked me over the edge to the cusp of unconsciousness.

Hammer on spike.

Spike/spike/spike.

Here be dragons.

Hic sunt dracones.

No.

Hic sunt daemones, laired beneath the earth in a chamber carved by magma, by the earth's blood climbing up through vessels, through veins, making tubes and vents and pipes as it released gases and ash.

The cinder cone under which I lay was partly made of iron. And also partly sulfur.

Hammer/hammer/hammer of the spike through the eye, through the brain, and out the other side.

I got up again. I walked again. I staggered, I tripped, I fell.

And I got up again. Walked again.

Nearly fell again. I clutched my head, but walked.

Demons under the hill.

I walked, and I recited. *"Exorcizamus te, omnis immundus spiritus, omnis satanica potestas . . . Exorcizamus te, omnis immundus spiritus, omnis satanica potestas . . ."*

Not much. Not enough. All I could remember: "Exorcise you, every unclean spirit, every satanic power."

Surely by now my eye was bleeding. The pressure inside increased.

I felt it, then. Felt Remi inside my head. He gave me new words. Knowing him, from the Bible.

. . . *they will lift you up in their hands, so that you will not strike your foot against a stone.*

I walked again and did not fall. Did not strike my foot against stone.

Light before me. I halted, turned off the Maglite to be certain.

Flame ahead. I smelled smoke, and oil. Scents neither sulfur nor perfume, the odor of other demons.

My eye ached with a fierce, bright pain. It skewered through my head. One-eyed, guarding the other with a cupped hand, I saw lava tubes twisted one upon another. They framed themselves on a circle, made a curved chamber within, rimmed with torches. The walls were the rich color of blood, shining wet and slick in torchlight.

Because my one eye was blinded, I had not seen that the tube walls on either side of me had transformed from rough, natural stone patterned by the lava to walls redefined by design.

I looked at the wall beside me, saw something glinting in the corner of my good eye. I turned on the Maglite, flashed it across the wall.

Someone had carved a symbol. Better yet, sculpted. It was deeply chiseled into the stone so that it looked similar to a firefighter's axe hanging on the wall. I stepped to it, touched it, because I had to.

It was stone only, but carved in very high relief. The straight haft, plain, ran through the doubled head, blades facing away from one another. A *labrys*, the twin-headed axe of Minoan Crete.

I turned sharply, looked back the way I had come. What I saw now was different. It was not the tube I had followed. I could go forward. I could go back. I could get lost, and die.

I shut my eyes a moment, turned back. I touched the stone, touched the deep-carved shape of the *labrys*.

Oil and flame came rushing from behind me, filling the tube. To survive, I could only go forward.

With one eye yet weeping, I walked into the circular chamber as the fire sealed the sole entrance and exit, but came no farther. I saw within the huge chamber an altar, as expected, a massive white stone block stained with red, perhaps six feet tall, three feet deep, eight feet wide. Remi was upon it. Remi as tribute to the god.

But he was not tied down, or shackled, because he was meant to provide entertainment even as I was. He stood upright, untethered, atop the altar as Shemyazaz had stood upon the bar at the Zoo. I wondered inanely if Remi knew how to pirouette.

He saw me, waved his arm, gestured for me to come farther into the chamber. He was hatless, but otherwise exactly as I had last seen him. A Texas cowboy.

"Come on!" he called. His voice echoed. "You're holding up the show."

I grimaced. "Can we skip the show?"

"I don't think so. Not if we want to get out of here."

I nodded, watching him. He was undoubtedly unarmed. I, on the other hand, was not.

"You know what this is," he said.

"Of course I know what this is. The two-headed axe in the wall was a dead give-away. And the tubes funneling me in one direction. And now, of course, I can't escape until the task is done." I walked farther into the chamber, examined the bright paint on the rounded walls, the torches, the carved altar. "It's Daedalus's labyrinth, made for King Minos in Crete at the Palace of Knossos, which was built, umm . . . around 1900 BC. I think. If I remember correctly. I mean, this isn't the *real* labyrinth, but close enough."

"So you know what you gotta do?"

"Yeah." I reached back and tightened the elastic band around my ponytail. "I have to kill the Minotaur."

He's here somewhere," Remi said. "Legion, or Iñigo Montoya, or Jack the Ripper. Not sure when he might make an appearance."

I began to pace out the chamber. My eye still wept, my head still pounded. "So, I am apparently proxy for Theseus—and you might be Pirithous, his bestie. They caroused together. But only Theseus fought the bull-man. So maybe you're taking the place of the nine Athenian kids 'donated' to Minos."

I placed one hand on the walls, felt their slickness as I scraped across it while I walked the stone circle. The ruddy base color was rich. Bright frescoes highlighted the walls: dolphins, flowers, young men. The doubled-headed axe. And bulls. Bulls everywhere.

People are used to seeing the ruins of ancient cultures unpainted, lacking detail. But in Egypt, Crete, Pompeii, other places, the walls, columns, and statuary were painted in brilliant colors. Time leeched pigments away with no surviving creators or cultures, to freshen them. Left behind were the faded remains of architectural and artistic glory. But here beneath the earth, undamaged by sun, weather, and vandalism, the glories were visible.

So, bulls. And one bull in particular.

I kept pacing out the circle, looking high into what appeared to be a tier overlooking the ring. The roof overhead was domed. "The story of Pasiphaë and the bull who impregnated her is physically impossible, of course. We know bestiality exists, but for a woman to be mounted by a bull, and then give birth to a child who is half-beast, half-human? Not happening."

I stumbled, caught my balance by stiffening my knees. Pressed the heel of my hand against the eye. I was certain it felt swollen, bulging out of the socket and in need of lancing. I turned into the rounded wall, pressed my forehead against it with hands spread beside my head. It was easier just to lean there against cold stone.

I drew in a hard breath. "I can't see out of this eye."

"I know," Remi said. And maybe he did, through the *primogenitura*.

I moved then, turned to look at him atop the huge block. I'd intended to say something else but the pain in my head intensified. I went down to one knee, bent forward, felt my belly heave.

Remi shouted, and it reverberated inside my skull. "Gabe—get up! Get up!"

I stood, using the wall to provide support. I heard heavy breathing, the rumbling snort of a very large animal.

"Gabe!"

Ah. Enter the bull from Stage Left.

I pressed myself off the wall, hoofed it hard to the altar in the center of the chamber, and used sheer panic coupled with adrenaline to scramble my way up the carved stone block until I reached the top, where Remi stood. He reached down; I grabbed his arm, pulled myself to my feet.

The bull was big and black with a thick set of curved horns and a rolling, angry dark eye. No question of his gender. From the top of his skull between the horns to mid-back, a mane curled against his body, black as the rest of his coat. Between his shoulders rose a hump.

Remi helpfully ID'd the bull's pedigree. "Brahma cross. The rodeo escapee, I do believe."

I tried to clear my eye of tears. "You know him personally?"

"We ain't on speaking terms, if that's what you mean. But I've seen plenty like him in rodeo arenas. Mean suckers, some of 'em. Twisty and fast and almost impossible to ride the full eight seconds. Hard to escape once you hit the ground, too."

The bull circled the altar. His nose was broad with slick, wide, fluttering nostrils, and dark eyes watched us standing atop the large stone block.

"Conjured," I said. "The Minotaur was myth."

"Nothing conjured about this son of a bitch," Remi said. "Well, 'cept for the carpet on his back. Anyway, you got a plan?"

I slipped a hand inside my jacket, drew out the revolver. "Gonna shoot him."

CHAPTER THIRTY-NINE

E ven as I assumed the stance, gun at the ready and the bad eye closed, a voice reverberated throughout the chamber. It had an odd metallic sound, slightly distorted, and either the guy was using a metal speaking tube from inside a statue, or he wore a mask.

"Your bullets will have about as much effect on my bull as they did on Cerberus! By the way, I am *totally pissed* that you killed my dog. You've hurt me to my soul. He was a good boy!"

And I remembered the note written in red on the photo of Remi: *'My name is Iñigo Montoya. You keel my puppy. Prepare to die.'*

I lowered the gun and turned my head so Remi could hear me clearly. "Well, that answers that. He's not a demon. He's a god."

"What god?"

"Some called him Pluto. Others called him Hades." I raised my voice again. "So, what's the deal with Lucifer taking over? Did you retire?"

"We're sharing the kingdom," Hades answered. "Right now he's got Tartarus. Everything else is mine. I've come to earth on vacation, thanks to the hell vents, but I haven't retired. Still got stuff to do. And Persephone's on a tear right now. I figured it was better that I give her some space for a while, hang out in my mancave."

Okay, so he wasn't a gloom-and-doom villain.

Torchflame roared, spilled additional light throughout the chamber. It also allowed Remi and me to *see* Hades. He'd been in the shadows, seated in what looked very like a theater box overlooking what we now knew was a bull-ring. He was clothed in black, though I couldn't see details, and wore a mask of gold. Real gold, I felt certain. It was shaped to resemble the face of a bull. All features but the mouth were flattened, without depth. The mouth, however, was a speaking tube, if abbreviated.

"In this scenario, I'm King Minos," he announced, "who had leprosy, wore a bull-faced mask."

"You kill all those women? You here to kill us?" Remi called.

"I'm here to kill *everybody*," Hades replied. "Yes, I killed those women. Would have killed Mary Jane Kelly, too, but decided it was more fun to lead you guys on for a while. I did claim you two in the fantasy draft—and yes, it's a real thing. Lucifer and I co-developed it along with some game designer demons. But let's stop monologuing! Oh—and don't say I didn't give you a chance. You kill the bull, you walk out of here. I'm a god of my word." He waved a hand, pale in the dimness. "Have at it."

I turned, aimed two-handed, shot a first bullet at the bull. The round did not quite hit what I aimed at, so the gun's sight *was* a little off. No bother. I altered my aim, emptied four more chambers.

Didn't do a thing.

Well, except for pissing off the bull. "Well, shit," I said, as it started pawing at the ground.

"Knives, now, right?" Hades called. "Could work. Might not.

Remiel, you are the bladesman. How about you take what Gabriel's got on him and give it the old school try?"

"He's too calm," Remi said to me. "Hades is, I mean. He's not about to tell us how to hit him where it hurts, but nothing harmed Cerberus until another dog took him out. I'll take your knives, sure, but I'm bettin' we'll do no better."

"What happened to *your* knives?" I asked.

"Hospital security took 'em. And my gun. Rules, you know. Then I got escorted out by a few Hades's guys, and here I am, naked. So to speak."

"I give you the knives," I said, "and we got nothing."

"Give me one knife. The Bowie. The target's pretty damn big. I just have to hope I hit something vulnerable. Even just bleeding, if I hit him right, will slow him down. I figure if we're fast enough we can run through the fire in the tunnel."

I didn't like that at all. "We don't know how deep that fire blockade is!"

Remi and I both startled as a whining, soprano sound reverberated throughout the polished stone chamber. Not the bull, who appeared to be working himself into a charge. It was—an organ?

"Baseball?" Remi's tone was disbelieving. "He's playing the baseball park organ?"

Well, it *was* that four-beat measure starting high, then low, then two chords bridging the distance between the two, to fill time and rouse the fans. ONE-two-three-four, ONE-two-three-four. And the six-beat measure at the end, the *Off To The Races* fanfare.

The next sound was a deep strangled grunting. It rose in pitch and tone and was unrelenting. I heard heavy inhalations, blatting trumpet-like exhalations.

"Bull's getting pissed," Remi said.

Into my right eye, a wash of red came like a tsunami. I went to one knee again, cupping the right side of my face. The migraine was back full-force.

"Get on with it!" Hades wasn't joking anymore. "Don't waste my time. If you want to walk out of here, Gabriel, you'd better get cracking."

The bull's serenade ran up high and loud, expelled explosively. He sounded like a damn donkey with that unremitting honking squall. I thought cattle 'mooed,' or 'lowed.' What the hell was this noise?

I yanked the Bowie from its sheath, put it into Remi's hands just as the bull charged. Its lowered head slammed into the altar, shifting it slightly. I suddenly realized that being up in the air guaranteed nothing save perhaps a harder fall.

Remi's knees were flexed. "Let him come," he said. He did not stand at the edge of the altar, but near enough all the same. "C'mon, you son of a bitch, come on back, try that again."

The bull was accommodating. It trotted away, rounded the ring, then once again charged.

I'd never been up close and personal with an actual bull to judge overall size and weight, but this thing was *massive*.

As it zeroed in on the altar, Remi let fly with the knife. It rebounded, tumbled to the dirt. Gritting his teeth, Remi stuck out his hand. "Gimme your KA-BAR."

I unsheathed it. "I thought you were leaving it with me."

"Was. Now I'm not. Got an idea."

Well, he sure as hell was better than I at throwing a knife. I handed it over.

"This time," Remi muttered, "I'm goin' for an eye."

"Won't that just make him angrier?"

"Wouldn't it you?"

"Well, yeah, but is there an advantage to it? If we lose the knife, I mean?"

"There's an advantage in that a one-eyed bull is easier to run the hell away from. How are you seeing out of the eye that's weeping blood?"

"Not so good." I blotted gently at my eye. "I take your point."

"So part of your field of vision is blocked. That's the goal here, too. I'd like to put this through his eye into his brain, but blinding him'll do."

Once again Remi stood with knees flexed, blade held in fingers. I decided to help. I pushed myself back to my feet, squinted the bad eye closed, began waving my arms. "Come on you, bovine bastard! Come 'n get us!"

That horrific strangled, blatting donkey trumpet filled the ring again. The bull lifted its head, scented with gaping nostrils, then dropped it low and charged again. Just as it came straight in toward the altar, Remi leaned forward just a little. Then he let fly.

Well, shit.

Unfortunately the bull dropped his head just a shade lower as it crashed into the block of stone. The blade struck him, but the best we got was a gouge between the eyes. The bull backed off, shook his head hard, then charged again.

This time when the massive animal plowed into the altar, Remi went right off.

Oh shit. Oh shitohshitohshit!

In the dirt, Remi lurched back to his feet, cast a glance over his shoulder, ran from the bull. He ducked, dodged, twisted his torso like a Spanish bullfighter, and if he went down he rolled, bounced back up. The bull's giant head was lowered, hooking with blunted horns but horns nonetheless.

I saw Remi eyeing the altar as he ran and realized what he was going to try. I dropped to both knees and one hand, moved as he did, tried to position myself as best I could. As the bull made another charge. I dropped to my belly, thrust one arm over the edge, and Remi caught it. I pulled with all my might as he scrambled up, felt myself slide toward the edge. But Remi came up the side in full scramble and dove for the middle of the altar, breathing like a bellows.

I rolled away from the edge, pulled my arms to my chest, and lay sprawled on my back panting. More stress than effort, probably. "Holy shit," I croaked.

Remi was face down. He levered himself up on his elbows, peered over the edge to mark where the bull was, then hung his head, shoulders bunched.

"Close call!" Hades shouted through his mask. "Almost had you, Remiel!"

Remi suggested hoarsely that Hades do something anatomically impossible with the mask. Then he said to me, "I got an idea."

"Does it get us out of here?"

"If it works, it will."

"If it doesn't?"

"Well, he'll stomp us. Hook us. Bash us with his head. Smash both front hooves into our chest."

"Pretty much kill us."

"Yup."

The pain in my eye had backed off. I'd arrived at the conclusion that Hades was the trigger for the pain, and all the *red* and *red rum* and *red death* had been in response to whatever spell or power he was wielding. If we kept him busy, he might forget all about my migraine. Might stop messing with me.

I sat up, placed myself carefully in the precise center of the altar. The bull was trotting along the curved walls of the ring, head hooking back and forth, clearly looking for something. His shadow darkened frescoes, made them appear to be moving. "What's your idea?"

"You feelin' fleet of foot?"

I frowned at him. "What do you—oh, hell no!"

"Ever been to a rodeo?"

"Once when I was a kid, but—"

"Remember the clowns?"

"Yeah, but—"

"One or two were just regular clowns, mostly, playing to the audience."

I shrugged. "Okay. Yeah. But—"

"The other clown is different. He's the one that runs up on the bull when the cowboy comes off, tries to distract the bull while the cowboy runs like stink to the chute or the wall to get out of range. We call him a bullfighter, just like in Spain and Mexico, but he's not lookin' to kill the bull. Just keep it away until the outriders can use their horses to run the bull back into the alley and out of the arena."

I stared at him with eyes wide, mouth open. "You want me to be the bullfighter!"

He nodded.

"And what will you be doing?"

"Riding him to a standstill."

"Riding *the bull*? You out of your fucking mind? You can't ride that thing!"

Remi was clearly surprised by my vehemence. "Sure I can."

I flung out my hand to indicate the bull. *"That?"*

His slow grin appeared. "I ain't sayin' it'll be easy, mind—but this is what I do at rodeos, Gabe. I ride broncs and bulls."

Okay, maybe he had something of a shot. Like, a two percent chance of survival. *"Then* what?"

"You find that Bowie, and that KA-BAR buried in the dirt, and you stab him in the throat. Or the eye. *And* the eye." Remi read my expression. "There's no buzzer here to tell the bull it's over. No outriders to push him to the alley. No nothin,' but us. You gotta run, duck, dodge, twist. You gotta dance with that bull, keep him moving, keep him annoyed. Make him expend energy. We have to tire him, Gabe. Have to exhaust him. That's my job, too, to be the burr beneath the metaphorical saddle. And then you can waltz right up and kill him."

I sat there with my mouth open for several long seconds, trying to marshal words to tell him he was batshit crazy. What I managed was, "How long is this going to take?"

Remi shrugged. "Never done it before to know. The bulls are loose in the arena after the cowboy comes off maybe ten to fifteen more seconds. Twenty at most, unless he decides to take a victory lap. They do that sometimes. So while it's an eight-second ride if the cowboy makes the buzzer, the bull only works hard around twelve, fifteen seconds at most. That's it—twelve or fifteen *seconds.* He'll throw a few farewell bucks just because he can. This means I gotta stay on him considerably longer than eight seconds. And since he *will* throw me, I'll have to get back on him as many times as I can. Your job, when I come off, is to divert him so I have time to get back up on this altar. I can't mount him from the ground. Gotta be above him."

I could not believe he was so calm about all of it. "But don't you guys hang on to something?"

"Got a rigging, yup. A handle, loop of rope." He shrugged. "But here, we got nothin.' I don't know why Hades gave him that mane, but he's got one, and I aim to hang onto it."

Okay, something I could address. "I know where the mane comes from. I read a story once about Theseus and the Minotaur, when I was young. Because he was a beast, not truly a man, he wasn't like other bulls. Or men. The drawing with the story showed a man from the waist down and up to mid-chest, and he had a big curly pelt from the hair on his head to his ass. And, well, a weird head that was half-bull, half-human. And horns."

"Okay." Remi stood up, slapped dust from his pants. "I reckon this'll take us a good while. We'll probably be hungry when we get all done. I'd recommend brisket, but bulls don't make good eating."

I rubbed the back of my hand against my eye. The migraine had died to a dull roar. I affected a drawl. "Well, then, let's git 'er done!"

Apparently colossally bored by our lengthy planning session, Hades played "Take Me Out to the Ballgame" on the house organ.

Then he roared, "The seventh inning stretch is OVER!"

CHAPTER FORTY

I stripped out of my leather jacket, out of the shoulder harness and gun. It left me in a long-sleeved Henley pullover shirt, leather motorcycle pants, boots. Fleet of foot undoubtedly did not describe what I'd be doing while wearing leather pants and heavy-soled leather boots.

So I took the boots off, too.

I lingered at the altar's edge, staring down at the big animal. "The goal is to be total idiots and make him mad."

"The goal is to make him run hell-for-leather all over the ring. He won't do that if he's happy. You gotta piss him off so he's trying to dump me and stampede you all at the same time. That'll wear him down."

I nodded, distracted again by the bull who was not-mooing and not-lowing but working his way through the bovine vocal scale of low chesty moans clear to a high-pitched scraping sound of extreme emotional discord. He sounded nothing like a cow. He sounded like a monster.

"Do they all sound like that?" I asked. "Or is this Hades playing around?"

"Oh, hell—this ain't nothin.' You should hear a herd bull warning off the younger boys." Remi moved close to the altar edge. "Okay, this is going to take some doing. How about you get that jacket of yours and wave it here along the edge, let him see it. He ought to come over to give it what for, and I will at that point endeavor to slide myself down onto his spine right behind the hump."

The moment nearly overwhelmed me. "You can't do that! Remi, we can't do this. It'll get you killed! You don't land right, he's got you right under his hooves!"

Remi looked at me steadily. "And then it's your turn, son. You got to get his attention and lure him away."

"Oh, my Christ. Hell with a gun—I want a grenade launcher!"

The bull bellowed, hoarse and heavy.

"Wave that jacket," Remi told me. "Make him see it. Make him come."

"My jacket's black, not red."

"Bulls are red/green colorblind. They come to the movement, not the color."

"Then why do matadors use a red cape?"

"Drama, son. Sex appeal. Now wave that jacket. I will stay on him long as I can, but you've got to be down in the dirt and ready for when I come off. Then we'll do it all again."

The bull's screeching, honking, donkey-sounding bellow reverberated in the ring. I leaned down, flapped my jacket. "Here, kittykittykitty. Come to papa."

The bull answered at a trot, then broke into a charge. God knows what noises I was making, but as he came up I whopped him in the face with the jacket. In his shock, he paused.

Remi slid off the altar and onto the bull's back.

———

Seconds. That's what Remi said it lasted, a cowboy's ride on a bucking bull. For the bull, twelve to fifteen seconds from chute gate opening to heading down the alley. But to me it lasted *hours*.

Remi came off. Remi came off so many times I'd lost track. Sometimes he came right off as the bull accelerated into hard bucking as soon as Remi clamped left hand in the mane and feet in the ribs behind the bull's forelegs. Sometimes he made it longer, bent at the pelvis as he leaned back hard, right arm thrust into the air for balance. He got whipped hard in all directions. The bull bucked so hard and high he was almost vertical, butt so upright I thought he'd flip over for sure and come crashing down on Remi. Sometimes he just spun one way, then spun back the other. The power in the beast was incredible. Not only was he huge, but he clearly knew how to use his body.

God, I ran. Ran and ran. Looked and looked for the knives. Dodged one way, ducked the other, whacked that bull with my jacket as hard as I could right between the eyes. Then he yanked it away from me, dropped his head, hooked it, swept it right out of my hands. Now I had nothing.

Knives. Find the knives. But the dirt of the bull-ring was deep, and I saw nothing of my blades.

Remi was still aboard. The bull shook his head, jacket hanging off a horn. Every time he moved his head, the jacket swung forward to cover one eye. Not for long, but it was enough to ramp up his annoyance.

"Yes!" Remi shouted.

So I didn't even try to rescue my jacket. I let it hang there as the bull wildly swung his head, shook it hard, dropped it down low. I didn't know how long the jacket might remain hung up on the horn, so I took my chance and ran up to him from his blind side, then darted sideways and smashed my fist into his good eye.

The bull scrambled back, head thrown up in the air. Remi was swearing in between catching breaths.

Come on, knives. Show yourselves. Fighting Remi, fighting me, fighting the jacket might well exhaust the bull so that I had the opportunity to stab him in the eye, or slice into his throat.

The bull bellowed, tossed his head, and the jacket flew off. Crap.

Knifeknifeknife.

I took too long eyeballing the dirt looking for my knives. Remi shouted, sounding panicked, and I glanced up in time as the bull came in, head tipped sideways to hook me with a horn.

I flung myself away, landed hard, scrambled up, felt a horn rub by me. Blunted, the horn did not puncture. It wasn't a gore. But it was like being punched by a house.

I thrust myself up, tried to run. Overbalanced and went down flat on my face. I needed *not* to be where the bull might expect me. I bounced up, threw myself sideways rather than attempting to run a straight line.

Remi came off, landed hard. I saw him tuck down and roll himself up like a pillbug, hands and arms guarding his head.

I pushed up again, kept my feet, ran after the bull while shouting breathless, broken insults and vulgarities at him. I scooped up my jacket, reached the animal just as he prepared to shove his horns either beneath Remi to lift and roll him, or to drive one horn down into chest or abdomen.

Matadors were sometimes gored, then picked up and literally thrown by the bulls. Thick blunted horns couldn't do that, as Remi had pointed out, but crush him?

I caught up to the bull and snapped my metal-zippered jacket up between splayed hind legs, cracked it whip-like into his low-hanging fruit as hard as I could.

Remi rolled, sprang up, staggered out of the way, fell down and got up again. Sweat plastered his shirt to his torso, hair to his head. His eyes were fixed on the bull. The wobble in his legs, the break in the knees that he caught, then snapped back into place, told me how exhausted he was.

The bull turned on me, and I couldn't find the knives.

The altar represented respite, a chance to catch our breath, to regroup and begin again. Except I wasn't sure either of us had any gas left in our tanks to leap and scramble our way back up onto the flat surface.

Exhaust the bull, Remi had said.

Yeah. And us.

The animal, head lowered, eyeballed Remi, turned to me. I swear, and I'll swear to my dying day, that his eyes were brilliant, burning red, and his hooves glowed silver like steel. He was no longer just an escaped rodeo bull.

From one of his hips, black hair stood up. Hair burned. Flesh burned. I could smell all of it. The red-eyed bull threw back his head and filled the chamber with a bellowed roar of agony and anger.

The new brand on his hip was raw, bright red. Curvilinear.

666

It glared at me. And in his eyes was the intelligence of a man.

Knives wouldn't harm him. He was no longer just a bull. Hades had made him much more.

"Remi . . ." Out of breath, I pantomimed instructions. Sideways sweep of arm directing him to the altar. My bent body, linked fingers, the upward jerk. We met at the altar as the bull began to charge. Remi stuck one booted foot into my linked hands, went upward as I boosted. He made it. I didn't.

The one horn hooked around my ribs. It *hugged* my ribs. I felt the tremendous power in the animal's body, felt the heat of his breath, the burning saliva. The crimson eyes were bright and sharp and calculating.

He flung me away just as he had my jacket. I hit hard, rolled, grabbed at dirt and tried to climb to my feet, tried to push myself upward to run again.

"Here!" Remi shouted in a wrecked voice that broke halfway through. I ran for the altar, reached for his arm, nearly pulled him off the edge as I scrabbled my way back on top.

I stood bent over, hands on knees, in the center of the block. At some point the elastic holding my ponytail had broken so I had loose hair hanging free. "I don't think . . . I don't think we've got another climb up this thing in us."

"He break anything?" Remi asked, panting hard.

I felt at my chest, my sides. "—don't think so."

"No knives?"

I shook my head. "In the dirt, under the dirt." I sucked in another breath. "I've been looking. Too much running. Dirt and ash is all broken up. Buried. No time . . . no time for a real search. And any more . . . I think neither knife nor gun would stop him."

The massive bull stood a good fifty feet away from the altar, head lowered as he watched us, weighed us, with red, roiling eyes. The brand on his hip still smoked.

"Did you see it?" Remi asked.

"I saw it."

"Ain't a natural bull anymore."

I shook my head and looked up at Hades. It was stupid, but I did it anyway. "You're an *asshole!*"

"Yes," he called.

I swallowed hard and heavy. Shouted again. "You know we can't kill this bull. It's not a bull anymore!"

His voiced echoed. "Monsters can die. Theseus killed the Minotaur. He walked out of the bull-ring. You and Remiel can do the same. Kill the Minotaur, Gabriel. You just have to figure it out."

I looked at the torches.

Hades sounded cheerful. "Bolted down. You have to be cleverer than that. Nothing so prosaic as a flaming torch to distract the monster, or burn out an eye. You'll have to do it another way."

I had little voice left, and almost no breath. "I'm just a guy. Not Theseus. And that was *mythology!*"

"So am I," Hades called. "Or was. This is not Star Trek's holodeck. This is real. Or, well, as real as you can *make* it. If you take my meaning."

The bull charged. He crashed into the big stone block and knocked it sideways, scraping one horn across stone. Remi and I went sliding. He managed to hang on. I did not. I went right off the edge onto the devil's front porch.

"One more—?" I shouted to Remi. I dodged the bull. Dropped, rolled, came up. Staggered another direction. "You got one more ride in you?"

Remi grinned. "Hell yeah, I do!"

I pulled off my shirt and pressed my chest against the altar block, making myself flatter. Smaller. "You ready?"

"Born that way!"

"Minotaur's coming."

And he was, a freight train on four hooves. I waved my shirt like a madman. The red eyes fixed on it. One horn scraped the block, screeching like metal. I slipped around the edge, heard Remi's grunt of effort. The bull spun away, and I saw again the scorched brand on his hip.

Eight seconds. Eight seconds, maybe twelve.

As real as I could *make* it, Hades had said.

I ran. I ran through the gate, through flames that did not burn, to the carved Minoan axe cut into the wall, the sacred double-headed *labrys*, Lady of the Labyrinth.

"Be real," I rasped. "Be fucking *real!*"

And I yanked it out of the wall.

Stone flaked away. I saw the gleam of ancient metal. I ran back through the flames, back into the ring, and right up to the bull.

I registered the shock on Remi's face. I saw red eyes and the whip of heated slime, heard the steam engine of his breath, smelled the stink of hell, the stench of burning hair, the reek of bubbling flesh.

With two shaking hands and all the power left in my shoulders, I swung the *labrys* up like a scythe over my right shoulder, then brought it down on the diagonal into the neck between jaw and shoulder. The blade cleaved skin, muscle, spine, sliced through veins and vessels. Blood shot into the air in arterial spray. *"Yippie-ky-ayy, motherfucker!"*

Remi fell off the collapsing bull. I just fell over.

CHAPTER FORTY-ONE

I lay on my back in the dirt and didn't care. I probably lay on my back in bull shit, too—*actual* bull shit—and I didn't care. In fact, when Hades came walking across the dirt, mixed with or without bull shit, I also didn't care about that. I had nothing left in me *to* care. Nothing, nothing, nothing.

I just lay there on my back and stared up at him as he stood over me. And I laughed. I couldn't help myself. I was too worn to help myself. I was utterly spent.

"What the hell?" I croaked. Dirt and blood was in my mouth.

"I know," Hades said. "But it's dramatic. One of the best entrances ever filmed."

I swallowed, tried to reclaim some of my voice. "Darth Vader . . . does not wear a Cretan bull-mask. The least you could do is dress up like Hercules." I waved a limp hand. "You know, in leather."

"I think you have the leather market cornered," Hades said. "Boots, pants, jacket, gun harness. Though right now you seem to be limited to leather pants."

"I ride a motorcycle. Get over it."

"You've left bits of yourself spread all over the bull-ring."

Hades switched his glance from me to Remi, who was apparently eschewing lying in the dirt—with or without bull shit—and was attempting to sit up.

Primogenitura came roaring in, and this time I could move. *This* time I could defend, because Remi was at stake.

I reached for the axe haft, scrambled back onto my feet, stood up holding the *labrys*.

Even through the cut out metal eyeholes, Hades gave me an amused stare. "I'm not going to harm either of you, you idiots. I didn't draft you just to kill you off. I'm going to turn you out onto the field, or the gridiron, or the pitch, or the track, now and then, and just have fun with you."

I did not let go of the axe. "You killed all those women."

"Did I?"

"You said you did."

"Did I?"

"Those were extremely graphic photos."

"Special effects are amazing these days."

I tensed my hand, flexed my shoulder. "You sent us a human kidney."

"You can buy them on the black market." He put up a single finger, wagged it at me. "No. That axe is too heavy for you, now. It's game over."

The axe *was* too heavy. I couldn't keep it in my hands. It landed in the dirt, then dissolved. I wondered if it was back on the wall, or if Hades had stuck it somewhere else.

He turned back to Remi, now standing. Dirt and blood clung to every part of his person. His hands, I saw, were trembling. He was barely on his feet.

"My compliments," Hades said. "Never in my wildest dreams did I imagine this type of denouement. A cowboy? Riding the *Minotaur*? Inspired. And it speaks well of your chances of a longer survival." He swung back to me and his Vader cloak swirled. "Yes, it's a game! My consortium and I drafted your team—sorry not to let you know—and we're betting on you against other teams. But enough of the post-climax monologue. We need an *epi*logue. But that's up to you, to heaven's bastards. Time for me to go." He bowed, flourished an arm across his chest, then stripped off the gold bull-mask as he straightened. Beneath it he wore the Guy Fawkes mask, not his own face. "Not yet," he said. "Too soon blunts the impact. I'll show you one day."

He didn't have wings to shroud himself in. He just— disappeared.

I looked past Remi to the huge black heap near the altar, head almost separated from its body. "There's your brisket. We could take it back to Ganji. He said he'd fix us steaks."

Remi wiped briefly at his shirt, quit when it served only to make bloody mud. The next attempt was a forearm across his face, which was no more successful. He squinted, spat lightly to the side, then gave all of it up as a bad job.

He eyed me. "Well, at least I'm fully clothed. You look like a male stripper who's been mud-wrasslin' a pig, and the pig won."

"Do you really say that in Texas? 'Wrasslin'?"

"We say whatever we want in Texas. If we say it, it's Texan."

I took a couple of steps, staggered a little, waved a hand in Remi's direction. "See if you can find my weapons. I'm just gonna pick my clothes up off the floor, like Mom always told me to."

———

We mostly staggered through the lava tube, occasionally grabbing one another to keep from falling down. Remi, weaving a little, was mightily impressed by the environs. He *ooh*ed and *ahh*ed over it until I finally asked if he hadn't noticed something as large as a subway tunnel on his way in.

"I wasn't a sentient person on the way in, bein' shanghaied by minions, rendered mostly unconscious, and dragged in here."

"What were you on the way in if not a sentient person?"

"Pretty much a potato."

It made me laugh. "Mashed or hashed?"

"I also wasn't semantically inclined on the way in to sort out what version of food I felt like."

"Are you semantically inclined to sort out what you feel like now, food or otherwise?"

"I might could be."

"Well?"

He stopped walking, tucked his chin and looked down at himself. Then he raised his head and presented me with an expression of exceptional blandness. "What I am is as down to earth as horse shit in a meadow."

We wobbled onward some more, and the echoing acoustics continued to fascinate him. But after intoning *ooh*s and *ahh*s *for a while*, he began to sing instead. And then he sang a little louder.

"Nonono!" I cried, and it carried down the tube on the heels of his singing. "Not *that* song!"

"It's a good song. I like it. Johnny Cash sang it, among others."

"But it's the red eyes and the steel hooves and the burning

brand and the devil's herd! Again." I half-turned, pointed stiffly over my shoulder. "And we just did that *for real*!"

"Yes."

"And the yippie-ki-ays!"

"You did your *own* yippie-ki-yay in there!"

"I quoted Bruce Willis!"

"And I am quoting 'Ghost Riders in the Sky.'"

"Country. *Country*, Remi." I stumbled, caught myself. "You know, it's your call when we're in your truck, and we now live in a cowboy bar with a jukebox full of country music and a live band playing country music and open mic night with people singing country music, *all of it* country. Can we just *not* do country when we're, like, walking through a lava tube after meeting up with the god of the underworld?"

Remi considered that. "Well, what do you like to listen to? In your heart of hearts—hell, let's just make it your guilty pleasure. Who would you pick?"

My time to consider. "Heart of hearts? Guilty pleasure? *Really* guilty pleasure?"

He bobbed his head, eyes bright. "Sure. Heart of hearts, guilty pleasure."

"You won't tell?"

"Well, unless you're gonna inform me that it's Liberace *and* we're in a bar full of bikers, because it would be just too stinkin' funny to announce it, I won't say a word."

I told him.

Remi stared back at me. "That's it?"

"That's it."

He blinked, and his smile grew into an exceedingly broad grin as teeth showed very white against the bloody, muddied face. "Well," he said, "I never promised not to *sing* it!"

Which is why we tromped the rest of the way out of the lava tube with Remi singing John Denver's "Sunshine On My Shoulders" at the top of his lungs.

The bike would not start.

After five tries and checking things mechanical, I informed my bike that I would get off, get down on my knees and pray to Jesus, Mary, and Joseph, and all the angels dancing on the head of a pin, if it would please start, please run, and please drive us back to the Zoo, where it could then go on strike if it wanted to.

But the bike was already on strike.

I looked at Remi, who was hiding a smile behind fingers supposedly scratching his lip. "Your phone?" I asked.

Remi blinked at me a moment. "If you're hauling a guy off to see the god of the underworld and meet the Minotaur, all against his will, do you leave a phone with him?"

"Well, you had two phones."

"*Had* being the operative word. What happened to yours?"

"One of mine got broken when Shemyazaz knocked it out of my hand in a fit of pique, but I do have the other. Gotta put the cards back in it."

"Yaz is back?"

"Yeah, he wanted to pick on me." I pulled the angel phone out of a pocket, examined it for damage. It appeared to be fine. Then I unzipped my secret pocket and pulled out SD card, SIM card, and also the flash drive.

I looked at the drive a moment. Things were no longer amusing.

Remi sensed the shift. "What?"

I displayed the flash drive. "There's a story about this. Things have undergone a sea-change, and I have lots to tell you about the drive, Cassandra, Grandaddy, Greg, but not right now." I tucked the drive away again, thinking about Cassandra. Then I zipped the pocket closed, placed the cards back into the phone and waited for a signal.

When it came, I called Ganji. "Can you come get us?" He said yes. "Okay, we are at the gate by the visitor center at Sunset Crater. You'll see us." I hung up. "He said he'll come get us."

Since we had to wait fifteen to twenty minutes, Remi and I attempted to enter the men's room, which was locked, made do with a couple of trees. Then we hit up the drinking fountains to clean the blood off faces and hands. I'd tied the torn Henley shirt around my hips and wore the jacket over my bare chest. Jacket was a little scuffed by its up close and personal activities with the bull, but nonetheless in one piece.

Ganji still hadn't arrived by the time we were back with the bike. I frowned down the road with hands on hips. "What's he doing, walking?"

"It's a nice day," Remi observed.

"It can be a nice day when we've showered, eaten, and imbibed alcohol, too. If we ever get there." I called Ganji again, attempted to smooth the impatience out of my voice. "Do you know where the loop road is?" He said he was on it. "Okay. See you in a few."

As I was tucking the phone back into my pocket, Remi started chuckling.

I looked at him. "What?"

"You asked Ganji if he could come get us."

"Yeah?"

"You did not specify if he should come get us *in a vehicle*."

I snapped my head around. Sure enough, the Mighty Lord of the Volcanos was ambling down the asphalt road on foot. I stared at him blankly for several long moments, then abruptly turned and began unbuckling the saddlebags from my bike. Remi just hooted.

Ganji arrived. "A beautiful day," he proclaimed, "near one of my children." He gestured to the cinder cone with pride, then looked us up and down. "Though perhaps the day has been particularly hard on you."

I slung the saddlebags over my shoulder. "Did you know this particular child has a labyrinth inside?"

"The lava tubes? Of course." His smile was sweet. "Now, despite your dirt, shall we enjoy a pleasant walk back to the Zoo?"

I did my very best to enjoy our pleasant walk back to the Zoo, because no one picked us up. Hell, *I* wouldn't pick us up. Once back at the dancehall, I raced Remi up the stairs and jumped into the shower first. Probably I won because he didn't know we were racing and I had a head start.

He yelled at me from the other side of the door. "Is that any way to treat a world champion cowboy who beat the bull who couldn't be rode?"

I turned the water on, ran it to get it warm. "Are you a world champion cowboy?"

He sounded a little chastened. "No. Not enough weekends. And school got in the way."

Well, that made me feel bad. "I'll buy you a beer," I promised, shouting over the water. "To celebrate the world champion half-angel cowboy who beat the bull who couldn't be rode."

"Tequila!"

I agreed it could be tequila, then stepped under the water.

EPILOGUE

It was after midnight, and the Zoo was closed. Ganji was off communing with his volcano, soothing her after the insult of two earthquakes that had disturbed her rest. Remi lasted through two glasses of tequila before he set the bottle aside and observed that if he drank any more he'd probably fall down the stairs and break his neck. That was not, he said, what the man who beat the bull who couldn't been rode would do.

I told him I'd collect him at the bottom, carry him up, and dump his ass in bed before I called 911. "Because that's what a hero would do."

He eyed me askance. "Have another whiskey, Gabe. Might could drown your sorrows about your bike."

I'd managed half a glass more than he had. Ganji made us burgers before he left—Remi said he'd have his brisket another time—so at least we had something in our bellies to soften the booze, but we were both feeling it. "Cisco said he'd meet me out there in the morning, haul it in. And I'd like to have a little talk with the kid. Meantime, shoot some pool?"

"Sure." Remi slipped off the barstool, headed toward the jukebox. "I'll see if I can find some John Denver for you."

"Oh, c'mon now, you said you wouldn't make a thing out of it."

"I said I wouldn't tell anyone, not that I wouldn't make a thing out of it. Besides, I doubt there's any on here."

I slid off the stool, intent on finding the cord to the jukebox and unplugging it. Then someone knocked at the front door.

"Oh God," I muttered. "Please let it not be Shemyazaz. I'm not up to counting pirouettes." I went over, stood close, but did not unlock or unlatch the door. "Who is it?"

"It's Mary Jane!"

Much better than Yaz. But was it actually her? After meeting up with Hades, I wasn't taking chances. I unlocked and unlatched, pulled it open as far as my planted, booted foot, which was about five inches away from the jamb. Saw it was indeed Kelly. She wore a fuzzy pink hat pulled low over her head to hide the shearing, but also a big grin.

I turned my head to shout over my shoulder. "Mary Jane's here!" And I asked her if she wanted whiskey or tequila.

I closed the door behind her as she came in. She wore a jacket and had a daypack hooked over her shoulder. I assumed that meant she anticipated staying the night. And probably not alone, or on the sofa bed.

"Can I have beer instead?" she asked.

"You can have whatever you want." I smiled blandly as Remi came up. "In fact, why don't I just pour a draft while you and Remi get much better acquainted."

She actually blushed. Remi, still hatless until he got it cleaned, just smiled slow and sweet. I figured they'd be moving to a booth, maybe to sit nice and close, but Kelly climbed up onto a barstool as I moved behind the copper-topped bar to take down a beer glass. Music came on in the background; I hadn't unplugged in time.

Remi slid onto the stool beside her. "Be nice," he told me. "It's not 'Ghost Riders in the Sky.' I figured that'd be pushin' it, in view of the circumstances."

I set the beer in front of Kelly. Remi shook his head when I asked a question with raised brows; he was done for the night.

"You're okay?" I asked her.

She nodded, touched the hat with one hand briefly as if self-conscious. "I'm okay. I'm good. He didn't really hurt me. I mean, my scalp is tender, yeah, but considering what he could have done to me, a sore scalp is fine."

I thought back to Hades standing over me in the bull-ring. We had a name, now. No more Jack the Ripper. No more Legion, or Iñigo Montoya. We had the god of the underworld.

"Wasn't a demon," I murmured. I caught Remi's eyes. "*Hic sunt daemones.*"

"What?" Kelly asked. Then she waved her hand to dismiss the question. "Never mind. Listen, I brought something for you guys, to say thanks for saving me."

I snorted. "I'm not sure we saved you."

"You did." She nodded. "You did. Anyway, this is something my grandmother left me. She told me I should save it for a special occasion. I figure this is about as special as occasions come." She reached down and pulled something out of her daypack, set it on the bar.

It was a jar. A jug, actually, big gallon jug, stoppered in cork and sealed with wax. Someone had haphazardly mosaicked the exterior, as if for a school project. Kindergarten.

Kelly saw the fleeting expression on my face. "Yes, it's my artwork," she admitted. "Grandma let me practice on it with broken pottery. I know it's not any good. She said she would put her most precious thing into it for me. Anyway, this is a special occasion and I want to open it." She picked at the wax with a thumbnail.

"Here." I slid the jug close, took a bar knife to the wax. "Easier this way." I cleared the seal, slid it back to Kelly. "There you go."

She thanked me, started working at the cork. It was deeply seated, and she scowled.

"Here." Remi this time. A little thumb pressure applied, and the cork popped off.

"Bless you." Kelly's face lit up. "There!"

I expected the odor of old hooch to permeate the air. Instead what we got were shiny red beetle-things boiling out of the jar.

Remi scrambled off his stool and backed away. I took two long steps, ran into the ornate barback. I looked away from the beetles to see ecstasy transforming Mary Jane Kelly's face.

She looked at me and laughed. "You were so easy, Gabe! Didn't even realize each time you took the ibuprofen I put in the bathroom, you had a 'spell.'"

The crimson beetles flowed down the sides of the jar, across the bartop, to the edge, then abruptly took wing. The swarm broke out the front windows and flew into the night.

Kelly released a sigh that bordered on afterglow. "All those evils you'll have to chase down." Her eyes were laughing as she looked at me, then she turned her attention to Remi. "You of all people—a Biblical scholar!—should know they were never *cockroaches*. They're locusts!" She shrugged. "Yeah, okay, they're a different breed so they look a little different." She gave me a limpid glance as I closed a hard hand on her wrist. "You can't hold me, Gabe. I'm clay, not flesh."

She felt solid enough. "You're not a demon. Demons can't come in here."

"That's why they sent *me*." She smiled, removed her hat, and the wealth of brown hair with its bright gold streak tumbled free. "Hades never hurt me. That was for the picture. I'm in the consortium." Grinning, she *crumbled* out of my grasp as she put her hand on the jug and stroked it.

I didn't waste time in trying to grab her again. "Who are you?"

She indicated the jug. "It was never a box," she declared firmly, reassembling clay dust into a woman's arm.

Remi reached for her, but she crumbled aside, made herself whole again.

"My name, obviously, isn't Mary Jane Kelly, though there is a real park ranger by the name." She did not much resemble that false version of herself. Something a little wild, a little mad was in her eyes. "Neither am I Legion, or Iñigo Montoya—yeah, Hades told me about that little conceit. But he bet I couldn't get *you* two to open the jar. Hah! Won some money off him!" She stopped short, got right up into Remi's face. "My name is *Pandora*. And it was a *jar*, not a box. Some idiot so-called scholar couldn't read his ancient Greek."

Then she kissed him hard, crumbled into dust, and simply blew away.

It took me a moment to find my voice. "Hephaestus," I said finally, because I could think of nothing else. A streak of clay dust lay in my palm.

Remi, white-faced, looked at me, totally bewildered. "What?"

"In the Bible, it's Eve. The first human woman. In Greek mythology, it's Pandora. Hephaestus made her, on Zeus's order, out of earth and water. She was so perfect the Olympian gods gave her many gifts, among them a box. Jar. She was expressly told never to open it."

Remi nodded slowly. He still looked stunned. "Told never to eat the apple."

"Pandora opened the jar."

"Eve ate the apple."

I looked into the jug. Then I stoppered it with the cork, thumped it tight with the heel of my hand. "We *will* have to go after all the evils she let loose, which of course was her plan. In our copious spare time when we're not killing demons."

"All the evils *I* let loose."

"But hope remains." I patted the stopper. "In the tale, Pandora closed the jar before hope could escape. I just did the same."

He stared at the jug, then lifted his eyes to mine. And hope wasn't just in the jar. It lived in Remi, too.

I poured whiskey, tequila, admonished his burgeoning refusal with a scowl, and when he raised his glass I tapped mine against it. "Hope is all we need." I paused with the glass halfway to my lips. "Well, that and John Denver."

Readers well-versed in mythology, folklore, religions, and various cultures will notice I have cherry-picked specific details in service to the story I want to tell, while I have altered others. Those with questions may seek out the original texts, tales, and resources.

The dog who takes out Cerberus was inspired by a pit bull who became dear to many of us. He literally threw himself into a friend's life by running down the middle of the street heading for a collision with her VW bug. (The car would have lost.) She took him home to work up Found Dog posters and make some shelter calls.

Two hours later, as a man tried to break into the home, the pittie ran him off in defense of five female college students. When his owner never came forward, my friend adopted the dog. So began a two-and-a-half-year journey with Peter Pittie of Instagram and Facebook fame, as his exploits entertained us all. His loss to cancer still saddens all of his vast human family.

I have a love/hate relationship with computers (mostly a severe hate relationship), and thus I must thank Brian Gross for backing me up on what little techspeak is included. And while I have over 40 years of serious dog experience behind me, I nonetheless called on fellow Cardigan Welsh Corgi breeder Dr. Barbara Merickel, a veterinarian, to, well, *vet* my canine first aid.

While I have never been a bullrider, I had horses and knew cowboys back in the day, and used to attend a lot of rodeos. (And cowboy bars.) I took great pleasure in merging the legend of the Minotaur with Remi's modern-day bullriding.

The lava cave and tubes are real, and just outside of Flagstaff, though not where I placed them in the book. Check out Lava River Cave on Google to see amazing photos. There *is* an ice cave in Sunset Crater National Monument, but it is closed. As for the bull, I did not make up the sound effects. Just Google "angry bull sounds."

Next in the pipeline is *Sword-Bearer*, Volume 8 in the SwordDancer saga, followed by the further adventures of Gabe and Remi in Volume 3 in the Blood & Bone series.

I may be reached via my website at *www.jennifer-roberson.net;* my e-mail at *booksartdogs@gmail.com,* as well as Facebook, where I am extremely active, and Twitter.

Life and Limb, Vol 1 of the Blood & Bone series, is available in paperback, e-book, and audiobook formats.